Troubled Waters

The sight of the old farmhouse conjures up
all those reasons she left…

Troubled Waters

RENE GUTTERIDGE

Troubled Waters

Hendrickson Publishers Marketing, LLC
P. O. Box 3473
Peabody, Massachusetts 01961-3473

ISBN 978-1-59856-982-5

Troubled Waters © 2003 Rene Gutteridge.
This edition by arrangement with the copyright holder.

First Hendrickson Edition Printing — March 2012

Cover Photo Credit: ©ZenShui/Alix Minde, PhotoAlto Agency RF Collections, Getty Images

For my sister, Wendy,
and in special memory of my grandmothers,
Flora and Jacquelyn.

About the Author

RENE GUTTERIDGE is a talented playwright and award-winning novelist with over twenty novels to her credit. She has served as the director of drama at an Oklahoma City church and has written over five-hundred sketches for use in services.

Rene and her husband make a home for their two children in Oklahoma.

Visit www.renegutteridge.com.

Prologue

S he debated with herself as to whether or not this was a sin. Writing the final thoughts down, she turned the paper in order to get a perfect slant to the handwriting. She paused before signing it. Her hand was trembling a little. She glanced at her daughter's old school paper, eyeing the name at the top right. The *M* was bubbly. The *Y* had a little curl at its end. She copied it perfectly.

A finger, swollen from the July humidity, tapped her thin lips and then rubbed the edge of her chin. She swallowed hard and continued.

Pinching the corner of the paper, she crinkled it a bit. She bent it backward and forward and then backward again. Her coffee cup made a perfect half-circle stain when she placed it on the opposite corner and pressed down. She lifted the cup to her lips, hardly noticing the coffee was barely warm anymore. The cream had even risen to the top in a white circle.

The old wood floors creaked beneath her as she stood with much effort and walked to the kitchen sink, where she turned on the water and stuck a finger in the stream. Back at the table, she sat down, dabbed her finger on the edge of the paper, smudging the ink ever so slightly. She did this precisely four times.

If this wasn't a sin, then she was attending to detail. If it was a sin, then she could chalk this up to being deceptively calculating.

The ceiling above groaned, and her heart stopped with a breath-taking sting. She glanced to the stairs, pushing her glasses up her small nose, but there was no shadow to be seen. Another sound from above assured her no one would be coming down any time soon. Jess could hardly sit up enough to eat soup, though that didn't keep her from thinking maybe, just maybe God had answered his prayers and healed him. The ceiling became silent again, and she had to assume that Jess was still in bed and Patricia, his nurse, was still upstairs caring for him.

Carefully folding the paper three ways and sliding it into the envelope, she tried several times to moisten the envelope with her tongue, but her mouth was so void of any moisture that she ended up sticking a finger in her coffee and running it along the glue before sealing it as tightly as she could.

Then she set it down on the table and stared at it.

It stared back. Or maybe glared. Her guilt consumed her, but only for a moment. An unfamiliar peace ushered the guilt out, and she knew this was what she had to do. *Had* to do, or *needed* to do? The guilt returned seconds later.

Grabbing her purse off the table, she stuck the envelope deep inside. With a different pen and a different pad of paper she wrote a note to Patricia, telling her she had to run into town and would be back soon. She left out details so she wouldn't have to lie.

Then she walked out the back door of her house, eased herself down the cement steps that had given her problems for fifteen years, and shuffled along the dirty sidewalk and scorched grass to their old Pontiac. Lowering herself into the seat just about took all her breath away, so she rested a bit before pulling the car door shut. Thankfully it started without trouble. She slowly backed the car down the driveway.

The upstairs bedroom curtains moved, and she knew Patricia was looking out to see who was coming or going. But she pretended not to notice as she shifted the car into Drive.

Fifteen or so minutes later, she was at the post office. She didn't bother going inside, thankful there was a drop-off box. Yet her arthritis and back problem kept her from being able to reach far enough to drop it in without getting out of the car. She managed to rock her heavy frame back and forth until she was out of the car and on her feet. She looked down and smiled. She was still wearing her house slippers.

In front of the mail drop, she prayed silently. This was wrong and right all at the same time. She'd never done anything like it in her life. When she was fifteen she'd secretly given Herbie Templeton a quart of milk from her daddy's cow, because he said he couldn't afford any. But that was it. Could this really be what God wanted her to do?

A brief thought passed through her conscience, a thought that in doing this maybe she was speaking of things that weren't, as though they were. But it was crowded out of her mind by the next thought, that she didn't trust her God enough to allow Him to work things out in His way.

A warm southerly wind picked up, flushing her cheeks and tearing her eyes. She wiped at them and turned to find something serene to look at. In the distance she could see acres of wheat fields waiting to be harvested. The wheat waved at her as the wind swept through. The combines would be here in a couple of weeks.

Velma Peterson stepped out of the post office then and waved at her, too. Luckily the drop box was located on the other side of the street, and the wind was blowing hard. Velma always worried about her hair, so instead of walking toward the drop box to say hello, she hurried off to the shelter of her car.

Fear gripped her at the thought of anyone approaching her or asking what she was doing. Simply mailing a letter was *not* what she was doing. Sweat trickled down the side of her face and collected on the skin of her thick neck. She wished she'd brought her hanky. June had been comfortable, but now it looked like July was going to be oppressive.

The wheat fields caught her attention again. It had been a long time since she'd noticed their golden beauty. The wheat moved back and forth, as if God Himself were walking along, His giant feet parting it effortlessly. Her life was about to change in a way she'd only imagined in her darkest dreams. She wondered if she would survive the pain.

She also wondered if she would survive the guilt of what she was about to do. The drop box blurred from the heavy tears in her eyes.

It was time to make a decision.

One

I don't ask a lot. At least I don't think so. I ask for loyalty. I ask for consistency. I ask for a little hard work for fifteen minutes every morning. I don't think that's asking too much. In fact, I think you have it rather easy, don't you?"

Macey Steigel gestured dramatically at her CoffeePro, willing it, wishing it, demanding it to make coffee. But on this steamy summer morning it stared lifelessly back at her, refusing her simple request. Macey stood up from her bent position and sighed heavily. She turned and wondered if she could actually make it out the front door without any java in her system. Doubtful. She turned back around and slapped the thing on its side. The hard plastic stung her hand, and she winced in pain.

Bending back down to its level on the kitchen counter, she said, "I paid eighty bucks for you. For your reliability. For your satisfaction guaranteed. And you know what? Most people don't pay eighty bucks for coffee makers. No. In fact, most people don't pay for coffee makers at all. You know why? Because most people get them for wedding presents. I, however, as you know and witness every morning as I get up and roam this apartment by myself, am not married and cannot seem to carry a relationship for as long as it takes you to make me coffee. So I'm sure you can see how upsetting it is when you, of all things, refuse to stick by me and do the one thing that makes me happy in the morning. Make me coffee." She glared at it furiously. "MAKE ME COFFEE!" But the fancy plastic box in front of her never made a sound. She flipped the switch on and off, unplugged and plugged it back in, shook it back and forth as hard as she could, only to watch it sit on the counter and do nothing. "I have no coffee and I'm talking to inanimate objects again. I probably shouldn't leave the house today," she mumbled as she scooted toward the shower.

She waited ten minutes for the water to warm up, an inconvenience the apartment manager failed to mention when she signed the lease a year ago. The ten minutes gave her plenty of time to mull over the message she'd come home to on her answering machine last night.

"Hi, Macey . . . it's me, Rob . . . Yeah, listen, I think it's better we don't see each other for a while . . . okay? Who am I kidding . . . we shouldn't see each other, period. You're a nice person, and I mean that from the bottom of my heart, I just don't think I can do this anymore. You know what I mean? I hope you know what I mean. You're probably thinking I'm a coward for doing this on the machine, but I didn't want you making a scene, and I felt like I needed to get this off my chest. So, that's it. I'm sorry to have to do this. It's just . . . it's just time to say good-bye. Good-bye."

I just can't do this *anymore*, Macey recited inside her head. It was a line she was familiar with, as if all men were reading from the same script. Danny had said he couldn't do *this*. James couldn't do *this*. Lee couldn't do *this*. Bobby Watson had said he couldn't do *that*. She was pretty sure what *this* was. *That* wasn't quite as well defined. In her own definition, *this* meant act like an adult. Make mature decisions. Be responsible, loyal, reliable, and consistent. She wasn't asking too much, was she? WAS SHE? She must be. This was her third relationship in a year, not the kind of track record to go bragging about. At least he hadn't cost her eighty bucks.

The water finally hit a tolerable warmth, and she got in and steadied herself. Her head was already pounding without the coffee. If she wasn't careful, she might fall back asleep. The showerhead poured water from its spout, and she adjusted its strength. "Now, *you* are reliable," she said dully. "I need a guy like you. You're a little slow to warm up, but maybe the best ones are. Not once have you failed to give me water. Not once have you failed to do your job. Not once—AAAAHHHHH!"

The water went ice cold, though at first Macey thought someone had stabbed a hundred knives through her body. "What—?"

She jumped out of the shower and grabbed a towel, slipping and falling onto the tile floor with a thud. She pulled herself to her feet and growled as she yanked her bathrobe off the back of the bathroom door. She slung her wet, matted hair away from her face and walked into the hallway and then into the kitchen just in time to see a heavyset man emerge from underneath the sink.

"Who are you?" she shrieked, though it came out barely a whisper. The man hiked his jeans up to his waist and wiped some grease onto his shirt. He looked fairly harmless.

"I'm sorry, ma'am. I didn't know no one was here."

"Anyone was here." She likened bad grammar to fingernails on a chalkboard.

"I can see that now."

Macey rubbed her eyes. Was this some kind of mirage, the ill effects of no coffee? No, this man was real. "What are you doing here?"

"Fixin' your plumbin'. But I have to say, I didn't find nothin' wrong."

"I didn't report a plumbing problem."

"Ain't you 754?"

"Seven fifty-*three*!" Macey snapped.

"Well, good grief, excuse the daylights out of me. I'm as sorry as can be, ma'am."

Macey smiled tolerantly as the man stooped to gather his tools, revealing the predictable plumber's stigma. She covered her eyes until the man stood back up.

"I'm sorry fer the mistake, ma'am."

"That's okay."

"Hey, aren't you the lady on the TV?"

"Yes, I am."

"I'll be outta your way now."

"Thank you."

"Say, you don't happen to have any coffee goin', do ya? I'm dyin' for a cup."

"You and me both, pal," she said as she went to the door to open it for him. He shuffled along the floor, banging his toolbox into almost every piece of her fine furniture while creating black scuff marks on her recently waxed tile. "You wouldn't happen to be able to fix a coffee machine, would you?"

"Only if it's a CoffeePro Deluxe."

"What?" Macey nearly stumbled standing still. "That's what I have! A 432!"

"Then I can fix it for ya."

———— ◆ ◆ ————

"Yeah, these CoffeePros have a little quirk in 'em that my wife and I found out about in the Deluxe 132 that we got for our wedding. I figured it was somethin' like a wire loose, and it was. This little wire here"—he held it up for her to look at—"just pops loose and disables the whole stinkin' machine. I can't believe they haven't fixed this problem by now." Donald put the bottom back on her coffee maker.

It wasn't long before Macey was enjoying a hot cup of coffee and talking to Donald as if they'd known each other for years. He had two kids, been married twelve years, and actually enjoyed being a plumber. He found it challenging.

"Ya see, it's like a jigsaw puzzle every time I go to a job. Something's not workin', and I gotta look at all the pieces and figure out what the problem is."

Macey couldn't quite identify how that was like a jigsaw puzzle, but it didn't matter because she was now drinking hot coffee, her mind in caffeinated bliss.

Macey poured coffee into a large Styrofoam cup for Donald, then added cream and sugar at his request. The plumber glanced at his watch. "Good grief, I better get goin'. The lady who made this call is prob'ly waitin' on me."

"Are you sure you can't stay a few more minutes?" Macey found it only mildly pathetic that she was so lonely the company of a plumber with bad grammar seemed reasonably delightful.

"No, ma'am, but thanks for the coffee. Have a good day." Donald shut the door behind him and Macey felt a twinge of sadness. But that soon left when she realized how late she was running. She slicked her hair back into a style somewhat professional looking and threw on her newly dry-cleaned suit. Finishing off her last drop of coffee, she thought to herself, *There is a God.*

* * *

Her Lexus sped past domestic and foreign cars alike, and she hardly noticed her eyes were on the clock more than the road. She practiced her breathing like her shrink had taught her and was proud of the fact that she hadn't yet cussed out a fellow driver. Cussing, her shrink had told her, only further exacerbated the anger. It was only two months ago that she'd done a special report on road rage, secretly humored by the irony of it all. Three tickets in the past four weeks kept her speed to ten miles above the limit.

Breathe and release. Breathe and release. Breathe and release. Deep breath. Repeat.

A red Ford Bronco cut in front of her. She slammed on her brakes and screamed he was a moron, all the while passing him on the right and covering her face with her hand so she wouldn't be recognized.

She was forty-five minutes late and quite sure she was experiencing at least five of the eight common signs of stroke. Mitchell was going to freak.

———— ◆ ————

"Do you know how late you are? Do you know how freaked out Mitchell is right now?"

"Do you know that the CoffeePro Deluxe 432 model of coffee maker has an inherent glitch in it dating back to the first model ever made? It completely shuts off the whole machine."

Beth followed Macey around a corner, so close Macey could smell the mint in the gum she was smacking. Beth was mostly tolerable because she was an apple-polishing, fame-seeking intern who thought Macey hung the stars and the moon.

"It might make an interesting story, you know. Maybe *Dateline* would pick it up. I mean, the makers have to know about it, right? So they're deceiving the public. There's a good investigative story in that."

"Right, sure. But you're on in twenty minutes, and Mitchell is losing it!"

"It's good for him to squirm a little, don't you think?" Macey kept the facade of someone unruffled by a tense environment. It's what everyone expected of her. She was actually on in seventeen minutes. Beth was clueless as to how important every second was in this business. She just had to remember, when she got to her desk, to pop an aspirin to thin her blood. They walked into Macey's office.

Just then, Mitchell Teague, her beloved and enigmatic producer, entered like a storm blowing in. "Macey! Seventeen minutes! You're on! Do you know there was a shooting last night? Do you know there was a traffic accident? And a homicide?" The hair he had combed over his bald spot was standing straight up and doing a little wave. Macey waved back and laughed to herself.

She glanced in her mirror to make sure her face was powdered adequately. "Since when isn't there a shooting, accident, or homicide in Dallas, Mitchell? I can do the updates with my eyes closed. Besides, the meat isn't until the noon broadcast. I've got two hours."

"You know how I hate this! You of all people. You live and die by the clock."

The thing Macey appreciated about Mitchell was that he had always wanted to be a producer and was good at producing, so he never envied the anchoring job, a rare find in the industry. Many producers were producers only by default, presuming they could do the anchoring better themselves, and they probably could. But they either lacked the grace or looks or both, which put them behind the scenes, in a small room full of expensive equipment, to run the show with little to no credit. Often the result was cutthroat envy, so much so that even with all his eccentricities, Mitchell was a breath of fresh air.

"Mitchell, I'm sincerely sorry. There was a strange man in my apartment this morning, and it delayed me a little."

Mitchell frowned. "A stranger in your apartment? Are you okay?"

"I'm fine. We had coffee and talked. But I can't predict when I'll have tie-ups like that, and you're just going to have to cut me some slack now and then. I don't do this all the time."

"Did you call the police?"

"No. I felt indebted to him for fixing my coffeepot."

"What?"

"Mitchell, if you can't keep up, then don't ask, okay? Now, can I at least look at some notes or something?"

Mitchell remained flustered, nodding and mumbling as he left her office. Beth arrived again shortly with notes and script in hand.

"Thank you, Bethie. You're the queen. How do I look?"

"Marvelous as always."

"Good," Macey said, glancing over the notes. "Shooting on Harvey, go figure. Accident on Beltline, at least once a week. Homicide downtown. So, where's the fire?"

"It's happening right now at the Xerox plant. We'll probably lead with breaking news."

"No kidding?" Macey smiled. "All right, give me some time to look this over."

"You've got ten minutes."

"Twelve minutes."

Beth pointed to a small sticky on Macey's desk. "Did you see that?"

"What?" Macey started moving papers aside. "This?" She picked up the note and looked at Beth. "Are you serious?"

"Called this morning."

"His assistant?"

"*Him.*"

"*Him*? Thornton Winslow called here for me?"

Beth beamed. "Yep. I covered for you. Said you were out on assignment."

"This is the real thing, isn't it?"

"I think so. You're on your way to the top, baby!"

"Does Mitchell know?"

"He was standing there when I took the call. He couldn't be happier, you know, even though he's not going to let you see that."

"Am I supposed to call Mr. Winslow back?"

"No. He said to let you know that he called, that he's interested in talking with you, but that he'd have to call back in a couple of days because he was leaving for London. He said to make sure and tell you they have your demo tape and were very impressed."

"Seriously!" Macey jumped out of her seat. "Beth! This is huge!"

"You could be in New York! You could be doing really big stories! I mean, you could be in the same building with Jane Pauley!

Stone Phillips and Matt Lauer! Do you think Katie Couric's a snob? I bet she is."

Macey fell back into her chair and stared at the ceiling. "This is unbelievable."

"Yeah, and now it's 9:55. You better get to the desk. I've got to go answer the phone."

Macey walked to the newsroom, hardly touching the floor she was walking on. As they did sound tests and mike checks and powdered her face and touched up her hair, Macey dreamed of New York and the network.

The floor director gave her the three-minute warning, and Macey ran over the script one more time. She hated the idea of cold reads. The five and ten o'clock anchor, Emma Patrick, a longtime Dallas anchorwoman and the mother hen to all the "youngsters," had been doing cold reads for fifteen years. But she'd been in the business for twenty-five years. At fifty and three plastic surgeries later, she still held the coveted five and ten spots. No one dared even to attempt sliding into her position. The woman would rather be dead than give it up. Eight years ago she did a week's worth of broadcasts with full-blown influenza just so another younger, hipper anchor wouldn't get exposure. It seemed Emma Patrick had invaluable connections, and Macey would be forever stuck as the "nooner." She glanced down at the note with Thornton Winslow's name on it and smiled. Or maybe not.

Suddenly Beth was by her side.

"Beth, what are you doing? We're on in less than three."

Beth looked a little pale and avoided Macey's eyes. "Um . . . I have a message, but it can probably wait. . . ."

"From who?"

"Really . . . it can wait. You've got two minutes."

"Beth, for crying out loud! Who's the message from? Thornton?"

Beth hesitated, then finally answered, "Diana Wellers. She said you knew her as Diana Parr."

Macey shook her head with disbelief. "Diana Parr? I knew her in high school. I haven't seen her in almost twenty years. What in the world is she calling me for?"

Beth hesitated again and glanced at the director as he gave the thirty-second signal and waved at her to move out of the way.

"*Beth*, what is it?"

"Um, I don't think—"

"Beth!"

Beth swallowed and said, "She called to . . . to tell you that . . . I guess your father has died."

Beth looked at her one second longer and then stepped away from the news desk. Macey felt as if someone had punched her in the stomach. Her mouth went dry. She watched Eddie give her the ten-second sign, his face bewildered as he eyed Macey.

Five . . . four . . . three . . . two . . . pull it together . . . one. . .

"Good morning, Dallas, this is Macey Steigel with a News Channel 7 update. This morning, fire officials are reporting a fire at the Xerox plant north of the city. No injuries have been reported, and officials aren't saying what started the fire. . . ."

Macey read the teleprompter with professional accuracy, all the subtle nods and gestures in place as if she were talking to a person and not a camera. She raised her eyebrows to underscore an important fact and softened her expression before she pitched the weather. She made a lighthearted joke to Walter the meteorologist, smiling back at him as if they were the best of friends.

The tips of her fingers tingled in the strangest way. The news that her father was dead made her go numb inside, though she didn't really know why. In her mind he'd been dead for nearly seventeen years.

Two

Macey tried to gather her things and stuff them into her brief-case, maneuvering around the three-person crowd that now occupied her office.

"I don't need time off, Mitchell," Macey protested.

Mitchell's eyes shifted to Beth's, whose shifted to Walter, who simply stared at the carpet. Mitchell cleared his throat. "You're not going to the funeral?"

"It's complicated, okay?" Macey eyed each of them. "And don't anyone sit here and judge me for it, either."

Mitchell's chest heaved in a reluctant sigh. "All right, fine. But don't hesitate to change your mind. We'll work things out." Someone screamed at Mitchell about some crisis with camera number two, and Mitchell was gone before anyone knew it.

Walter tilted his head to the side, the tilt that indicated he had no words or advice, and he shuffled out of the office with his head hung low. Unfortunately, Beth wasn't so quick to leave. She smoothed out her ponytail, a sure indication she was thinking of some way to state something she shouldn't.

"Beth," Macey warned, "please don't. I don't need to hear whatever you're about to say."

"But he's your dad—"

"Beth—"

"You're his only child—"

"*Beth*—"

"And he's dead."

Macey looked up, her eyes cold and tired. "Yes, he is."

"So . . ." Beth managed carefully, "whatever he did to you in the past, he can't do to you now. Dead men can't do much, you know."

Macey crammed more papers into her briefcase. "I wouldn't be so sure about that."

Beth's eyes lowered. "He must've been a horrible person." She glanced up at Macey. "I mean, to not want to go to your own father's—"

"Beth, really. I know you're trying to . . ." Suddenly the whole thing overwhelmed Macey, and she turned away and closed her briefcase. Her father was dead. The reality was sinking in. A reality she'd thought little of over the past seventeen years. She wondered how he died. He would've been sixty-seven in three weeks.

Macey snapped the locks on her briefcase and thought Beth had asked her a question. She turned around to head for the door. "What?"

"I said, what about your mom? Is she still alive?"

The tears were now escaping. Macey rushed past Beth and out the office door. She took the back hallway and the stairs that led directly to the door where her car was parked.

She quickly opened the door and threw her briefcase onto the passenger seat. Before the car door closed, all her emotions collapsed onto one another. For an hour she sat hunched over the steering wheel, unable to do anything but cry.

———— ❖ ————

Evelyn Steigel wasn't sure when her tears would run out, but she had little energy to try to stop the ones that still flowed. Patricia opened the front door for her, bumping it with her hip because it always stuck when the humidity was high. She helped her in, and Evelyn was grateful for the warm touch of another human being.

"Here, sit down there at the table," Patricia instructed softly, "and I'll make us some coffee."

Evelyn's whole body quivered. The house was so silent. But she appreciated the way the early evening sun glowed through the windows and warmed the room. The smell of freshly brewed coffee awakened her a bit so that she smiled as she watched the coffeepot fill up with the dark liquid. They had talked about getting an automatic coffee maker for three years before finally buying one at the Sears in Joplin. Jess had always insisted on grinding the beans fresh. She was going to have to learn to do that now.

Patricia brought her a warm mug, perfectly flavored with cream and no sugar, and joined her at the table as she stared blankly out the window. Finally the silence was more than either of them could bear.

"I sure love the flowers you picked out, Evelyn. Jess would've, too."

Evelyn's eyes blinked lazily. "You know Jess. He wouldn't have wanted a big fuss made over him. I think I got the cheapest casket they had. He's not there anyways. But I thought it might be nice to have some color with the flowers. I didn't spend that much on 'em."

Patricia agreed with a warm smile. "Well, the service is going to be lovely. Just lovely."

"Pastor Lyle's going to be coming over in a while. I guess I better get something prepared."

Patricia stopped her from standing. "Evelyn, we have more food here than could feed Willie Bartlett's pig farm. Margie Potter brought over her famous chicken and potato casserole. Let's just warm that up and be done with it."

Evelyn agreed and watched as Patricia moved about the kitchen. "Patricia, I'm sorry if I haven't told you how grateful I am to have had you around these past few weeks." Patricia looked over her shoulder and nodded. "I suppose you'll be moving on now, yet it was nice to have you here, just want you to know that."

Patricia turned the oven on. "Evelyn, you know I'll be around. I just adore you, and I adored Jess. I can't just leave because the job's over. Nursing, it's more than just medicine."

Evelyn stared at the picture of her and Jess on the baker's rack. "You did a good job taking care of him. You're like a daugh—" The words caught in her throat, but Patricia was kind enough not to turn around.

"Listen, why don't we make some of them buttermilk biscuits to have with the casserole. Pastor Lyle always does like biscuits with his meals." Patricia went on reminiscing about Lyle and his love for biscuits, about the time when at the church picnic no one brought biscuits. But Evelyn wasn't paying much attention.

Instead, she was praying. She hoped she didn't sound too angry or too harsh. But her prayers, her deepest longings, hadn't come true. And now it was too late. God could never answer that prayer. He'd rejected her most precious request.

A car pulled into the drive, the sound of rolling gravel an indication it was Pastor Lyle. Ever since he got that new Ford pickup, he drove way too fast.

"I'll get the door," Patricia offered, but Evelyn stood anyway. It was awfully rude to stay seated when someone was paying a visit to one's house. Her daddy had taught her that.

Pastor Lyle hadn't even knocked yet when Patricia opened the door and let him in. He was a round man, with a red face and silver white hair that was parted and slicked with a pastor's precision. He walked over to Evelyn and took her hands.

"Dear, how are you? What can I do for you? Are you ready to talk about the funeral? It can wait. I'm very sorry for your loss."

Evelyn guided him to the kitchen table and motioned for him to sit, which he did, huffing and puffing like he'd just run a marathon. Everyone had expected Pastor Lyle to pass on years ago. He'd already had two bypass surgeries. Still his blood pressure elevated if he did anything other than sleep. And he was a closet smoker, something everyone pretended not to know about.

"Pastor Lyle, you're kind for coming by," said Evelyn. "Patricia's warming up Margie's chicken and potato casserole."

Pastor Lyle glanced toward the oven. "Any biscuits?"

Patricia smiled as she brought him a cold glass of water. "Of course."

His attention shifted back to Evelyn. "The funeral is set for the day after tomorrow, at ten in the morning. It's all cleared with Newt. I wish we could've had it at the church but I just don't think we'll be able to hold the crowd."

Evelyn nodded as she lowered herself back into her chair. "We have coffee if you want."

"Nah. Water's fine. But I will have some of them biscuits and casserole when it's ready."

Patricia stooped down and peered into the oven. "Lookin' like about ten minutes."

Pastor Lyle sipped his water, blotted his brow with his hanky. "Boy, every summer I think it *cain't* get any hotter, but then it does. You'd think by evening it'd cool down a little."

"Not till that sun goes down. Maybe we'll get some breeze then," Patricia said as she made up a pitcher of lemonade.

Evelyn tried to focus on the chitchat, which most of the time she loved. But today her heart was breaking, and there wasn't too much that interested her. Pastor Lyle set down his water.

"Evelyn, again, I'm so sorry for your loss. We'll all miss Jess something terrible." Evelyn nodded but didn't look the pastor in the eyes. "Have you thought of some people that might want to speak at his funeral?"

Evelyn wiped a lone tear away and took a few sips of her coffee. She was trembling so badly she had to steady the mug with both hands. "I thought maybe Roger Layton. And of course Jess's brother, Howard."

"Howard just lives over in Chanute, doesn't he?"

"You're thinking of his sister, Barb. Howard lives in Parsons."

"Will Barb be able to make it?"

Evelyn shook her head. "The last stroke really did her in. She's in a nursing home now. Hardly knows where she is."

Pastor Lyle nodded and patted Evelyn on the hand. "Well, I'll call Roger, and maybe you could call Howard."

"I've already talked to Howard, and he said he'd be honored to say something."

Pastor Lyle let go of her hands while Patricia set the casserole down and hurried back for the biscuits. "Oh! I just love Margie's casserole! I never told Shirley when she was alive. You know how they always had that cookin' competition thing. But Margie's casserole just cain't be beat. And that's sayin' something because my wife was a good cook." He scooped out a large portion and plopped it onto the plate Patricia had set in front of him, then grabbed three biscuits from the basket. He blessed the food before Evelyn or Patricia had served themselves and went right to eating without any hesitation.

Pastor Lyle was famous for putting food before God. Most of the time someone had to remind him to bless it before digging in. In his sermons, when he talked about heaven, he always in some way mentioned how much turkey would be there.

"The ladies will be bringing the food for the reception," he said between bites. "I'm assuming you'll want it here at the house?"

"That'll be fine," Evelyn said, chewing food she could hardly taste. "We've got so much food here as it is, Pastor. Tell them not to bring too much. It'll just go to waste." She'd said this without thinking, for food never went to waste. Pastor Lyle always took it home. Ever since his wife died, the community paid him in few dollars and lots of food, an arrangement he was perfectly fine with. At least once a week someone had him over for dinner and made extras for him to take home.

"And you've made all the arrangements with Newt Castles at the funeral home?"

"Yes, we'd already bought our plots. Right between our parents. And anyone's welcome to come to the graveside. I want people to know that."

"Sure," Pastor Lyle said, nabbing two more biscuits. Patricia refilled his water and brought him a fresh glass of lemonade.

A quietness settled over the table, and Evelyn tried not to think too much about Jess's painful last days. The man had believed God would heal him, up until he took his last breath. Evelyn had tried as best she could to believe it, too. Now she decided to think more about how thankful she was that she'd been able to say good-bye. How thankful she was that he was with the Lord. She only had to live without her husband a few short years. She figured she wasn't likely to live that much longer anyway. Lately her health had been failing her. Even though her mama had lived to be eighty-six, she felt she wouldn't make it past seventy-five. So ten years alone. Maybe she'd be lucky and the Lord would bring her home before that.

She smiled to herself as she wondered how her daddy and Jess were getting along up in heaven. They never much liked each other down on earth. They managed to be cordial enough for the sakes of the women in their lives, but Daddy always thought Jess made too many risky decisions about the farm, and Jess always thought Daddy never trusted him enough.

Pastor Lyle had managed three more helpings of casserole as Evelyn and Patricia were finishing off their first. Evelyn was quite sure she saw him sneak two biscuits into the pockets of his pants.

Patricia rose from the table and went over to open the oven, revealing a new batch of biscuits. "Well, Pastor, looks as if I baked way too many biscuits. Please take some home."

"Oh, I couldn't," Pastor Lyle recited.

Patricia played the role. "Oh, you must. The fridge is packed. We'd just have to toss them out to the chickens."

"Well, if you're going to throw them out . . ."

"I'll wrap up the rest of that casserole for you, too." Patricia cleared the table while Pastor Lyle poured himself water and Evelyn more lemonade.

The sun was lowering itself toward the horizon. It was the time of day when she and Jess would sit on their front porch in their new rocking chairs and listen to the sounds of the evening. The crickets would begin their song, the locusts compete for their place in the chorus. The sun's orange rays met with the stars of the night, creating a sky that looked painted by God himself. Usually Evelyn would've made a pie, and the two of them would enjoy it silently, conversing together without ever making a sound.

Pastor Lyle cleared his throat and lowered his voice. "Evelyn, what about your daughter?"

Evelyn looked down at the table. "I don't know. I, um, I don't think she'll be here. She probably doesn't even know."

"I can try to contact her if you'd like me to."

Evelyn couldn't speak. She didn't know what to do. Tears splashed onto the table, and she grabbed her napkin to try to stop them. Pastor Lyle's soft blue eyes melted with compassion.

"Whatever you think is best, honey. I just wanted to ask."

Evelyn nodded. Patricia rescued her by bringing the wrapped casserole and biscuits back to the table. Pastor Lyle accepted them graciously and then stood to leave. He hugged both Patricia and Evelyn, held the food like a newborn baby, and left the house quietly.

Patricia wrapped her arms around Evelyn. "I'm sorry your daughter's not here. I wish I could do something."

Evelyn shook her head, waving her hand at the absurdity of her reaction. "I don't know why I expected anything else. Macille doesn't want anything to do with us. She never has. I just thought . . . I just thought maybe God would . . ." Her voice broke and her eyes shut. She let herself cry about it a few minutes longer while Patricia held her hands.

Patricia finally pulled out a chair and sat down. Evelyn dried her tears, looked out the window and said, "Sometimes, Patricia, God says no to your prayers, and you have to be okay with that."

Three

It was almost a high for her. The busyness. The chaos. The swarms of people milling about with no regard for one another. Macey bought a salad, then seated herself near gate 7 at the St. Louis airport and watched it all. She tried to keep her mind occupied with thoughts of the network. Her dream job was within her reach, and after she returned home from Kansas, things would move forward. Now, though, she was waiting to fly to Joplin. It made no sense that the flight to Joplin would take as long as the flight from Dallas to St. Louis. She glanced at the clock, which said 11:44.

The voice over the speaker announced her flight was ready to board and for first-class passengers to approach the gate. Macey always flew first class. She needed to be around people who recognized that a plane trip wasn't the time to make a new friend; rather it was a time to work. She swung her carryon over her shoulder, adjusted her sunglasses, and was soon striding down the jetway with six men, all carrying laptop computers.

During the flight Macey found herself distracted by the thoughts of returning home after so many years. It was ultimately the thought of her mother being alone that had made her choose to return. At least that's what she guessed. Her mind had changed suddenly, and she wasn't sure why. Deep inside her throat, a tightness still clung and threatened to escape at the most improbable moment. So she just stared out the window and admired the patterns of clouds of an approaching thunderstorm far beneath the wings of the plane.

She wondered what her mother looked like, if she'd aged much. If the house still needed painting. By now, their old dog, Sandy, was gone. But she wondered if they had a new one. If the chicken coop still sat twenty yards from the barn.

The memories overwhelmed her, a bitter reminder of why she'd kept herself from thinking about such things all these years. The continual clicking of the computers around her brought her mind back to the present and ushered her on to escape into daydreaming about the network again. Very few reporters and anchors ever got to work for a network. Many were intimidated by the whole prospect of it all. But Macey wasn't afraid. She knew that by getting a job with the network and moving to New York, once and for all, she could leave behind everything that haunted her and start over.

This trip back home certainly put a crimp in the plan, yet the humanity in her couldn't bear to think of her mother dealing with her husband's death alone. Her mother had devoted almost her entire life to the man. Macey intended to return home, make sure her mother would be all right, and then leave again soon after. Perhaps in the future they would stay in touch. It would be okay if that happened. As long as she wasn't expected home every Christmas. A network job would be relentless. There would be little time for social gatherings on a farm in Kansas. She checked her watch. 1:21.

Before she knew it, the plane's wheels were bumping the runway in Joplin. After collecting her luggage, she went to check in at the car rental counter. Less than fifteen minutes later she was sitting in a four-door compact, the thick air suffocating every breath she tried. She rolled the windows down and switched on the air-conditioner, not wanting to look like she'd gone for a swim before even getting there. Flipping open her briefcase, she found her Bruce Springsteen CD. She'd thought about bringing Eric Clapton's *Reptile,* but Springsteen's *Live in New York City* was a double CD, and she thought she might be listening to an awful lot of music in the two days she was planning to stay.

Without much effort, she found herself driving along on a steamy Highway 166. Her heart began pounding at the thought of the reunion soon to take place. What would she say? Thanks for the cards? Sorry I didn't forward my address after leaving San Antonio? She sighed and realized she couldn't prepare herself for all that might occur. She just hoped her mother understood the reasons why she hadn't returned home for so long. Her mother was naïve and pure, but she wasn't stupid. It had never been discussed out loud, she guessed, between her mother and her father. Even so, everyone involved knew. Macey hoped her mother knew enough not to talk about it.

The sun shone down bright and harsh, so Macey slid her sunglasses back on. The air-conditioning on high proved barely adequate to ward off what Macey guessed to be 102 degrees or higher heat outside. Already her skin felt sticky and moist. She sat up straight to separate her shirt from her lower back.

She turned north on Highway 169, almost without thinking. In this part of the country, she was pretty sure time moved backward. She drove by some of the familiar towns she'd once known so well: Morehead, Thayer, Earlton, and Chanute, where her aunt used to live. Barb had probably passed away by now.

The golden wheat outside her car windows, the endless pastures, served to calm her spirit a little. It was truly beautiful here, where the land was sacred and appreciated for all it could give. It had been a long time since she'd seen so many cows.

———— •◆• ————

The drive took about an hour. She had no trouble finding the old house. There it sat, one of only seven houses in a square mile.

It still needed painting and looked as if it had aged a century. Her mother had been faithful in planting some flowers, however, and the porch appeared as bright and inviting as ever.

After turning off the engine, Macey took a deep breath and slowly opened the car door. The exhausting heat rushed in, and she felt drained the second it hit her. She pulled her shoulder-length hair up off her neck and decided to leave all her baggage in the car for now. She couldn't leave it too long, though, or everything would melt.

She imagined her mom hurrying out the door and embracing her with hugs and kisses. Then she imagined her mom peeking through the window, pretending no one was home. As she walked up the porch steps, she noticed two new-looking rocking chairs her father had probably made himself. He had always been masterful with wood.

Macey knocked lightly and waited. The barn was still intact, and she was pretty sure she could smell the chicken coop, though it had apparently been moved, to someplace upwind no doubt. She knocked again and listened for any movement inside the house.

One more knock and then she decided to try opening the door, which of course was unlocked. No one ever locked their doors around here. The knob turned but the door stuck. She had to push it with her hip till it gave way.

The house quietly creaked, and Macey was afraid to say anything. Everything from her vantage point looked exactly the same as when she left, not surprising her at all, although she was shocked to see an automatic coffee maker on the kitchen counter. At least she could count on good coffee while she was here.

She moved farther into the house. "Mother?" she called softly. No answer came. Macey wondered where her mother could be in the heat of the day. She walked around the house, gazing at pictures and knickknacks. It was as if she were frozen in time at the age of eighteen. It surprised her to see pictures of herself still sitting around. Had her father not insisted that all traces of her vanish?

A framed photo of her mom and dad sat on the baker's rack, and Macey bent closer to get a better look. It showed her father as an older man, his brow creased deeply, his eyes tired. He was almost completely bald. Her mom looked much heavier than the last time Macey saw her. Yet it was no shock to see that her mom had a weight problem. Her whole side of the family was heavy, and her mom had always insisted on cooking with lard, something Macey had found to be startling only *after* she'd left Kansas.

Two different sofas replaced the ones she remembered. Both looked old. A quilt lay on the back of one of them, its colors in contrast to everything else around. Macey wasn't sure if the TV was the same, but this one had knobs and imitation wood, so she assumed it was old. Her mother's orange blown-glass "art" decorated the shelves and coffee table, along with fishing, hunting, and sewing magazines in a basket and the current *Guideposts* balanced on the arm of the sofa. In a smaller basket next to the rocking chair were her mother's knitting yarn and needlepoint supplies. She walked to the large bay window, which displayed a perfectly manicured lawn and the edge of the riverbank.

All seemed to be in order, dusted, arranged and in place. A feeling of sadness swept over Macey as she realized whatever homecoming she'd anticipated wasn't going to happen now. She decided to wait to explore the upstairs portion of the house. Instead, she went out the back door and walked across the lush lawn toward the river.

The rushing sound of the water brought her some comfort. From where she stood she could see that Stone Bridge still crossed over the Neosho River. On the other side, the old abandoned two-story house still stood, the house she used to play in as a child. Her mind echoed thoughts of children laughing and playing inside its walls. But the laughter soon faded, and her heart mourned the more recent memories. The truth was, the very last memory of that house had ruined her life.

The coop was rather quiet, the chickens listless in the heat of the day. She strolled along the river, admiring the blueness of the water as it bounced along the riverbed. The river was down, as it always was this time of year. Still, it flowed with a strong current.

When she finally arrived at Stone Bridge, she could see the old house across the river a little better. Tall and threatening, the house captured her curiosity, just as it used to when she was a child, guiding her feet along the smooth stones of the bridge until she reached the other side. Her heart throbbed at the thought of approaching it after all these years.

That's when she saw the laundry line, the articles of clothing moving up and down in the light breeze. Could someone actually be living in the old house?

She stepped carefully around the weeds and rocks and made her way toward the house. Being daytime, she couldn't see a thing through the windows. As she neared the back of the house, the grass became greener and shorter. The place didn't look abandoned, but it certainly didn't look like it should be occupied, either. The grayish brown wood siding was all cracked and dry.

Moving around the side of the house, she gasped when she saw the obvious signs of occupancy: flowers, lawn chairs, a tire swing hanging from the old oak tree. Quickly she started to leave when she heard a loud *snap*. Her body whirled around just in time to see a large man wearing only a pair of overalls walking toward her. Over six feet tall, he was muscular with long hair tied back in a ponytail. The only thing missing was an ax.

"Um, so sorry... I'm... I thought..." Macey took a deep breath and tried a little humor. "I thought you were a ghost."

"That's funny," he said in the deepest voice she'd ever heard, "I thought you were a burglar. If you'll stay right here, I'll go get my shotgun."

Macey blinked and swallowed, then realized the stranger was showing the hint of a smile. "I don't look like a burglar, do I?"

"It depends. How much do I look like a ghost?"

Macey was soaked in sweat. Once again she lifted her hair up off her neck to try to cool down. "I'm sorry to bother you. I thought this house was abandoned. It used to be. I used to play in it as a child."

The man gave her another half smile, and she noticed paint on his hands. "Well, as you can see, I live here now."

"Yes, again, I'm sorry."

He looked her up and down and said, "It isn't often we see a lady like you dressed up like that in these parts." His accent wasn't as thick with laziness as she expected it would be. In fact, it didn't really sound like a local accent at all.

Macey smiled tolerantly. "Yes, well, I don't plan to stay long. I'm here visiting my parents . . . my mother, I mean. Excuse me. I'll get going."

"Are you Evelyn and Jess's daughter?"

Macey had already turned around, but she stopped and turned back. "Yes. You know them?"

The man stepped forward. She could see that he had a few small paintbrushes sticking out of his overalls. He pointed toward her mom's house across the river. "They're my neighbors. Of course I know them. But I don't know you. Why is that?"

The man made her uncomfortable. His eyes were intensely blue and seemed to look into her soul. "You paint?" Macey pointed to the colorful smudges on his pants.

"I do."

"Listen, I was noticing my parents' house is in desperate need of some paint. I'll pay you whatever you charge."

He grinned and wiped his hands on a dirty rag hanging from a front pocket. "I don't paint houses."

"Oh. What do you paint, then? Cars?"

"Canvas."

Macey tried not to let her mouth hang open, but she couldn't help tilting her head to the side. If there was anyone who didn't fit the image of an artist, it was this man. A woodcutter, maybe. But an artist, no. He must be joking.

"It surprises you that a painter might use canvas?"

"No," Macey said. She noticed the easel now, just a few yards away. "It's just that you don't really look like an artist. Do you have, um, formal training?"

"I have instinct and quite a bit of natural talent, which has gotten me pretty far."

Macey felt pity for the man. Perhaps if he'd left this part of Kansas, he could've been somebody great. She offered a bit of unwanted advice. "Well, instinct and natural talent can't teach you some of the finer points of painting, now can they? I know out here people don't have too much of an appreciation for higher education, but you should consider it. It might take you places."

The man stared at her, his eyes perfectly still, as though he were receiving some silent message from her and interpreting it as it came. He nodded as an afterthought, then said, "I have strengths and weaknesses. More strengths than weaknesses. I know color, for example."

Macey was growing aggravated. She could feel the suffocating humidity melting her makeup and flattening her hair. Sweat dripped down the sides of her temples, rolling over her cheeks and gathering in the hollow of her neck. Did she really have the energy to debate artistry with a man who couldn't even find an undershirt to wear with his overalls?

"Color," Macey responded, her intolerance increasing with each bead of sweat. "That's handy if you're going to be a painter. What do you know about color?"

That same small smile she'd seen before crept across his weathered lips. "Oh, for example, a brunette should never wear that color eye shadow with that color blouse and expect to pull off pink lipstick. It washes you out."

Macey's eyes narrowed in disgust. Here she was trying to help the poor guy out with some friendly advice, and he was insulting her choice of lipstick? She tried to think what color of eye shadow she had on. Her blouse was purple. Was it the blue eye shadow she put on this morning? And what in the world did her brown hair have to do with it?

"I didn't realize Mary Kay had representatives this far into nowhere land." It was the best she could come up with, but it didn't seem to have fazed him. He fiddled with one of his paintbrushes and stared at her with complete social ineptness.

The sun was making her dizzy. Was it the sun or the giant beast of a man standing in front of her? She could feel her cheeks flushing from the heat; she was probably getting a sunburn. "Well, it was nice talking with you," Macey offered in the dullest voice she could find. "I'm sorry again for trespassing."

He shrugged. "Oh, no, listen, my house is always open to people who just want to wander around and snoop. In fact, if you're not busy tomorrow, maybe you could sneak over and dig around in my personal belongings."

Macey crossed her arms and narrowed her eyes again.

"You are not a very nice person."

"I suppose you've mistaken me for someone with a strong intellect, like yourself. After all, I know a higher education can at least make a person *nice*. Isn't that right?"

"I'm leaving now," Macey said, stomping her heels into the dirt as she rounded the corner of the house, back toward Stone Bridge.

"I'm sorry, I didn't catch your name," he said, but Macey didn't turn around.

What a facetious, arrogant hick! She quickly made her way through the grass and weeds and back to the bridge, where she was able to catch her breath for the first time. Halfway over, she looked back at the old house.

She had always imagined it haunted when she was a child. Now, as a young adult, the ghosts she'd created there still haunted her to this day. She had hoped the house would be torn down, but to no avail. There it stood, dark against the horizon, reminding her of the biggest mistake of her life.

Four

H er sweaty feet made it impossible to walk in heels with any grace, so Macey was now barefoot, enjoying the soft grass between her toes. Her mind replayed clever insult after clever insult, thinking of all the ways she could have, should have, thrown the lipstick comment back in his face! She glanced at her watch. 3:50.

A few blue jays swooped down low and harassed her and each other before moving back into the trees. They were mean birds, sort of like the one across the river. She glanced over her shoulder one more time. The house was smaller and no longer detailed.

She walked through a grouping of tall elm trees, feeling their bark and admiring their strength. She remembered how much imagination was set free in the midst of all these trees. She looked around at the tops and there it was! Her old tree house. She couldn't believe it had resisted years of storms and wind. She also couldn't imagine how she'd ever climbed up so high. Her father had built it for her when she was six.

Shuffling her feet through the grass again, Macey looked up and was startled to be so close already to her mom's house. There in the driveway sat the old maroon Pontiac. Could she still be driving the same car? She barely had time to process this when she looked toward the back door of the home, and there, standing in the frame, was her mother.

She was large, even more so than the pictures revealed. A lightweight sleeveless summer dress hung loosely around her and moved in the breeze. Macey could see her face, which was bright and glowing, causing Macey to pick up her pace with no regard for stickers or rocks.

Then, as she neared the back door, Macey hesitated. She watched her mom hold on to the railing and ease herself slowly down the steps, wincing in pain every time her knee bent. Macey took a few more steps forward until they were face-to-face.

Macey offered a smile.

"Macille! You're home!" Her mother's strong arms embraced her, and Macey patted her lightly on the back. "You're home!" She released her daughter and cupped her shoulders in her hands. "You're beautiful! As beautiful as I could've ever imagined you to be. And you still have that thick brown hair of yours."

"Hi, Mom." Macey smiled again, thinking of the six or so times she'd cut and grown out her hair in the past seventeen years. Her hands found their way into the pockets of her pants. She didn't know what to do. She wasn't used to being hugged. Or even being touched, for that matter.

Her mom put her arm around Macey's waist and guided her toward the back steps. "The heat's unbearable. Let's go inside. I'll make us some lemonade."

The shuffling of her mom's feet against the cement indicated she couldn't do much more than walk, for she could hardly pick up her feet. Macey slipped her heels back on and finally matched height with her mom, who had always been a tall woman. When they got to the steps Macey took her mom's arm and helped her up the steps while her mom complained of arthritis and tendinitis and several other *itis*es Macey had never heard of.

They walked into the kitchen, and her mom grabbed the pitcher off the baker's rack and began filling it with water. She then turned and looked at Macey, tears sparkling in her eyes. "I wasn't sure you would come. How did you find out your father had passed on?"

Guilt stung her heart. "Um, Diana Parr. You remember her?"

"Oh, yes. I see her mother at least twice a week at the grocery store."

"Yes, well, we've kept in touch, sort of. I mean, not regularly. I guess I've only talked to her twice since high school. But she called to let me know." Macey paused as she watched her mom stir the lemonade. "I'm sorry I didn't forward my address to you after I left San Antonio. Things got crazy. I just lost track of time." Four years of time? Hardly an excuse. Her mom didn't seem to care, though. She set the lemonade on the small kitchen table with a grin and went to the cupboard for glasses and to the refrigerator for ice.

"So you've been livin' where now?"

"Dallas." She took the glass from her mom. "Nice city. I like it much more than San Antonio."

"Still doing the TV personality?" She watched her mom lower herself carefully into the chair.

"Anchoring, yes. I anchor the noon news." The ice in her drink melted almost instantly. The conversation ended, and her mom simply stared at her and smiled as if trying to recreate all the time that had passed while separated from each other.

"You're just so beautiful. And sophisticated. That suit looks so expensive—you look like a model! I see you wear your makeup like the department store women try to show me. I can't ever get it to look right. But you look just perfect. The pink lipstick is just wonderful. I could never wear a color like that."

"Apparently neither can I," Macey said with a chuckle, then wondered if it might be time for an updated look if a woman on a farm in Kansas thought her makeup looked like someone in a department store had done it.

"I'd always dreamed of wearing suits and high heels," Evelyn said with enthusiasm. "But sometimes all your dreams can't come true."

She shrugged and smiled again. "It's so good to have you home." Her hands messed with her short curly hair. "I must look like I've aged a hundred years."

"Oh, Mom, no. You look fine. Really." She glanced around the kitchen and into the living room. "The house has hardly changed."

"That's your father's doing. Never did like change. Of any kind." Macey noticed her eyes moistened a little. "But did you see our coffee maker?"

Macey laughed. "I noticed it. Who says you're not modern?"

Evelyn smiled and then giggled, and Macey's heart melted with hearing her mom laugh. They both enjoyed the quietness of each other's company for a bit, and then Macey felt compelled to fill the silence. Silence made her uncomfortable, she guessed because when on-air even a second of it was too long.

"Have I missed the funeral?"

"No, no. It's tomorrow at ten. Pastor Lyle's doing it."

"Pastor Lyle is still alive?"

"Oh, yes. He was over just last night for casserole and biscuits. The man must be doing something right for the Lord, since the Lord refuses to take him home. I guess it goes to show that His timing is all that matters." Evelyn poured another glass of lemonade, and her eyes became distant in a reflective thought of some sort. "I'm sorry I wasn't home. I had to make a few more arrangements for the funeral." She looked up at Macey with tear-filled eyes again. "I'm just so glad I didn't have to come home to an empty house. Your timing couldn't have been better." The tears fell and dripped down her cheeks. Macey was speechless. She had little experience in comforting others.

"Um . . . can I see upstairs? Is it still the same?"

Evelyn wiped the tears away and seemed embarrassed.

"Your room is all ready for you! Haven't changed it a bit, either. Do you have any luggage?"

Macey groaned as she sorted through lipstick that had turned to liquid. It had seeped into her eye shadow and powder so that everything was now a sticky mess. Evelyn busily wet paper towels to try to help her daughter clean up the assortment of melted makeup colors.

"I knew I shouldn't have left my luggage in the car," her daughter lamented. "I know what this kind of heat can do."

Evelyn handed her another paper towel, trying not to be too obvious in staring at her. She was just so pretty. "Well, we can go into town and get some more. It's probably not the fancy kind, but it'll do for now."

Macey nodded and wiped her hands off with a towel. "Let's leave this. I still want to see my room."

Evelyn smiled and let her go first up the stairs. Macey was gracious enough not to race up before her, but took her hand and helped her climb each step. They finally topped the staircase, and she watched her daughter's eyes take in all the pictures and rooms with one turn of the head. She then walked straight down the hallway to her room, with Evelyn following close behind.

Macey stood in the middle of the room and gazed at all the knickknacks, pictures, and keepsakes from high school. She seemed to be speechless. Evelyn was out of breath herself from the climb, so she shuffled over to the bed and sat down, patting the comforter.

"The sheets are washed and cleaned. Everything's dusted. I even waxed these old wood floors. 'Bout broke my back, but at least they're shiny."

Macey turned to her. "But you didn't know I was coming."

"Well, I prayed that you would," said Evelyn, "and I wouldn't have too much faith if I didn't prepare like the Lord was going to answer those prayers." She pointed to the shelf above her bed. "All of your high school ribbons and awards are still there."

Macey walked over and took a ribbon down. "Track. First place."

"Do you still enjoy athletics?"

"I run eight miles almost every day," her daughter said with a smile. She then walked around the rest of the room, even looking out the window for a moment. "I suppose I took for granted this view from my room. Look at those beautiful fields."

"The combines will be here soon for harvest. I'm sure you remember all the rumbling that causes. It's like we're having an earthquake for a month! We don't have to mess with them anymore since your father retired and sold the fields." Evelyn paused, thinking of what a painful time it had been for Jess. The drought had lessened the value of the land drastically, but with his health he couldn't afford to keep up with it all.

Macey opened the door to one of her closets. She turned to Evelyn and said, "My clothes are still here?"

Evelyn shrugged. "Didn't know what else to do with them. I didn't want to give them away. I thought you might call and need them."

Macey pulled a high school T-shirt off a hanger and grabbed some cutoffs from the shelf. She held them up and laughed. "I can't think of anything more comfortable to wear in the world! I feel like I've run a hundred miles. Mind if I take a shower and clean up?"

Evelyn rose, steadying herself on her feet, and went to the linen closet. "Here's a towel and washrag. You take your time. Relax. Take a nap if you need to. I'm going to go start dinner." She handed them over to Macey. "Make sure to check for ticks. It's that season and you were out barefoot in the grass."

Macey thanked her and moved to the bathroom. Evelyn stood in the hall long after the door had shut and the water had been turned on. There was joy yet there was also sorrow. Her daughter was home, but she'd come home too late. Wounds couldn't be mended now.

As tears streamed down her face, she wondered what in the world God could be up to, because she knew one thing for sure: He was never late.

The water relaxed her. It was a steady stream, just like she remembered, and she found herself complimenting the showerhead and comparing it to the one at home. The water warmed up quickly, but she turned the hot down and let the cool dominate. Even in the air-conditioned house, the heat remained suffocating.

Afterward, Macey stood at the window of her bedroom, looking out at the fields glowing with golden hues. She mindlessly towel-dried her hair and studied the beauty before her. She hadn't ever remembered taking the time to stand here and appreciate it all like this.

But soon enough a haunting voice chilled her spine, and she turned to watch the memories she'd tried so hard to escape play out before her in vivid images. Her breath escaped her and she closed her eyes, forbidding any more to be recalled. Except she could still smell the distinctly sweet aroma of the tobacco from his pipe, the one he somehow justified against all the strict rules he'd been so loyal to.

It was a long moment before she felt it safe to open her eyes again. She stood motionless as she observed her room again, this time without the watchful eyes of her mother nearby. She imagined her mother begging her father not to touch the room, her father relentless in insisting they take everything out of it and burn it. Somehow everything had remained intact. It was as if seventeen years ago she had walked out and the door hadn't been opened since.

Suddenly she realized how much her feet hurt and how her back and shoulders ached. She lay down on her bed, on top of the frilly white-and-pink comforter, and closed her eyes. Her feet almost hung off the end, and it seemed so much smaller than she remembered. Montsey, her favorite stuffed animal—a large white animated bunny with floppy ears—was much smaller than she remembered.

Rolling over, she opened her eyes and it hit her that she couldn't stay in Kansas long. The funeral was tomorrow. She would stay another day after that, to help her mom get settled and make sure all her finances were in order, and then she would leave.

But all these thoughts couldn't silence the one voice she hated to hear. She wrapped the edges of the pillow around her ears. As her mind sank into the darkness of sleep, her last thoughts pondered how a dead man could still be so alive and how his words could still sting so much.

Five

The heap of mashed potatoes hit Macey's plate with a thud. She watched her mother cut off a two-inch square of butter and slap it on top of her serving, followed by an overwhelming helping of salt. Evelyn then salted and buttered her own potatoes with as much.

Next came the gravy. It screamed "heart attack," and Macey swallowed hard as her mom poured a lumpy scoop of it over the potatoes while mumbling about how Margie's gravy was always as smooth as silk.

Evelyn went back into the kitchen, and Macey thought she was going to be sick. The smell of grease permeated the air.

"Honey, this is the best fried chicken you'll ever have in your life!" Evelyn exclaimed, setting in front of Macey a large platter of what appeared to be at least two chickens. Paper towels underneath the chickens soaked up the grease. "This is Oda Yeager's recipe, and it's won the Chanute County Fair blue ribbon for three years in a row."

Macey tried to sound grateful, but she'd become somewhat of a vegetarian and was working on eliminating almost all fat from her diet. Eyeing the fried chicken platter, she asked, "Mom, how many chickens did you fix? It's just you and me."

Evelyn chuckled as she stirred the iced tea. "Well, I figured it's probably been a long time since you had a good home-cooked meal. Besides that, you're too thin. You need some meat on those bones!"

Macey clutched her napkin, folding and refolding it, thinking about how much it would hurt her mom if she elected not to eat the food. "Is there a vegetable?"

"Of course!" Evelyn took a large pan off the stove and set it on a hot pad. "Green beans. We always have a vegetable with our meal. Vitamins are important, you know."

Macey agreed and scooted the pan close to her plate. But before she could scoop out a serving, her heart sank. Peering into the pan, she could see three pieces of bacon floating on top of coagulated circles of grease. She glanced up at Evelyn, who was eagerly waiting for her to serve herself. Macey took a small helping and pushed the pan away.

"Sugar in your iced tea, dear?" Evelyn asked as she poured.

"No thanks," Macey said, deciding the ice tea might be the only thing she could stomach at this meal.

Evelyn smiled and poured her own glass. "Good for you. Too much sugar can rot your teeth." She hurried back to the oven and opened the door. "One more thing. Some piping hot biscuits." Evelyn pushed the biscuits into a bread basket and brought them to the table. Macey was afraid to ask what else was on the menu, but finally her mother sat herself down and arranged her napkin on her lap. "Shall we bless it?"

Macey lowered her head, and her mother thanked the Lord and asked Him to bless the food, still praying the same prayer she'd prayed since Macey was a child. Most of the time, however, it had been her father who said grace, and if an ounce of food was touched beforehand, she would be sent to her room without any at all. It had taken Macey years to feel comfortable taking the first bite without blessing it.

"Amen. Dig in, darling!" Using her knife, Evelyn flicked a slab of butter onto her own helping of green beans and asked Macey to pass the salt. Macey could tell any sort of hesitation might hurt her mother's feelings, and on the eve of her father's funeral, perhaps she should at least attempt to take a few bites. She started with a green bean.

They ate in silence for a little while, and Macey was amused at the way seventeen years could go by and still there wasn't much to say. Perhaps there was a lot to say, but none of it suited a mealtime discussion.

Macey was working on holding down the three or four bites she'd taken when she noticed her mother had hardly touched her food. "Mom? You're not eating? You fixed a ton of food here."

Evelyn shook her head and stared at the platter of chicken. "This was your father's favorite meal. I don't know why I fixed it tonight. I guess it just hasn't sunk in that he's not going to be here anymore. I ironed his shirts this morning, for goodness' sakes. But I always iron his shirts on Thursday mornings, so I didn't know what else to do." She looked up at Macey, a bewildered expression passing over her saddened face. "Tomorrow is his funeral. At ten. He always used to meet for coffee and play dominos with the boys on Fridays at ten."

"Mom, I'm sorry," Macey said, setting down her fork. "This must be so hard for you." Her mom looked away and with her index finger put streaks through the sweat on her ice-tea glass.

A few uncomfortable moments passed. Evelyn sat up straighter and picked at her chicken. "You might meet Patricia tonight. She said she'd come by later on this evening. I need my hair done. She said she'd even paint my nails."

Macey spread her food around her plate, hoping it would look like she'd eaten more than she had. "Who's Patricia? Your beautician?"

Evelyn shook her head. "No. Your father's nurse." Her mom finally took a small bite of potatoes, just as Macey's stomach rumbled with hunger. Evelyn pointed her fork at the chicken. "Eat up. There's plenty."

Macey managed a smile and another green bean. "Nurse?"

"Hospice. She used to work in Joplin and then she moved to Parsons. Now she lives just east of Fort Scott and commutes to all her patients. We've become good friends over the past few months, so she's promised to stay in touch. Sweet lady, Patricia. Your father adored her."

Macey's throat grew tight. She took a bite of potatoes, the butter beginning to grow on her. "Dad was sick, then?"

"Lung cancer."

"Oh."

A faint rumble of thunder filled the silence. Evelyn's eyes turned to the window. "Could storm tonight," she said. "It's awfully muggy. Probably too muggy for anything wicked."

Macey twisted her fork in the mound of potatoes she had left on her plate. Through all the pain of the last several years, the thought of her father suffering for months with cancer brought her no comfort and even more pain. Her heart was hard. She knew that. She'd spent years deliberately building up the walls, so it was a little perplexing that it bothered her so much. Maybe it was the thought of her mother knowing her husband of more than forty years was going to die. This hurt her in the deepest places of her soul, and she felt a familiar guilt creeping in. She should've been here for her mom.

Macey watched her carefully. Her mother's eyes were distant. Sitting on the other side of the table, her mom seemed so lonely. So out of place. Anger grew inside Macey, and she wasn't sure what to do with it. She seemed unable to direct it to its source. But there it was, cinching her heart like it had all these years. From time to time it crept into her life, usually at the most inopportune moments. Often the anger resulted in her making a new enemy from some innocent bystander.

Evelyn smiled uneasily at her. Macey knew her face was not concealing her feelings. It never did.

"Are you okay, dear?" her mother asked cautiously.

"I'm fine."

More silence. More anger welled up.

Evelyn shoved the chicken platter toward Macey. "Eat some more. Like I said, this is the best fried chicken this side of Kansas City."

Macey's face turned red. "I don't want any more chicken, Mother."

Evelyn almost dropped her fork. "You don't like it?"

"No. I don't like it. I don't like any fried chicken. Do you know how much fat must be in one piece of this chicken? Not to mention the way you butter and salt the potatoes! And you know what? When you cook green beans in bacon fat, that sort of makes the vitamins in them obsolete! Aren't you watching what you eat, Mother? Don't you care that you're probably clogging an entire artery with this one meal?"

The words shot out faster than Macey could pull them back, and when it was all over, her mother's eyes were filled with tears and Macey's stomach ached with a piercing regret. Macey covered her face and shook her head.

Evelyn stood, wobbling and feeble, and began clearing the table. "I'm sorry. I didn't know. I thought you might like . . ." The rest of the words got choked away. "Let me make you something else. Anything you like. I could run to the market. Maybe we could make a fresh salad or I could get some strawberries."

Macey peeked up at her mom, watching her as she spoke with great fluster, her cheeks bright with embarrassment. Macey wanted to bury herself alive.

"Mom, stop. Please, just stop." Macey rose and took the dishes from her. "I'm sorry. I shouldn't have said those things."

Evelyn shook her head and laughed, but it was a laugh to hide the pain. "Oh, dear, you're probably right. Look at me. I'm a big fat pig. And it's not because I've been watching what I eat."

"That's not what I meant."

Evelyn went back to the table to clear more dishes. "Well, you don't get to lookin' like this by eating carrot sticks, that's for sure. Your father, now he was always a lean man, as you know. He could eat anything and not put on a pound. But he worked hard out on the farm. He needed a good meal at night—"

"Mom, please don't apologize. I'm being ridiculous and completely ungrateful. I'm not sure where that came from." Macey stood in the middle of the kitchen, holding a platter of chicken and a pot of green beans, not knowing what else to do.

Evelyn refilled Macey's glass with ice tea as Macey carefully set the food back down on the table. "You're probably just tired. You made quite a trip today, and here I am fussing over you like you've never eaten a meal before. I should've just asked you what you would like for dinner instead of assuming you like the same meals you did when you were younger." Evelyn stopped and blotted her forehead with a napkin. "It's mighty hot this evening." She stepped over to the kitchen window. "I keep hearing thunder. For sure a storm's coming, but it's a ways off still."

Shame and guilt consumed Macey, and she felt like she might break down. "I'm going to go get some fresh air. Just in the back. Okay?"

Evelyn smiled, a warm smile considering how Macey had just cut her to the quick. Macey tried smiling back and then quickly walked out the back door and down the porch steps. In the plush green grass were two lawn chairs. She imagined her mother and father sitting there, watching the river, talking about fried chicken and state fairs.

A few tears escaped, releasing the giant knot in her throat. Macey fell into one of the chairs and closed her eyes, swearing to leave tomorrow after the funeral. Coming back, though not the worst mistake she'd ever made, certainly wasn't going to make life easy for her. Too many memories. Too many regrets. Too much hate.

About a hundred and fifty yards downriver, on the other side, sat the old house. There didn't seem to be much activity at the moment, but it was hard to tell from this distance. She had to admit she was curious as to what the man, the *artist*, had done to restore the inside. The last time she'd been in the big house, there had only been two rooms on the main floor. Half the wood had been rotting out, and the place had smelled like mildew.

She wondered what else the man on the other side of the river did for a living. Was he just yanking her chain when he said he was an artist? Maybe it was just a hobby. Very few people could make a living painting. Who bought art in this part of the country, anyway?

A warm wind swirled the treetops, and thunder rumbled in the distance. A few minutes later lightning struck from within a towering billow of clouds. For the first time Macey could see the storm approaching and smell the rain. A fresh scent and something she wasn't used to, having lived in the big city for so long.

"Care for some pie?"

Macey startled and turned in her chair. She hadn't heard anyone approach. Standing above her was a very short, thin woman with black braided hair and bony features. Her dark brown eyes were open wide, and her thin lips spread into a smile.

"Pardon me?"

She sat down in the chair next to Macey. "I'm Patricia Steele, your father's nurse. I brought your momma her favorite pie. Apple. I thought you might want a piece. And then I thought I sure would like to meet you. So I killed two stones with one bird by bringing ya out a piece and sayin' hello. So . . . *hello*."

The woman's accent seemed to indicate she'd lived in this area her whole life, and the fact that she could kill two stones with one bird made Macey wonder what kind of training she had as a nurse. She stuck out a skinny arm and small hand for Macey to shake.

"I'm Macey."

"Yes, I've heard about you. I'm so glad to finally meet. So where-abouts are ya from?"

"Dallas."

"Oh. That's a big city. Been there once. Didn't like it. Too many people."

"Yes. I sort of thrive on that sort of life."

"Do ya? Your momma tells me you're on the TV. Got your own show and everything." Suddenly the woman raised her hand and slapped Macey on the neck. Then she drew her hand back and showed Macey her palm, which was bloody with a black spot in the middle. "Mosquitoes. They'll eat ya alive." She wiped her hand off on her jeans.

The sting from the slap hurt more than the bite from the mosquito and Macey rubbed her neck, keeping a close eye on Patricia's next move.

"Here," she said and passed the small dish with a large piece of apple pie on it. "It's just as delicious as you can get. And I melted some American cheese on the top."

"Oh. Thank you." Macey looked down at the pie. It had been a long time since she'd seen apple pie with cheese on top, and a long time since she'd eaten pie at all. Her stomach growled. Macey figured she couldn't possibly be rude twice in less than an hour. She took a bite and it melted in her mouth. "You made this?"

"I love to bake. I enter the Chanute County Fair every year. I've got two blue ribbons."

"It's delicious." Macey took another bite. Her stomach muscles relaxed with thankfulness. "How long did you take care of my father?"

" 'Bout four months."

Macey stared out at the river. "Did he . . . did he suffer?"

"The last couple of days weren't pleasant. Your daddy, he believed God was going to heal him, all the way to the end. I ain't seen faith like that in a long time. My guess is he was pretty surprised to find himself in heaven. That's how much he believed God was gonna heal him. A strong man, your father."

Macey swallowed hard. "I haven't been home in a while. I guess they told you that."

Patricia smiled warmly and patted her on the back. "Well, you're home now and that's what's important. Your momma, she's an awfully sweet woman. She's tryin' to be strong. But she's grieving. Your comin' home has probably helped more than you know."

The ground vibrated as the thunder clapped loudly. A few bolts of lightning flashed into the fields across the river. "I suppose we should go inside," Macey said as she scooped the last bite of pie onto her fork.

"Yep," Patricia said, standing. "This un's gonna be a boomer."

Macey glanced over near the barn. They still had the storm shelter. Heavy drops of rain pelted their skin, and veins of lightning scattered above them in the clouds. The wind picked dirt and leaves up suddenly. Patricia covered her eyes and shouted, "C'mon! It's gettin' ready to pour!"

Macey hurried toward the porch but looked back once more before going inside. Miles away, lightning danced from cloud top to cloud top, waltzing in rhythm with the thunder and illuminating a dark shower of rain against the horizon. She lived among tall buildings and busy streets, where it's impossible to see a storm approach. No one had time to look to the sky, anyway.

She heard Patricia beckoning her, yet she stood a few seconds longer and let the raindrops thump against her cheeks. The dirt that the wind had blown into her face began to wash away.

———— ◆ ————

Evelyn folded the shirt as neatly as she could, as if putting it in the drawer for Jess to wear the next day. But instead she was taking it out of the drawer and putting it into a box for someone, some stranger, to wear. It would be someone in need, and that brought her some comfort, but each shirt, each pair of pants, each sock, each shoe had a memory attached to it. It was hard for her to believe he'd never be wearing these again. His clothes had that distinct smell, the smell of Jess. Her lip quivered at the thought of not smelling that smell again. It was pipe tobacco and soybean fields and river water. With a touch of Stetson.

"You okay, Evelyn?"

Evelyn turned to find Patricia and Macey standing in the doorway. Patricia was holding a pot of coffee and Macey had three mugs. "Thought you might like some coffee," Macey said.

"Oh, dear, thank you."

Patricia poured and handed her a mug. "You want some help with all this stuff?"

Evelyn stared into the next empty box waiting to be filled. "That would be fine."

For the next two hours, as heavy rain pounded the roof, they packed away Jess's clothes and listened to Macey describe her life as an anchorwoman. Evelyn was amazed at the life her daughter lived. Every second was vital, her days filled with endless activity.

She tried not to think of each item she packed away as she listened to her daughter describe the day when a gunman broke into the newsroom in San Antonio and threatened to kill everyone. Fortunately the building was equipped with trapdoors so no one got hurt. Patricia was about to fall down with excitement.

"What was his beef?" she asked.

"He owned some apartment buildings and he wasn't keeping up with the maintenance. So we reported on the side of the residents."

"Well, I guess he was already a few fries short of a Coke."

Evelyn glanced at Macey, who laughed a little. "I guess so."

Patricia continued to quiz Macey on the adventures of her career. Evelyn admittedly was enjoying the conversation and realized it would be an awfully sad time without it. As they talked, she smiled to herself, thinking of how Macey had come in from the rain and asked if she could have some leftover fried chicken. Evelyn had almost thrown it all out, only she always found it hard to throw away food. Her daughter was still the precious little girl she remembered. She knew that had been Macey's final attempt at saying she was sorry for what she'd said earlier. But Evelyn had forgiven her long before that. Macey had eaten two entire pieces, commenting that she could understand why it had won the blue ribbon at the county fair. Evelyn explained the secret was in the spices and the way the batter was made, and that Oda had given just two people the recipe: her own mother and Evelyn, the only two she trusted.

Evelyn tuned back in to the conversation, suddenly noticing Patricia fold Jess's shirts with carelessness. She had to look away. "We've never had nothin' like that happen in these parts," Patricia said. "Oh, there was that time when Becker Bronaham's gun went all possessed and started shootin' on its own. Remember that, Evelyn?"

"Who could forget?"

"It was the craziest thing. They were out huntin' quail, and for some reason Becker's gun, which was lying in the bed of the pickup truck, just went off and kept shootin'! It was ricocheting off the pickup and sending the men flyin' for cover." Patricia was laughing hard. "Bobby Sunchen said Dale Jessett peed in his pants, but Dale swears that didn't happen. 'Course, Dale swears Bobby was crying like a baby, so they probably both just made up stories on each other. It was still funny, though."

"Did anyone get hurt?" Macey asked.

"Buck Stanley took some buckshot in the hand, and poor Pete got his kneecap blown off. But it coulda been a lot worse." Patricia shook her head. "That all happened before I moved to Parsons. But I swear, people all over these parts know that story."

Macey laughed, then looked at Evelyn. "More coffee, Mom?"

"Thank you," Evelyn said. Suddenly she realized everything was packed. She went to the closet and saw it was empty of all his things. The sight was like an illusion, and her mind wasn't comprehending it. A gentle hand patted her shoulder—Patricia's. It had done that a lot lately.

"I better get to bed. It's been a long day." Macey stood on the other end of the room, pouring Evelyn's coffee. "Here you go. I'll set it on your dresser."

Evelyn left the closet. "The covers are pulled back for you. Fresh towels are on the end. And I left a glass of water on the nightstand, because you used to like that."

Macey walked to the large bedroom window. "This is a big storm. Are you sure we shouldn't have the TV on? Just to see how bad this is supposed to get?"

Evelyn joined her at the window. "The reception is no good during storms anyway. It'd only be static." She touched her fingers to the pane. "Have you lost all your instincts?"

Macey laughed a little. "Instincts?"

"Sure. Don't you remember what your dad taught you? You both used to be able to predict weather as good as those weathermen, and without all the fancy equipment."

Her daughter turned to look outside. "The rain isn't going sideways."

Evelyn smiled and hugged her from the side. "See? It's like riding a bike." She left the window and picked up her coffee mug. "No. This one isn't going to be too bad. Just noisy."

Patricia gathered her things. "Well, I best be going."

Evelyn looked at her. "What? It's pouring rain out there! Why not stay the night? Your room is still there for you."

"I'll be fine. I've driven in a rainstorm or two."

"But it's a forty-five minute drive."

"Evelyn," Patricia lectured, "it's time you start taking care of yourself. Not everyone else. I'll see you tomorrow at the funeral. You need to get plenty of rest." Patricia hugged her and then proceeded down the stairs. After a few seconds they heard the front door open and close.

Macey said good-night, told her mom they could move the boxes in the morning, and went to her old room, quietly shutting the door.

Evelyn was left alone, only the sound of the thumping rain to fill her ears. She shuffled back downstairs to wash out the coffeepot and caught her reflection in the bay window. She hadn't done much looking at herself in the past few years. There in front of her stood an old woman. She pulled on a curl or two of her hair, all of it gray now. She'd stopped coloring it some years ago when she was spending so much money trying to keep up. And then there was the whole cancer scare about hair dye.

The window distorted her image, and she wasn't sure if her dress was wrinkled or not. She tried to smooth it out. What in the world would she wear tomorrow? She didn't own a thing in black. None of her old church dresses fit her anymore. Maybe she could wear the blue dress with lace she'd made a few years ago. Jess liked it. Maybe

Macey would help her with her makeup. With all the talking going on this evening, she'd forgotten to remind Patricia about her hair and nails.

A bolt of lightning brightened the room for a second, followed by a clap of thunder that shook the china. Evelyn moved from the window, tired of staring at the image in front of her. With all the humidity, there wasn't going to be too much anyone could do with her hair anyway.

She thought about going to the kitchen and finishing up the dishes, but instead she sat down on the sofa and let the rain soothe her. She imagined Jess in front of the TV, banging on the side of the old box, trying to get a picture to come through. And just like she always did, she'd tell him it was useless and that he might try picking up a book once in a while. He'd keep banging and she'd go make sure some meat was thawed out for the next evening's supper.

Instead, here she was, sitting alone, listening to a storm pass on through.

She could hear Macey upstairs getting ready for bed and thought about going up to see if she could get her anything, but she decided against it. She could see the pain in her daughter's eyes. She could see she didn't want to be here.

Her heart sank. She wondered again if she had done the right thing with the letter. Could things be different now? Maybe her daughter would want to stay longer. Maybe they could talk about the past.

She shook her head and squeezed the pillow on her lap. She knew it wasn't best left alone. Just like back then, though, she didn't know what to do now. Her own fear of confrontation might keep her daughter away for seventeen more years, and Evelyn doubted she had that much time left.

Upstairs, the noises stopped, and Evelyn guessed Macey had finally turned in. Now the house was quiet. Even the storm was dying down, only a light rain misting the windows.

She took a deep breath and looked around. This was how the rest of her life would be. Quiet and lonely.

Six

Macey was used to getting up early, and this morning was no exception. The sun coming in her window woke her before 6:30. She washed her face, gazing at puffy eyes and blotchy skin. She'd slept hard.

As she opened her bedroom window, a light morning breeze pushed the lace curtains to the side. The fields of wheat, still wet from the night's storm, glistened in the early morning sun.

Today was her father's funeral. Why was she here? What had made her return home? Her mom had Patricia for support and all her friends at the church. It had been so strange how she'd willed herself not to come home, yet here she was, standing in the same bedroom in which she'd packed her suitcase seventeen years before.

She stretched her arms far above her head, then slowly touched her toes, a technique she'd learned when she was in her yoga phase. She'd become more limber but certainly never found any inner peace. These days she did kickboxing. Again, no inner peace, although it sure felt good punching things.

She pulled on her running shorts and tied her shoes. She'd have to get her exercise before it got too hot. She'd probably run up north, see if anything had changed. Doubtful. It hadn't changed in the eighteen years she lived here. And no one expected it to change for another hundred years. There was always the possibility of a flood, but sometimes even that didn't work.

Downstairs, her mother stood at the stove, never hearing her come down. Macey cleared her throat and she turned around.

"Good morning! Hope you're hungry!"

She was, and she quickly glanced at the table, hoping to find something that wouldn't sit heavy in her stomach.

Evelyn rushed to the table. "Now, listen. We've got sausage and bacon. I know, I know. But there's also fresh strawberries and some cream. Right now I'm whipping up some pancakes. You do eat pancakes, don't you?"

Macey pulled the strawberries closer to herself. "Mom, you don't need to make a big breakfast. You shouldn't even be cooking. This is a hard day for you."

Evelyn lifted a pitcher of orange juice. "Freshly squeezed. No sugar added."

"Thank you," Macey said. "And, Mom, I'll eat a couple of pancakes if you make them."

Evelyn grinned and turned on the griddle. She brought over a basket of biscuits and some gravy. "Just thought you might like some biscuits and gravy. We had quite a bit of gravy left over last night. Biscuits aren't going to kill you, are they?"

Macey smiled and took a biscuit, thankful for the peach preserves sitting on the table. Evelyn went back to the griddle and poured out the batter. "Honey, you can borrow a dress of mine if you'd like. I have several that don't fit me anymore. They might be a little big on you, but no one would notice."

Macey looked down at herself, then chuckled. "I brought a dress. This is what I run in. I thought I'd run up north, see what's going on."

Evelyn flipped a pancake. "Oh, you should! Benny Trailor just built himself a new tractor store. It's bringing in business from miles around! And the old feed store's still there. Lester's granddaughter runs it now. She's always been good with numbers so she does his books, too."

Another pancake sizzled after being flipped, and the smell of homemade pancakes made Macey's stomach grumble with anticipation. The strawberries melted in her mouth. Macey mused at the fact that her mother talked of these people as if Macey hadn't been gone for all those years. The fact was, she hardly remembered anyone.

Her mother offered her a bowl of blueberries and a banana, then brought over the pancakes. Macey spooned a few blueberries on top of a pancake and started cutting up the banana, eager to dig in. "Mom, aren't you going to eat?"

"You don't worry about me," Evelyn said, pouring more batter onto the griddle. "I'm not going to waste away."

It had been a long time since she'd had someone fix her breakfast like this, a long time since she'd had anyone to eat breakfast with. She sat up straight and held her fork properly. All these years of singleness had wreaked havoc on her manners. Half the time she didn't even use a napkin. She looked at the one sitting next to her plate and picked it up, gently placing it on her lap before starting in on the feast. Her stomach was accustomed to an everything bagel with no-fat cream cheese. She hoped she could run with this much food in her stomach.

Finally her mom joined her at the table. She sighed heavily as she poured herself a glass of orange juice. She then put a biscuit on her plate and spread gravy over it, but did nothing more than stare at it.

"How about some strawberries, Mom?" Macey pushed the bowl toward her. But Evelyn waved a hand at it, her bright blue eyes hazy with tears.

"I'd never really imagined Jess would go first." Evelyn filled another orange juice glass to the top, though she hadn't even taken a sip out of the first she'd poured. She glanced up at Macey. "You think about these things when you get older. Who'll go first. I always thought it'd be me. Maybe I just always hoped." Her fork scooped up the gravy around the biscuit and put it on top. "It's unfair to love someone for all these years and then have to live without them. It's a cruel thing . . . real cruel."

Macey's hunger subsided, and she set her fork down. She didn't know what to say. She had no idea how to comfort her mom. All the contempt she felt for her father made it particularly hard. She knew her mother grieved. She knew she should be grieving, too. But she wasn't. At least not the way her mom was.

"I'm glad you have Patricia," Macey said after a bit, and Evelyn agreed with a brave smile. "She's quite a fireball."

"Yep. Good woman, that Patricia." But this was all that was said, and Macey's head pounded with stress. Finally Evelyn looked up and said, "You better go on that run of yours. We don't have much time. I'd like to get there by nine so I have time to say one last good-bye."

Macey swallowed. She'd hoped to arrive a few minutes late so she could slip in the back unnoticed. Of course her mom expected them to ride together, and she couldn't let her own mother drive to the church by herself to bury her husband.

"I'll be back in plenty of time," Macey assured her, then downed the last of her orange juice.

Evelyn wiped a few tears from her cheeks. "I'm so glad you're here. I couldn't imagine doing this without you. I hope you can stay awhile."

Macey smiled but said nothing. She opened the front door by giving it a little tug to get it unstuck. Outside, the morning air was still fresh and remarkably still. She could hear her mom following behind until she too had come out the front door.

"At least it's a beautiful day," Evelyn mused. "It would be terrible to have it pourin' down rain."

Macey agreed and bent down, stretching her back muscles and hamstrings, and then stood back up, reached around, and grabbed an ankle to stretch out her thigh. "I miss this air," she said, rolling her head from side to side. "It's so fresh here and easy to breathe."

Evelyn took a few more steps out onto the front porch, pulling her old tattered robe closed. "I suppose I just take it for granted. I've never known nothing else." Evelyn looked west. "I was born in a farmhouse two miles up the road. They tore it down about four years ago. We had a storm come through. But nobody'd been livin' there for twenty years. I think maybe Jed Burnhill used it to store his hay."

Macey knew the house well. She thought it was funny how her mom would tell her the story nearly every time they passed it when she was a child, as if she'd never mentioned it before. Not too many things change. Macey dropped her heels off the edge of the step to stretch her calves.

"Your flowers are beautiful, Mom," Macey said, pointing to the three flower beds along the walls of the house. "I've never had much of a green thumb."

Evelyn started laughing. Macey smiled a little, not knowing what was so funny, but her mom was now laughing so hard she was turning red in the face, her eyes tearing faster than she could wipe them. "What a hoot!"

Macey laughed. "What?"

Evelyn turned to one of the flower beds and pointed to it. "They're all fake!"

Macey looked down. "Fake?"

"Silk flowers I bought at Marie's Craft Store." She took a step down, still laughing. "Your father was always such a stickler about having flowers planted every year. But this last year when he got so sick, I just couldn't keep up with the gardening and taking care of him. So I planted these!"

"Are you serious? They look so real!"

Evelyn nodded and laughed some more. "I pulled the whole thing off like a regular scam artist! I even stood out here and watered them, waving at your father while he sat up there in the wheelchair looking out from the window. I suppose I'm going to have to pull them out before winter or the whole town's gonna know my secret!" Evelyn roared with laughter again, hanging on to the railing. "He even commented that he'd never seen our flowers look so beautiful."

Macey laughed again, getting more of a kick out of watching her mom laugh about it. The laughter finally died down, and Macey did one more stretch. "Well, I better go run. Be back soon."

Evelyn said good-bye as Macey took off down the driveway and onto the road that ran in front of their house. She headed north, waving to her mom, who still stood in the doorway watching her. Her mom's pleasant smile and beautiful laugh filled her mind. How could she do anything but cry on a day like this? Her mom's strength amazed her.

As the sun rose higher in the eastern sky, it warmed the air and left Macey's back damp as she tackled the steep hill before her. This certainly beat running the track at the fitness center or twenty blocks of sidewalk downtown. Picture perfect trees towered above her, their long limbs stretching across the road toward one another, almost sheltering her from the low sun. All this beauty, yet so much darkness.

She would stay the weekend, but that was it. Monday morning she would be gone.

◆

Evelyn kept busy by cleaning up the dishes from breakfast, the whole time scolding herself for fixing too much food. She always fixed too much. She poured all the fruit into one bowl, wrapped up the biscuits, dumped the leftover pancakes into the trash, and wiped the table clean. It was almost seven-thirty and she hadn't done a thing to get ready. She didn't want to. And she still didn't know what she would wear.

Evelyn scrubbed the dishes and dried them until they sparkled, so consumed by her washing that she didn't hear Patricia come in. Her presence was soon revealed, however, when she knocked over a chair, startling Evelyn half to death.

"Sorry, sorry!" she chimed. She carried three plastic grocery bags that hung from her arms. "Evelyn Steigel, just what do you think you're doing?"

Evelyn smiled, setting down the dishes to help Patricia with her load. "I didn't hear you come in. Guess I had the water running."

They put the bags on the table. "You're not even dressed!" Patricia poured the contents of one of the bags onto the kitchen table. Evelyn picked up nail polish, lipstick, and curlers. She looked at Patricia. "Bet you thought I'd forgotten, didn't ya?" Patricia said as she organized the mess on the table. "I thought you might've enjoyed conversing with your daughter more than curling your hair last night. I figured I could come over early this morning and fix you all up."

Evelyn sat down at the table, tired already, and the day had hardly begun. "Thank you, Patricia. I'm so glad you came."

"Where's Macey?" Patricia had already spun Evelyn around and was picking at her hair.

"Went out for a run."

"Now, I thought we'd use the number three curlers. You know that always gives you a lift. We might try a little rouge today, too. I know you ain't keen on color, but I think you're going to need some rose in them cheeks of yours."

Evelyn sat still in the chair, her hands lifeless on her lap. "Whatever you want."

Patricia pulled and stretched her hair, securing rollers faster than anyone she knew. She never once dropped a hairpin. She coated the curlers in White Rain hairspray, careful to shield Evelyn's face, then scooted a chair in front of her and took a hand, filing each nail with speedy accuracy.

"Are you doin' okay, honey?" Patricia asked, squeezing the hand she was filing.

Evelyn nodded but couldn't speak. Today she would bury her husband. It was the darkest day she could imagine.

"I brought over Race Car Red and Pretty in Pink. You decide which color you want on your nails, and I'll put on a coat of clear first."

Evelyn looked at the two colors, didn't really care which one, but chose the pink. While the first coat dried on her nails, Patricia powdered her face and applied the makeup. She rubbed rouge into her cheeks and put a little of the color over her eyelids, as well.

"You know old Samson Titus died?" said Patricia, stroking the pink polish carefully onto each nail.

"Oh, I hadn't heard."

"The funeral'll be Tuesday."

"Give Bea my regards," Evelyn said. She stared down at the hand that was finished. "How long was he ill?"

"Couple of years. Had him in a nursing home since May. I think Bea's gonna have to go herself soon." Patricia shook her head, sucked on the end of a Q-tip, and carefully removed some polish from the edge of Evelyn's finger with it. "Be glad you're still independent, Evelyn. You have your freedom. Those nursing homes ain't a place someone like us should be."

Evelyn silently thanked the Lord that she was not in a nursing home and that they'd been able to at least afford some medical insurance. Patricia stood and instructed Evelyn not to move her hands for ten minutes. She then began removing rollers and picking her curls out.

"Don't make it too big," Evelyn said. She reached up and touched each curl Patricia had already picked out. "I've always thought Margie's hair was too big."

"Well, she's a Texan," Patricia pointed out. "You'd expect that from down there."

Evelyn took a mirror off the table and studied her reflection, while Patricia chided her about being careful not to touch her nails to anything. "I look tired," Evelyn sighed.

"You look perfectly beautiful. So, what are you planning to wear?"

Evelyn laid the mirror on the table. "I haven't a thing to wear. Nothing appropriate for my own husband's funeral, that's for certain."

"I betcha we can find something in that big closet of yours."

Evelyn shook her head. "I can't fit into most of it."

"What about that pretty blue dress you wore to Beck and Nina's sixtieth wedding anniversary party?"

That old thing?"

"It was wonderful. And who says you have to wear black to a funeral? We know we can celebrate that Jess is up in heaven and having himself a good ol' time."

"Kay Timmons will have me beheaded. She's such a traditionalist."

"Well, Kay can wear black at her own funeral. This doesn't have nothin' to do with her."

Evelyn nodded, and then, without warning, the tears came. They ran down her face in streams and her chest heaved.

"Oh, honey! Oh, Evelyn." Patricia rushed to her side and held her shoulders. "Now, now. Goodness' sakes, your mascara's gonna run."

But Evelyn couldn't stop the sobbing. She already missed Jess so much, and he'd only been gone three days. She turned and clutched Patricia and cried harder than she'd ever cried before. She knew she'd scuffed a nail, but she didn't care.

Macey slumped against a tree, her heart pounding wildly in her chest, her side cramped with pain. The bark scraped her back through her clothes as she slid down it, her body finally resting against the soft grass. She closed her eyes and caught her breath.

She'd run too hard. She knew her limits, and she'd passed them two miles before. Her chest hurt as her lungs struggled to draw air. Her hair fell into her face, dripping with salty sweat.

She moaned and lay down on the grass, her chest heaving up and down. Above her, unseen birds chirped and sang a melody. With shaky hands Macey separated her T-shirt from her skin.

A soft breeze rustled the leaves in the trees, cooling her a bit. Mingling with the sweat were the tears, and her body now shook with grief and pain instead of exhaustion. There was hardly a building in sight, and Macey let her sobs escape without restriction.

Sounds of her own laughter as a child replayed in her mind as she wept. She could see her father swinging her around and around in the backyard of the farmhouse. She squealed with delight, begging him to do it again.

One mistake. One horrible mistake had ended it all. But she still didn't know whose mistake was worse. She still didn't have the answers her heart had longed for.

Now she never would. In a few hours, her father would be deep inside the earth, silenced forever.

Seven

Macey's legs trembled as she climbed the porch steps. An unfamiliar car was parked in the driveway, and when she opened the door, she knew it was Patricia's. Her mom stood by the kitchen table, dressed in a pastel blue dress with a lace collar and pearl buttons. It wasn't the type of thing Macey would wear to a funeral, but her mother's expression indicated that she should approve immediately.

"Mom, you look beautiful," Macey said, grabbing a kitchen chair and sitting down.

Evelyn touched the string of pearls around her neck. "Are the pearls too much?"

Macey glanced at Patricia, who was shaking her head. "Of course not," Macey said. "And the earrings are a nice touch, too."

"I'm not sure too many people will approve of wearing blue to a funeral," Evelyn said as she smoothed down the collar.

Macey saw her own black dress hanging on the coat closet door. Evelyn didn't miss a beat.

"I ironed it for you. Packing does quite a number on clothes, doesn't it?" Her mother looked at her, obviously hoping she wouldn't be mad.

Macey wasn't accustomed to people going through her belongings. Today, though, she'd just have to let things go or she might fall apart. "Well, I hate to iron, so thank you."

Evelyn walked to the closet and took the dress off the hanger, gently laying it over her arm. "You better go get ready."

Macey looked at her watch. It was 8:09. She knew for a fact she could shower and dress in precisely twenty-two minutes, but instead of stressing her mother out, she decided to take her advice and go upstairs. First, she went to the kitchen to get a drink of water. Patricia joined her.

"I can hang around and do your hair and nails, too, if you'd like," Patricia offered. "How I'd like to get my hands on that beautiful brown hair of yours."

Macey smiled and then gulped her water. "That's okay. But thank you for offering."

"Alrighty. I'll be off, then. I gotta go check on Mrs. Williams before heading over to the funeral home." She looked at Evelyn. "Are you sure you don't need anything else?"

Evelyn nodded, and Patricia packed her sacks and left. Macey was just finishing the last bit of water when something caught her eye—the corner of a piece of paper barely showing on the top of the cupboard. Macey rose to her tiptoes to try to reach it. After three attempts, the ends of her fingers moved it enough so that it fell off the cupboard and floated gently to the floor.

She was surprised to find it to be an old school paper of hers, probably from her sophomore or junior year. It was from English class, a story she'd written about a moth named Abigail who was in love with a beautifully colored butterfly named Prince. Macey stared at all the carefully-thought-out descriptions. No one knew what this story really meant. No one knew who this story was about. No one but Macey.

"What are you looking at?"

Macey jumped and set the paper down quickly. Her mother stepped around her, glanced at the paper, and grinned. "Oh, one of your school papers."

"From English class," Macey said and moved to the other side of the kitchen for a second glass of water. She gripped the edge of the counter to keep her hands from shaking. "It was on top of the cupboard. That's strange."

She watched her mom pick up the paper and look at it and then at her as if she knew something she shouldn't. Macey turned and filled her glass with ice. Her mother couldn't possibly know what the story was about. To anyone but Macey it was just a silly story about an ugly moth and a beautiful butterfly.

"I better get ready now," said Macey, avoiding her mother's eyes. "We don't want to be late."

Upstairs, Macey showered, dried off, and slipped her dress on and carefully buttoned it. She combed and pinned back her wet hair. She realized then she had no makeup. She found her mom downstairs, sitting quietly in the living room and staring out the bay window.

"Mom?"

Evelyn turned as if snapping out of a trance. Macey noticed she was still holding the school paper. "What? I'm sorry?"

"Can I borrow some makeup?"

Her mom thought for a second. "Well, let's see here. I have a little compact of pressed powder, and I think I have a lipstick somewhere." Evelyn rose from the sofa and found her purse. Digging through it, she said, "Patricia, she has a whole store full of makeup. I don't have much these days. It doesn't seem to make too much of a difference. I do have some wrinkle cream, though." Her hand emerged with a tube of lipstick and a compact of powder.

Macey took the lipstick and looked at the color. "Hot Mama Red?"

Evelyn's blue eyes glowed bashfully. "Your father always did like that color."

"I guess this is going to have to do," Macey sighed and headed back upstairs. Facing the mirror, she moisturized her face, put only a dab of color on her lips so she wouldn't look like she'd just left a Broadway stage, then used the lipstick to create some color on her cheeks and brow bone. She wasn't here to win any beauty contests. Meanwhile she rehearsed what she would say to the guests at the funeral. A tight smile and a "Thank you so much" would probably do for most comments. She had no idea what anyone knew about why she'd left so many years ago, and a funeral wasn't the place to discuss something like that anyway. But Macey was smart enough to know there would be a few old women who would make what was none of their business their business.

She could maneuver through a crowd, act busy, seem occupied, serve coffee, sit in the bathroom—all tricks she'd learned at social functions. She was a master at seeming present without really being there.

After a quick check in the mirror Macey went downstairs and was ready to leave. Her mom was dusting.

"Mom, should you be cleaning house?"

Evelyn began strategically placing coasters on all her wood furniture. "I'm going to have a houseful of guests here in a few hours. I can't have my house looking messy."

"The house looks fine," Macey assured her, steering her away from the furniture and taking the feather duster from her hand. But Evelyn immediately went to the dining room table.

"This silver hasn't been polished in over a year. I think I need to—"

"Mother, please," Macey said, exhausted just watching her, "let it alone. It's your husband's funeral today."

Evelyn stopped. "I know, I know." She shook her head. "Maybe I'm just trying to forget that."

Macey looked at her watch. 8:37. "You said you wanted to be to the church by nine."

Evelyn took her purse off a chair. "It's at the funeral home, not the church. It'll be a twenty-minute drive. They thought too many people would come, and the church only seats a hundred and fifty, comfortably that is. They can pack more in, but in July you risk people fainting."

Macey spent another five minutes convincing her mom that the house was in order and that Margie and all the women would be able to find everything they needed for the reception. By the time they made it outside, the sun had dried the final dampness from the steamy ground and the temperature had reached at least the upper eighties.

She helped her mom to the small car, pushing the passenger seat back as far as possible before helping her to sit down. Carefully closing the door, Macey hurried around, got in herself, and started the car. They waited a minute for the air-conditioner to blow cold.

"Nice little car you got here," Evelyn said. "Does it have power steering?"

"It's a rental."

"Oh. Our old Pontiac doesn't have power steering."

"You've had that thing for years."

"Yes, well, it still runs. No need to get a new one until the only other option would be walkin'. I don't do that too well these days."

For the first ten minutes of the drive, Macey was thankful that her mom was content to point out landmarks and acquaintances' houses. It was easy conversation, the kind where one could nod, raise an eyebrow, ask a leading question, all without any emotional effort.

But soon the conversation ran dry, and the only noise was the constant hum of the air-conditioner. Macey tried to think of anything they hadn't covered but there was nothing. They'd talked about the house needing painting, the chickens hating the heat,

Patricia's dating life, the 112-degree temperature they'd had on this day last July. So Macey just drove, and her mother just sat.

Seventy Horn Horse Ranch blurred as they sped past it. Macey thought about posing a question that might get a conversation going again, but then decided against it. The atmosphere turned solemn. Her mother's eyes were dark with grief. The silence, while stifling, was the best they could do. So Macey kept the air-conditioner on high, fixed her eyes on the road ahead, and thought about butterflies.

———— ◆ ◆ ————

"Evelyn, my deepest sympathy for you and yours." Newt Castles, a very small, nervous-looking man with a bald head and thick wire-framed glasses, shook Evelyn's hand deliberately and then shook Macey's.

"Thank you, Newt," Evelyn replied, gripping her purse and fiddling with the lace collar on her dress. She'd met Newt only a few times before. He ran Castles' Funeral Home and Cemetery in Chanute, where pretty much everyone buried their loved ones. His father and grandfather and great-grandfather had run the business before him, so Newt was a very proud mortician.

"Everything's arranged," said Newt, twitching his eyes and licking his lips. "The flowers are here, and we put out extra chairs, just in case. I've already talked to Pastor Lyle and also Howard and Roger. You're welcome to sit behind the divider or wherever you like."

"We'll just sit in the front row," Evelyn said. She squeezed her daughter's hand. "If that'll be okay."

"Just fine." Newt seemed to be able to run down a checklist and still convince you he was sorry for your loss, all in the same breath. "You've requested a closed casket. And you would like Pastor Lyle to invite everyone to the graveside, which will follow immediately after the service."

Evelyn nodded and searched for her handkerchief in her purse.

"Now," Newt said, "the casket will already be there at the front, and we'll bring you and your daughter in after everyone is seated."

"Is that necessary?" Macey's voice was tight and terse.

Newt glanced at Evelyn. "Whatever you want, Evelyn."

"Oh, um . . . whatever Macey wants."

"It's not up to me," Macey said. "I'm just not comfortable walking down the aisle like it's my wedding day. Can't we just come in the side? And maybe a few minutes before the service starts so we're not the main attraction."

Evelyn stared down at her newly painted fingernails. She didn't necessarily want to be marched down the aisle, but in these parts it was customary for the widow to be the last one seated. Newt's eyes darted to each of them, and Evelyn blotted her forehead with the back of her hand.

"What? Is there some sort of protocol that must be followed in order to get someone into the ground?" her daughter asked.

Evelyn didn't know how to respond. Her daughter's sudden agitation caught her off guard. A painful expression in Newt's direction gave him permission to handle the situation.

"It's of course at your discretion, but normally the family—"

"Well, this isn't a normal family, so let's just be seated before the service starts. I need some air. Where's the door?"

Newt motioned to the left, but Evelyn stopped her with a gentle pat on the arm. "I'm going to view the body. I was hoping you would come with me." Macey's eyes were cold and startled, and Evelyn let go of her arm. "It'll be the last time I see your father. The last time you see your father. At least on this earth."

Painful indecision flashed across Macey's already flushed face. She glanced at Newt as if she wished he wasn't standing there and then looked around the room.

Evelyn could tell this was the last thing on earth she wanted to do. "Listen, it's okay. If you don't want to go—" Evelyn tried to keep her voice steady and calm, but inside she felt her heart quiver with disappointment.

Macey's chest heaved as she took in a breath. "Fine. Let's go view the body."

"One more thing, Evelyn . . ." Newt's brow glistened with perspiration. "I always like to settle the account before the funeral starts. You don't need to be thinking of money during or afterward."

Evelyn nodded and reached into her purse. "Of course, Newt. I apologize. What do I owe you?"

"Five thousand, one hundred and three dollars and fifty-eight cents." Newt glanced at Macey and back to Evelyn. "That of course includes the casket, the funeral home expenses, the graveside—"

"What kind of funeral home makes you pay before you bury someone?" Macey grunted. "Can't this be handled later?"

"I should've done it yesterday," said Evelyn. She quickly wrote out a check. "No need to explain, Newt. It's perfectly fine. You've been in business for decades, and it's not because your family is a bunch of thieves." She tore out the check and handed it to him with a smile.

Newt folded the check, sliding it into the front pocket of his suit jacket. "Thank you, Evelyn. It's always uncomfortable to ask, but it has to be taken care of. Now, let's go see Jess, shall we?"

"I'm sorry. I just . . . just can't." Macey stood in the doorway of the viewing room, her eyes glassy.

Evelyn turned to Newt, hoping to express her need for them to be alone without having to mention it. Newt graciously backed out of the room without a sound.

"Dear, I'm sorry," Evelyn said.

"No, it's not you." Macey's arms extended from her body as if keeping some unknown object away from her. "But I just can't do it. I don't like dead . . . I haven't seen . . . and I don't want my last image of him to be . . . because it's been a long time, and . . ." Her voice trailed off, and she covered her mouth, shaking her head and still keeping her free hand extended in the air, making it difficult for Evelyn to decide if she needed to be hugged.

Evelyn finally approached, but instead of embracing her, she took her shoulder and guided her out of the room. The poor girl was shaking all over. "Sit down here and take a deep breath."

Macey looked up with tears in her eyes as she mindlessly collapsed into the chair. "I'm sorry. I wanted to be here for you. I intended to be here for you."

"Don't say another word," Evelyn said, patting her on the knee. "You don't worry about a thing. I shouldn't have asked, and I realize not everyone wants to see someone who's dead."

Macey's hand swiped furiously at the tears that fell from her eyes. "You need closure. I understand that. Do you want me to go get Mr. Castles or something? Or call Margie or Patricia?"

"No, no. Don't disturb them. I'll be fine." Evelyn's knuckles turned white as she gripped the handles of her old leather handbag. "It's just a body. He's not there. He's in heaven, probably shootin' quail or something like that."

That put a small smile on Macey's face, though her eyes remained tearful. She'd found a box of Kleenex under her chair and was pulling tissues out one by one.

"Go get yourself some air, if you can in this heat. I thought I saw a pop machine in one of the offices. I'll just be a minute or two."

Macey nodded and stood, started walking down the hallway, clutching the box of tissue, staring absently at the wall as she passed

by. Evelyn waited till she was out of sight and then opened the door
to the room again.

The lighting was dim and focused, the casket set up against the
far wall, surrounded by silk flowers. Evelyn batted at a fly that had
followed her in. Her legs felt weak as she approached the casket.
His face, pale and somber, looked peaceful enough. She wondered
if he was comfortable. He never liked to sleep on his back. Her head
shook at the absurd thought.

He'd lost so much weight during the chemotherapy that he
hardly resembled himself. His cheeks were sunken and his forehead
and chin protruded unnaturally. Still, his eyes, though closed now,
kept him familiar and warm.

A small speck of dust on the shoulder of his suit distracted
Evelyn and she flicked it off, then creased the collar and smoothed
the material. They'd parted his hair on the wrong side, so she found
a small comb in her purse and corrected it, an easy task considering
there wasn't much there.

As she'd requested, his old tattered Bible lay next to him, along
with some memorabilia from the Masons' Lodge and his favorite
handkerchief his mother had made him.

Evelyn was hardly aware of her tears. She was more in awe that
this would be the last time she'd ever touch him, ever look at his
face, ever hold his hand on this earth. He was cold, but it didn't
matter too much. His hands had always been cold because of poor
circulation.

Poignant and poetic she wasn't, although she wished she had
something elegant to say. Instead, her throat was swollen with disbelief and sadness, so anything she wanted to recite would never make
it out anyhow.

Her eyes rested on the Bible next to his body. How he'd
combed through its pages year after year. He loved the Word and

devoured it like it was a meal. A righteous man, he'd always believed in following God's law with absolute strictness. Evelyn had tried her hardest and best to do the same. But she never did it like he did. No one did.

But it had been that very Bible, that very law, that had torn him from his daughter all those years before. If he could have only . . . Evelyn shook her head. She couldn't ask him to be less than who he was. She'd always relied on God to make things right. Tears welled in her eyes as she thought about how God hadn't made it right. Here she stood over his casket, their daughter not able to stand by her side, all because God hadn't made it right.

Sorrow seized her heart, and she turned and wept into the tissue she'd stuffed into her pocket. God knew she wasn't strong enough to make things right, or to know what to do, or to mend the wounds. She was a simple woman, with a simple heart and a simple way of life. The complexities of the heart were matters she could not pretend to know how to solve.

Evelyn glanced over to Jess again, and suddenly her heart burned with anger that God had not taken her first. God had made her stay. Why? What good could she do without Jess? He was what she had lived for and worked for, had loved for. Could there be any good reason at all for her life to go on without him?

Evelyn found a small chair in the corner. She sat down, her legs tired, her body aching. She could still see Jess, but just barely. His strong Roman nose and the top of his brow were all that were visible.

Fifteen minutes passed while Evelyn sat in the chair, almost as lifeless as her husband. The tiny black, dimly lit room brought her some comfort. The walls were close and secure. Anything beyond the door was unknown and dangerous. She'd closed her eyes and maybe even dozed off for a bit, her head resting comfortably against the wall the chair sat against.

Before long she was aware of faint voices and knew that people were beginning to arrive. She still sat in the small chair for a few moments longer, her purse on her lap, her hands folded against her chest.

But the voices grew louder and so, after a few attempts, she stood. She put her purse on the chair and opened it, pulling out an envelope. She glanced to the door to make sure no one was about to come in. Then she walked back over to Jess, patted his hands, smoothed his hair one more time, and adjusted his tie to perfection.

"I never sent it," she said softly, the envelope damp with the perspiration from her hands. "I wanted to. I wanted to make things right. I stood there in front of the post office and thought hard about sending it to you. I imagined your face as you read the letter. I knew these words would be the ones you'd longed to hear all these years. You never said so, but I knew. I sometimes would watch you from the top of the stairs, when you didn't know I was there. I'd watch you stop by the mantel and look at her picture. Sometimes you'd look at it for a long time.

"I never will understand all this. I suppose the good Lord will show me someday. But mostly, I'm sad that you died and never got to see her again. She's beautiful. A real lady. And smart, too. Just like you'd expect." Evelyn's chin quivered but she maintained herself for a moment longer. She slipped the envelope into the inside pocket of his suit and stepped back from the casket. "So there. You can read it if you want to up there in heaven. They're not her words. They're mine. Maybe I should've sent it, I don't know. But I didn't and that's that."

Evelyn stood silent, then, and held her husband's hand as tightly as she could. She didn't ever want to forget what this felt like. She wanted to mention how much she would miss him, how she hoped they had the good kind of fried chicken up there, and to ask the Lord to take her home soon, but she suddenly had the realization that she was in the room by herself. Alone. So she squeezed his hand, picked the last speck of dust off his coat, and turned toward the door.

At the door, she stopped herself, dug through her purse and found what she was looking for. She walked back to the casket. Opening her husband's hand, she carefully placed the gold necklace with the little gold cross into his palm and folded his fingers around it. Then, for some reason she didn't know, she took the envelope out of his pocket and stuffed it back into her purse. She moved back to the door in silence.

Turning around once more, she managed to whisper good-bye and then quietly shut the door behind her.

Eight

Macey shifted her weight in the rusty steel chair, slowly and carefully, so as not to draw attention to herself or cause the old thing to collapse. A south wind picked up a little, cooling her off. Even though a large elm tree nearly shaded them all from the sun, the humidity was rising quickly, and everyone in their black dresses and dark suits was beginning to perspire noticeably. All the elderly women were fanning themselves, the men blotting their foreheads. The only person who didn't seem to care or felt it inappropriate to do so was Pastor Lyle, who was reading faithfully from his little black funeral book a psalm she didn't recognize. It was apparently her father's favorite, something about mercy and forgiveness.

The funeral had been hard. Her mother had wept, and Macey comforted her the best she could. Men stood up and spoke of her father in a way one might speak of a saint, calling him "good and decent," "a man of God," "stoic," and "compassionate," of all things. By the time the service ended, her jaw muscle ached like she'd chewed a hundred pieces of gum.

Her uncle Howard, who sat next to her during the funeral, had smiled and told her it was good to see her, but nothing more was said, and the greeting could've fit a complete stranger. He wasn't cold, just indifferent. But then again, so was she. She'd smiled and echoed his words back to him. In one sense, she had hoped things would be different. Maybe relationships could be mended. But much more of her wanted pleasantries to be pleasantries and to remain in the same obscurity she'd been caught in for the last seventeen years. While staring at her father's casket, she wondered who knew what.

Had her father told anyone what really happened? Or had he lied to cover up the dark family secret? If she had to guess, no one asked and he never explained. That was the way things were done.

Now at the graveside, Macey could see the solemn faces of those who had been close to her father gathered around the casket, their eyes teary. She tried not to stare. She should have been weeping and mourning. But instead she just sat there, careful not to make her chair creak, careful not to do anything but sit.

So this was it. This was the day her father would become "ashes to ashes and dust to dust." As Pastor Lyle rambled on about God's love and Jesus' sacrifice, Macey imagined the casket being lowered into the ground, a small shovel thrusting handfuls of dirt into the hole in steady rhythm. The distinct *thump* of the dirt hitting the top of the casket pulsed with her heart, and she closed her eyes in hopes of ridding herself of the sound. But the thumping continued, only it grew softer, more muffled. In her mind's eye she suddenly realized the person she saw in the casket wasn't her father, it was herself. The box was cold and black, and it wasn't the dirt falling onto the casket that made the thumping noise but her fists pounding against the walls, hard and fast. And she couldn't speak, couldn't scream. Her voice had been silenced, as it had been all the years before. Her fists pounded harder, trying to let someone know she wasn't dead but was alive, breathing and awake.

Then the air left, and her mind swirled with dizziness. Her hands were no longer curled into fists; they now scratched lightly at the side of the casket. With her last breath she wondered why everyone thought she was dead. Why was she in a casket? Why was she being buried?

"Amen," the small crowd said in unison, and Macey opened her eyes. There in front of her was the ongoing graveside service, and before she could think about anything else, her mother was standing. So Macey stood, too.

Evelyn approached the casket and placed the white rose she had in her hand on top of it, and Macey followed instinctively, placing her rose carefully next to her mother's. She helped Evelyn back to her chair as the rest of the crowd took the roses in their hands and set them on the casket, as well. Macey suddenly felt very tired. Her eyes closed and opened with great effort. It was as if she were in a dream, watching the scene from afar. Was it really that different, after all? She'd placed a rose on top of the casket as a gesture of love for a man she never understood. They'd talked of him as if he was a hero of the faith. Was this the same man whose cold eyes had pierced her fragile heart? The same who had told her she'd done the unforgivable? *This* man?

The service ended, and Macey found herself standing next to her mother, greeting a small line of people. They hugged Evelyn but simply patted Macey on the shoulder or cocked their heads to the side and smiled with pity. She supposed she wasn't very approachable, and no one could figure out what to do with her.

She was surprised when suddenly two firm hands grabbed her shoulders and pulled her close. It was only after they let go that Macey realized it was Patricia. She couldn't help but sigh in relief and smile. At least someone cared enough to embrace her.

The crowd had begun strolling back through the cemetery to their cars. Her mother was talking to some old woman a few feet away who'd apparently lost her husband a few months before and had taken up bird watching to pass the time. Macey turned back to Patricia.

"Honey, you okay?" Patricia's intense brown eyes matched Macey's.

"Sure." Macey glanced away, looking at nothing in particular.

"You look me in the eyes and tell me that," Patricia instructed, but Macey knew that wasn't going to be possible, so she stayed silent and stared at the flowers lying on the casket. For being such a petite woman, Patricia had quite a bit of muscle and guided Macey away from everyone as if she were a feather. "Now listen. I'm going to take your mom back to the house for the reception. Why don't you take a few moments here by yourself."

Macey's eyes began to fill with tears, though she successfully willed them to stop. "Why would you think I need some time alone here?" She glanced at her mom. "Mom's going to need some help back at the house. You know how she frets."

Patricia gently punched the bottom of Macey's chin, like a trainer might do to a boxer. "Hey, I ain't no spring rooster. There may be this certain way things are done, and certain things that are said and not said, but that doesn't mean that that's the way it should be." Patricia's firm smile and pointed eyebrows gave the pause a mark of emphasis. "So what I'm sayin' to you is that you need to take some time here for yourself, away from everybody who's just following all the etiquette. Get what I'm trying to tell you?"

Macey frowned and tried to decipher the message. Was she saying what she thought she was saying? With Patricia it was a little hard to tell. "Are you sure you don't mind taking Mom back?"

"We'll be fine. Maybe you'll be lucky enough to miss the beginning crowd. When the food's gone, so are most of the people, if you catch my draft."

Macey nodded and smiled. She didn't realize the tears were falling until one curved around her nose and fell into her mouth. She quickly wiped them away and composed herself. "Okay," she said.

"Okay then." Patricia gave her one more strong pat on the shoulder, then turned and found Evelyn, guiding her to the car and explaining along the way. Macey turned away so she wouldn't catch anyone's eyes, and before long all the cars were gone and she was left alone in the cemetery with a shiny casket and two creaky chairs.

She looked around, thinking maybe somebody would be by soon to lower the casket or take the chairs, but no one was in sight.

The cemetery was huge, extending several acres in every direction. She imagined everyone who had ever lived even near Chanute was buried here. Toward the west, the gravestones looked older, while toward the east the plots were obviously newer. Macey looked down and realized she must be standing on the plot reserved for her mother. Then she noticed the two headstones of her grandparents on her mother's side. Her grandfather had died a few weeks before she was born, and her grandmother when she was two. She had no memory of either of them, but they were kept alive by her mother, who reminisced as if they'd never passed away.

She focused on the two headstones on the other side of the casket, where her father's parents were buried. Her grandmother had died of cancer even before her mother and father married, when her dad was twenty. She remembered her grandfather, though. Grandpa Porter. He was a very tall, skinny man who loved horses and hated cats. He'd died tragically in a train accident near Chicago, one of his only trips outside of Kansas, when Macey was ten.

She'd attended the funeral at the church but wasn't permitted to go to the graveside. She remembered her aunt Barb remarking she'd be too fidgety. So she stayed behind and played near the church with the other children until the reception, where her mother had been horrified at how dirty her dress was.

A low-lying cloud passed slowly in front of the sun, giving some temporary relief from the heat. She'd been breathing shallowly, she discovered, so she took in a deep breath and blew the air out toward her forehead.

She almost had to laugh at the absurdity of her standing here in the middle of a cemetery, making peace with a casket. Even in the daylight she didn't relish the idea of being in a cemetery alone.

The cloud that a moment ago had provided her precious shade now moved on, and the sun began scorching her skin again.

Grandpa Porter's grave caught her eye a second time, and her heart saddened at the thought of her being only ten and losing him. Then, with no warning, the anger overtook her, and there was a moment when she thought she might scream at the top of her lungs and release all the frustration that had built up over the last two decades.

At that instant an unexpected breeze swirled the tops of the trees and then dipped low, knocking off several of the two dozen or so roses that lay on top of the casket. Macey absently walked over to pick them up and place them back on the casket, but then she stopped. Her face burned with hot tears, and before she knew what she was doing, she'd gathered up all the roses off the casket, marched over to Grandpa Porter's grave, and placed them carefully against his headstone.

Macey walked back to her car, started the engine, and let the air-conditioner blow the tears and sweat away. Heading home, thirsty and even a little hungry, she hoped there would be a vegetable tray.

———◆———

She hadn't expected the commotion. It was more like a twenty-year reunion than a funeral reception. People were talking loudly, and her mother seemed invigorated by the houseful of guests. She smiled and served coffee while everyone complained about how she should be sitting and resting, to which Evelyn remarked she wasn't the one that died, and this caused quite a bit of laughter and nodding of heads.

For the next fifteen minutes or so, Macey managed to exist as a wallflower, munching on carrots and drinking cold glasses of water. But soon everyone's coffee was filled, and suddenly her mother found her in the dark corner of the dining room. She took her hand, guiding her to the middle of a crowd.

"Twenty, I want you to meet my daughter, Macey."

"Macey! My goodness!" the loud, boisterous man with short fuzzy hair and chubby cheeks exclaimed. "I haven't seen you since you was a little girl. Aren't you all grown up and just as purty as you can be."

Macey blushed and looked her mother's way, who laughed and patted the man on his back. "We call him Twenty because he lost a bet when he was a teenager—"

"My papa's two favorite horses for twenty bucks," Twenty butted in. "Boy, was he angry." Macey smiled. The man's charisma was a little contagious. "I hear you're some big celebrity or something," he said, his words muffled as he stuffed an entire finger sandwich into his mouth.

"Just an anchorwoman," she replied, then wondered if she needed to explain what that was. She didn't have a chance, because her mother had pulled another person in.

"And this is James Tomlin, but we call him Tom-Boy. He does all our plumbing, plus he's been mowing our lawn."

He shook Macey's hand vigorously. "Pleased to meet ya, ma'am. I'm sorry for your loss. Your daddy was a good man. I served as an usher and deacon with him for fifteen years over at the church."

"Tutie! Come over here!" Evelyn called, waving her hand above the crowd. "Come here and see my daughter." A thin older woman, with silver hair and a cane to match, maneuvered around the people over to where Macey and her mom stood.

"I'm Tutie," she said in a deep shaky voice. "Probably don't remember me. But you sure have grown up. I used to do your mom's hair before the arthritis got the best of my hands and I had to retire."

"Oh." Macey couldn't think of anything else to say.

"I'm called Tutie, but my name is Gertrude."

"I can't remember anymore how Tutie came about," said Evelyn. "I've just always called you that."

The old woman shrugged her bony shoulders. "Well, I guess you just have to live with some things. Can I get you something else to drink, dear?" She pointed to Macey's empty water glass.

"Oh, no thank you. I'm fine."

"How about some coffee? Cream or sugar?"

Evelyn urged her with a small nod of her head, so Macey smiled and asked for both sugar and cream. Tutie turned and headed toward the beverage table, and Evelyn whispered, "Don't count on getting any. She always gets distracted on her way and forgets. I'll go get you a cup."

"Mom, that's okay. I don't need any coffee."

"No trouble at all," Evelyn replied as she began moving away. "Besides, I want you to meet Pepper."

"Pepper?"

"Long story. I'll be right back."

Macey shook her head and mumbled, "Does anyone around here go by their real name?"

She heard a deep laugh and then, "I do."

Looking up, she saw her tallest nightmare. There he was, long hair tied back, white shirt with no tie, smiling at her as if he knew something she didn't.

He cleared his throat. "I'm not sure I got a chance to introduce myself the other day when you were trespassing. The name's Noah."

Macey put her guard up by crossing her arms, then said, "As in the whale?" She smiled to herself, glad she could at least remain witty around him.

He grinned. "Actually that's Jonah. I'm more at home in an ark."

Macey closed her eyes with embarrassment. How could she get the two mixed up? She'd had to practically memorize both stories in Sunday school. She was just nervous. "I knew that."

His blue eyes sparkled with childlike defiance. Annoyed, Macey's muscles tightened, but at the same time she couldn't help notice how handsome he looked when he wasn't in a pair of tattered overalls. She shrugged off the thought and avoided his eyes.

Just then two blond, brown-skinned little girls ran up squealing, "Daddy! Daddy!" Long shiny curls rolled down their backs. They looked identical, both with emerald green eyes. One wore a red summer dress, the other yellow. Macey guessed them to be five or six.

"Hi, girls," Noah said, hugging each as they wrapped themselves around his legs. "What've you been up to?"

The one in the red dress replied, "Twenty took us out to see the chickens."

"I miss Jess, Daddy," the other one said.

Macey's throat tightened in a painful lump, and then she realized Noah and both little girls were looking at her.

"This is Savannah and Stephanie," he said, nodding first to the one with the red dress. "Girls, this is . . ." Noah waited for Macey to introduce herself.

She smiled tolerantly at him but then openly to the girls. "I'm Macey."

"She's Jess's daughter," Noah added, and Macey shot him a questioning look.

"Jess had a daughter?" Savannah said. Both girls stared up at her.

"Why didn't we ever see you before?" Stephanie asked as she rocked on her heels.

Macey was about to explain how long and complicated it was, but Noah rescued her and said, "Why don't you two go find Tutie. She was asking about you."

The girls squealed again and ran through the crowd, disappearing within seconds. Macey had trouble finding words. Finally she said, "Those girls are yours?"

"The joy of my life," he said, his tone pleasant, unassuming.

"They're beautiful," said Macey, now feeling extremely uncomfortable and wondering where his wife might be. "I should probably go find my mom."

Noah looked across the room, his head towering above everyone else's in the room. "She's fine. She's over there talking to Pepper." He winked at Macey. "Who, incidentally, is nicknamed for her allergy to it."

"Oh."

"*Macey*—is that a nickname?"

"It's short for Macille."

"I see why you'd go by Macey." He smiled and winked again. Macey was growing nervous as she was sensing an unlikely bit of chemistry forming between them, perhaps due to all the winking and grinning he was doing.

"Is your wife here?" She'd said it straightforwardly, just to make sure there was no miscommunication between them.

"She died," he said, and his lively eyes dulled a little. "When the girls were born."

The frustration of the day and the embarrassment of the moment came to a head for Macey, and her eyes suddenly teared. "I'm sorry."

Noah nodded and rocked on his heels, just as his little girl had done. "It was a while back. I'm glad to have these two munchkins, though. I can't imagine my world without them."

Agitated and exhausted, Macey could no longer carry on the conversation. Everything that had exchanged between the two of them seemed to spark something else, and on this particular day her fuse was shorter than normal. So she nodded obligingly and said, "Well, I think I'll find a quiet corner and drink a nice cup of coffee. I seem to be saying all the wrong things, and quite frankly I'm too tired to match wits with you."

His lips fell into a straight line. Macey wasn't sure if this was due to pity or indifference, but she didn't care. She spun around in order to make her way through the thinning crowd when she heard, "One more thing."

A small part of her told herself not to look back, to keep walking instead. But the vivaciousness of his blue eyes had a certain power over her, a power she was comfortable in denying existed. Nevertheless, she turned on her heel, her eyes meeting his.

"What?"

He bit his lower lip before saying, "You've got a tick the size of Detroit feasting off the blood of your scalp."

Nine

W atch the fire, Pepper! You're going to burn the poor girl to the ground!" Tutie's voice screeched next to Macey's ear. Macey closed her eyes, clutched the bottom of the chair she was sitting in, and counted backward like her psychiatrist had once taught her. She hated to think how many people were standing around staring at her scalp. Her ears burned as her blood pressure rose, creating a nice shade of red that crept slowly upward from her neck.

"I'm not sure the lighter is a good idea," came another deep voice, this time Noah's. "If someone'll get me some tweezers, I'll pluck the sucker right out."

"Make sure you get the head. If you don't get the head, it just keeps sucking and causing an infection," an unfamiliar voice chimed in. "It's just weird the little things don't need a body. I guess the only thing the body's used for is to hold the blood."

"I can get some bleach," her mother said. "Bleach kills pretty near anything."

A sharp pain pierced Macey's stomach, and at that moment she thought she would rather be dead than be the center of this crowd's attention. "Mother, I don't want to be a blonde."

Pepper, whom she hadn't officially met yet but who was leaning over her like a surgeon, replied, "I heard you're supposed to burn them off. If you don't use heat, a boil will form and you'll lose your hair."

She hadn't noticed Noah had left until he returned with a pair of tweezers. "Pepper, I don't think it's a good idea for you to be playing with fire around this young woman's hair. You know how your hands shake."

Twenty pushed his way forward, saying, "Yeah. Remember when you 'bout burnt Peedley's nose off trying to light his cigarette for him?"

The crowd laughed, and Macey could only be thankful it wasn't at her. Her stomach grumbled with nausea at the thought of a tick sucking her blood. She began feeling clammy, and her palms started sweating. She closed her eyes for a moment to try to steady her spinning head. The next thing she knew, everything went black.

"You killed her! You killed her!"

Macey's eyes flew open. A few of the women gasped as Macey came to realize she was lying on the hardwood floor near the dinner table. What looked like a hundred faces peered down at her, eyes wide and mouths open. A large hand took her shoulder and helped her to sit up.

"Get her a glass of water," the voice instructed. Macey identified it as Noah's. "And step back. She needs some air."

Macey rubbed her eyes. "I passed out?"

"For only a minute."

The water came quickly, and she sipped it as best she could.

"I didn't get that fire anywhere near her!" A sharp voice rose over the mumbling crowd. Everyone turned to see Pepper, middle-aged and over six feet tall, and Tutie glaring at each other.

"Why else would the poor girl faint like that?" Tutie was leaning forward on her cane and using her free hand to point at Macey.

"Well, do you see her head smokin'?" Pepper shot back.

"Ladies, ladies," Noah said. "Do you mind?"

The two gave each other one more hateful glance before shifting their attention back to Macey, who was feeling her part on the top of her head.

"I got the little critter while you were passed out," Noah said. "I thought it'd be easier that way. You'll have a scab."

Macey swallowed and closed her eyes for a moment.

"Macey, dear, are you okay?" her mother asked, and Macey looked up. She couldn't quite get herself to nod. Physically she was fine. Emotionally she wasn't sure yet.

Noah's firm grip raised her to her feet and then moved her through the group of people, out the back door, and onto the porch. Macey leaned against the rail and was actually thankful to be out in the heat. It felt cooler than what she'd been feeling inside. She looked at Noah, who was smiling.

"That was one of the most humiliating things ever to happen to me," she said, then walked down the steps and sat in a lawn chair, her knees shaking. Noah followed her.

"Listen, it happens all the time in these parts. We just know to check for ticks when we've been out in the grass, that's all."

"Yeah, I guess I forgot. You'd never know I grew up here." She shook her head, then looked at the sky. "The last thing I wanted was to draw attention to myself. So, what horrible disease can I contract from a tick?"

"Well, it's unlikely, but if you start feeling like you have the flu, we should probably get you to a doctor."

"Nausea? Headache? Hot flashes? I'm already feeling that way!"

Noah handed her the water she'd set down, and she sipped it absently. She would pack her bags and leave tomorrow. She needed the comfort of the hectic insanity that was her life back in Dallas. The fact that a bloodsucking tick could cause this much excitement perplexed and annoyed her.

Her mother would be fine. She'd probably relish a few phone calls and cards. But each additional hour she was here, things just got worse. She'd buried her father and supported her mother, and now it was time to go home.

Before she knew it, the water in her glass was gone and only a couple of soft ice cubes remained in the bottom. She noticed then that Noah was staring at her.

"What? You see another tick?"

He laughed and shook his head. "I just think you need a break from all these people. How about you walk across the bridge with me? I'll show you my house."

Macey's eyes grew large. Could she step inside that house? Looking at it from the outside was one thing, to go in quite another.

Noah must've read her expression, because he said, "I'm inviting you, which means you'll not be trespassing, if that's what you're worried about."

Macey gazed across the river at the old house. "It was so run down as I remember it. You must've done a lot to it to make it livable."

He nodded. "It was almost a yearlong project. My wife and I worked on it together, before she had the girls. It has three bedrooms now, a nice kitchen and dining area, and even a playroom."

She was just about to decline the offer when the back porch door flew open and Pepper stepped out. "Macey! I found some peroxide and cotton balls. We need to do a good soakin' of your scalp or else an infection could start and you could lose all your hair. We have a nice wig shop in town, but nobody wants to have to see you use it."

Macey looked at Noah. "I'd love a tour."

The front door creaked open as Macey waited for Noah to enter before she did. Her feet, heavy with fear, barely lifted at her command. Noah looked back and waited. Finally Macey stepped forward, across the threshold and into the main entryway.

The inside of the old farmhouse looked brand-new. The walls of the entryway had been painted a country blue and decorated with family pictures. From the entry she could see the breakfast area, large kitchen, and dining and living rooms. She followed him in and noticed a stairwell, lushly carpeted in beige.

She stopped and oriented herself for a moment. As she remembered it, the stairwell had caved in, and the bottom level was divided by one long wall that apparently had been knocked down. There were very few windows before, though now several allowed the sun to glow in a beautiful crisscross pattern throughout the open rooms.

Artwork hung on the walls above the sofa and up the staircase. The one above the sofa was an impressively large landscape depicting a desert storm. Other pieces were smaller and varied from portraits to impressionistic paintings. Noah turned around to watch her.

"I don't normally pass out," she said. The statement came from nowhere, making her feel like a bumbling idiot. Noah's tolerant, steady smile only served to reinforce the feeling. "I'm just saying I don't do that. I don't pass out. I've never passed out in my whole life." Again, he only smiled. "What? You're looking at me like you don't believe me."

"No. I'm only looking at you. You read more into my expression than is there."

"You're trying to tell me that mischievous, smug expression on your face is normal and everyday for you?"

Noah shook his head and walked toward his kitchen. "You are something else, Macey Steigel. What can I get you to drink? Coke, tea?"

Macey hesitated. She'd geared herself up for a debate, and now he was offering her a beverage? "Tea sounds good."

She stepped farther into the living area. A large television, two leather sofas, and three antique-looking side tables occupied the

room. Fresh flowers in what appeared to be an expensive vase sat
on one table, while the two others had only coasters or magazines
on them. On the opposite side, across from the living area, was the
dining room. The polished mahogany table and chairs shined in the
natural light, with another fresh arrangement of flowers placed perfectly as a centerpiece. She strolled carefully between the two areas
and into the kitchen, where Noah was busy making tea.

Macey leaned on the large butcher-block island in the middle
of the kitchen and watched him drop fresh mint into the crystal
pitcher. She was astonished at the wealth inside the home. When
she'd first met him, she'd figured he was a poor struggling farmer or
mechanic who painted for a hobby. Now she was starting to suspect
something different. She just didn't know what.

"Your home is beautiful," she said.

"Thank you." He handed her a glass of tea, lightly sweetened
with raspberry. "Is it like you remember it?"

Macey shook her head. "Not at all. I remember it as a dump. I
can't believe you were able to restore it like this."

He winked and said, "I'm pretty handy with a hammer and saw."

Macey turned and took in the main rooms again. "I like how
open it is, how the sunlight pours in through the windows."

"It was my wife's idea not to have any shades or curtains. She
loved natural light."

Macey stayed facing away from him, feeling uncomfortable at
the thought of his poor wife dying. She walked over to the dining
room, where a large mahogany buffet sat with pictures crowded together on its top. She picked up a picture of Noah standing next
to a tall, blond, fresh-faced woman wearing an expensive-looking
pantsuit and gold jewelry. He had his arm around her, and his hair
was quite a bit shorter.

"That's Emily," he said.

Macey jumped, not realizing Noah was behind her. He slowly took the photo from her and looked at it himself, as if he'd never seen it before. He smiled before putting it back on the buffet.

"She was beautiful," Macey managed, her eyes scanning the rest of the photos. "How did she die?"

Noah walked back to the kitchen for his glass. "During child-birth. She was actually carrying triplets. One of them died, too. Her name was Sierra."

Macey shook her head as she picked up a picture of the two identical girls, who looked to be about two years old at the time the picture was taken. They were hugging each other in the middle of a wild-flower field. "I'm so sorry."

She could hear the sound of more tea being poured into his glass. "Actually it brings me great comfort." Macey turned around, and Noah explained. "To know Emily and Sierra are together in heaven—they have each other there. And we have each other here. Someday we'll all be together again." Noah brought the pitcher over to Macey and refilled her glass. "The girls know they have a sister. They knew it long before I had a chance to explain it. It was strange. Every time they'd play dolls or have a tea party, there would always be a third place set, and when I asked who it was for, they'd say their sister." He shrugged and walked back to the kitchen to set the pitcher down. "How's the tea?"

"Amazing. Tastes like raspberries."

"I have raspberry bushes on the west side of the house. Your mom has made some great raspberry cobblers out of them."

Macey smiled and then sipped the tea again, thinking how wonderful it would be to have her own raspberry bushes.

"Let me give you the tour," said Noah. He was halfway to the stairs when he noticed she'd hesitated and wasn't following him. "You remember when these were collapsed?"

Macey laughed. "Sure do. And the ones that remained looked like they couldn't hold the weight of an ant."

They walked up together. Directly at the top was the girls' room, painted pastel colors and adorned with frilly lace, the exact replica of a dollhouse. Macey gasped in amazement. "What a fairy tale!"

Noah opened the door wider and motioned for her to step in. Hundreds of dolls and stuffed animals lined the shelves all around the room. Golden butterflies painted delicately on one wall seemed alive with motion. Two twin-sized beds on opposite sides of the room had plush white comforters and three or four pillows each. Noah walked to a bed and straightened one pillow a little. "This was all Emily's doing. She had the vision for it and made it happen."

"How old are your girls?"

"Six. They're small for their age. But they have the personalities to make up for it."

Noah went on to show her the upstairs bathroom, his bedroom, and the girls' playroom—a giant room filled with toys—all the while explaining how each room was transformed and what they had done to make it special and unique.

They walked back downstairs, where Noah, with Macey right behind him, rounded the corner of the stairwell and opened the door beneath it.

"This is my studio."

Canvas, easels, brushes, tubes, rags, and other paint supplies cluttered the room in a semiorganized fashion. Noah waited for her to come in, but Macey couldn't take another step forward. Displayed before her were beautiful landscapes, breathtaking colors, serenity caught on canvas, yet all she could see was darkness. Her stomach cramped as painful memories surged through her mind. She backed out of the room and went to the front door. Noah followed her.

"Are you okay?" he asked, his large hand on the small of her back.

"Fine." She forced a pleasant smile. "I just realized I should go check on my mom. I didn't even tell her where I was going."

"Of course," Noah said, opening the door for her. The heat had increased dramatically since she'd entered the house, and it surprised her as she tried to catch her breath. "I'll walk over with you. I have to get the girls."

They strolled in silence, and Macey appreciated the way this man could somehow sense she didn't want to talk right now. On Stone Bridge they stopped for a moment to look and listen to the river and then continued on. As they made their way toward the farmhouse, the innocent giggling of the twin girls brought their attention to the tree with the tree house, where the girls were hanging like monkeys from the lower limbs. Noah and Macey laughed at the sight.

Macey could already tell that many people had left the house. She heaved a sigh of relief. Noah looked down at her, seemingly reading her mind.

"Looks like the crowd's thinning," he said.

Macey nodded and tried hard not to make a cynical remark. Instead, she made an impulsive request. "Come to dinner tomorrow? You and the girls?"

Noah glanced down at her again, his eyebrows raised. She was about to give an explanation as to why she had asked him when he said, "You cook?"

Macey bit her lower lip. No, she didn't cook. And no, there wasn't a Boston Market down the road. Her heart raced. "Surprised?"

"You just don't seem like the type that cooks."

"Well, maybe you've got me pegged all wrong."

"Maybe," Noah said as they approached the porch steps. "But are you sure your mom's up for more company?" They both glanced through the back window, finding a group of guests pressing in around Evelyn as if she were a celebrity.

"I don't think she'd have it any other way."

Ten

Evelyn stood a few feet away, watching her daughter carefully organize and then nervously reorganize all the ingredients on the counter top. Without turning around, Macey said, "Mom, please go and lie down. You've had an emotional couple of days."

"I'm fine. Stop fussing over me. Everyone has been fussing over me." Evelyn went to the refrigerator for a cold glass of water. "Tell me again what you're making?"

"Nothing fancy," her daughter said, rearranging the ingredients again. "Just spaghetti and some French bread. Green beans. That and a little wine should make for a nice meal."

Evelyn sat down at the kitchen table, her legs shaking from exhaustion. The truth was, she had never been more tired, but she didn't want to miss any opportunity to spend time with her daughter. Last night she'd gone to bed early after sorting through some more of Jess's things. She'd woken up seven or eight times throughout the night and then risen early, before the sun, just to get away from her tortured sleep.

She'd spent the day with Macey as they'd sifted through Jess's old books and collectibles, deciding what to keep and what to give away. It had felt good to spend the quiet time with her daughter, even given the painful circumstances of their task.

"I've never had canned spaghetti sauce before," Evelyn said, and Macey turned around, a scowl bunching up her features. "Is it good?"

"I like it," she answered flatly.

"Does it come with meat?"

"No, Mother. Not every meal has to have meat. I have freshly shaved Parmesan cheese, mushrooms, and parsley. I plan to make garlic bread."

"Goodness, I hate for you to have spent all the money. We have fresh tomatoes and oregano out back. We could've just whipped up our own sauce, let it be simmerin' all day. And I've got beef in the freezer in the garage we could've thawed."

Macey held up her hands. "Mom. Please. I'm preparing a simple, inexpensive meal. You should learn to do the same. Not every meal has to be an event." Macey was chopping the parsley furiously, so Evelyn sat and sipped her water for a minute.

Then she said, "Well, I'm just so happy you got a chance to meet Noah. He's just as sweet as can be. Those little girls are just dolls. I'm glad you invited him to dinner."

"He told me his wife died."

"It was so tragic. She passed on shortly after he and his wife fixed up the house. She was a lovely young lady. Noah had the funeral elsewhere, since they didn't know too many people around these parts yet. But he stayed living here and has been raisin' the girls just the best that he knows how, and he's doin' a good job of it, too."

"Where did they move from?" Macey asked, rinsing mushrooms under a stream of water at the sink.

"New York City," Evelyn answered. Macey turned around while wiping her hands with a dishrag, her eyes large and quizzical. "Yes, they were apparently tired of the big city life and wanted to get away from it all. It was quite a change for them, but when we found out who he was, we all were just so excited to have him living here."

Macey set the dishrag down and frowned. "Who is he?"

"He didn't tell you?" Evelyn shook her head, laughed and took a gulp of her water. "That boy's a humble one."

"Who is he?"

"Well, I'd never heard of him before, but apparently he's some big artist. That's according to Louise Belltrap, do you remember her? Her husband was the—" Evelyn sensed her daughter's impatience and continued, "Anyhow, she follows art and says he's very well known, and his oil paintings have sold all around the world. Anyone who knows anything about art knows—"

Macey almost dropped the knife she'd just picked up. "Kauffman!" She walked forward, her eyes wide with disbelief. "He's Noah Kauffman?"

"You know him?"

Macey threw her head back with laughter. "I know *of* him. I was at a fund-raising auction once, where one of his paintings sold for fifty thousand dollars. He wasn't quite as well known then, but I've heard him mentioned here and there over the years. He's definitely established a name for himself." She covered her mouth, her head still shaking with disbelief. "That explains the house."

"Oh! Did you get to see the inside? Wonderful, isn't it?"

Macey nodded and went back to chopping mushrooms. "I can't believe it. He's *the* Noah Kauffman."

Evelyn shrugged, walking to the fridge to refill her glass. "Well, he's mostly just known as Noah around here. He doesn't want to be treated special, and we've never taken to treatin' him special. 'Course, his girls are spoiled rotten because of us, but that's another story." She poured a glass of water for Macey and started a fresh pot of coffee. Her eyes stung with exhaustion, yet she was still exhilarated by being in the presence of her daughter. "What did you think of our little grocery store?"

Macey smiled. "It was fine—it had everything I needed. Not quite the selection I'm used to, but who needs five hundred varieties of spaghetti sauce, anyway?" She wiped the counter with the dishrag and then sat down at the kitchen table and glanced at her watch.

"We have a couple of hours before they'll be here." She picked at a hangnail and said, "I thought the funeral was nice."

"It was, it was," Evelyn said with a deep nod of her head. "Everyone was so kind. They always are." The coffee began dripping, filling the room with the soothing aroma.

"The graveside was nice, too."

"Yes. It was hot, but the shade from the tree sure helped."

"It did. I noticed that."

Each sipped her water, Macey at the table and Evelyn at the counter. They stared out separate windows for a while. A crow was making a furious racket out the front window, and Evelyn smiled a little at the thought of how much her husband used to hate crows.

"Mom, I'm leaving tomorrow."

Evelyn set her glass down. "So soon?"

"I have a job. They expect me back, you know. I'm sorry. I wish I could stay."

Evelyn's eyes moistened, but she nodded and tried to smile. "I understand. You're a busy woman. That's good. I'm glad you're successful in what you love to do."

"I'll call, though. I promise. And write. Maybe I can arrange for you to come out and see me sometime."

"I'm not the big city type. You know me." She turned to the sink, hoping to find some dishes that needed washing. There were only a couple of bowls and spoons. She took up the rag and started scrubbing them.

"But before I leave," her daughter said as she stood and approached the sink, "I want to make sure your finances are in order. Did Dad have a will?"

Evelyn sloshed the soapy water around in the bowl. "A will? I don't know, dear."

Out of the corner of her eye, she could see Macey scratch her head. She then said, "We need to find that out. We're going to need to know exactly what your assets are. And over the next few months, I can help you decide what you want to do and where you want to put your money. I've got an excellent financial planner, and I can get his help in all this. Some things are going to have to change in your finances, Mom. Okay?"

Evelyn nodded but wasn't sure what Macey was talking about. Jess always handled the money. She never had a thing to do with it.

"Do you know of any IRAs? Maybe some CDs or bonds? Stocks?"

"I don't know."

"What about property? Do we still have that land on Frontage?"

"It's good for nothing as far as I know." Evelyn handed the bowl to Macey to dry. "We need to check and see if your tick bite's infected. You're not feeling like the flu, are you? If so, we should take you to the doctor."

"Mom, don't change the subject." Macey put the bowl in the cabinet and turned to Evelyn. "I'm sorry. I'm not trying to overwhelm you. Let's just forget about it until after dinner. After Noah and the girls are gone, we'll sit down and go through everything."

Evelyn agreed, thought about pouring herself a cup of coffee, then changed her mind. She didn't even have the energy to do that. She was glad Macey was fixing dinner, even if it consisted of canned spaghetti sauce.

"Mom? You okay?"

She felt Macey grab her elbow and realized she might have just nodded off while standing up. "Fine," she mumbled, but Macey was already guiding her toward the stairs to help her up to her bedroom.

"You're not fine," Macey lectured as they slowly made their way to the room. Macey continued to hold on to her until they made it to the bed.

"Oh, my feet," Evelyn moaned.

Macey quickly bent down and removed her mom's shoes. She took Evelyn's feet and steered them up onto the bed, placing a pillow underneath them, and fluffed a second pillow for her head. "You must rest," she said sternly.

Evelyn looked to the other side of the room where Jess's wheelchair and hospital bed used to sit. She'd grown so accustomed to the clutter that the room now looked open and empty. Her hand moved to the vacant side of the bed. She'd had to sleep alone since his move to the hospital bed, but it crushed her that she'd be sleeping in this bed, in this house, all alone from now on. She tightly closed her eyes to keep the tears at bay and heard Macey quietly shut the door as she left.

Tomorrow she would go and put fresh flowers on the grave and make sure everything was in order. Though it was nonsense to think of Jess lying still under all that dirt, she would do it nevertheless. She didn't know what else she was going to do with her time.

As her eyelids became heavier and her mind swirled with indiscernible images, she wondered briefly if this were all just a dream. Perhaps she would awaken and life would be normal again. But, before drifting off, her last thought was of heaven and that maybe it would be better if she awoke there instead.

———◆———

The spaghetti sauce popped and sputtered itself out of the saucepan and onto the stove top, while Macey frantically tried to reach around it and turn the heat down. It was too late, though. The stove top was splattered with bright red Ragu sauce as were her silk top and khaki shorts. She seethed with anger, throwing down the saucepan lid and grabbing at a dishrag. She couldn't even prepare a simple meal such as spaghetti without making a mess!

"Dear? Are you okay?"

Macey whirled around to find her mother creeping down the stairs, a little hunched and looking very old. She grumbled, turned back to the stove, and resumed cleaning up the mess. She quickly resigned herself to the idea that her shirt and shorts were unsalvageable. Her mother was next to her before she could cover up the evidence of her incompetence. Evelyn had already taken a towel and was beginning to help her wipe it up.

"That sauce can bubble before you know it, can't it?" her mother said with a smile and a light tap on her daughter's back.

Macey sighed and went to finishing folding the napkins for the dinner table. "I just wasn't paying attention, that's all."

"Well, it smells marvelous. It practically woke me up from a dead sleep!"

Macey finally felt the tension release from her shoulders. She managed a smile and said, "Really? It smells good?"

"Wonderful. The garlic. The oregano. Do I smell cheese?"

"Yes. I'm making garlic cheese bread, remember? Nothing fancy, but it tastes good."

"That's what counts," Evelyn said cheerfully. "Can I help you with anything?"

"Do you have any candles? I like to eat dinner by candlelight," Macey said, though it was a lie. She mostly ate by herself at restaurants or on her couch in front of the TV. She hoped she wasn't being too obvious with the candlelight, but it was her mom's house, so maybe Noah would think it was her mom's idea.

Evelyn started hunting in the pantry. "I think we have a candle or two in here. I don't know if any of them match. We usually only use them when the electricity goes out."

Macey heard only every other word of her mother's muffled voice, but when she emerged with two red candles, complete with brass holders, Macey grinned and handed her mother the matches. "Perfect."

Dinner was just about complete. The pasta was all ready, so she poured it through the colander, the steam melting what little makeup she had on. She quickly transferred it to a serving dish, carefully poured the hot spaghetti sauce over the middle, and added fresh parsley for more color. Finally she topped it off with the sautéed mushrooms. Even though Andy had dumped her over a year ago, the one thing she took from him was how to make a simple meal look fancy. He'd taught her the art of garnish.

She opened the oven door and pulled out the garlic bread, the cheese bubbly and hot. Evelyn approached and peered over her shoulder. "My goodness! What a feast!"

Macey handed her the dish of pasta to take to the table while she scooped the bread into a basket. The canned green beans were heated through, so she seasoned them with a little sugar, salt, and soy sauce, and poured them into a serving bowl.

Just as she was about to check her watch to see how much time she had to go change, the doorbell rang. Evelyn opened the door, and in walked Noah and his two girls. Macey stared down at the mess on her clothes and shyly greeted each of them.

"Come in. Dinner is ready. Perfect timing," she said, trying to cover up the stains on her shirt.

"Had the heat on too high, did you?" His finger pointed to her clothes, and that wicked little smirk of his was accompanied by a sparkle in his eyes.

"Thanks for noticing," Macey quipped and then asked her mother to prepare the drinks while she flew upstairs to change.

As she climbed the stairs, she looked back down at Noah. His tall figure towered over her mother's, and his booming voice had a soothing effect. The two girls beside him made her smile, but then a feeling of despair wrenched her heart and she looked away, taking the stairs as fast as she could.

With Macey, guilt always arrived at the most inopportune times.

———◆———

It felt good to laugh. It wasn't the type of laughing that's concocted to impress a boss or to look casual in front of the camera when Walter the meteorologist makes a crack. And it wasn't the type of laughing done alone, in front of the television set, to the predictable, mindless humor of a sitcom. This was laughter from the heart, and Macey made herself enjoy it.

Noah was sharing his previous life in the New York arts scene, telling unbelievable stories of greed and selfish ambition while trying to help his young girls eat, not wear, their meal. Macey leaned back in her chair and listened intently, laughing each time he made a funny remark, thankful that her mom seemed to be enjoying herself. It was hard to believe they'd buried her father just the day before.

Stephanie and Savannah asked if they could go outside and play in the tree house, and Noah told them to run along. The table, once elegant and organized, was now strewn with napkins, dirty plates, a half-empty basket of cold bread, and melting candles. Macey loved it all the same.

Evelyn went to the kitchen and returned with a fresh pot of coffee. The temperature in the house was finally cooling as the evening sun settled down through the windows, mellowing the day's intensity. Macey doctored her coffee with precision and found herself staring at the man across the table. His deep-set blue eyes captivated her, his humor even more engaging. She had lost herself in thoughts of Noah when suddenly she heard him say, "And what about you?"

Macey blinked and realized how awkward she must look. She tried to smile, bringing her coffee cup to her lips. "Me?"

"I've been talking about myself all evening."

"Well, you're terribly interesting," Macey offered, setting the cup down and twisting the napkin in her hands.

"Evelyn mentioned you're a television anchor in Dallas. That's pretty impressive."

Macey shook her head and glanced at her mom, who was grinning with pride. "It's not bad," Macey said softly.

"Not bad at all," Noah acknowledged. "That's a big market. How long have you been there?"

"A few years. I came to Dallas from San Antonio. But there's a chance—" Macey stopped and wondered if the two people sitting across from her would understand how big this really was—"there's a chance I'll be going to the network."

Her mom smiled, nodding as though she knew what Macey just shared was something good but didn't know what it meant exactly. Noah, however, leaned forward and raised his eyebrows. "No kidding? New York?"

"Probably. There's a chance I may go with cable, which is in New Jersey. I don't know much yet. Just that they're interested in me."

"How did this come about?" Noah asked. "I know enough about the network to know they don't just seek out any news anchor."

Macey smiled. She was glad he knew it was a big deal. "Well, I think I caught their eye during the Dallas fire last year."

Evelyn sat back down after clearing some dishes. "I remember hearing about that."

"Sure," Noah added. "It looked like half of downtown was burned."

Macey nodded. "Yes, it was really intense. I'm the noon news anchor, which of course isn't the prime spot to be seen by talent scouts. But when the fire broke out, it was at eleven in the morning and so I was the one who covered it. The story went national, and there I was on every TV in America, covering the fire. It was sort of a fluke, I guess you could say."

"But it wasn't a fluke that they saw talent in you. They must've seen something good."

Macey shrugged, avoiding his gaze. "Maybe. They want to talk to me. It would be a big break, that's for sure." Macey glanced over to see her mother staring into her coffee.

Evelyn looked up and said, "So you're moving to New York City?"

"Nothing's for sure yet, Mom. They just want to talk. There's a whole lot of talking that goes on in this business. Only every once in a while does it mean something's going to happen. There's also a lot of competition. It's horribly cutthroat."

Evelyn's eyes dropped back down to her coffee, and although her mom wore a small smile, Macey knew she wasn't pleased. She sighed and stirred her own coffee, the atmosphere thickening almost immediately.

Then Evelyn stood up. "I bet those girls would want some ice cream, Noah. I've got strawberry out in the freezer."

Noah laughed. "Evelyn, they've been filled up with junk all day, but I bet they're not going to say no."

Evelyn laughed a little but not in her usually gleeful way. She mumbled that she would go ask them and then went out the back door without another word.

Macey kept stirring her coffee. She watched her mom through the back bay window, talking and laughing with the girls. A deep-seated sadness swept over her, and she tried to take in a few deep breaths. She glanced at Noah, who she saw had been watching her all along.

"Your mom doesn't approve," he said.

Macey shrugged. "It doesn't matter. I care for my mom, but I'm not going to pass up an opportunity for my dream job just because

she doesn't want me living in New York. I haven't seen her in seven—"
Macey stopped, realizing she was saying more than she should.

"It must be hard for her, knowing she's going to be alone from
now on."

Macey set down the spoon she was using to stir her coffee. "Are
you trying to make me feel guilty?"

"Oh, I hardly think I need to contribute to that. You seem to be
doing fine on your own."

Macey's eyes narrowed. "Why would you say such a thing?"

Noah fiddled with the tablecloth and, without looking at her,
said, "You're right. This is an opportunity of a lifetime. How could
you pass it up?"

Macey folded her arms against her chest. "It must seem so cut
and dried to you. But I assure you, this . . . this whole thing, it's complicated. I'm sorry my mom's going to be alone, but it's not my fault.
None of it's my fault."

"You're right," Noah said curtly.

"I don't expect you to understand. You weren't here when it all
happened and . . ." Macey paused, swallowed. She'd done it again
and was about to say too much. She looked at Noah.

"When what happened?"

"Daddy! Daddy!" The girls' squealing made Macey's heart
jump. She hadn't heard them come in. She looked to the back door
and saw her mom slowly making her way up the steps. "Evelyn said
we could have ice cream! Can we?"

Noah hugged both girls and told them they could. They ran
to tell Evelyn and then skipped behind her out to the garage to the
large freezer. Noah's eyes followed them, a grin spread across his
face. Macey stood and began clearing the rest of the dishes.

"Can I help you with that?" he asked from behind her. She nodded, though she really just wanted to be alone. Noah moved back

and forth between the table and kitchen counter with dishes and leftovers in his hands. Macey stood at the sink, filling it with hot water, adding the soap. Evelyn and the girls came back in with a gallon of ice cream and cones, but Noah told them they had to eat their ice cream out on the back porch, so all three went back outside again. Macey started in on scrubbing the dishes, while Noah stepped to the sink to dry them.

It was silent for a time, except for the excited screams of the two girls and the gentle instruction from Evelyn on how to hold an ice cream cone so the ice cream doesn't fall off. They both listened to the distant conversation until Noah said, "The candles were a nice touch."

Macey handed him a plate. "Excuse me?"

"The candles. I've eaten here many times before and never seen candles on the table. They were nice."

Macey swallowed. Was he being serious or giving her some coded message like he was apt to do? Was he seeing right through her? And why did he have to stare at her like that?

"You're dripping water everywhere," she pointed out, and he smiled as he went back to drying the dishes.

As they finished the last glass and Macey began putting the dishes back in the cupboard, she suddenly felt compelled to say, "I'm leaving tomorrow."

He looked at her as if he wasn't the least bit surprised. He just nodded and continued to hand her dishes.

"You probably think I'm horrible."

"Why would I think that?" he said innocently.

She frowned and closed the cupboard. "Because I'm leaving. I should stay. Be the loyal daughter. Take care of my grieving mother. Et cetera."

His expression, as usual, gave her no indication as to what he was thinking. But it was a moot point, as the girls and her mother were on their way back inside, laughing and complaining about how sticky they were.

"Look at you two!" Noah said. He scooped them up with no regard for their dirty hands. He kissed them both, set them down, and ordered them over to the sink. "It looks like you rolled in the ice cream! Did any of it get into your stomachs?"

They both giggled as they fought over who would wash their hands first. Evelyn helped sort them out and made sure they both had soap. The whole idea of the evening—a romantic dinner with the stranger from across the river—mingled with the reality of why she'd returned home, leaving Macey standing in the kitchen feeling suffocated.

She quietly moved to the living area unnoticed and stared out the bay window, only half listening to the sounds in the kitchen. Her tired mind pondered the last couple of days, what it all had meant. She was shocked at the impact all of this should've had, yet how so much had been left unresolved, and always would. Tomorrow morning she would pack her things, kiss her mom good-bye, promise to call and write more, and return to her life in Dallas, the life she was accustomed to. She would pretend, as she had for the better part of seventeen years, to live day to day and lay aside matters of the heart.

A tugging at the bottom of her shirt made her look down where she found one of the twins, her dramatic emerald eyes wide and engaging. "I'm Savannah," the girl announced, apparently feeling the need to make clear which one she was. "You didn't eat any ice cream."

Macey smiled and bent to her level. She wanted to reach out and touch her silky white hair. Instead, she nodded and said, "No. But I should have. A person should never pass up ice cream."

Savannah agreed with a grin, then turned serious again. "You look sad."

Macey looked around to see if anyone had heard this, but the rest were still in the kitchen and out of earshot. She didn't know how to respond, so she asked, "I do?"

"Your eyes. Daddy says you can always tell people are sad by looking at their eyes."

"Oh." Macey tried to think of a way to change the subject. But Savannah continued.

"Are you sad because your daddy died? My mommy died. But I was a baby and I don't remember. I just see her in pictures. My daddy says she was a wonderful mommy. Are you a mommy, too?"

The questions overwhelmed Macey so that tears moistened her eyes. She didn't know how to answer the little girl. Savannah had barely taken a breath before she asked, "Have you prayed to Jesus?"

Again Macey was caught off guard and thought to herself how uncouth children could be. Didn't they understand you shouldn't talk about personal relationships or religion with people you don't know very well?

"Jesus helped my daddy when my mommy died, and we pray to Him every night before we go to bed. There was this mean boy at school and Stephanie and me prayed that Jesus would help that boy not be mean, and now he doesn't pick on me anymore."

Macey nodded, tried smiling, but inside she was trembling.

"Your daddy was a nice man," said Savannah, pointing up at a picture on the nearby TV. "He always took us out to the farm. He loved Jesus, too."

Macey ran her fingers through her hair and stood, afraid she wasn't getting enough oxygen. Savannah stared up at her with questioning eyes. "Are you okay?"

"Yes, fine," Macey said. She wondered why in the world everyone was staying in the kitchen so long. "You like school, do you?" The attempt to change the subject somehow didn't faze the young girl, and now she was cocking her head to the side and folding her arms together.

"Jesus lives in my heart. Is He in your heart?"

Just as Macey was going to make another attempt at changing the subject, Noah walked in, smiling as the other girl clung to his leg. Macey sighed in relief, believing Noah would step in and quietly mention to Savannah that it's not polite to ask people about their religious beliefs. But instead, as Savannah continued to talk about Jesus, Noah simply listened and beamed with pride.

Savannah's speech finally ended with, "Are you saved?"

Swallowing hard, Macey looked at Noah, who seemed just as intent on hearing the answer as the three-and-a-half-footer standing in front of her. Even Stephanie showed some interest while fiddling with the change in Noah's pocket.

Macey bit down on the thumbnail on her left hand, not knowing what to say.

Savannah turned to her father and said, "Daddy, she isn't answering the question. Is this the time I should tell her about hell?"

Macey's eyes widened in horror. She waited for Noah to reprimand his daughter, but he simply told her lightheartedly, "No. This is the time you should tell her about how much Jesus loves her." He glanced at Macey and said, "This is making you uncomfortable?"

Her eyes narrowed just as she tasted blood. She swallowed the pieces of fingernail in her mouth and said, "You know, if she could just throw in a question about my political affiliation, then I'd be feeling really comfortable. Religion *and* politics. That'd be just perfect."

Noah's large hand found Savannah's shoulder. "Well, around these parts, no one has to ask what someone's political affiliation is. We all know. As far as religion, I think it would be hypocritical of me to raise my family Christian and then ask my children not to share their faith. Don't you?"

Macey didn't respond but instead gazed out the window to avoid his eyes and said, "It's starting to get dark outside. I'd hate for you three to be crossing the river in pitch black."

Evelyn, having just entered the room, said, "Oh, it's no big deal. They do it all the time." She obviously didn't catch the meaning behind Macey's sharp look.

Noah took each girl by the hand. He stepped closer to Macey and then looked down at Savannah. "Why don't you invite Macey to come to church with us tomorrow, Savannah?"

Savannah didn't have time to repeat the question before Macey said, "Thank you, but I'm leaving early in the morning."

Noah winked at Savannah. "We'll pray tonight that she changes her mind." Then he thanked Evelyn and told her to call him without hesitating if there was anything he could do for her. The three of them left through the back door, and Macey watched as the two girls bounded across the grass and Noah casually strolled behind them.

Blood still oozed from the corner of her thumbnail, now pink and raw. She hardly noticed it. Without taking her eyes off Noah and the girls she said to her mother, "I guess we need to talk money."

Eleven

S he noticed her hands were shaking. With her daughter peering over her shoulder, the tiny key was bound and determined not to slide into the tiny hole. Evelyn tried to take deep breaths, but the key still missed its mark by an inch.

"Here, Mom, let me," Macey insisted and snatched the key from her before she could try again. Evelyn backed away and sat on her bed, watching her daughter unlock the small safe and open the lid while lecturing her about why she shouldn't keep valuables in the house, even in a box that locks.

"It's fireproof," Evelyn retorted softly, but she doubted Macey heard. She was already going through the contents inside, mumbling about mortgage papers and other things.

Her daughter also asked about balances and stock portfolios. Evelyn's mind wandered elsewhere. She thought of the letter she'd written a few days ago. For a moment her heart stung, thinking she might have put the letter in the safe, but then she remembered she'd stuck it in the drawer of the table next to the bed. Her shoulders dropped a little, and she simply watched her daughter.

Perhaps they could talk. *Really* talk. Evelyn could make muffins, and they could sit together on the porch and watch the fireflies dart in and out of sight. Her daughter would leave in the morning and probably never be back. Could Evelyn really live out the rest of her life without acknowledging the past? Without trying to resolve their future?

It was the hateful glare that could instantly pass through the glimmer in Macey's eyes that kept Evelyn's boldness in check. She couldn't bear the rejection, so she sat silently on her bed, hands folded in her lap, listening to Macey talk about things she didn't understand. What she did understand, though, was the tension rising in Macey's voice. She tuned in to her words just in time to hear ". . . not a single item here indicating how many assets you have, Mother."

Evelyn blinked. She reached for the glass of water on the end table by the bed and saw that her hands were still trembling. She attempted a sip but ended up just staring at the water as it swished in the glass.

Macey's eyes were disturbed. "Mother? Did you hear me?" Macey stood, envelopes and papers bunched up in both of her hands. "We have to get this settled before I leave. Don't you have any record of your stocks and bonds?"

Evelyn frowned and wondered if maybe she did. She couldn't remember. Jess never talked to her much about money. He'd always maintained that it was his job to support the family and she needn't worry about money. There were plenty of other things around the house for her to worry herself about. So she didn't worry. Not once during the many years they were married. And not once had Jess failed her.

"Well, honey," Evelyn said, "I think you just worry too much. I've always been taken care of. There's no reason to think I'm not going to be now. The good Lord's going to—"

Macey's hands flew up and she closed her eyes, a tense expression flattening her features. "Please, can we just not talk about that? If anyone says another word about religion, I'm going to flip out." She dropped the papers onto Evelyn's nightstand and then rubbed her face vigorously, causing red splotches to break out across her cheeks and forehead. "Now," she continued, her voice low and controlled, "how about a bank statement? Can I at least see a bank statement?"

Evelyn rose and went to the bedroom door, where she'd hung her purse after the funeral. She normally hung her purse off one of the breakfast table chairs, but for the reception she'd brought it up-stairs. Her mama had always taught her to keep her purse safe and closed when men were around. She'd taken to heart her mother's advice, and never once had anything been stolen. Once she thought her coin purse had been snatched, but later she found out it had fallen out of her purse in the parking lot of the old IGA. Another good reason to keep one's purse closed.

"I don't know about any bank statements," Evelyn told her as she dug in her purse, "but this is our checkbook. Will that help?"

Macey took it from her and flipped to the register. Her curled lip released slightly, and her eyes even looked happy. Evelyn breathed a sigh of relief. "Well," she said, flipping back and forth through the small pages of the registry, "looks like you at least have enough money to get you through a couple of months." Macey looked up at Evelyn. "Your register shows five thousand, two hundred and eight dollars, plus some change. How much do you usually spend on bills a month?"

Evelyn shrugged. "Don't know. Your father always did the bills."

Macey's eyes rolled in apparent annoyance. "You're going to have to do it from now on, Mom. Or get Patricia to. But you need to be aware of what you're spending every month. I know you and Dad own this house and your car, so you don't have to worry about that. But you have utilities, property taxes, insurance, and of course food and clothing. But I imagine you're not a big spender." Macey smiled at her mom, and Evelyn's heart melted. She nodded in hearty agreement. "Good. Let's try to figure out how many assets you have and where they're located, and then we'll put together an outline of what we want to do with them. I have an excellent financial planner, Mom, and if you don't mind I'd like to have him look over your portfolio and put together a plan for you. Things are different now, and your money is going to have to last you until you die, which means that adjustments will need to be made. Okay?" Evelyn nodded. Macey continued, "Now, I'd like you to think hard and tell me where Dad might have filed information on any stocks or bonds. Is there a possibility they're in a safe-deposit box?"

Evelyn scratched her forehead and realized her ankles were swelling, as they almost always did in the summer months. Sometimes even into September if the summer turned out to be long. She shuffled back over to the bed to sit down and remove her shoes. Peeling off one of her knee-high nylons, she looked at Macey and said, "I can't say that I have any idea where that might be. But I do know the name of our banker. Ira Plato. Very nice man. He can probably tell you more than I can."

Macey paced the floor of the bedroom. "Mother, I'm leaving tomorrow. You can't tell me anything about your money? Do you have any idea at all how much you have total?" She stopped and turned to Evelyn, who couldn't find any words to explain. "Mom, what about savings? How much do you have in your everyday savings account?"

Evelyn pointed to the checkbook. "Well, you already saw that."

"This?" Macey held up the checkbook. "This is your savings? I thought this was your checking."

Her other foot invited the air as the second knee-high got removed. She wriggled her toes, turned her ankle from side to side. She should've taken the hose off when she'd lain down for her nap. "It's both, I think. We just put money into the one account and then wrote checks out as needed. That's all we have as far as I know, but I don't know much."

Macey's fingernails scratched methodically at her hairline. She stared down at the checkbook in her hand. "Okay," she said in the middle of a sigh, "well, that's a start. At least I know you've got over five thousand to start you." Macey's eyes then grew dim with some silent and sudden fear.

Evelyn stopped rolling her stockings together when she noticed her daughter's change in demeanor. "Macey? What is it?"

With her shoulders hunched, her brow creasing wrinkles into her forehead, Macey slowly lifted her eyes to meet Evelyn's. "Mom?"

"What? You look like you've just seen a ghost, dear."

Macey looked down at the checkbook in her hand. She opened it back up to the register, and it was on the last page where her eyes lingered for a long moment.

Evelyn had no idea what could possibly be causing Macey to react like this. Perhaps there was a subtraction error. She wouldn't know. She never did anything but simply write out the checks. That's why, several years ago when they came out with the carbon copy checks underneath, Jess was ecstatic. Evelyn was always writing checks and forgetting to record the amounts in the register. With the duplicate checks, she could just write them and let Jess handle things from there. She guessed she was going to have to start doing the math, too. A heavy sigh escaped unnoticed.

"Oh, no . . ." Macey said, snapping the checkbook closed and lowering her head. "Oh, no."

"What is the matter?"

The old rocking chair in the corner creaked and rocked as Macey fell into it. She stared at her mother as if she were a stranger. Evelyn couldn't begin to interpret all this, so she just waited for an explanation, her hands twisting the nylon stockings.

"You forgot to enter the last check written, Mom," Macey said quietly, obviously assuming Evelyn would catch the meaning. After a few beats, she said, "Don't you get it?"

Evelyn could only shake her head.

"The last check you wrote was for five thousand one hundred and three dollars, to the funeral home. Don't you remember? If you wrote a check for fifty-one hundred and three, and you had fifty-two hundred and eight dollars in your checking account, that means you have only a hundred and five dollars left!"

Evelyn sat motionless as her daughter stood abruptly from the chair and started pacing again, mumbling to herself. She didn't know what to say. She owed the funeral home the money, and they'd always paid people they owed. What else was she to do? Money had been the furthest thing from her mind, and she just figured that Jess had taken care of everything. He always had before.

The skin on Macey's neck had turned red and blotchy as she sat in the chair again and stared at the ceiling. Evelyn couldn't quite understand all the fuss. Surely there was money somewhere else. Jess would've seen to it.

"Life insurance!" The rocking chair halted as Macey turned back to Evelyn. "Right? Dad had life insurance, didn't he?"

Again Evelyn had no answers, so she stood and walked to the bathroom to rinse out her stockings in the sink. The thump and creak of the rocking chair started up again, this time at a faster pace, and Evelyn found herself washing her stockings more thoroughly than normal.

But she couldn't stay in the bathroom forever. Finally she laid them over the bathtub, lotioned her hands up, then walked back into the bedroom.

"I'm sorry I can't be of more help to you, dear. But don't you go worryin' about me. Everything will work out. It always has. It always will."

Looking at the floor, Macey said, "I wish I could believe that."

"Don't make such a big fuss. I'll be fine. I don't want you worryin' about this."

"I can't just leave you in this predicament. I can't just believe things are going to *work out.* Things in my life have never just worked out. I've always had to work them out myself." Macey rose from the rocking chair slowly as if an old woman. "I'll stay until Monday. We'll meet with your banker Monday morning and figure out what's going on, and then I'll talk to my financial planner when I get back to Dallas."

"You'll stay?" Evelyn couldn't hold in her excitement. "Thank you! Thank you!"

Though not warm, a small smile spread across Macey's lips. She walked out of the room then, closing the door behind her. Evelyn was left standing in the middle of the hardwood floor. Soon she heard another door open and close again. Her daughter's bedroom.

Evelyn went back into the bathroom, shed her clothes, and struggled to put on her nightgown, her muscles aching and unco-operative. With a little wiggling and twisting, the gown slid down over her large body. She blotted away her forehead's perspiration and began applying her night cream, welcoming the familiar scent. The mirror, however, angered her. She smoothed the thick cream into her sagging skin, wishing it did everything it promised. But the wrinkles told the tale of all the worrying she'd engaged in through the years, while the dark circles under her eyes mirrored the recent days of grief. And the rolls under her neck exposed a few too many pieces of apple pie.

She brushed her teeth, not as thoroughly as normal but good enough to make her feel she was ready for bed. The nap earlier had taken the edge off her tiredness, so she took a minute to arrange some things around the bedroom, fold the quilt her mama had made for her, and count out her vitamins for the next day. After these were done, she couldn't find one other single thing left to do in the room.

She decided to listen to some music and went to the old record player in the corner. Squinting to read the label of the record already on the stand, she decided to just play the thing and see what came out. Kenny Rogers. He was singing about being a gambler, and Evelyn chuckled to herself. It must've been a year since she'd played a record. She watched the black disk spin smoothly around and around, then decided to move the needle ahead four notches. It had been a long time, but she knew the album by heart. There was a pause, followed by the low, guttural yet soothing melody of "Desperado," which instantly filled the room and helped to relax the tension built up in Evelyn's shoulders. She sat on the edge of her and Jess's bed and listened to the music, the vivid memory of her husband's burial but a day ago pressing heavily on her mind. A few tears escaped, but she let them. She reckoned these wouldn't be the last.

She forced herself to think of the good memories of Jess, and as "Desperado" ended and "Don't Fall in Love With a Dreamer" began, Evelyn lay back on her pillow, pulled her feet onto the bed, clasped her hands together, and resolved to sleep in this room tonight. A part of her wanted to go downstairs with her mama's quilt and sleep on the couch, but she would have to find the courage to face her fear, so she prayed silently that the room wouldn't feel so empty. Then she closed her eyes and drifted off to sleep on top of the comforter, mouthing the melody about love and dreamers.

"Don't act like this isn't a big deal. It's a big deal." Macey held the cell phone close to her ear. The reception was terrible, but Macey felt glad to be able to get a connection at all. She was in the middle of Toto land, for crying out loud. "Speak up. I can't hear you. . . . What? . . . No, I'm fine, and I'm not being demanding."

Macey listened to Mitchell try to explain that a couple of more days off would be just fine as she leaned an ear against her bedroom wall. She swore she had heard "The Gambler" playing earlier, only now the wind had picked up, so she could only make out faint murmurs of music.

"Alexis is filling in for you and she's doing great. So there's no need to hurry back."

Macey hardly heard a word Mitchell said. "It's just that my mother is in this apparent financial situation," she said, "and you have to know my mother—she's clueless about these things, and I can't just leave here without helping her sort it all out."

"It's fine, Macey," Mitchell said again, and Macey could hear the microwave beeping in the background. Mitchell, having never been married, always ate dinner late and could barely fix a meal even when using the microwave.

"Another frozen dinner, Mitchell?"

"What else?" he replied, and then the phone fumbled a bit on his end, and she smiled, knowing he was trying to handle a hot tray.

"I can be in by Tuesday. Make sure you tell Alexis that. Are you listening, Mitchell?"

A pause, a clanging of silverware, and another beep, followed by, *"Yes, yes. I'm not a two-year-old. You don't have to repeat yourself. Jealousy, by the way, does not become you."*

"What?" Macey stopped listening for music at the wall and paced the length of the bedroom. "What on earth would make you say that?"

"Because, Macey, you're obsessing about taking time off, and instead you should be concentrating on your family situation. Quit worrying about how much time Alexis is spending at the anchor desk. She's a reporter, not an anchor, and everyone here knows it. So just let it go and do what you need to do."

A tight heaviness pressed against the inside walls of her chest, and she made herself do her breathing exercises briefly before she responded. "Mitchell, this has nothing to do with Alexis the Lexus, and you know it. I hate being away from work. I always have—"

"*Because you're a workaholic.*"

"Which has taken me to where I am today, and I won't apologize for it. Just tell Alexis the anchoring's over Monday, and that I'll be back in Tuesday."

"*Fine, fine. You're the boss.*" He said this sarcastically, as he always did, and Macey smiled again.

"Don't I wish it. Has New York called?"

"*Twice.*"

"Twice? What did you tell them?"

"*The truth—that you had a family emergency.*"

"What did they say? Word for word, Mitchell."

She could hear him chuckling softly on the other end. "*It was Thornton Winslow again, and they want to meet you a week from Tuesday.*"

"That's not word for word."

"*Beth scheduled you a flight out next Monday at noon, I think.*"

"Who's filling in for me?"

"*That's not your concern.*"

"It is my concern."

"*It's not your concern and I've got to go. Cheese enchiladas with bad Mexican rice and bland refried beans can barely be tolerated when hot.*"

"Are you mad?"

"*Mad?*"

"About the network. Nothing's for sure yet."

Macey could almost see him grinning through the phone. "*You know this is my dream for you.*"

She fell backward onto her bed, her feet flying up in the air like a teenager on the phone with her prom date. "This is unbelievable is what it is!"

"*You deserve it. You're the best of the best, and that's who works for the network.*"

"Thanks, Mitchell. Please tell Bethie to call me on my cell if anything changes."

"*I will.*" She could hear him beginning to eat as he said, "*And come back when you need to. I'm serious. If you need to stay a couple of extra days, then do it.*"

Macey stared at her toenails, made a mental note to get a pedicure when she returned home, and said, "See you Tuesday."

After hanging up with Mitchell, she lay on the bed for a while, wishing she didn't have to stay another day, worrying about her mother's financial situation, and dreaming of New York all at once. She halfheartedly did stretches while lying on her back and wondered if anything would ever come of her relationship with Noah if she stayed here or he moved back to New York. She admitted to herself it was a silly thought to entertain, but such thoughts were the safest—the ones that had little or no chance of ever coming true.

The few pleasant thoughts that did come were instantly shattered by the intrusion of a violently loud memory of the last time she saw her father. His words echoed crisply, as if they were spoken in person.

"*How could you betray me like this? How could you betray God like this?*"

She sat up abruptly, breathing hard, drawn to the blackness of the night sky. She walked with trembling legs over to the window and pushed up the sash, letting in the thick sticky air. Outside, the stars were as vivid as anything she'd ever seen, and she appreciated the way the country's scarce light allowed the sky to show off its own.

After a few minutes, she closed the window and moved back to her bed. Unzipping her suitcase, she felt around the small pockets of her makeup bag for the familiar bottle of sleep aid. She found it with little trouble and swallowed two pills without water.

Quickly she changed into a cotton T-shirt and boxer shorts, washed her face, brushed her teeth, and crawled into bed. For a moment she thought she heard Kenny Rogers belting out "Lady," but she didn't have long to think about it. The music met her dreams, dancing together as if lovers, while she drifted off to sleep, never moving a muscle.

Twelve

Oh how He loves you and me . . .'"

Macey couldn't help but hum along. She knew the words by heart, and although she didn't believe a single one of them, she felt an odd comfort in following along with the melody. The rest of the small congregation sang loudly and off-key, but with enthusiasm.

Across the aisle, seated at the end of the pew two rows in front of her, sat Noah and his two girls. With the third and final verse Pastor Lyle lifted his arms, indicating the congregation should rise, which they did in perfect unison. Macey welcomed the stretch. Her back muscles had begun aching twenty minutes into the sermon, and forty minutes later she had still been sitting in the same position, waiting for Pastor Lyle to conclude.

She'd hardly listened. She found herself watching Noah's every move instead, which wasn't much. Occasionally he'd glance down at his girls and quietly hush them, and once he took a piece of paper from his pocket and wrote something down. Other than that, he sat motionless and listened intently to the sermon, as if the president of the United States were standing behind the pulpit.

Her mother, too, took great interest in the short man up front, so Macey endured the boredom, fanning herself with her bulletin and admiring the colorful stained glass. She'd sat in these pews more times than she could count, between her father on her left and mother on her right. To her left was an empty space now. She couldn't decide whether this comforted her or saddened her.

The song finished, and Pastor Lyle made a hurried announcement about watermelon and chicken as church members turned to one another and pumped hands as if business deals were being made. Widespread grins glinted across the crowd. Macey decided to stare at her expensive Cole Haan shoes, hoping not to see a hand poked out at her, or a flashy smile, or a sympathetic tilt of the head. She managed to look up once and was surprised to see Noah turning and squeezing his way through the slow-to-disperse crowd. As he emerged, Savannah popped up at his side, an endearing grin revealing one missing top tooth.

"God DID answer our prayers, Daddy!" she said, looking up at her father and then back at Macey.

Macey smiled but didn't quite understand. She clasped her hands in front of herself and tried to look graceful.

"You, here at church," Noah explained, patting Savannah on the shoulder. "We prayed you would come to church."

Macey wanted to point out that it was because of her mother's financial mess, not a divine act of God, but instead she kept quiet and tried to maintain her smile.

"Sorry about the heat," Evelyn said, moving to the side as another member squeezed by the outside of the aisle. "We have air-conditioning, but it makes such a racket that no one can hear Pastor Lyle speak. So we voted several years ago that we'd rather endure the heat than miss a single word from the sermon. They keep it running right up until the service starts and then they turn it off. Normally that's sufficient, except on the hottest summer days, when all these bodies just heat the place up."

Patricia suddenly emerged from the swarm of bodies.

"Well, let's go, people! The food's not going to eat itself. What are you waiting for—a formal invitation? Them flies are gonna help themselves if we don't get out there."

Stephanie, now standing next to her sister, said, "Daddy! Can we go?" Noah nodded, and the girls slid through the crowd with ease.

Evelyn turned to Macey. "It's the church picnic. There's more food than anyone can dream of."

Macey wasn't sure what to say. Were they going to go to the church picnic two days after the funeral? The last thing she wanted was to have to see all those people again and listen to all their drippy condolences. What were the chances of the church's summer picnic falling on the one day she decided to show up at church? Pleasant memories of calmer, serene times flooded her conscience, but she immediately pushed them out. That was then. This is now. A lot had changed.

Evelyn cleared her throat. "Well, we probably should get back. Macey probably doesn't want to—"

Macey was just about to nod in agreement to whatever her mom was about to suggest when she felt a strong hand take her forearm and begin leading her toward the door. "Of course Macey wants to stay," Noah was saying, and Macey found it odd she wasn't fighting too hard against his attempt to persuade her. "Don't you?" He smiled mischievously.

"I'm tired," she replied, but it was a lie. She'd slept like a rock the night before. Then, before she knew it, she was standing outside on the church lawn, along with a hundred or so other bodies lined up at three long tables of food. She'd once heard that the chances of getting food poisoning at a potluck event were one in four, but she had a stomach of steel. It came from years of stress. She prided herself in being able to tame an upset stomach as if it were a helpless mouse. She could almost will the nausea to disappear.

Macey listened to Noah instruct his girls from several places back in the line on how to carry their plates without spilling baked beans on their pink dresses. They nodded and tilted anyhow, but an elderly man with a pleasant demeanor came to their rescue and steadied their plates while guiding them to a nearby table.

Noah laughed. "Thanks, Mack," he said before shifting his attention to Macey. "So it's been a while since you've been to the church picnic."

Macey stared at the table in front of her, inching forward with the line. "Seventeen years."

Noah handed her a plastic plate and fork and took the same for himself. They parted at the table, each one taking a different side, and excused themselves as they reached for the same dish. Their knuckles slammed together directly over the coleslaw.

"You like coleslaw, too, eh?" Noah said, shaking off the pain in his hand.

Macey smiled as she scooped a large portion onto his plate, then served herself. She continued on in the line, trying to find anything that seemed less likely to kill her after being left out in the heat. Noah, on the other hand, piled his plate high with everything he could cram on. Somehow he got through the line before she did. He stood and waited for her while she debated over whether or not to try what obviously was Oda Yeager's blue-ribbon fried chicken.

"A leg or a thigh?"

Macey looked up across the table to find Twenty grinning at her and holding a fork over the decorated tub of chicken. He was missing a tooth, something she hadn't noticed before, and for a moment he seemed vaguely familiar. It was as if he'd asked that exact same question twenty-five years ago when she stood in line at the identical summer picnic.

"A thigh," she finally answered.

Twenty pierced a piece of the chicken and said, "I always love a good thigh," then plopped it on her plate. Macey couldn't help but snicker at Twenty's innocent remark.

She joined Noah at the end of the serving table. They walked a few yards together toward an open table under a large shade tree, somewhat isolated from the rest of the crowd. He waited for her to sit before he took a seat next to her.

"The food's already blessed. We just missed it because we were inside." He picked up a dinner roll, took a bite, and looked at her as if she were about to say something, which she wasn't. So she started in on the coleslaw and kept her eyes on her plate.

The low roar of a feisty crowd was enough to fill the silence at their table. It amazed her how acceptable silence was out here. Back in the city, silence was avoided at all costs. If there was even a second of silence during a broadcast, heads rolled. Even at home she always had the radio or TV switched on—sometimes both. And at night she went to sleep listening to one of a thousand CDs she owned. The morning started with her favorite talk radio program blaring out from her clock radio. But here it was okay to sit and eat and not say anything. It made her nervous, but she endured it.

One table down, she watched Patricia listen intently to the elderly people, who were complaining of their many aches and pains. Her eyes were fierce with concern, and Macey marveled at how Patricia actually seemed to care. She figured this was why Patricia always talked loudly. Most everyone she knew was nearly deaf. Back in Macey's world the elderly were often brushed aside as a mere inconvenience. She'd once watched a middle-aged businessman shove an old man out of the way to get to a taxi. And most every time elderly people fumbled around a bit in their wallets or their purses, or couldn't understand how the gas pump worked, or needed help seeing where to sign a credit card slip, heavy, intolerable sighs would escape from nearly everyone around.

At another table nearby, several younger women, even some teenagers, listened as a middle-aged woman described the new sewing machine she'd purchased from Sears. At this same table men were laughing boisterously as someone told a fish story. Though Macey had lived half her life here, now the place felt foreign to her. At least partly. Deep inside it touched her as warm and familiar, but she wouldn't allow herself to think too long about the familiar part. With just a glance over to the back side of the church, she could see herself running across the plush grass, barefoot and free, with all the other little children. In another glance, there she was with her father, attempting to fly her first kite on a nearly windless day.

Pastor Lyle had been the pastor of the church but a few years before Macey left. Pastor Rolley had been the pastor before him—elderly, stoic, and almost perfect in Macey's eyes. He died peacefully at age seventy-seven while taking a nap on a Sunday afternoon, three hours after he'd preached a sermon on perseverance. Macey had cried desperately at his funeral, and even her father, not a man of much emotion, had excused himself from the reception afterward.

Pastor Lyle carried his plate from table to table, greeting everyone and mooching some items he'd missed on his first two passes through the line. Her mother sat with Pepper, Patricia, and Tutie, all of them looking particularly interested in what might be going on at her table.

Macey gave a short wave to all of them and then looked at Noah. "Looks like we're being studied," she said, and Noah looked up and waved at the ladies, as well. They giggled and turned away as though they were all fifteen and the high school quarterback had just looked their way. Macey shook her head.

"What?" Noah said.

"You. You've got this whole town wrapped around your little finger. They all love you."

"I love all of them," he said softly, then glanced over to check on his girls, who were both busy eating watermelon and spitting the seeds as far as they could, which was mostly just to the edge of their little chins. "My life was such chaos before. But now it's peaceful.

Good. Pure." He said the words with such conviction, Macey had to look away. She hardly knew what any of these words meant anymore.

She wiped her mouth and pushed her plate away. "I couldn't wait to get out of this place." She glanced at Noah, who didn't appear to be fazed by her bluntness. "This town had nothing to offer me."

"Well, I guess you're quite a success story. A big time anchorwoman. Possibly going to the network. I suppose all of this isn't your cup of tea."

"Why'd you move here? I mean, the middle of nowhere hardly seems a place an artist like you would land. The scenery here's nice, but by no means is it breathtaking."

"Storms."

"Storms?"

"There's no other place in the world where you can see storms like you can in Kansas. Plus, I like the way of life here. And the river."

A crowd had gathered at a nearby table, and laughter erupted after Macey overheard the words *fire* and *hair*. She hoped they weren't talking about her tick incident. "Interesting," she said to Noah.

Noah sipped his tea. "So that's why you left? Because this town wasn't big enough to hold all your dreams?"

Macey stared hard at him. "You think you've got me figured out, don't you?"

He shrugged and smiled a little. "No, not completely. I can't figure out why you're always so defensive."

Macey frowned as her eyes narrowed. "Defensive?"

"See?"

Her jaw clenched. "I asked a question. That's not the same as being defensive." But the tone in her voice made this response sound defensive, and now her arms were crossed tightly against her chest. "I'm not being defensive!" He only smiled and cut into his carrot cake. This man was infuriating! "I just hate it when people think they've got me pegged. That they've got me all figured out. Things aren't always what they seem, you know."

The small piece of cake was already gone. Noah found his napkin, wiped his mouth, and asked, "What things?"

"Just things—big things, small things. Things." His soft stare melted her heart and enraged her both at once. "Like me, here today, at church."

"You're not here at church?"

"*Nooo.* What I mean is that I'm not here at church because I woke up this morning and felt the glory of God shine through my window, beckoning me back to a place that I—" She stopped herself. A light southerly wind picked up just in time to dry the beads of sweat that had just formed on her forehead.

"So why are you here? Free food?"

"My mom needs my help. I'm going to have to stay one more day. She wanted me to come to church. So here I am."

Noah glanced over at Evelyn, who was in conversation with some of the other women. "She looks fine to me."

"She's not fine."

"Well," he said, suddenly standing, "then I guess it's a good thing you're staying."

"Where are you going?"

"To get us some more tea." He smiled as he took her glass, his arm brushing against hers. "I'll be right back."

Macey watched him walk over to the coolers. Then she covered her eyes in humiliation. This man was a walking paradox, and he was about to drive her crazy. Yet, when she got tense and angry, he didn't seem bothered by it. Every other man she'd known couldn't handle her mood swings, her fury. She never blamed them, either. Not for that, anyway.

Noah returned with the drinks and then told her about last year's picnic and how the girls had gotten into a fight with eight-year-old Timmy Willows over ice cream. As she listened, it dawned on her that all the tension she'd felt before was now melting away like the ice in her tea. The tables of food were now swarmed with flies, but no one seemed to care. With the hot sun high in the sky, and laughter and joy mingling among animated conversations, Macey suddenly realized that, for the first time in as long as she could remember, she had no idea what time it was. Nor did she care.

———•◆•———

The heat had done a number on both of them. When they arrived back at the house, Macey, sticky with sweat, was astonished to find that it was already four o'clock. She'd always thought time moved so slowly here. Evelyn had collapsed into her easy chair, and Macey made sure she had a tall glass of cool water next to her.

While her mother "rested her eyes," Macey used the kitchen phone to make a few calls, to see about rearranging her flight schedule. It took thirty minutes, but she managed to get a flight out at one in the afternoon the following day, still leaving her plenty of time to go to the bank, resolve her mom's financial situation, and then head home to Dallas.

She was climbing the stairs to go put moisturizer on her sunburned skin when she heard the faint ring of the phone. She realized it was her cell and tripped twice trying to get to it before the voicemail kicked in. She pounced on her bed and reached for it, hitting the middle button with the blue line across it.

"Hello?"

"*Macey Steigel?*"

Yes.

"*This is Thornton Winslow, from the network.*"

Macey's heart stopped. "Mr. Winslow. Hello."

"*I understand your father died.*" His voice came through thick and distinguished.

"Yes. I'm here in rural Kansas, wrapping up a few things for my—"

"*Can you fly to New York on Thursday?*"

"This Thursday?"

"*I understand we'd set something up for a week from Tuesday, but that's not going to work for me.*"

Macey swallowed. "Thursday's fine."

"*We'll arrange everything from this end.*"

"All right."

"*Good. Then we'll see you Thursday.*"

"Okay. And thank—" The line went dead. Macey sat on the edge of the bed and took a deep breath, running her fingers through her tangled, windblown hair. This was going to be a tough business, but she was up for it. She once heard that famed journalist Peter Tollenhause had missed his own mother's funeral to cover an assignment in the Middle East. The network wasn't interested in an employee's family matters or personal problems. You served them with your whole heart or you didn't serve at all.

A stark beep from her cell phone told her that she'd forgotten to end the call. She pushed the button and fell back into the pillows. She should call Mitchell and Bethie right away, but she decided to wait until tomorrow. She didn't have any other close friends to speak of and was a little disappointed at the anticlimax of it all. She then thought of her mom and got up to go downstairs to share the big news with her. Though she wouldn't understand just how incredible it all was, at least she'd smile and nod and be happy for her.

At the top of the stairs Macey could hear her mother talking with someone, whom she assumed was either Patricia or Margie or some other church member who had stopped by. As she headed down, though, she realized her mother was on the phone.

"Why, thank you," she heard her mother say and then laugh. It was nice to hear her mom laugh. "Yes. I am very concerned about that sort of thing."

The conversation went on as Macey stood at the living room bay window and looked out across the river. From the window she couldn't see Noah's house. She thought about stepping outside just to do this very thing but then quickly dismissed the thought and continued to listen to her mother on the phone, wondering which friend she was chatting with.

"Well, no, it's a long tale, and I'm sure you've got better things to do than listen to an old woman's sob story.... You're so kind. Are you from around here?"

Macey frowned. Perhaps her mother wasn't talking to a friend. Staying put in the living room, she listened more carefully.

"My goodness! You must be racking up quite a phone bill then. ... Oh, well, aren't you so nice.... No, no, I live by myself now. My husband just recently passed on."

Macey decided to go into the kitchen. She found her mom standing at the counter, the short phone cord barely reaching across the narrow room. Evelyn smiled and waved her over to the fridge, mouthing she'd just made some tea. Macey nodded and started to reach for a glass to pour herself some so she'd have a reason to stay in the kitchen and not look like she was eavesdropping.

"Oh, thank you. You're very kind.... Yes, that's what my daughter keeps saying." She winked at Macey and then stared back down at the floor. "Uh-huh ... uh-huh ... Yes, that sounds very simple to me.... Uh-huh ... No, no, dear, I'm not too savvy on things like this. But this does sound like a good idea."

Macey forgot to pretend to be interested in tea. Instead, she stood near the fridge, listening to Evelyn.

"Okay, sure, that would be fine. You sound like a very decent young man. Are you married? . . . I've got a beautiful daughter and she's very successful. . . . That's true. You are quite a ways away. . . . What's that? . . . Oh, I'm sorry, you needed what now? . . . Okay, well, my memory's not what it used to be. Let me see if I can recall it. . . 442-77—" Evelyn stopped and looked to the ceiling as if searching the far corners of her mind—"is it 41 or 44?"

Macey suddenly realized what was happening. "Mother!"

Evelyn startled and turned to her daughter, frowning and confused.

"Mother!" Macey said again loudly. "What are you doing? Are you giving out your social security number?"

"Hold on," Evelyn said into the phone and then covered the receiver. "Dear, what are you ranting about?"

"Mom, you're not giving your social security number to some stranger on the phone, are you?"

Evelyn looked squarely at her. "Well, yes. This man on the other end, I think his name is Mark, he told me that if I give him my social security number and bank account number, he would be able to double my money in three months, and after that, he could triple my money in five months."

Macey snatched the phone out of her mother's hand and screamed into the receiver, "You listen to me, you pathetic piece of—" She glanced at her mom, lowering her voice a bit. "I know what you're up to, and if you EVER call this number again, I will personally hunt you down and—"

The phone clicked. The man had hung up. Macey was breathing hard. She wanted to finish giving the jerk a piece of her mind, but instead she was left with an operator instructing her to hang up and try again. She firmly placed the phone back on the wall cradle and swung around to face her mother, whose eyes were wide and distraught.

"What in heaven's name did you do that for?" she asked.

Macey rubbed her temples and reminded herself she was talking to her mom, not the crook on the phone. "Mother, listen to me. Are you listening to me?" Evelyn nodded. "Don't *ever* give out any personal information, especially any numbers, over the phone or to anyone you don't know you can trust. Not your social security number. Not your bank account numbers. Not your driver's license number."

Her mother was still nodding, but Macey knew it was out of nervousness and confusion, not because she comprehended what she'd just told her. She clasped her hands together in front of her lips, drew a deep breath, and asked her mom to sit at the kitchen table with her. Evelyn obeyed, and Macey sat down with her, remembering suddenly how gentle and understanding Patricia had been with the elderly people at the church picnic.

"Mom, I'm sorry. I shouldn't have yelled at you. Please forgive me."

Her mom's trembling lips formed a weak smile. "I'm sorry. I didn't mean to do that . . . whatever I wasn't supposed to do."

"I know that man sounded friendly, but do you know what he was doing?"

"He said he was a financial planner, just like the man you'd mentioned last night. He sounded very knowledgeable, and he was also such a kind young thing."

Macey shook her head. "No, Mom, actually he's a crook."

"A crook?" Evelyn laughed. "How could you tell that over the phone?"

Macey made her tone stay firm yet quiet. "Because he asked for your bank numbers and social security number."

"But he said he needed those in order to double my money and secure my financial future."

"What he needed your numbers for was to steal your money and also your identity. People like him sound friendly, Mom, but they're not. They go through the newspaper looking at the obituaries with the purpose of preying on recently widowed women, hoping they'll trust anyone who comes along and promises security—what they call financial independence. He was planning to take you for everything you had." Macey studied her mother's soft eyes in hopes a light would come on. Instead, Evelyn's brow dropped low across her eyes, and she looked as if she was worried about Macey. "Mom, that 'kind young thing' was not a good person. He was a thief. Do you understand now?"

"Well, maybe such a thing happens in the big city, but this is a small town. We don't have that sort of problem here." She tapped her fingers lightly against the table. "Besides, he said he was from Connecticut. How would he know I was widowed if he was in Connecticut?"

Macey bit her tongue for a couple of seconds to keep herself from losing control. "They have ways of finding things out, and chances are he was probably not from Connecticut. For all we know, he could've been calling from Parsons."

Evelyn studied Macey with a worried expression, and Macey could hardly keep from exploding. Her mother wasn't getting it; she probably thought Macey was paranoid, the result of living in the "big city" for too long.

"Well, whatever the case may be, he's gone now and I'm getting a little hungry. What sounds good for dinner? I can thaw out some beef."

Evelyn began to rise and go to the fridge, but Macey said, "Mom, please." Evelyn turned around. "Promise me you'll never give those numbers to anyone you don't know."

Evelyn's features turned bright and cheerful. "Macey, I'd do anything for you. You know that."

Macey was about to explain that it wasn't about *that*, that it was a common sense issue and that her mother was much too naïve, when the phone rang again. Macey grabbed it. "Hello."

"*Uh . . . Macey?*"

"Yes?"

"*Hi, uh . . . it's Diana. Diana Parr. I'm married now, but I was just. . . well, how are you?*"

Macey swallowed. She hadn't expected any friends from the past to be calling. "Fine."

"*Good, good. Listen, I was thinking if you were going to be in town awhile, maybe we could get together? I'd love to see you. Oh, sorry about your dad.*"

Macey closed her eyes and wondered if she'd rather spend the evening lecturing her mother about telephone thieves or listening to Diana reminisce about the past. She twisted the cord several times around her left index finger and listened to her own breathing through the mouthpiece.

This was not going to be an easy choice to make.

Thirteen

There were going to be questions. A lot of questions.

The dusty wind made her eyes tear, but she kept her speed high and constant, her hands tightly gripping the handles. It had been years since she'd ridden a bike. The exercise felt good, especially since she hadn't had a run since Friday. Her heart pumped vigorously, and her muscles throbbed with a dull ache. Even so, she kept pedaling. She'd always been able to push herself.

It took almost twenty minutes to ride into town by bike. Once she reached Main Street, she pulled the bike onto the sidewalk, steadying it around a curve. She couldn't believe she'd found a bike in the barn. It was a little rusty, but the tires were inflated, and it pedaled nicely.

Though it was almost seven o'clock, the sun, starting to lower toward the horizon, still warmed the air enough to make her sweat. Wisps of hair clung to her temples, and her T-shirt stuck to her back. She licked her lips, wiping all the salt away, only to have it return seconds later.

Not many people were around on this Sunday evening. Most of the shops were closed, while the teenagers always escaped to Parsons to hang out. At least they did when she was their age and living here.

She hopped off her bike and strolled alongside it, window-shopping while letting her heart rate drop slowly. The shops along Main Street had changed. New clothing boutiques. A bookstore, a music store. The hardware and floral stores still remained, though.

Two blocks away was Edna's, a greasy diner and town favorite. It was one of the few establishments that stayed open on Sundays, even though a hundred deacons had warned Edna she'd go to hell for it. Rumor had it that Edna once decked a deacon right after telling him that if flipping burgers on a Sunday would send her to hell, then it probably wouldn't hurt her to punch out a deacon while she was at it.

Macey slowed her pace, checking her watch. 6:54. She had a few minutes yet. She stopped at a little children's shop and peered through the glass. The store's interior was dark except for a few racks of summer clothing that were highlighted by the evening sun. Her stomach growled and then stung in pain as she second-guessed her decision to meet with Diana.

What would she say to Diana? How would she explain? She'd spoken to her maybe twice since leaving, and even then it was pleasantries and chitchat. That was easy over the phone. But in person, things were a little harder to hide.

They'd been friends. Not good friends. Not best friends. But friends, one of only a few Macey had known in high school. When she was younger, friends seemed easy to come by. In high school, for reasons she still couldn't figure out, her friendships became complicated. Relationships were harder to maintain. It wasn't long before she was lonely and standoffish. She'd been burned by a few too many so-called friends, therefore she had isolated herself, retreating inward, to a place no one could understand. Not even her.

From where she stood, she could see the edge of Edna's bright pink neon sign. The smell of diesel trucks filled the air. Being only a mile from the highway, this was a favorite of truckers, too, though they had to park six blocks away and walk. None of them seemed to mind. The booths were always filled with heavy men sporting trucker hats, eating greasy hamburgers, and drinking Cokes.

Macey crossed the street, walked another block, and leaned her bike up against the brick wall of the restaurant. The air already felt thick with grease, even outside the restaurant. Fleeting memories of the place passed through her mind.

A tall burly man opened the door for her, grunted, and waved her in. She'd thought she would just stand outside a few more minutes, but she didn't want to be rude so she stepped in, relieved at least to be in cool air.

Scanning the room for anyone resembling a woman she hadn't seen in nearly twenty years, she saw that all eyes were on her. She tried to look pleasant and unassuming, imagining that any new customer was probably something to gawk at. After another quick look around the restaurant, she decided Diana hadn't arrived yet.

A thin freckle-faced blonde who couldn't have been more than seventeen approached, her hair high in a ponytail that swung from side to side.

"Can I help you?"

"I'm waiting on someone."

"Me too. You." She winked and smacked her gum. "You wanna sit down?"

"Okay."

The girl grabbed two menus and took Macey to a booth by the window. She slid the menus onto the table, and Macey sat down, brushing the crumbs off the vinyl seat first. The girl raised an eyebrow at that and then said, "Your waitress will be here in a sec."

The stench of cigarette smoke made it hard for Macey to breathe. She knew better, though, than to ask to sit in the nonsmoking section. The sign across the room said Nonsmoking, but the lack of ventilation left a thick haze hovering in every corner. Still, she didn't feel too put out, for the place *was* air-conditioned.

Macey carefully handled the menu, which was stained and sticky, and decided to get just an order of French fries and a Coke. She figured it would be enough grease to last her a few years. If they still fixed their fries the same way, they had a certain bite to them that made them particularly good. If they still fixed their hamburgers the same way, that meant the state health board hadn't visited in a while. At Edna's there was no such thing as well done.

Judging by the expression on the woman's face, an old crank of a waitress approached, pulled out a pad and pencil and stared down at Macey, who realized this was her cue to order. "I'm waiting for someone. But I'll start with a Coke."

"Pepsi."

It was a statement, not a question, so Macey just nodded. The woman walked off, and Macey glanced up just in time to see an extremely large, jovial-looking woman entering the diner, carrying a sizable fake-leather handbag, wearing cutoffs and a blue T-shirt that barely fit over her thighs. Macey tried not to let her jaw hang open. In high school Diana hadn't been thin, but she wasn't even close to obese. Could this be her?

The woman glanced around, and when her eyes met Macey's, she smiled and, after Macey waved to her, shuffled over to where Macey sat.

"Macey Steigel?" she asked, out of breath from the walk over.

Macey stood and smiled. "Diana Parr? I mean, Wellers?"

Diana gripped Macey by the shoulders and pulled her into a bear hug, then let her go and took a moment to fit herself into the booth. She laid her purse next to her and grinned with bright eyes. She seemed as mirthful as ever, her large jowls ruddy and her smile small and sweet. "My goodness," she exclaimed, "you look just wonderful! All sophisticated."

Macey swallowed, trying not to glance at Diana's kinky permed hair, pulled back in a barrette, or her overly hair-sprayed bangs. "Oh, you too."

Diana laughed embarrassingly and shook her head, avoiding Macey's eyes. "I've gained a few pounds. You probably noticed." She glanced up. "I have five children."

"Five?"

"Yep. I guess I told you that time we talked on the phone that I married Willie Wellers, remember? He's from Chanute." Macey nodded her head. "Well, anyway, our first one was a honeymoon baby. Willie Junior. And then came Stella. Bobby. Bradley, who we call Beaker, and Obert is our baby—five years old." Her eyes were kind and happy. "Could've had more, but I had some female troubles and then I had the surgery, and so that ended that."

Macey nodded, unsure whether this was good news or bad. The waitress returned with her Pepsi and asked for their order. Diana ordered a double-stack bacon burger with extra onion, large fries, and a diet Pepsi, all without looking at the menu. "I'll just have the fries," Macey told the waitress and then looked at Diana, who frowned a bit.

"You're not eating?" Diana asked.

"I'm not?"

"No, I mean, you're just having fries? That's hardly going to fill ya up."

"Oh." Macey fidgeted with the menu. "Well, I ate a ton at the church picnic, so—"

"That explains it." Diana chuckled while she looked around the room as if to see if anyone she knew was there. She looked back at Macey. "So, how ya been?"

"Um, fine. Just working in Dallas. How did you find me, anyway? The last time we spoke, wasn't I in San Antonio?"

"It was sort of by luck, actually. Remember Barney Petsel?"

Macey nodded but didn't remember. The name sounded a little familiar; that was it.

"Yeah, well, he married Thelma Stonehouse, if you can believe that. What is she, a hundred years older than him? Anyway, then he started driving trucks. He was at some stop in Dallas and saw you on the television. But that was a few years back, so I wasn't too sure you were still there, and I had a hard time trying to figure out which station you were at." Her cheeks jiggled as she laughed. "But I have a way with people, so I finally got the information I needed."

"I see." Macey tried to smile back. "Well, thank you for calling."

Diana shifted her large frame uncomfortably in the booth, her eyes darting about. Macey thought about how to keep the conversation going. If Diana was anything like she used to be, she could always talk about nothing. "Tell me again where you met your husband?"

"Willie? A family friend. My daddy used to buy farm equipment from his uncle, and then one time during the harvest, I had to drive the machine and Willie was out there, too. That was in high school. You don't remember?"

"High school was sort of a blur."

The waitress delivered Diana's drink. She slid the glass closer to herself and sipped through the straw, her eyes locking with Macey's. "Yeah, you took off out of here pretty quick."

Macey was working on what to say next when the waitress returned with their order. "I remember these fries being great," Macey said in an attempt to change the subject once again.

Diana agreed heartily. "The best. It's a secret spice Edna won't reveal."

Diana dug into her food while continuing to talk, explaining where each of her children was conceived, providing much more information than Macey wanted to know, yet this was a far better topic to be discussing than why she'd left town so long ago. Diana then veered off into how the river flooded in '89 and Blamer's Warehouse burned down, both in the same year, followed with details of some lurid affair that had gone on between the mayor of Chanute and Peggy the dog groomer. Macey, masterful at facial expressions, nodded, raised eyebrows, smiled, and even asked probing questions, all to fill the time with Diana and to keep her talking about nothing of interest to her. It was practically what Macey did for a living.

This killed enough time for Diana to finish her burger and fries, and Macey was thankful that she might be able to slip out without discussing the past. But then Diana said, "You gonna finish them fries?"

Macey looked down at her basket. She'd only eaten a few. She shook her head, and Diana pulled the basket toward her, salted them with great delight, and said, "So, Macey, I've always wondered . . . why'd ya leave?"

It seemed almost as if the rowdy restaurant crowd hushed a bit following the question. Macey actually had to turn around to make sure people weren't staring. She glanced back at Diana. "Oh, you know . . . I just had to get out of here." Macey watched Diana's eyebrows curve upward, creating a look of skepticism. "You know, I wanted to go to college, pursue a career."

Diana licked the tips of her fingers. "That's not what I heard."

The waitress came with fresh drinks and the ticket, dropping it onto the middle of the table. "You girls need anything else?"

"No, thank you," Macey managed.

"Checkout's up front," the waitress said and then left.

Suddenly the air-conditioning felt too cold, the smoke too thick, the fries too heavy on her stomach. Macey couldn't imagine how she would give an answer to what Diana was suggesting. There was no avoiding it. She didn't even have a fry to pop in her mouth to create a brief pause. She looked at Diana, who was eating the fries and staring at her like she might be next.

Maybe it was time. Maybe she should just tell the truth, talk about it, get it off her chest. It had been seventeen years, and she hadn't spoken a word about her past. Could it be that in the middle of a stuffy run-down smoke-filled diner she was ready to bare her soul?

Diana pushed the empty basket away and leaned on the table, tilting the whole thing toward herself. "I heard that you flunked out of algebra."

Macey blinked and tried to keep an even expression. Diana heard she had flunked out of algebra? Was that what the town thought, that she left because she flunked algebra?

"I mean, you were the best student ever. That must've been tough. And a little embarrassing, I reckon. We all felt bad because none of us would've said nothin' about it. But you were always so hard on yourself." Instantly Diana's eyes turned soft and kind. "You obviously finished a degree somewhere 'cause of your career and everything."

Macey couldn't think of what to say. Did they really think she left town before graduation because she flunked algebra? But then again, what else could they think?

"My goodness' sakes, I've put you on the spot, haven't I?" Diana reached over and patted her on the hand. "Listen, honey, we all have our dark secrets." She lowered her voice a little. "Willie Junior, he was conceived a little before the honeymoon, if you know what I mean." She winked and sipped her Pepsi, and Macey could only nod and feel relief that Diana was confessing her dark secrets and Macey wasn't having to confess hers. "So, how long you stayin' here?"

Macey was just about to happily answer the question when she glanced up, and in horror, watched a man she thought she'd never see again push his way through the glass doors of Edna's and look around the place. The drink glass slipped from her fingers and clunked against the table, tilting and spilling a little before Macey could set it upright again. She and Diana grabbed for napkins, and together they quickly sopped up the spill.

"Girl, you look like you just saw a ghost," Diana said, handing her another napkin as she swung around to see what had caused Macey to act so alarmed. "Oh, there's Harley Preston."

Harley was looking the other way, although he'd glanced over briefly at the racket she'd made, obviously not recognizing her. He continued to scan the room for whomever he was looking for.

"It just slipped," Macey said, her hands shaking uncontrollably. She hid them under the table and watched Harley walk over to the other side of the restaurant and join a group of men who were all smoking and drinking beer.

Diana laughed as she told Macey of the time three of her five children spilled their drinks all at once at a restaurant. Macey was only half listening while trying not to stare across the room at Harley. He seemed taller and was definitely heavier than she remembered. He certainly still dressed the same. Tight jeans, cowboy boots, and a T-shirt. Macey looked at Diana.

"What in the world is Harley Preston doing here?" she asked, hoping to sound only casually interested, even though she clutched the edge of the table to keep her hands from trembling. "I heard he moved." She hadn't heard that, but it was all she could think of to say.

"Yeah, you know, he married Ellie White and they moved to Kansas City with his job. They had three kids and then got a divorce a year and a half ago, so he moved back here to help his dad with the hardware store. I guess it was a pretty ugly divorce. He barely gets to see his kids."

Macey shot a glance across the room. "No kidding? I always imagined he'd end up being some professional football star."

Diana rattled the ice around in her drink. "Nope. I guess he wasn't as good as we all thought he was. He couldn't even get a scholarship to any big-name schools, and then he and Ellie married and I guess he had to go get a job. You know how that goes." Macey nodded. "I see him from time to time, but he doesn't talk to me all that much. I wasn't really in his crowd, you know. Plus, I think he's pretty bitter from the divorce. I've heard he's a changed man."

"Is that right?" Macey willed herself to keep the questions and her tone light.

"Yeah. Hey, you went out with him once, didn't you?"

Macey took a deep breath. "A couple times, I guess. It was no big deal."

"No big deal? He was the quarterback of the football team. Any date with Harley Preston was a big deal." She smiled a little. "I remember being jealous of that."

Macey laughed, "Jealous?"

"Of course. You didn't really talk about him much, but even one date with Harley was like a million with any other guy. That was spring of our senior year, right?"

Macey nodded, unaware that she was now shredding the napkin in front of her. "He wasn't my type."

Diana chuckled. "Boy, you must've had some pretty high standards if Harley Preston wasn't your type."

"Well, listen," Macey said, shoving the pieces of napkin to the edge of the table and grabbing her wallet, "I should probably get back to my mom." Macey took the ticket. "Please, let me buy."

Diana smiled warmly. "Thank you. That's very kind."

They walked to the cash register, and Macey kept her back turned to Harley. She doubted Harley would recognize her, yet she didn't want to risk it. Her heart pounded as the cashier slowly counted her change back to her. Diana was explaining why she hadn't made it to the funeral, and Macey hardly heard a word she said.

Outside the restaurant, Diana still talked on as Macey hopped on her bike. Finally Diana gave her a hug and told her it was good to see her. Macey said the same and then lied about how she would try to stay in better touch. Diana slowly made her way down the sidewalk to her car, while Macey turned her bike and rode off in the opposite direction.

She turned left on Brighton, then took a right on Bixby and found an alleyway where she coasted to a stop, her feet planted on either side of the bike. She was out of breath, though not from the bike ride. Her chest heaved. The alley was quiet and deserted, which was perfect because she couldn't risk being seen by anyone. The last thing she wanted to have to do was explain why she was about to burst into tears.

After catching her breath, she headed west, back toward home. She peddled as hard as she could, all the while thinking how ironic it was that Harley Preston wasn't a big football star but instead worked in his father's hardware store. He wasn't happily married, making lots of money. He was divorced and bitter. He wasn't popular. He was just another guy.

If only she could've seen that seventeen years ago.

———— ◆ ————

Something made her stir. Evelyn opened her eyes and realized she still had Macey's baby book on her lap. The last thing she remembered was praying. She must've fallen asleep. Nothing new at her age. So much for burning the midnight oil.

She gently closed the album and set it on the coffee table next to her. She checked her watch. A little after eight. After three tries, she finally lifted herself out of the easy chair, making a mental note to look into getting one of those chairs that did the lifting for you. She and Jess had talked about it a few times before.

As she stepped onto the back porch to get some air, she recalled what she'd been praying about before falling asleep. Macey. She'd prayed that somehow she would have the courage to talk to her tonight. This would be her last opportunity, after all, to try to make things as right as they could be. If she didn't at least try, she would always regret it. Yet, every time she remembered that icy stare Macey could give, her confidence dwindled to nothing.

The humidity had dropped enough that now the air felt pleasant and mild. Evelyn began praying again. She had to. It was only going to be through God's strength that she would be able to talk with her daughter.

The back door opened suddenly, and Evelyn jumped. Macey stood in the doorway. She looked hot, tired, and drained. "Hi, Mom."

"My goodness! Did you bike all the way to Missouri?" Evelyn motioned for her to sit on the porch swing. Macey about fell into it.

"Thank you," her daughter said in a half breath. "I think I've gotten enough exercise today."

Evelyn sat down on a wicker chair a few feet away. Should she just do it now? Or wait? Or gradually work her way into it? She tried to read her daughter's mood, not an easy task.

"Diana has five children," Macey said after drinking most of the glass of water she'd brought out with her.

"How is she?"

"Fine, I guess. Married some guy named Willie Wellers. She looks happy."

"That's nice," Evelyn said, wringing her hands and twisting her wedding ring. Now? Should she say something now? Her daughter's face was emotionless. "So—"

"Where'd the bike come from?" Macey asked suddenly, then added, "I'm sorry—you were about to say something."

Evelyn paused. "No, um, it's . . . your father bought the bike at a garage sale for ten dollars. I never knew why. I don't think he did, either. He was always just buying junk for no good reason. Just because it was cheap."

Macey smiled. "It's a good bike."

"So you rode all the way to Edna's?"

"Yeah. Took me twenty minutes."

Evelyn nodded. Unable to come up with anything to say next, she continued to twist her wedding ring and stare at her daughter's tired eyes. Evelyn was just about to start again when Macey rose and went into the kitchen for another glass of water. Evelyn followed her. Soon Macey was in the living room, punching on the TV.

"Hey, *I Love Lucy* is on!"

Evelyn followed her and watched her daughter plop down on the couch and tuck a pillow underneath her head and then kick the one on the other end of the couch under her feet.

"They don't make sitcoms like this anymore. These are so funny." Macey's eyes were glued to the TV, and she laughed at Lucy, who was frantically pulling a smoking turkey from the oven.

Taking a seat on the opposite couch, blinking at the tube for a while, Evelyn was caught up in thought about what she should say to Macey, and when. Macey made a few remarks, about not having a remote and that cable would fix the fuzzy picture, to which Evelyn nodded and smiled.

The fresh aroma of coffee filled the air. She'd forgotten she'd even made a new pot. Evelyn figured she'd go pour herself a cup, but then realized that was just a distraction. She should focus on what she needed to do. So she gathered her dress in her hand, scooted to the edge of the couch, and said, "Macey, honey . . . can we talk?"

Macey glanced over at her, frowned, and said, "Mother, you look worried. Are you worried about tomorrow? Don't be. Listen, I know it all seems overwhelming, but we'll talk to your banker, get all your money sorted out, and things will be fine. I probably overreacted yesterday and I'm sorry about that. I don't want you to worry." She sat up on one elbow and looked intently at Evelyn. "Let's just sit back, watch *Lucy,* and relax. I think right now what we both need is an easy, uncomplicated evening." She smiled as if to punctuate this last sentence. "And I'd even be willing to eat a bowl of ice cream."

Evelyn smiled broadly, but it was forced. Her daughter went back to watching the tube, and Evelyn leaned back into the cushions of the couch. Uncomplicated. She looked at the TV and wondered if it was so bad having their last evening together filled with laughter and ice cream. She put her feet on the coffee table and arranged a pillow behind her back, closing her eyes briefly to clear her mind of her former intentions.

As her daughter chuckled at the antics of the red-haired comic in black-and-white, Evelyn made a mental note to be sure to let the ice cream soften a bit before she scooped. It made her wrists hurt if she didn't.

Fourteen

Ira Plato was older, but with black hair and a uni-brow to match. His wide grin and small eyes made his face disproportionate. When he laughed, he sucked air through his clenched teeth, which made a sort of slobbery wet sound. He seemed to have only two expressions: plain and dramatically gleeful.

"What a beautiful young lady your daughter is," Ira said to Evelyn, who sat next to Macey on the other side of his large mahogany desk. He winked at Macey, and Macey wondered if he was going to offer her a lollipop. Evelyn gushed and patted Macey on the knee.

Mr. Plato flashed his dentures at them both and then said, "Now, what can I do you for?"

Macey decided to let her mother speak. Evelyn glanced at her daughter and, after clearing her throat, said, "Well, my daughter here is a little concerned about how much money I have, so we're here to set her mind at ease."

"Ah." He typed a few commands into his computer. "We can sure find that out for you now."

"Thank you, Mr. Plato."

As he typed he said, "I was so sorry to hear about Jess. He was such a nice man."

"Thank you," Evelyn said again, though this time with not as much pep.

Macey sighed and wished the man would just stick to the business at hand.

"Yes, you know, I'd known your father for nearly twenty years," he said with a glimpse in Macey's direction over his reading glasses.

Well, that's three more years than I knew him, if at all. Good for you.

"Alrighty, it says here you've got one hundred and five dollars and seventeen cents in your checking account." He looked up and grinned as if he'd just saved the world.

"I know how much she has in checking," said Macey. "What about savings? Do they have a savings account?"

The man typed on his computer some more. "I thought I remembered that they do," he said as though this would somehow impress Macey. She guessed small-town bankers relied heavily on the personal touch. A couple of more keystrokes were followed by Mr. Plato saying, "Yes, here it is."

Macey breathed a sigh of relief. At least they had some savings. Though it had been foolish of her father to keep all his money in the bank, that didn't matter now. She would get Chad on it as soon as she returned to Dallas and divide it up suitably. "Great," Macey said, glancing at her mom with a smile. "How much?"

"Eight hundred and seventy dollars and a little change." He thumped two pencils against the desk like a drum accenting a punch line.

Macey popped up from her chair, and Evelyn looked up at her with soft inquisitive eyes. "Dear, what's the matter? Isn't it good that your father put savings away?"

Macey's hands found her face and she scrubbed at it. "Yes, yes, of course. But, Mother, don't you see that eight hundred dollars isn't even close to being enough?"

Her mother shifted her attention to Mr. Plato, whose jaw was hanging open. He obviously hadn't seen such a display of emotion in a while. Macey shook her head, sat back down, and leaned into her chair, trying to come to terms with the dilemma before it got the best of her. Mr. Plato began chewing on the end of one of the pencils he had been so happily tapping just a few seconds earlier. He gave them a half smile, but his eyes showed his uneasiness.

"Mr. Plato, what about a safe-deposit box? Did my dad have one? Maybe he's got bonds or something in there."

Plato nodded, pecking at his keyboard again. "Why yes. Number 587."

Macey turned to her mom. "Do you have the key?"

"The key? Oh, um . . ." Evelyn began searching in her purse, yet Macey knew immediately her mother wasn't aware they'd even had a safe-deposit box.

A heavy sigh of frustration fled Macey's lips in the form of what sounded like a growl, surprising not only Mr. Plato and her mother but also a nearby secretary who'd obviously taken great interest in their predicament in an eavesdropping sort of way.

Mr. Plato stood and said, "Listen, Evelyn, don't you worry about it. In light of the current situation, being that your husband has passed away, we'll unlock the box for you and at no cost."

"Thank you," Macey said dully and began following Plato to the room where they kept the safe-deposit boxes.

He disappeared for a moment to retrieve the proper keys, then emerged as if he'd found gold. "Okie-dokie, let's see what we've got . . . I mean, you of course." He led them inside the vault. "This is a private matter, and"—he unlocked the box and stepped aside—"I'll be at my desk if you need anything."

Evelyn watched Mr. Plato round the corner, but Macey was already digging into the box. She sifted through the papers, trying to figure out exactly what kind of dire straits her mom was in. After quickly reading over the last piece of paper, a letter about their mortgage insurance, Macey leaned hard against the wall and shuddered. Evelyn took the papers from her hand and looked at them. "What in the world is all this junk?"

Macey shook her head. "Just junk. Nothing of any value." She watched her mom gently thumb through each piece and then put them back into the box. "This is a nightmare," Macey added. The edge in her voice was intentional. Her mother must understand the seriousness of her circumstances.

But Evelyn only smiled and closed the door to the box. "Macey, this isn't your problem."

Macey glared at her. "Mother, you're practically broke. What's your problem is my problem."

"It's not my problem, either."

Macey's eyes rolled and she stared at the ceiling. Could her mom possibly be this ignorant about the situation? Maybe she was suffering from a bit of dementia. Her head throbbed at the thought of how massive this problem really was.

"It's God's problem."

"It's God's problem? That's all you can say? It's God's problem? Yeah, you're right. It *is* God's problem. It's going to take a king-size miracle to get you out of this predicament." The sarcasm dripped from her tone.

But Evelyn only held her pleasant smile as if she held some secret solution to everything, which she wasn't yet ready to share with Macey. This infuriated Macey all the more, and she stomped past her mom, back to Mr. Plato's desk.

"Is there *anything* else you know of, Mr. Plato?" Macey asked, her palms flat on his desk, her eyes ablaze with intensity. "Any assets? Anything at all?"

Plato seemed to hold his breath. "I'm sorry, but we don't show anything else." Macey was about to turn and leave when the banker added, "Miss Steigel, your parents have had a rough time the last few years." Macey waited for him to continue. "The farming business has suffered badly, as I'm sure you've been reading about. Your father's was hit pretty hard. He almost lost his home. As I'm sure you know, he had to sell most of the land."

Macey's breath became shallow.

"In fact, your father drove to Parsons three times a week to work at the local Wal-Mart. He did that for three years. Then he got sick."

Macey swallowed back the unexpected surge of emotion. She glanced up to find her mother slowly making her way down the hall. She looked back at Plato. "He worked at Wal-Mart?"

Mr. Plato nodded. "As a greeter."

Macey frowned and shook her head, frustration and anger building pressure in her chest. She looked the banker squarely in the eyes. "He's left my mother in a horrible financial predicament, Mr. Plato."

He folded his hands neatly on top of his desk. "Jess was a fine man. I know him well enough to know he wouldn't have left something like this unresolved."

"Well, you didn't know him as well as you think. He left a lot of things unresolved before he died."

———— ◆ ————

Even though the fifteen-minute car trip back to the house was driven in silence, Macey's head was filled with the clamoring of angry thoughts and retaliatory conversations. How could her father do something like this? How could he be so stupid? If only she could speak to him, oh the things she would say.

She was angry, but not at her mother. This wasn't her mother's fault. No, her mother was more a victim of time and culture, trained to be a lowly housewife, to not ask questions about matters only men should be handling. She was taught to take her place behind the ironing board and at the stove, bred to be obedient and submissive. Macey cringed as she thought of the implications of all this.

Her mother was broke and had no way of doing anything about it. All because she did what she was told by a man who was supposed to provide for her.

Macey steered the car up to the side of the house and killed the engine. Seconds later she was helping her mother out of the compact's front passenger seat. Evelyn clung to her arm as they slowly walked the old weed-grown sidewalk up to the front porch. Climbing the concrete steps, Evelyn mentioned that she was sure a nice cold glass of pink lemonade would "make everything better." Macey pushed open the front door for her mom, and just as she was about to step inside, her cell phone rang. Evelyn turned to see what it was Macey fumbled in her purse to find.

She opened the line and said, "Macey Steigel."

"Mitchell here."

"Mitchell . . . um, now's not really a good time. Can I call you back?"

"Macey, you're coming home tonight, right?"

"Uh . . ." At the front door still, Macey watched her mom trying to locate her glass pitcher in the kitchen.

"We just broke news that Senator Brandt is having an affair."

"You're kidding! With whom?"

"Audrey Stevens."

"The socialite?"

"Yep. And get this—her husband turned up missing yesterday. It's an amazing story. The networks have been calling nonstop for more information. We need you here, Macey. We need you here now."

Macey gulped as she stepped outside and closed the front door behind her. "Mitchell, some things have happened here. My mom is . . . is in some financial trouble."

"I'm sorry to hear that." There was a pause, followed with, *"So, you want me to let Alexis have this one? Probably the biggest political story of the year?"*

Mitchell was playing dirty. Could she expect anything less? "I'm slated to fly to New York Thursday instead of next Tuesday. They called and wanted me to move the meeting up. It was Thornton. He sounded interested," she lied. He hadn't sounded interested; he had sounded cold, like a machine.

"Let me get this straight. What you're saying is that you don't need this?" Mitchell's tone turned severe. *"What if I need this, Macey? What if I need you here?"* His voice lowered, and Macey could almost see him looking around as he drew nearer to his typical state of panic. *"You know Alexis can't handle this. She didn't even know whether Brandt was a Republican or a Democrat. When she heard Audrey Stevens was involved, the first comment she made was about the woman's hairstyle!"*

Macey smiled a little. It sounded like something Alexis would say. "You hired her, Mitchell. Besides, just feed her through the IFC. Make her sound like she knows what she's talking about. It's what you do best."

"It's too risky," he growled. *"The network may even go live with the reports, I don't know. It's pure chaos here. I need you."*

Macey closed her eyes. She felt dizzy. How could all this be happening, and everything at once? She leaned against the front door and said, "I can't guarantee anything. I can't just leave my mom like this, with the way things are."

"You haven't seen your mom in twenty years!" he screamed into the phone. *"I've been loyal to you since the day you came here. I practically sold you to the network! And here you are telling me you can't guarantee anything!"* Macey stared at the dusty porch as Mitchell continued to rant. *"Yet I'm sure you're all too willing to adjust your schedule for a Thursday flight to New York, aren't you?"*

"Mitchell," Macey said in her most soothing voice, the one she used when interviewing a family who had lost a pet, or an elderly person just taken for a large amount of money. "I was prepared to come back today. You know that. I'm sorry for the delay. I really am sorry."

There was a brief pause and then Mitchell said, *"I'm turning around."*

Macey frowned. "You're turning around?"

"Yeah. So you can take the knife out of my back." With that the phone went dead. Macey's head dropped.

The front door squeaked open, and Evelyn stood holding the now-filled glass pitcher, smiling. "Well, how 'bout some pink lemonade?"

———— ◆·◆·◆ ————

It took two and a half more hours for Macey to confirm her worst fears: her mother had no assets other than her home and her car. She'd dug through every drawer and file that might contain even the smallest inkling of hope. Her eyes were swollen from her allergy to dust, and her nose itched uncontrollably. All the while she played scenario after scenario over and over in her head as to what might happen if she didn't return to work by tomorrow. Why couldn't she just leave? Never in her life had she been unloyal to her career. She'd once even dropped a relationship with an attractive attorney because he couldn't cope with her hours.

She clomped downstairs to find her mother sitting at the dining room table, arranging a vase full of fresh flowers. Evelyn looked up and smiled. "Look at the petunias! Aren't they beautiful? They practically grow wild down by the river."

Macey stood over her mom, her foot tapping. Her mother might not eat next month and all she thought to do was arrange flowers? She pressed her fingers to her lips to keep from saying something she shouldn't. But then an explosive sneeze escaped, followed by two more. Evelyn grabbed tissues from her pocket and handed them to Macey. "Dear, do you need an antihistamine?"

Macey shook her head. "No. They knock me out, and I definitely don't need to be sleeping right now."

Evelyn just stared at her like she didn't know what else to say. Macey sneezed one more time and then said, "I think I need some fresh air. Mind if I drive around for a little while?"

"Of course not. I know how much trouble I've been. I'm sorry."

Macey sat so she was eye level with her mom. "Mother, this isn't your fault. Not at all. Please know that."

But Evelyn's expression didn't seem any less heavy. Macey stood, found her keys, and faced the muggy outside air again. Walking to her car, she took in a deep breath. She'd already missed her flight. She knew she couldn't return to Dallas. Not now. Not with her mother in this circumstance. She decided to go to the cemetery. After all, she hadn't really gotten a chance to pay her last *respects*.

Fifteen

Some of it she'd said out loud. Some she dared not let escape her lips. One elderly woman placing flowers at a nearby headstone looked up once but thankfully didn't stay long. It didn't matter much to Macey who was around, though. She had a lot to get off her chest. Seventeen years' worth. An outdoor thermometer hanging on a tree not far away read 105 degrees. As far as Macey was concerned, she might as well be in hell.

She was somewhat taken aback at what had shot up to the surface. There was a lot of anger, which of course wasn't surprising. But there was some sentiment as well, and weak moments of regret and shame. There was even laughter, albeit brief and tainted with frustration. It ran the whole gamut.

Yet, after forty-five minutes, standing over the fresh dirt of her father's grave, she felt no better than she had before. Her face was wet and streaked by tears. Her shoulders ached. She checked her watch—3:25. Squatting to the ground, she stared hard at his grave. It irritated her that she could go through all the emotional turmoil and not feel better. He met her now just as he had in life: with a cold, icy silence. His headstone, a dull gray, was the exact color of his eyes. She noticed the date of his death wasn't etched in yet, and she wondered how long ago her parents had ordered their headstones. Her mother's had been set beside his. What an odd thing it must be to order a headstone.

She shuddered, unsure as to why. It seemed a reaction to all the thoughts of the past. She shuddered again, touched her face, and realized she'd stopped sweating. Her eyes rolled back into her head for a moment as she tried to stand.

She was going to have to find water. She walked back over the dirt of her father's grave in the direction of her car. Once inside the car, with the air-conditioner's cold hitting her face, she leaned back and thought about how lucky he was that she had to go get herself some water. But in reality there was nothing more to say.

She drove around for an hour. She'd been afraid that if she drove back to her mother's house, her bags would practically pack themselves and she would come up with some way to justify her leaving.

At 5:12 she found herself on the other side of the Neosho River, driving up the long road toward Noah's house. She didn't know why, but she was compelled to see him. As the car approached the house, she thought about turning around. What was she thinking? What good was this going to do? But before she could think twice about it, she saw him next to a nearby tree, with easel, canvas, and brush, waving and smiling.

She got out of her car and slowly walked up to him. "Hi."

He finished a stroke and said, "Hi there. What a pleasant surprise." He glanced at the car. "A little too long of a walk for you?"

She laughed. "I've been driving around. I found myself on this side of the Neosho so I thought . . ." She shrugged and looked away.

"I thought you'd be gone by now."

"Me, too." She walked to the other side of the canvas to see what he was painting. She gasped at the beauty of it: a field of wheat with a distant line of trees and beautifully colored sky. She looked up to see if he was painting an actual scene, and there it was, right in front of her, precisely represented on the canvas. She hadn't seen the

Kansas landscape like this before. The fields, the trees, the skies—they somehow all became extraordinary when brought to life by oil paints. "It's wonderful," she told him.

Noah resumed his painting. "You know, when I lived in New York, I thought I had to travel to all these remote, exotic locations to find something to paint. Don't get me wrong. They were nice. But I must have fifty paintings just from standing outside my house here and looking out over the fields. And these—the ones I've done in Kansas—have sold the best."

"Do you still travel?"

"Not too far. I've been to Texas and Colorado, but I haven't been overseas since the girls were born. I make it to New York twice a year." He glanced her way. "I'll look you up on my next trip. I mean, if it turns out you move there and take a job with the network."

She smiled and continued to watch him in silence. He was masterful the way he controlled the paint and the color with each stroke, working the textures as if the brush were an extension of himself. After a few minutes, he wiped his brush and said, "Can I offer you something to drink?"

Macey shook her head. "I'm sorry. I don't mean to bother you. I just stopped by to . . ."

"To what?"

"Just stopped by." She smiled bashfully. "Don't people do that here—stop by for no reason?"

He laughed and put down his brush. "Come on. Let me get you some water. It's a hot one today."

She followed him inside the house, and as they passed his studio door, she stopped him. "Noah, may I see your studio?"

He turned around. "I was rude the other day . . . I mean, when I had to leave so suddenly. I really am interested in seeing your work."

"Sure," he said. "But first let me get you a glass of cold water."

He poured her a tall glass and then led her back into the studio. Although cluttered, it did appear organized. Canvas and other paint supplies lined the walls and shelves, and there must have been seven or eight unfinished works at different stages. He explained that he had to have several paintings going at once or he got bored. Several large windows filtered light in from various angles. Other than supplies, shelves, and canvases, there wasn't much in the way of decoration.

She walked around the room, her hands clasped behind her back, looking at each individual piece. They were all so beautiful. A horse standing at a pond. An old barn with cows all around it. One in particular caught her attention. It looked as if it had been painted from the top of a tree. There was something eerily familiar about the picture.

"What about this one?" she asked. "Where is this?"

"I actually climbed a tree and painted from that view. I almost fell out twice."

"It looks familiar." She shook her head. "I don't know why."

He stood next to her, their shoulders almost touching. "It's from the big tree by your parents' house. The one with the tree house."

Of course. It was the view looking north, over the wheat fields, at sunset. Growing up, she'd sat in the tree house for hours, watching the sunrises and sunsets, sometimes even storms.

She continued moving around the studio. "You don't strike me as a New Yorker," she said.

"I'll take that as a compliment."

"You don't have the aura, or attitude, especially of an artist from there." She glanced at him. "I've known a few."

"I'm sorry," he said with a laugh.

"You don't even sound like you're from New York."

He trailed her around the room. "I'm not, originally. I'm from Minnesoooota."

Macey chuckled as she circled back to the studio's door. "Well, you don't really sound like you're from up north, either."

"Maybe I'm starting to sound like a hick."

"No, I'm not hearing that at all."

His eyebrows rose and he said, "Are you sure? 'Cause I'm fixin' to get ya some more water, little lady."

She giggled and followed him out of the studio and into the kitchen, where he refilled her glass. The fluids felt good to her body, and she gulped down the second glass nearly as quickly as the first.

"Where are the girls?" she asked, noticing the house was considerably quiet for having two six-year-olds around.

"At a friend's. They're spending the night there." He tapped his fingers on the small kitchen island. "Stay for dinner."

She looked up and almost dropped her glass. "Stay . . . for dinner?"

His eyebrows formed a worried arch. "You don't trust me to cook for you?"

"It's not that. It's just . . . I wasn't expecting you to—" She stopped her rambling, took a deep breath, and met his eyes. "Sure. I'd love to."

Noah picked up the phone in the kitchen, dialed four digits and said, "Hi, Evelyn. It's Noah. Listen, I invited Macey over for dinner. . . . Yes . . . Would you like to come?" Macey held her breath. "Are you sure? . . . Okay . . . I promise I'll have her home by dark. Bye." He hung up the phone, and his lips curved into a confident smile. "You have permission."

She shot him a look. "Right." She rinsed her glass in the sink. "I forgot you only had to dial four digits here."

"Yeah. Kind of a trip, isn't it? I mean, in many places now, you have to dial an area code even if it's not long distance, just because they've run out of numbers. Here it's only four. I love it."

"You love a lot of things about this place, don't you?"

"Sure. It's a nice place to live."

An awkward silence caught Macey off guard, and she wondered what kind of conversation she could expect to have during an evening alone with Noah Kauffman.

"So what's on the menu tonight?" she asked. Silence was something she was never going to be comfortable with.

A devilish glint in Noah's eyes was followed by a suspicious grin. "I guess that all depends on what I'm able to find and kill in the next thirty minutes."

＊◆＊

He was only half joking. The grill spat flames into the air when Noah flipped the rabbit and then the rattlesnake. Macey covered her mouth as Noah laughed. "You'll love it," he assured her. "I promise."

Macey stood several feet away from the grill yet close enough to hear Noah explain that he hadn't actually killed the rattlesnake or the rabbit, but that Twenty, who was a fantastic hunter, had done the killing, and that he was paid well for his meat.

"I just don't think I can . . . can eat. . ." She couldn't even finish the sentence. Noah went on with basting the pieces of meat, thoroughly amused the whole time, like a boy who had just introduced a tarantula to a frightened little girl. Suddenly Macey found herself craving her mother's fried chicken. What a transition she'd made in her life!

"These are best if cooked over a low heat for a while," he said as he closed the grill's lid, and Macey gladly followed him back inside. "I'll let you help me make a salad."

Macey washed, dried, and tore the lettuce, while Noah chopped carrots, tomatoes, and cucumbers, telling her at the same time about how Twenty goes to South Texas five or six times a year to hunt rattlesnake and that he'd even been bitten once and lived to tell the story. He told her if it had been a few months later, he would've fixed her venison stew. Macey just shook her head and continued to concentrate on the lettuce.

She'd just switched to washing the potatoes when Noah disappeared into the living room, and with his return a few minutes later, Simon and Garfunkel were bellowing out "Bridge Over Troubled Water." Macey listened silently as she scrubbed. It had been her father's favorite song, one that would make him pick her up and dance with her as if she were a world-class ballerina. As a child, she'd never paid much attention to the words. Now, as far as she was concerned, they were still meaningless.

Noah dried the potatoes, wrapped them in tinfoil, and stuck them in the preheated oven. He slapped his hands together, met her eyes with a crooked little smile, and said, "Well, I suppose I should start the appetizer."

Macey swallowed. "Appetizer?"

"Calf fries."

———◆———

Macey managed to talk Noah out of the calf fries, thankfully. She'd eaten them as a young girl, before she knew any better. Admittedly, they *did* taste like very tender chicken. But there wasn't a chance she was going to eat them now. Not even for the handsomely tall artist she was beginning to adore.

The sweltering heat of the day had turned into a muggy but only warm evening. Macey sat on the porch swing and watched Noah baste the rabbit, which lay directly on the grill, and the rattlesnake, wrapped in tinfoil close by. He used his own recipe for the barbecue sauce. It would all make for an amusing story to tell someday, she thought.

He joined her on the swing. "I'm sorry. But if I don't keep basting the meat, it'll dry out. You were talking about your life in broadcasting." He turned and looked at her, his eyes focused and seemingly interested in her life. This startled her. Most of the guys she knew talked only of themselves, then somehow later became threatened by her career.

She shrugged. "It's busy. Chaotic. Exhilarating."

"Why did you go into broadcasting?"

She thought about it for a moment. "I suppose because I thought I could make a difference."

"Really? What kind of difference?"

"Well, if nothing else, to keep people honest. To expose the bad guys and highlight the good guys. Maybe it's not that innocent, I don't know. There's a lot of exploitation in the business. The competition is fierce, to get the best story first. But in a small way I think I make a difference. I inform the public. That's important. That's what our whole system revolves around in America. Information. Accurate information."

He nodded. "If your life is busy and chaotic now, just think what it will be like with the network."

"Yeah. It sometimes scares me to think about it. I'm a hard worker, though, so that part doesn't bother me. I suppose I'm just a little afraid of all the politics involved, that I'll be able to survive it."

"How so?" His blue eyes touched her as engaging, dreamy. Macey had to look away to concentrate.

"Well, let's see. Back home in Dallas there's this weirdly mixed dynamic made up of producers, reporters, and anchors. Anchors get paid more, but probably, in most cases, don't know as much and aren't as smart as some reporters and most all producers. The anchors are paid to be the pretty face. And they're paid well. The producers and reporters do all the behind-the-scenes work, the dirty work, and get paid less. It causes a lot of backbiting and strife."

"I can imagine."

"The downside to being the anchor is when something goes wrong, no matter whose mistake it is, the anchor's the one who takes the blame. If I, say, report bad information my producer feeds me, mispronounce a word, call someone by the wrong name, or stumble because the teleprompter is behind, any of that—it all falls on me. I look bad in front of a million people, you know?"

"Wow. Sounds like a tough job."

"It is. And then there are days that you think you'll go crazy because you get a phone call from a woman who tells you if you wear your hair a certain way one more time, she's never going to watch your channel again. Or the guy who makes death threats."

"Death threats?"

"Sure. People take their anger out on the media. We get threats all the time. It's not unusual. We have trapdoors all over the station. So in case there's ever a gunman, everyone knows what to do, where to go. Even the receptionist has a trapdoor. Pretty high tech, eh?"

Noah nodded, completely fascinated. "I had no idea. I just thought you guys, ladies, reported the news and that's all there was to it. I never thought about all the behind-the-scenes things."

"Well, we're supposed to make it look easy. If you're thinking about anything other than the news, we're not doing our job." She shrugged and laughed a little. "Even if you're thinking about the color of my suit, we're not doing our job. I should never wear that suit again."

"So, in New York, all that is going to be multiplied by a billion."

Macey pressed her lips together. "Yes."

"And you're up for that?"

She nodded, though a little more apprehensively than she wanted to. "I put myself through college by working any job I could find. I even drove a garbage truck."

"You were a trash man?"

"For a little while, yeah. I was willing to do whatever it took to get through school, earn my degree. Collecting garbage pays fairly well, actually."

Noah shook his head. "I had you pegged wrong."

"Oh? And how did you have me pegged?"

He paused, then looked at her. "It doesn't matter. I have a lot of respect for someone who can endure a business like yours and someone who worked so hard to get there." He got up to check the meat and soon joined her on the swing again. "What drove you to work so hard?"

Macey swatted a fly away. "What do you mean?"

"I mean, there's usually some underlying factor that causes a person to do things like drive a garbage truck to get through college."

A confused look on her face, Macey shook her head and said, "I don't know what you're getting at."

"You're a smart woman. Of course you know what I mean. Did any of this, your pushing so hard, have to do with your leaving home so many years ago?"

Macey studied his eyes. What was he inferring? How much did he know? She hated that he always seemed to be one step ahead of her. It was like he could read her mind.

But before she could answer him, he said the words she was dreading the most: "It's time to eat."

———◆——◆——◆———

Why would she even *consider* doing this? For a guy? She'd made her share of sacrifices for a lot of men, and even a few shameful compromises, but eating rattlesnake? Had she hit a whole new low or maybe entered the Twilight Zone? She decided to take a bite of potato first.

"I've got sour cream and butter," he said, pointing across the table at each one.

"No thanks." She smiled, as calmly as possible. "I just take a little salt and pepper on mine."

"Ah. Health nut." He plopped both sour cream and butter on his potato.

"The camera adds ten pounds," she said, which seemed to appease him.

"Good," he said, using his fork to indicate her plate. "Rabbit and snake are both low in fat and high in protein. You should love that."

Macey took a bite of salad so she wouldn't have to respond immediately. She wiped her mouth, chewed until the salad was practically liquid, and then said, "You know, I'm not so sure—"

She stopped as his bright blue eyes dulled with disappointment. Was this a big thing for him? Was he really going to be hurt if she didn't eat the meat he'd prepared? Her pulse throbbed in her neck as she stared down at the small portions of rabbit and snake, each dripping with sweet smelling barbecue sauce. She could at least take a bite, couldn't she? After all, she'd tried squid once, and she ate sushi on a somewhat regular basis. What was one bite of snake?

Her stomach churned at the very thought. She quickly stuffed her mouth with another bite of potato. Suddenly the tune of "Little Bunny Foo Foo" played in her mind, but then she realized it wasn't her but Noah! He was humming it from across the table. She stared at him in disbelief. He just sat there, humming while slicing away at a hunk of cooked rabbit.

She had to laugh, and the laugh turned into an uncontrollable giggle, which ended in a full-blown roar with Noah joining in.

It took a good five minutes for them both to settle down. Macey leaned across the table and studied him. "This has all been a joke, hasn't it? You just wanted to see what I would do?"

A tight smile of satisfaction spread across his lips. "Well, it wasn't a total joke. We do eat these things from time to time. But from the foods you selected at the picnic, many of which you seemed to think might jump up and strangle you, I just had to see if you would really eat either of these." His face turned soft and pleasant. "They're good. You really should try them."

Macey shook her head. "I hate snakes."

"Yes, well, all the better to show them who's boss." His fork pointed down at her plate. "Tell you what. You take a bite of both the snake and rabbit, and I promise I'll stop asking you so many questions about your past."

Macey looked up at him with a surprised expression. "What?"

"I have to admit I'm curious. Why did you leave here all those years ago? Why didn't you come back until now, with the death of your father?" He set down his fork and wiped his mouth. "But I also have to admit, it would be something else to see you eat rattlesnake and Foo Foo over there."

Macey broke out into a cold sweat. Was he serious? She saw that there was something real in his eyes. Something pure. She scratched her forehead and tried to lighten up. "Quite a choice," she said.

He salted his snake. "Right." After taking a large bite of snake, he chewed and smiled at her all at once. Macey could almost hear the thing rattling inside his mouth. She bit down on what was left of her fingernails. Could she trust him enough to tell him about what happened so long ago? He might never talk to her again. But was that so bad? Was there any chance of more than a few days of fun with this man? Perhaps it was best to spill all her secrets to the stranger across the river.

She hadn't spoken a word of it to another person for seventeen years. She knew better than to think she could speak sanely about it all, as if merely talking about her drinking days in college.

She stared down at her plate and thought she might be able to psyche herself into believing she was eating chicken.

Noah's fork held a bite of potato in front of his face as he said, "Well, Foo Foo's getting cold. What's it going to be?"

Sixteen

A nd then there was Keith. Wow. Keith. He was something else. A doctor, really rich, drove a Porsche and a Mercedes and had two homes. But there was no chemistry between us, nothing. After Keith came Bobby. I thought it was true love with him, but then he dumped me out of the blue to date some up-and-coming actress. It took me some time to recover from that one, and I'm not sure I ever did completely. After that, I was a lot more cautious about who I dated. I never let myself take risks. So there was Alex, and then James, a construction worker if you can believe that, then Danny, and lastly Rob, who dumped me by way of my answering machine the same day I found out my dad had died."

Macey took a breath. She had to. She was feeling lightheaded because she'd been talking nonstop. He wanted to discuss her past. Well, this was her past. As he cleared her plate with the untouched portions of snake and rabbit, there was a small smile of satisfaction on his face. The questions were coming, she knew, but at least she could appease him for now with a few facts about her life.

She continued as they moved into the living room. "By the time Rob broke up with me, I was pretty much hardened, so it didn't really hurt that much. I sort of expected it. I'm occasionally too temperamental, my hours are wacky, and I've become calloused. Doesn't exactly make the perfect formula for a little housewife, does it?" Macey couldn't help but glance at the picture of Emily on the nearby end table.

Noah sat opposite her in a plush leather chair, his feet propped up on the ottoman, his coffee neatly balanced on his lap. He was listening, but Macey sensed he was deriving some amusement from something other than what she shared.

"I'm rambling," she finally confessed. She laughed to herself, embarrassed and feeling vulnerable. On most of her prior dates this would be the point where the male would begin reciting all of his past mistakes and disappointments, a common practice so both understood exactly what they were getting into. Everyone, in her experience anyway, had a long laundry list. Breakups, divorces, heartaches. But as she stared at the dark-haired man across the living room, she suspected this wasn't going to be any ordinary evening. She also suspected he wasn't going to have much of a laundry list.

She sipped her coffee, well aware that as she sat silently, Noah was reading her like a book. She'd never met anyone like him. It seemed it didn't matter what she said, he was able to sift through it all and find the truth.

She decided to fill the silence again. "You know those commercials—the ones where there's a group of people sitting around, all drinking wine or some other beverage, laughing and joking and hugging like they've been soul mates their whole lives?" She looked up at Noah for a reaction. He nodded. "I hate those commercials. Because none of it's true. I mean, do people really get together, everyone with the love of his or her life, and play games or sing songs or walk on the beach together and then roast marshmallows? Is there such a thing as three women, all the same age, getting along like sisters?" She shook her head. Why was she saying this? The words were pouring out and she couldn't stop them. "I wish, just once, a commercial would depict real life. For the most part women hate each other, and men are out for the chase. Couples eat their meals in silence because they have nothing left to say to each other. I've yet to sit at a dinner table with a group of friends and everyone clink their wine glasses and laugh at the pure joy of just being together."

Noah remained comfortable in his chair, his eyes sparkling with what seemed like compassion. She wasn't sure. It was probably pity. Then he said, "Well, I can't say that I ever expected my life to be about images."

Macey lowered her head and stared at the carpet. How humiliating. Now he was going to lecture her.

"But I know what you mean."

Macey looked up. "You do?"

"Sure," Noah said. "Much of New York is about just that—image. Greenwich Village, at least. Emily and I owned a loft apartment near there during our time in New York. It had twenty-five-hundred square feet, plenty of room for parties and social events. But we found ourselves having trouble finding even ten people we wanted to spend the evening with. Most of the time we sat on the couch eating pizza and watching movies. We were in the prime of our lives, in the middle of the New York City arts scene, and all we wanted to do was stay at home. How's that for imagery?"

Macey smiled, shrugged, and said, "That's a nice image, actually. Two people in love, spending time alone, pushing the outside world away."

"I suppose it is." He returned the smile. "You know, friends aren't hard to find if you just let it happen. Let the unexpected happen." He paused, then said, "My closest friends here are all over sixty."

Macey chuckled. "You're kidding."

He shook his head. "Every Tuesday and Thursday at noon I go have coffee with the boys. There were seven of us, until your dad died. We meet up at the Cracker Jack and have coffee and talk. That's it. Pretty simple."

Macey nodded and looked away. He considered her father a friend? How bizarre. She didn't take too long to think about it, though, because that would cause silence, and she couldn't afford for there to be any silence this evening.

"Sometimes I long for my childhood," she said carefully, hoping not to open a Pandora's box. "Things were simple then; friendships were easily made. Life was black and white. My biggest worry was whether or not the frog I'd caught was going to stay in the box I'd put him in." She followed the curve of her knee with her finger. "I used to beg to stay outside longer so I could watch the fireflies."

Noah's eyes engaged hers. "Sounds like you had a nice childhood."

Macey smiled with uncertainty. Yes. She did have a nice childhood. What a terrible setup for all that happened to her. She refocused on the carpet. "I just wish commercials or television or movies would tell the truth. Movies. There's one for you. Guy and girl love each other. Guy and girl have a fight. Girl runs out the door. Guy goes after her." She laughed, throwing her head back. "When has that ever happened? Guy doesn't go after her! Guy doesn't even call her! In fact, Guy has already moved on to the next girl because things just got 'too complicated.' " She realized her voice had turned edgy, and she took a breath and sipped her coffee, avoiding Noah's questioning eyes. "I'm just saying, it's like the whole world is out to set you up for disappointment. Cologne doesn't make you prettier. Makeup doesn't make you younger. Toothpaste doesn't make you happier. House paint doesn't bring you closer. New shoes don't solve every problem in your life. Whole-grain cereal doesn't make you feel better about yourself. Lower long-distance rates won't bring you freedom. Shall I go on?"

Noah laughed. "If you want to."

Macey shook her head and laughed a little at herself, too. "I guess I'll get off my soapbox now."

Noah uncrossed and recrossed his feet. "You're right about all that, you know. There's nothing tangible about the world. It's all smoke and mirrors."

"And that's why you moved out here, to get away from the smoke and mirrors?"

Noah paused. "Well, partly. But the smoke and mirrors are everywhere." His eyes narrowed as he spoke, and he glanced up at Macey. "There's always somebody trying to create an illusion."

Macey held her breath. What was he saying? Why was he staring at her like that? "I need to warm my cup." She went to the kitchen and poured a swallow of coffee into her mug, then set it down. She leaned on the counter to catch her breath.

"I'm sorry."

Macey jumped and turned around, her back up against the counter. She gazed up at Noah, who had somehow snuck up behind her. "Sorry for what?"

"Sorry you're lonely."

Macey swallowed. She wasn't lonely. She talked to inanimate objects because they carried on better conversations than most people she knew.

"Savannah thinks you look sad."

Macey's eyes darted away from him. "What do kids know?"

Noah moved away from her and to the sink, where he began rinsing his cup. Without looking up, he said, "You know, Macey, I'm here if you need to talk." He glanced back at her, then to the running water again.

Macey stuck her hands deep into the pockets of her jeans, her shoulders slumping with a sudden depression. "I thought you were going to ask me about my past. I didn't eat the meat. Aren't you going to grill me now?"

Noah smiled as he said, "I think I know all I need to."

Macey shook her head. She found her keys in her pocket. "I better go."

"Okay."

Macey walked to the front door, and after he opened it for her, she stepped out onto the small porch and said, "Thanks for the offer of being a friend. But I've got more baggage than any two people can carry."

"Oh, I hadn't planned on carrying your baggage for you. There's someone else to do that."

Macey frowned. "Who would that be?"

"Didn't you listen in church this Sunday?"

Her fingers ran through her hair and she shook her head. "So that's the solution, huh? God's going to take care of all this baggage? God's going to *heal* me?" She shot him an angry look. "Whatever. He's had plenty of time to do that. No, I don't think He's going to take my baggage. In fact, He's one of the reasons I have so much." She tried to smile. "Thanks for dinner. I had a nice time."

Macey spun on the ball of her foot and marched down the sidewalk and around the house to where her car was parked. Her fists were clinched into balls, and she looked as if she were carrying two imaginary pieces of luggage.

It took only a few seconds to get to her car and bend in. She turned the car around and headed down the long drive. She passed over a small hill that put her out of sight of Noah's house.

Her foot pressed hard against the brake as tears rolled down her face. Looking back several times in the rearview mirror revealed nothing but an inky sky. She should've known better. A man had never run after her once in her life. Not even her father.

Her tears were hot with anger as she thought of Noah's suggestion that it would be God who carried her baggage. The church always thought it had such simple answers. Faith, hope, and love would change everything, make it all better, solve every problem.

Didn't they know better? Didn't any of them see how life can pull you in, chew you up, and spit you out before you ever know what's happening? A spiritual Band-Aid wasn't going to do anything but attempt to cover up her ugly wounds. The Band-Aid would eventually fall off, and there the wound would be again for all to see.

She pounded her forehead against the steering wheel. She'd said too much. She'd poured out her heart too frankly tonight. And she hadn't even said much of anything! Anything real, anything of substance! It was all just surface stuff. Smoke and mirrors. Yet Noah seemed to know more of her than she revealed. But how?

She wiped her nose and swiped at her tears. A deep breath, then another one. One of her former flames, Bobby maybe, had once said she was a "pretty crier." She didn't exactly know what that meant except that perhaps she could cry one moment and look normal the next. She lifted her foot off the brake and slowly maneuvered the car out onto the dirt road that led to the paved street. She glanced one more time in her rearview mirror.

———◆———

Evelyn hummed along with the record player. A few decades ago, hardly anyone had *two* turntables in their homes. But Jess had always liked music, so they had one in their bedroom and several years later bought another for the living area. That was before the drought. After everything dried up, there hadn't even been enough money for a new record to play on the thing.

The scissors ran smoothly along the dotted lines of the coupon page, and Evelyn spent thirty minutes cutting and sorting. She usually cut coupons on Sunday, but Sunday had been rather hectic so it had to wait until this evening.

Patricia had called a couple of hours earlier, just to check in, and promised she'd come by tomorrow. Other than the call from Noah, the phone had been silent, and so had the house. The music sounded so good.

"Bridge Over Troubled Water" came on, and Evelyn paused, remembering how much her husband had loved the song. He'd never been the flamboyant, charismatic type, but this song moved him somehow. She guessed the words were rich to him.

She wadded the unused clippings of the newspaper and tossed them in the trash, cleaning up the table and filing away her new coupons. She'd have to make a run to the store soon. Could she remember not to buy as much food? How in the world do you cook a roast for one? She concluded that she'd have to start inviting a lot of people over for dinner.

Back at the table she scanned the front page of the paper for any new news. Most of it was about the new technological center, whatever *that* was, west of Parsons on the 160. Most people griped about it. It was an eyesore, that was for sure. Someone at church said it looked like Darth Vader had built it. She didn't know who Mr. Vader was, probably some high-classed snooty architect, but it was true that it did tend to loom over the horizon. It was a large grouping of dark shiny buildings, sort of ominous looking, that stood in the middle of what was once a wheat field. Many had protested the company coming and building there. Nevertheless, they bought the land and constructed their big complex. It was supposed to bring new jobs to Parsons and surrounding towns. She didn't know if it was doing that, but it sure was big. It had made for lots of lively conversation.

She flipped through the newspaper to see if there was anything else of interest and then came to the classifieds. She scanned it for upcoming garage sales in the area, then thought better about spending her money. According to her daughter, she was broke. She sighed and was about to close the newspaper when suddenly the job opportunity section caught her eye. She pressed the paper flat on the table and squinted as she tried to read the fine print with her bifocals. Maybe she could get a job! She ran her finger down the job listings. It was all so confusing, deciphering what each job title meant, and she was just about to give up when the back door swung open.

"Macey!" She smiled, but her daughter didn't smile back. "How was dinner?"

"What is it with that song today?" Macey said, nodding toward the living room. She plopped down at the table, looked at Evelyn, and tried to smile pleasantly. "It was just fine. Noah tried to feed me snake and rabbit."

Evelyn chuckled. "Well, my goodness. He doesn't know you very well, does he?"

Macey folded her arms and stared at the table. "I think he knows me a little too well, to tell you the truth." Her eyes focused on the newspaper. "What are you doing?"

"Oh, silly me, I'm looking through the classifieds. Thought about gettin' me a job."

"Mother!"

"What?"

Macey grabbed the newspaper and slid it closer to herself. "That's it! We can get you a job! All you need is living-expense money. It shouldn't be too hard finding you a job that'll cover your everyday expenses." Macey started scanning the listings. "Here's a job at a florist. Here's one at the school." Macey glanced up at Evelyn, her eyes bright with hope. "Why didn't I think of this?"

Evelyn cleared her throat. "Maybe because I haven't worked a day in my life, dear."

Macey's eyes fell back to the paper. She read and talked at the same time. "That's true, but there's no time like the present. Even a part-time job would help." She slammed her hands down on the table, and a wide grin spread across her face. "Step one. We need to figure out how much you're going to be spending a month. Let's get a paper and pencil."

Evelyn watched her daughter rummage through the desk drawer to find both. She returned with a small tablet and a leaky pen, which seemed to suit her just fine. She made some notes at the top, then looked at her mom. "Well, you better start some coffee, Mom. It's going to be a late night."

———◆◆◆———

Evelyn was on her third cup of coffee at ten past eleven o'clock. Her hands were trembling, from the caffeine she guessed. She was used to retiring around nine, but she relished the time spent with her daughter, knowing Macey was planning to leave tomorrow. She hoped that maybe if she didn't ask, Macey might stay a little longer.

Her daughter was busily typing away at something that looked like a gigantic calculator to her, but Macey said it was called a laptop. Evelyn had seen a few computers in her life, but this one looked awfully fancy.

Across the table, papers and all sorts of documents were strewn. They'd spent almost two hours just trying to figure out what kind of expenses she had every month. Macey had lectured her on setting up a budget, so while Macey "entered the data" into that laptop of hers, Evelyn had been trying to write down what she typically bought at the grocery store every month.

Macey looked up from what she was doing. "Are you finished?"

Evelyn stared down at her piece of paper. "I guess so." She was supposed to estimate how much each item cost, and she thought she'd done pretty well. She watched her daughter examine the paper as though she were looking for fleas on a cat.

She set the paper down and said, "That's good. But, Mom, we're going to have to put you on a monthly budget for food. You're not going to be able to afford all that meat you're used to."

Evelyn nodded. Who would she cook it for now, anyway?

Macey kept typing away and, after a few minutes, leaned back in her chair and clasped her hands behind her head. "There. That's a start."

"What?"

Macey turned the computer for Evelyn to see the screen. A chart of numbers stared back at her. It was much too sophisticated for someone like her.

"My goodness, what's this?"

"I've been entering all these figures into a program I have on my computer. It tells us how much we're going to need every month." Macey glanced over at it. "About eight hundred, low end. But I'd like to see you bringing in around a thousand, just for some leeway. Prescriptions can be expensive. I know you don't have a lot of medicine needs right now, but we want to be prepared, plan for things like that." Macey emphasized the word *prepared* by leaning forward and looking her mom in the eye.

"All right," said Evelyn. "But what kind of job is going to pay me a thousand dollars? That's a lot of money."

A thin, tolerant smile relaxed Macey's pursed lips. "We'll find something. We've got to."

Seventeen

Macey slammed the phone down and stared hard at the wall. While her mother sizzled bacon nearby, she tried to breathe in any fresh air she could find. She'd had a good run early this morning, but her stress level was already back up to its previous level. Nothing was working out. All the jobs listed were either filled or required a skill her mother didn't have. Evelyn could cook, clean, smile and chat, organize food for the bereaved, sew, and help coordinate a church picnic, but none of these skills seemed to be in demand.

"I thought I'd make us some grits," her mother, cooking furiously, said from behind Macey. "You probably haven't had grits in a long time, have you?"

Macey shook her head. Indeed she had not. She leaned against the wall and wondered if she should call Mitchell, try to smooth things over. He'd been terribly mad. Her stomach hurt at the idea that she was missing such a major news story. But Mitchell had been mad at her before. And what did it matter, if she ended up at the network?

She'd once again rebooked her flight over the Internet to leave early Wednesday morning. She would get back to Dallas, meet with Mitchell, and then catch her flight to New York without a problem. That left her only today to find her mother a job. Her stomach muscles tightened with anxiety.

"Breakfast is served," Evelyn said. Macey turned to find her mother standing over the breakfast table, her face jolly and bright. Macey sank into one of the chairs and took a sip from the glass of orange juice in front of her.

"I'm not having much luck finding a good job for you, Mom," Macey said as her mother brought the bacon to the table. It was stacked high on a plate, paper towels soaking up the grease underneath it. After staring down rabbit and rattlesnake, however, bacon didn't seem too bad of an alternative.

Her mother only smiled and nodded while continuing to bring platefuls of food to the table. "Well, then, I guess we're going to need our energy today. Eat up," she said, scooping some eggs onto her plate and then sitting down herself. "Banana?"

"Sure," Macey sighed and took the banana, along with a strip of bacon and two pieces of toast. "Mother, are you sure you haven't forgotten to tell me something that you might be . . . skilled at?" Macey tried to smile reassuringly.

Evelyn studied her eggs. "I was good at taking care of your father."

Macey peeled her banana and leaned back into her chair. As she ate, she looked over the classifieds one more time. Her eyes settled on the large ad for a company called American Standard Technologies. The ad indicated there were many job openings, and as she read it more carefully, she realized that AST wasn't too far away. Just off Highway 160. She'd skipped over it earlier, assuming a technology business would be no place for someone like her mom to work. But the ad said the company was new, that it had many different job opportunities, requiring a wide variety of skills. Macey slid the paper over to her mom and pointed to the page.

"Have you heard of AST?"

"Sure. Everyone has."

"What do you mean, everyone has?"

"It's the talk of the town. Darth Vader built it."

"What?"

"It's a group of huge buildings outside of Parsons. They bought the land, and lots of folks protested because no one wanted a big company like that moving out here. They did it anyway, and now I guess they're trying to fill the jobs. It was supposed to bring new jobs to the area, but I don't know if it's done that or not."

Macey's eyes widened. This was perfect! Maybe they had a job in the mail room or something similar. Perhaps a receptionist! Surely her mom could do that.

"Honey, I was hoping we could talk."

Macey looked up, midchew. "What?"

"Talk. I've been meaning to talk with you. I've been wanting to, I mean, it's just that . . ."

While her mother struggled to find the right words, all Macey could think about was AST. It would probably pay well and was only about a twenty-five minute drive from the house. She checked her watch. A little after nine. She should drive out there, check out the situation. She glanced up at her mom, who was staring at her nervously.

"I'm sorry. You were saying?" Macey wiped her mouth and quickly began clearing the dishes. Luckily she was wearing her good slacks and a nice blouse. She knew how to act in a corporate setting. Maybe she could talk with someone there, get her mom an interview. Macey went back to the table and found her mom still looking flustered. "Mom? You okay?"

Evelyn set her fork down. "Are you going somewhere?"

"Mother, this AST could be the answer! They're just starting out. They've got a ton of jobs to fill. I'm going over there to talk to someone in Human Resources and see what I can work out."

"Work out?"

"Yes, Mother. A job. For you. Aren't you following all this? I'm leaving tomorrow morning, and I've got to get you situated before I go."

Her mother smiled mildly and picked up with eating her eggs. What was with her? Why suddenly so solemn? Macey closed her eyes, gathered herself, and then said, "Mom, was there something you wanted to say?"

"No, no. You go on. See what you can find out."

◆

On the way there she tried to find some music that would get her focused, but nothing seemed appropriate, so she drove in silence. At least she tried to. Her mind became cluttered with thoughts of Noah, followed by thoughts of Harley Preston. She tried to shake them off, but they soon came back and brought along more disturbing thoughts each time. Her father's angry eyes flashed before her own more times than she could count, until finally she switched on the radio and settled into listening to two slow-talking men discuss agriculture as aggressively as politicians might a tax cut.

Fifteen minutes later Macey knew more about agriculture than she had ever cared to. But it was something to fill her mind.

As she cleared a large hill, suddenly she saw it. Three buildings, all with dark glass, sitting in the middle of a large field. They certainly looked out of place. The massive parking lot was only half full, and as Macey pulled her car into the complex, the towers seemed to disappear into the sky. No wonder all these farmers and ranchers didn't like this. It looked like its own city. To Macey it was exhilarating.

She checked her makeup and hair in the rearview mirror. Her face was slightly shiny, but wasn't everyone's in this humidity? She started obsessing over a wrinkle in her blouse, but then realized she wasn't the one seeking a job. All she had to do was convince the right person to interview her mom. That was the first step.

She walked briskly to the front door, and the dark glass parted in front of her with a *swoosh*. A blast of cold air greeted her. She stepped into a lavish lobby complete with marble pillars, lush furniture, and an ornately tiled floor. Her heels echoed as she approached the receptionist, a thin severe-looking woman with lips the color of blood.

"May I help you?"

She reminded Macey of a robot with her pale skin, glassy eyes, and her question, which sounded as if programmed. "I'd like to speak to someone in Human Resources, please." Macey made and held eye contact, a mark of confidence she'd learned long ago.

"Are you seeking a job?" the woman asked while thumbing through a stack of files. Her fingers emerged with a piece of paper. "You'll have to fill this out." She slid it onto the counter in front of Macey.

"No, I'm not looking for a job. But I need to speak with someone in Human Resources." The woman's eyes narrowed. Macey imagined she wasn't the standard visitor asking the standard questions. She'd obviously thrown the woman off a bit.

"What is the nature of your business?"

Macey paused. If she told the woman she was there to find her mom a job, she wouldn't get past the front desk. "I'm with KSCC in Dallas."

The woman didn't budge. "That doesn't tell me the nature of your business, ma'am."

Macey felt her muscles tense. She tried to stay cool by smiling. She was just about to try a different angle when suddenly she heard "Macey? Macey Steigel?"

She turned to find a long-haired, doe-eyed woman staring at her with a curious smile. "Yeah?"

"It's me!" The woman walked over and removed her glasses. Macey immediately recognized her.

"Kimmy Trout." Macey smiled as Kimmy hugged her.

"It's not Trout anymore. I'm a Harrison now." She flashed Macey her large diamond ring, and it glinted in the light. Lowering her voice, she added, "And I go by *Kimberly* in the corporate world." She grinned, her famously deep dimples marking each side of her mouth. "I suppose you're not Steigel anymore, are you?"

Macey scratched her hairline. "Actually, I am. Haven't quite found prince charming."

Kimmy laughed, almost dropping the stack of folders she was holding to her chest. Macey had to admit, she still looked amazing. Another of her acquaintances from high school, Kimmy had been a popular cheerleader and a church friend who would always make room in her life for Macey. Their fathers had been friends, too, at least until Kimmy's father cheated on her mother and then left the family. Kimmy was seven at the time. As the two girls grew older, they'd gone their separate ways, found separate interests. But Macey always liked Kimmy.

"You look terrific," Kimmy offered.

"Thank you. So do you."

"What are you doing here? Applying for a job?"

Macey steered Kimmy away from the receptionist and whispered, "I'm trying to help my mom find a job. My dad passed away last week, and she's sort of . . . desperate."

Kimmy's eyes widened with compassion. "Oh, Macey. I'm so sorry. You must be devastated."

"Mom doesn't have a lot of, well, worldly skills, if you know what I mean. But I thought since AST is a new company, they may need to fill all different kinds of positions. I was hoping I could speak with someone in Human Resources to get the particulars. Do you think you can help me?"

Kimmy grinned and said, "I think so. I'm the Human Resources director's personal assistant."

"This place is really something," Macey said as she followed Kimmy down a long corridor. Through glass walls, Macey could see different departments, their cubicles filled with brainy-looking people. "What exactly is AST?"

"Well, there are several components to it. We make pretty much everything that goes into a computer. They think up all sorts of cool things in the West building—they're the innovators. The East building is where most of the business is done—marketing, accounting, that kind of thing. This building, which is called Center, is all about computers. We make them, we build them, we service them."

They rounded the corner, and Kimmy stepped into a large office and walked behind the desk. "This is my office," she said with a smile.

"Wow," said Macey. It was about twelve by fourteen and included a small waiting room and a beverage counter. Expensive art decorated one wall.

"Through that door is Ms. Cunningham's office." Kimmy checked her watch. "She'll be in a meeting for about another ten minutes. I might be able to fit you in after that."

Macey nodded. "Okay. I'll take whatever I can get." Kimmy pointed to the chair in front of her desk while she took a seat in her own leather one. "I've never heard of AST."

"It's a Japanese company and goes by Japanese Standard Technology over there. They decided to start an American company as well, so this is it."

"Why build out here, in the middle of nowhere?"

"Coffee?" Kimmy said, gesturing toward the beverage counter.

"Sure. Black is fine."

Kimmy rose and went to pour them both a cup. "Well, AST is more than just a computer company. The plan is for it to become a community. AST bought over two hundred acres here, and they plan to develop apartments, housing additions, stores, movie theaters, pools and parks, things like that. It'll sort of be like its own little city. It's hugely popular in Japan. They're hoping it will be the same here."

Macey smiled. What a concept. She had a hard time imagining her mother working in such an environment. Yet, with this being her only option, she was going to have to give it a try.

"We couldn't interest *you* in a job, could we?" Kimmy asked as she brought Macey her coffee. "You were always so smart in school."

"No, thank you. Although it does sound interesting. Right now I'm working as an anchor for a television station in Dallas."

"No kidding? That's terrific! I always knew you'd do something important with your life."

"You look like you're doing pretty well yourself," Macey said, glancing around the office.

Kimmy sat back down and shrugged as she stirred her coffee. "I feel fortunate. I never graduated from college or anything, and before AST came here, I was working at a dry cleaners in Parsons. This was a big break for me."

There was an awkward silence as they both seemed to have run out of things to say. Before Macey could think of a way to continue the conversation on its present course, Kimmy said, "I've always been curious about something, Macey."

Macey steadied her coffee cup on her knee. She tried not to avoid Kimmy's eyes. "Oh?"

"Yeah. You left so suddenly after graduation. *Before* graduation."

Macey swallowed and attempted a smile, thinking she probably just looked nervous and timid. "Yeah, well, you know. Couldn't wait to get out of this town." This was becoming a standard answer, and it was truer today than it had been back then.

Kimmy nodded but didn't seem to buy it. She leaned forward on her desk. "Is that the only reason you left like you did?"

Macey could feel her eyes blinking nervously, so she stirred her coffee for something to do. "Um . . . didn't you hear all the rumors about my flunking math?"

"I never believed that." She leaned back into her chair, swiveling from side to side. "You were way too smart."

Macey met Kimmy's eyes, which seemed genuinely compassionate and curious. "I wasn't as smart as people might have thought."

"It was Harley Preston, wasn't it?"

Just the mention of his name made her heart hitch with anxiety, and there was no hiding her reaction. For seventeen years she hadn't heard his name uttered. Until Sunday. Seeing his face again brought a feeling of dread like it had all just happened a day ago. Now, hearing it once more, the sting wasn't any less painful. Macey didn't know what to say. She didn't know what Kimmy knew. She stared into her coffee and pressed her lips together.

"That jerk! I knew it!"

Macey had to look up. Kimmy was staring at the ceiling and shaking her head. *Knew what?*

"I dated him, you know," Kimmy said, and Macey shook her head. She was too shocked to even carry her half of the conversation. "Yeah. Right after graduation. And he broke my heart. He strung me along, even talked marriage, and then dumped me as soon as he knew he had me." She set her coffee down and looked hard at Macey. "That's what happened, isn't it? He broke your heart and you had to leave."

Macey set her coffee down, too. Her hands were shaking almost uncontrollably. *No, Kimmy, that's not what happened. I wish that's what happened.*

"He was such a ladies' man. At least he thought so. Apparently he couldn't even hold his marriage together to Ellie White. You heard they got married, didn't you?"

Macey nodded.

"Yeah, well, he's back here, and she's still in KC with their kids." She smiled. "I'm glad now I didn't marry him. That's what I would've gotten to look forward to. Being a single mom." Kimmy picked up her coffee again. "How long did you date him again?"

Macey finally found her voice. "Just long enough to know he was trouble." It was hard to keep the lies straight. Had she told Diana just once?

Kimmy laughed. "If we knew then what we know now, right?"

There wasn't a truer statement.

Kimmy was just about to speak again when the office door opened and a small, attractive woman wearing a striking suit and her hair in a fancy French twist walked in. Kimmy stood and cleared her throat. "Ms. Cunningham."

"Hello, Kimberly." Her voice was deep and a little scratchy. The woman looked at Macey. "Do I have an appointment now?"

"Um, no. This is Macey Steigel. She's a friend of mine from high school. She was wondering if she could speak with you briefly about her mother."

"About her mother?" They were speaking as if Macey wasn't in the room, which was just fine with Macey. She was still trying to recover from the previous conversation.

"Yes. Her father died recently and she was hoping there might be a job here for her mother."

Ms. Cunningham's expression indicated that Kimberly might have overstepped her bounds by assuming she was going to help every hapless person who needed a job, but she was gracious enough to try to hide it with a polite smile as she turned to Macey. "I see. Well, I think I've got about five minutes. Can we discuss it in that amount of time?"

Macey stepped forward. "I'm all about schedules, Ms. Cunningham. I'll do it in four."

Ms. Cunningham's eyebrows raised in surprised satisfaction, and she invited Macey into her spacious office, nearly twice as big as Kimmy's. "Please, sit down." They both sat, and Ms. Cunningham arranged a few pieces of paper on her desk before giving Macey her full attention. "So, your mother needs a job."

"Desperately, I'm afraid," Macey said. "I live in Dallas and I'm unable to take care of her. I could help pay the bills for a couple of months or so, but then . . . Unfortunately, my father has left her with little resources, so my mom is going to have to find herself a job. I read your ad in the newspaper and thought you might have something for her here."

The woman smiled as she put on her glasses for no apparent reason. "I see. Am I to assume your mother has been out of the work force for quite some time?"

"Yes."

"All right. Well, we do have a plethora of job opportunities here. What kinds of things can your mother do?"

"I think she'd be terrific as a receptionist. She's very friendly and warm. I'm sure she's also capable of secretarial duties. She can definitely organize and file, things like that." Macey was relieved to see Ms. Cunningham jotting down some notes. "She's a quick learner," Macey added, though she might as well have said she'd been a corporate executive. It was about as truthful.

Ms. Cunningham continued to write, then peered at Macey over her glasses. "Fine. Let me ask you this—is your mother capable of handling a fax machine?"

"Yes."

"Can she use a word processor?"

"Yes."

"Is she savvy on the Internet?"

"Yes."

"What about spreadsheets? Or perhaps Web design?"

Macey had to draw the line somewhere. She answered light-heartedly, "Well, that might be a stretch."

Ms. Cunningham smiled and took off her glasses. "Ms. Steigel, I can certainly appreciate your circumstance. My mother was in al-most the same position several years ago before she died. I think it's wonderful that you're here helping her try to find a job."

"Thanks."

"But I am curious. Do you really think a place like AST is suit-able for your mother?"

Macey swallowed. Of course it wasn't. "As I said, we're desperate."

"I understand, but this is a corporate environment. Your mom is elderly, right? Obviously grieving. Out of the work force for years. Perhaps there's a better option. An in-home caregiver maybe, or nanny? Things of that nature, you understand."

"There's nothing available. I've combed the want ads."

"Sure, but must you find a solution today?"

"It's just that I need to return to Dallas tomorrow, and I won't be returning to Kansas anytime soon."

Ms. Cunningham's face expressed surprise. "Oh?"

"Yes, and I've got a job opportunity in New York. If I take it, it'll be hard to come home and help my mother with this. But if I knew she had a steady, dependable job, I would feel much better about it."

Ms. Cunningham resumed writing notes. "How long a drive would it be for your mother?"

"Twenty-five minutes."

"That's a long way for an elderly person."

"I know." Macey leaned forward and looked Ms. Cunningham in the eyes. "I know this isn't our best option. It's just that right now it's our only one."

"Okay. I can't promise you anything, but I'd be more than happy to give her an interview."

Macey breathed a sigh of relief. "Thank you."

Ms. Cunningham opened a calendar on her desk, then called for Kimmy to come in. "Kimberly, what's Friday look like?"

Kimmy emerged with a calendar in her hand. "You've got a twelve-thirty, a two o'clock, and a three."

Ms. Cunningham thumbed through her calendar as she said, "Our appointments have been booking up quickly. I must be frank with you—a lot of people are interested in positions here."

"I understand," Macey said, but her mind was plagued with anxiety again. *Friday?* She was leaving tomorrow! How was she going to get her mother ready by tomorrow for an interview on Friday?

"Yes, Friday will have to do. Next week is filled with meetings, and then I'll be in Japan starting Wednesday, right, Kimberly?"

"Yes, ma'am. Your flight leaves at one."

Ms. Cunningham looked at Macey. "How about Friday, then, at one o'clock? What's your mother's name?"

Macey could hardly speak yet did manage to agree to the time and say her mother's name. The two women shook hands, and Macey said good-bye to Kimmy, promising to keep in touch, which they both knew was a lie. She took the elevator down and walked through the impressive lobby again. As the doors slid open, Macey Steigel thought that if she smoked, this would be a very good time for a cigarette.

* * *

"Goodness' sakes. Here, take this," Patricia said, and Evelyn took a tissue from her and dabbed her eyes. "I'm so sorry I haven't been here for you. Old Man Norton has been in terrible shape and takin' up all my time." She wrapped a strong arm around Evelyn's shoulder. They'd started the morning canning peaches, but Evelyn's emotions had gotten the best of her.

"Macey's being here has been so wonderful," Evelyn said as she tried to control her sobbing. "I can't tell you what it's like to have her home again." Tears welled up in her eyes when she said, "But she'll be leaving again."

Patricia moved a few inches away from Evelyn on the couch and patted her knee. "She'll be back. She seems like a sweet girl. Sensitive."

Evelyn nodded. "Oh, she is, she is. She turned out to be just delightful." Evelyn clasped her hands together between her knees. "No thanks to me."

She felt Patricia's worried eyes study her. "What are you talkin' about?"

"I've practically missed her whole life. Seventeen years, Patricia, gone, never to be seen again. I'd prayed long and hard that God would reconcile Jess and Macey before he died, but He didn't. I just wish Macey could understand everything."

Patricia handed Evelyn another tissue. She'd torn the first one to shreds. "Evelyn, I don't like to be pryin' into other people's lives, but I noticed that you and Jess never talked about Macey much, and certainly never talked about why it was she left. Or why it was she never came home."

Evelyn glanced at Patricia and began tearing the corners off her tissue again. Her chest shook in a spasm as more sobs were released. Patricia patted her on the back like she was trying to burp a baby. "I tried once to talk to Jess about it, but he wouldn't hear of it. And not for the reasons people might think."

"Well, honey, no one knows what to think. You two seemed not to want to talk about it, so we just never did." Patricia reached for Evelyn's ratty tissue. "Dear, you're gonna need to give this to me. You're making a mess."

Evelyn stared down at the tiny white pieces of tissue that lay in a pile at her feet. "I've made a mess outta more than just this tissue, Patricia. Now I don't know how to fix it. I don't know what to say."

Patricia knelt down by Evelyn and began cleaning up the mess. "You know, I took care of Jess for a long time, and although he never spoke of Macey, I think she was always on his mind and that he always did love her."

More sobs escaped, and Evelyn grabbed for another tissue from the box on the table. "He did, he did," she said. "He loved her more than he could say. It broke his heart the day she left. Maybe that's why he couldn't . . . wouldn't ever talk about it." The tears finally subsided a little, and Evelyn stared at her tissue, willing herself not to tear at it.

Patricia finally stood and dumped the old tissues in the nearby trash can. Her hands were placed confidently on her hips as she said, "Evelyn, I think you know what it is you need to do. Now, I don't know what that is, because I don't know the particulars or the history of all this mess. But you do and you got God on your side, so I'm suggestin' that you get down on those old knees of yours and receive that mighty power the Reverend's always mentionin' in his sermons."

Evelyn shook her head and stared at her feet. "I tried to this morning. I tried to say something, but then she gives me this look. It's sort of a mean look. Then I get all tongue-tied and can't even remember my own name. I'm guessing it's because I don't want her getting mad and stomping out that door, never to be seen again."

"You probably feel like you're walkin' on eggs. But leavin' things undone ain't in nobody's best interest. I see people die all the time. It's just a part of what I do. And once you're gone, you can't come back and do things over." Patricia's face was tense and serious. "Sure, Jess is gone now. But you're not. You're alive and well and still breathin', my friend. So as I see it, you got two options. You can let your daughter leave and pretend that all is well, or you can face your fears and talk to her about it."

A sudden surge of confidence entered Evelyn, and she sat up a little straighter and took in a deep, refreshing breath. She went back to the kitchen with the intention of finishing the canning, thinking hard about what Patricia had said. It was the truth and she knew it. For seventeen years she'd stood by her husband's side while battling her own moral dilemma. She'd watched him grieve in his own silent way and hoped for something that would never happen. Now here she was with the ability to change some things, to make a difference. A real difference. Like never before.

Yes. She would do it, even if it meant she'd be shaking in her boots. God was calling her to be bold. How could she fail Him now?

The back door creaked open, and suddenly her daughter was standing in the kitchen, looking tired and hot. Macey glanced at Patricia, who was cleaning something on the counter. "Hi, Patricia."

"Hi there, Macey."

Evelyn carefully removed a sealed jar from the pan of water. "How'd it go?"

"Well, Mom, let me ask you this. Can you tell me what the *e* stands for in e-mail?"

Evelyn didn't even know what an e-mail was, but she knew that whatever it was, she was going to have to know it. At that moment, though, she couldn't imagine what the *e* stood for and didn't even know enough to guess. So she simply stood at the kitchen counter, holding the tongs she used to handle the hot jars.

Her daughter ran her fingers through her hair, looked at her watch, and said, "We've got exactly fourteen hours to teach you about the modern world, Mother. Finish up the canning. It's time to get serious."

All the boldness in the world wasn't enough now. Her daughter had an agenda, and the way her brow lay straight across her face, perfectly horizontal with her tightened lips, Evelyn knew better than to try to distract her with what she wanted to say. She glanced at Patricia, whose eyes told her it would all somehow work out.

Evelyn attempted a smile but all that happened was her chin quivered. So she did the only thing she knew to do at that moment. She went to start a fresh pot of coffee.

Eighteen

It looked like a typewriter, and Evelyn had typed a few things in her life. It had been a while, but she imagined it was like riding a bike, and that it would all come back to her. When she thought about it, this was a poor example because she'd never ridden a bike, not even when a little girl. She'd always had a poor sense of balance.

Macey pushed a green button on what she called the keyboard, and a beep sounded, followed by some colorful pictures and words flashing on the screen. Evelyn said, "I didn't catch that. It's all going too fast."

Macey smiled and patted her on the back. "That isn't important. It's just stuff that shows up when you boot the computer." She glanced at her mom. "That means turn the computer on."

An image of a mountain at sunset came on and stayed for a couple of seconds. "That's a beautiful picture," Evelyn said.

"That's just wallpaper, not anything you need to know about right now."

Evelyn frowned. Was it the wallpaper in Macey's house? It didn't look like any wallpaper she'd ever seen before, but then no one accused Evelyn of being very modern. Maybe people were plastering pictures of mountains on their walls these days.

"Now," Macey said, pointing to some little pictures on the left side of the screen. "These are called icons. They're pictures that represent each program."

Evelyn nodded but was already lost. Program like was on the tube? Like *I Love Lucy*? That didn't make sense.

Macey looked at her again and said, "A program is like a function. For example, this program"—she pointed to an icon—"is a word processor. That's one program that we're going to need to learn about. A word processor is basically a fancy way to type letters and things like that." She took a breath and added, "It's like a piece of paper in a typewriter."

"Okay," Evelyn said. Her head hurt trying to take it all in.

"Now, this thing," she said, pointing to a small square on the side of the keyboard, "is called a mouse. It's a long story as to why it's called a mouse, and we won't get into it now, but basically it helps you move this"—Macey showed her the arrow on the screen—"around the computer and choose which item you want to click on."

Click on? What did that mean?

"You see, you can't just touch the screen to choose something. You have to move your finger on this pad and make the cursor move." Macey placed her index finger on the pad, and suddenly the little arrow darted all over the screen. "See? It takes a little hand-eye coordination, but you'll get the hang of it."

Evelyn's eyes were wide with wonder. How could something move that you weren't actually touching?

Macey said, "It's sort of like a steering wheel. You move the steering wheel on your car, right? But you can't actually see it moving the wheels, yet there's a reaction when you do it."

Evelyn smiled at her daughter. "I think you just read my mind."

"Good. Let's keep going."

Evelyn watched as Macey moved the little arrow around, which somehow made an almost white screen come up with little letters and pictures at the top. She called it a word processor or an electronic piece of paper.

Macey demonstrated how you typed the letters for them to appear on the piece of paper. She then pointed out a small machine next to the computer, attached to it with a cord. "This is the printer. This one is small because I carry it with me. It can also be used as a fax machine, which I'll teach you about later on. But see, I type words on the paper, then hit Print, and it will come out through the printer."

A few seconds accompanied by a series of beeps somehow made a piece of paper slide out of the machine with the very thing Macey had typed on it.

"That's awfully fancy," said Evelyn, staring at the piece of paper. "This is what everyone's using these days, is it?"

"Yes. You're doing yourself good by learning this, you know, Mom."

Evelyn smiled. Whatever it took to make her daughter happy.

Macey continued to show her how to open and close the paper on the screen and then the word processor program, all by pointing the little arrow to the tiny X on the top right part of the screen. Evelyn felt like she was comprehending the general idea up to this point, until Macey began discussing how to save her work.

"Once you've typed a letter, instead of filing it like you would if it were a real piece of paper, you do what's called saving it onto disk."

Evelyn swallowed. She felt like she was in a foreign country. And the house seemed to be getting warmer by the second.

"For practical purposes, the disk is basically the inside of the computer," Macey said as she studied Evelyn.

Evelyn stared at the screen. "So the piece of paper goes down into the computer?"

Macey chuckled. "Well, not really, though in a way it does. It remembers what you typed and then stores it away in its memory until you need it again."

"How much paper does it hold? It looks pretty small to me."

She could hear Macey sigh in her ear. "Mother, it doesn't hold actual pieces of paper. It just pretends to. It stores data." Macey rubbed her forehead. "It's kind of like a camera. It takes pictures of what you write. You don't actually have to understand how it works as long as you know how to work it, okay, Mom?"

Evelyn nodded. Good thing.

———•◆•———

Macey tried not to pace, but it was impossible. She stopped and looked at her watch. The ticking of the second hand practically resonated off the walls. It had been an hour and a half, and her mother still hadn't printed out the simple letter Macey had asked her to write. It had taken thirty-five minutes to show her mother how to backspace and correct an error. Then it had taken another ten minutes to explain how to use the arrow keys to move to a word without erasing it. Another five minutes was used up to explain the Insert and Delete keys, and forty-five minutes later she was still working on saving the document.

Macey peered over her mother's shoulder. "Mom, remember? You have to click on that little folder and make it open before you can save into that folder."

She watched as her mother's hands formed tight balls. "This is too hard."

"No, it's not," Macey said, scooting beside her mother. "It makes sense if you'll stop and think about it. If you were filing away a piece of paper normally, you would have to open the folder first. Same thing. Open the folder, then insert the piece of paper."

She watched her mother fumble with the mouse and then click on another set of folders accidentally. Macey once again had to back her out and start the process over.

"*This* folder, Mom. The one that says Temporary."

"I just can't get that little arrow to go where I want!" Her mother's voice was strained.

"Okay, listen, let's back off this for a moment, okay? Maybe stepping away from it will help."

Evelyn's hands dropped to her sides, and she leaned back into her chair. "Okay."

"Great. Now," she said, moving the computer in front of her, "I want to show you how most people communicate these days. Remember when I told you about e-mail?" Her mother's eyes looked glassy, but she nodded. "Well, the *e* stands for electronic. It works just like mail as far as going to different mailboxes. What's great about it is that it gets sent instantly and can go to anyone who has e-mail capability all over the world and in just seconds." Her mother was nodding and looking at her, yet Macey wasn't at all sure she was getting it. Macey checked her watch. It was almost four. "Let me give you an example." Macey stood and plugged the computer into the phone jack in the kitchen. "E-mail uses phone lines to transmit the data, just as if you were talking on the phone with someone, except you're sending information, not your voice." She typed her password and connected to the Internet, then opened Outlook Express, noting that she had received twenty-five new messages. Macey clicked on New Mail and typed in Bethie's name. "I'm going to send my assistant a message, and if she's at her desk, she'll send me one back. Watch carefully."

Macey typed a short message to Bethie and then clicked Send. She watched her mom's eyes try to take it all in. "Now it's traveling over the phone lines, and if Bethie's there, we'll get a reply message from her."

Less than a minute later, her computer beeped that she had a new e-mail. Sure enough, Bethie was at her desk. Macey opened the e-mail and quickly read it.

Macey, what are you doing? Mitchell is so mad! I've never seen him this mad. I think he's having a nervous breakdown or something. When are you coming back? Is New York still on? Was I supposed to decipher some coded message or something from that e-mail? Are you really just e-mailing me to say hi?

Evelyn was squinting as she read the text. She looked at Macey. "Who's Mitchell?"

Macey was typing and talking at the same time. "My boss."

"Sounds like he's pretty mad at you."

"He'll get over it." Macey pressed Send and waited for Bethie to reply, which she did instantly.

No, Alexis isn't permanent, although Mitchell might be leading you to think so. All he does is gripe about her all day long. The Senator Brandt story is huge right now. I can't believe you're missing it.

Macey tried to be sensitive to her mother's prying eyes as she typed out another e-mail to Bethie. *I know. Keep me updated. And keep your cell on you. Bye.* She clicked Send and turned to her mom. "That's e-mail. It's a very quick way to communicate with other people."

Evelyn frowned. "If you're using the phone line, why wouldn't you just pick up the phone and call her?"

Macey gave a half smile. Good question. "Because in this day and age, Mom, people are very busy and they don't have time for a lot of cordial chitchat and formalities. This way, you can send info and ask questions without having to commit to actually talking face to face, or voice to voice, with another human being. That can be quite time consuming."

Her mother's expression indicated that this had to be the most bizarre thing she'd ever heard. How could her mother possibly understand the pace of life outside this little farm community? How could she understand that people didn't want human closeness; they wanted information, and fast.

"Anyway," Macey said, "that's how you e-mail. It uses a lot of the same principles as word processing. We'll go over it more thoroughly later."

Her mother was staring into space like a zombie, and Macey realized how overwhelming this must be for her. Still, she couldn't let that distract her. This was her mother's only hope—a job at AST.

She thought for a moment about what might motivate her mother to concentrate and learn how to save a document. A smile spread across Macey's face, and she looked at her mother. "So, Mom, tell you what. As soon as you can save your document into that folder, I'll let you fix me a good old-fashioned home-cooked dinner."

Macey watched her mother's face light up and her eyes steady on the screen.

Country-fried steak drenched in thick white gravy was the home-cooked dinner Evelyn chose, and Macey had to admit that it was delicious. No one prepared country-fried steak like her mom. Sweet corn on the cob, lumpy mashed potatoes, and freshly baked muffins completed the meal. Macey could hardly eat fast enough. She couldn't remember the last time she had been this hungry.

"Does it taste okay?" her mother asked as she refilled the mashed potato bowl. Macey nodded and kept eating. There was something oddly soothing about this kind of meal. Just thirty minutes ago her nerves had been shot. Her mother had finally saved the file in the correct folder but in exiting the program had somehow deleted another file, a story Macey had been gathering notes on for about a month.

Macey stopped eating long enough to look at her watch. "It's 6:36. After dinner we'll take a few hours to get you familiar with faxing documents and also maneuvering around the computer without deleting everything on the hard drive."

Evelyn smiled uneasily at Macey while she buttered her corn. "I'm not catching on to this as quickly as you had hoped, am I?"

"It's not that," Macey lied. "I know all this is overwhelming to you. You're just going to have to concentrate, think on a different level." Macey set down her knife and leaned forward. "Mom, I mean, you realize that the whole world is connected by computers now, don't you? Everyone I know has a computer or works on a computer. You understand how vital it is that you're educated in this."

"Pass the salt, will you, dear?" Evelyn asked, and Macey handed it to her. "I suppose I am living in the dark ages here, aren't I?"

"A little."

"Well, if you think I need that job over at that AST, then by golly I'll try my best to get it." She smiled at Macey. "Don't let me forget I've got to gather the eggs tonight. I forgot to do it yesterday."

Macey nibbled at her corn as she wondered if there was any possible way her mother was going to learn everything she needed to this evening. The more she thought, the harder she nibbled, until soon all that was left was an empty cob.

Macey's plate was clean, and Evelyn was finishing up her portion. A mound of food still covered the table as Macey stood and began clearing the dishes.

"Dear, aren't you going to have another serving? Look at all this food I cooked!"

"Mom, we don't have time for second servings tonight. We've got too much to do. You still have to learn how to navigate the Internet, run a copier, and fax a document, and I probably need to at least introduce you to a phone system that has more than one line." She glanced up at her mother's rotary phone on the wall. "And explain push-button phones to you."

Evelyn set down her fork and knife and blinked at her plate. She looked sad, and Macey wondered if she'd hurt her mother's feelings. She wasn't trying to imply her mother was stupid; she was just behind the times. Macey approached the table. "Mom, I'm sorry. Are you okay?"

Evelyn's eyes glistened with tears and she continued to stare down at the table. "I'm disappointing you."

"No, no, Mom, not at all," Macey said, sitting in the chair next to Evelyn. "Am I giving you that impression? I'm sorry. You're not disappointing me. We've just got a lot to learn in a little bit of time. I leave tomorrow morning, and I have to teach you all this before I go. Your interview is Friday."

Evelyn looked up at Macey and shook her head, wiping the tears away. "Well, back in my day, interviews had to do with showing commitment and honesty. The people wanted to know if you'd work hard and be loyal to the company. If so, then they'd train you to do what it was they needed you to do. I'm honest and hardworking. I'm a loyal person—doesn't that count for something?"

Macey felt a sting in her own eyes. How was her mom going to make it in this world without her father? The lump grew in her throat the more she thought about it. Leaving her mother to fend for herself in the corporate world was similar to dropping off a toddler on the side of the street and hoping he had enough sense not to step into traffic. Yet there was wisdom in what her mother had just said, and Macey had to admit she wished things were that way today. Macey drew in a deep breath to steady herself. There didn't need to be two women carrying on at the same table.

"It counts for a lot," Macey managed, though her voice quivered a bit. "And I know you have all those qualities, Mom. They're good qualities. But in this day and age you have to know more. It's just the way it is."

Evelyn nodded, then said, "I guess I'll help you with the dishes."

———◆◆———

Macey had insisted that Evelyn let her do the dishes while she practiced faxing. Evelyn would have much rather done the dishes, but regardless she sat in front of the little computer and practiced using the mouse. Macey had explained that it was actually called a touch pad but that she still called it a mouse out of habit. At any rate, it took a delicate finger, that was for sure, and Evelyn tapped into some of her sewing skills in order to keep her finger steady and the pressure constant.

An hour later Macey had finished the dishes and brought Evelyn a fresh cup of coffee. "You'll be needing this," she said with a small grin. Evelyn loved to see her smile.

"Thank you. Well, I think I have this mouse thing down."

Macey pulled up a chair next to her and leaned on the table, supporting her chin with both hands. "Really? Let me see."

Evelyn maneuvered around the screen with the little arrow, clicking on different pictures and then closing them by clicking on the X. She turned to Macey. "What do you think?"

Her daughter's face was soft with surprise. "Mother! That's terrific. You have been concentrating!" Macey clasped her hands together and with excitement said, "Okay, now, let's review. I want you to type out your name on a document in the word processor, save it in the temporary folder, and print it out."

Evelyn sipped her coffee and couldn't contain her smile. She'd made her daughter proud. She looked at the computer screen and sat up tall. She could do this.

Thirty-five minutes later Evelyn still hadn't saved and printed the document as her daughter had instructed. Her eyes were becoming bleary, and her heart was heavy with disappointment. Why couldn't she understand this? Her daughter had shown her several times, yet she just couldn't remember all the little buttons to push. It was a sequence, and her memory wasn't so good these days.

She was starting over for the tenth time when it dawned on her that Macey was no longer in the room. But as she listened, she could hear her voice coming from upstairs.

"What took you so long to answer the phone? . . . Yes, I'm on edge . . . I know, I know, I read your e-mail . . . I was trying to show my mom, okay, never mind, it's not important. What *is* important is that I need you to rebook my flight . . . from here to New York. . . . Yeah, you've got the details from Thornton Winslow's office, don't you? . . . Just make sure I'm scheduled to be there in plenty of time. I'd prefer to fly out Wednesday night, but I can leave Thursday morning if I need to. . . . Okay, fine . . . Yeah, and just try to settle Mitchell down; he's making me nervous. . . . Okay, bye."

A thumping sound came from the stairs, and Macey emerged at the bottom, her face tired and strained. Evelyn kept her fingers on the keys like she'd been typing away. "Is everything okay, honey?"

Macey shuffled over to the table, swatting hair out of her eyes. "Yes. Why?"

"You just seem a bit tense. I heard you . . . um . . . talking to someone upstairs."

Macey sat down at the table and looked at the computer. "Did you get the file saved yet?"

Evelyn shook her head and hunched her shoulders in guilt. "No. Not yet."

"Okay," said Macey, rubbing her temples, "maybe we need to take a break from this and work on something else."

"There's more?"

Her daughter's eyes cut sideways to look at her. "Yes, Mother. There's more. There's a lot more. I've got to convince Ms. Cunningham at AST that you're qualified for a job that you're in no way qualified for." Her face reddened as she spoke. "I just can't believe . . ."

"What?"

Macey finally turned and looked squarely at Evelyn. "I can't believe Dad left you in this predicament. I just can't believe it."

Evelyn had no idea what to say. She hardly knew she was in a predicament until Macey pointed it out. They'd had a lot of financial problems since the drought, and then there were the doctor's bills. She'd never looked too far into the future. She knew if she did, she would see herself lonely and afraid. So she had just lived day to day, cherishing every last moment she had with Jess. And Jess had been so sure God would heal him. . . .

The dull look in her daughter's eyes told her that this was a serious situation, though, and that everything depended on her getting this job. She looked back at the screen and jutted her chin forward. She could do this. She *had* to do this. The words blurred now. It seemed like she'd been reading small print all day.

Evelyn felt her daughter's hand on her shoulder. She looked up into Macey's face.

"Mom, let's take a break and move on to something else for now. I know you're really trying hard."

Nineteen

The two hands of her watch formed a perfect right angle. It was nine o'clock. Macey twisted the band back and forth on her wrist as if trying to slow time down. An impossibility in their circumstance. If anything, time was speeding up.

Macey sat on the edge of her bed, the door to her room open enough so she could hear activity downstairs. She strained to hear the sound of the printer rolling the paper up or at least queuing a document. But there were no such sounds. Only her mother humming yet another refrain of "I Surrender All." It was a sweet melody, even with her mother's off-key rendition. It did nothing, however, to keep her muscles from knotting up, or her head from throbbing, or her hands from trembling.

Her fingers massaged her temples, and then her hands slid down her face and fell into her lap. A dry sting plagued both her eyes, so she closed them and fell backward onto her bed, plunging into the softness of the comforter as though it were a pool of water. She stretched her arms over her head and stared at the ceiling.

What am I going to do?

Above her mother's humming she could hear the soft tapping of the keyboard. At least she was doing *something* down there. They still hadn't covered the fax machine or how to use a copier or telephone system or voice mail. The list was endless and so was the hard, fast beat of her anxious heart.

Her fingers mindlessly tore through her hair as she tried to think of some other option, some other way she could help her mother. Admittedly AST was a bad idea. But everything was a bad idea at this point. At dinner her mother had suggested they pray about it, and Macey lowered her head while her mother blessed the food and asked for God's provision in the situation. But she hadn't been praying; she'd been thinking instead. She was still thinking. But nothing was happening. No solution came to mind.

She'd come upstairs for a break. She knew her mother needed one, too. Macey had been standing over her shoulder for hours, barking orders and repeating instructions. For a woman whose life consisted of cooking, cleaning, and church socials, this was probably more than she could take. And it didn't help that she'd buried her husband just a few days ago. Even if her mom got the job, could she really maintain the eight-to-five lifestyle required, all the driving? Just being there for thirty minutes, Macey had picked up on the pace of the office setting. It would run her mother over. One anxious thought pushed a previous one out of her mind, and each time the new one showed up much quicker. It was a freight train of fear building up speed.

She didn't know if leaving her mother alone with the computer was a good idea. She'd already erased one file. But maybe if she just had some time alone to mess around with it, see that it wasn't going to bite her, maybe she'd have a breakthrough or something.

Macey kicked her shoes off and stretched her legs. As she grabbed her ankles and rolled herself up to a sitting position, something suddenly caught her eye. It was her other closet, the storage closet. Macey slid off the bed and walked toward it, wondering what was in there.

She passed by the bedroom door, and her mother's humming and typing could still be heard downstairs but with no sound of the printer working. A sigh released as she moved closer to the storage closet door. She reached for the gold doorknob and then hesitated. What was she afraid of? It wasn't like a skeleton was going to fall out.

She had to grip the doorknob hard and turn it steadily before the door opened. It creaked with each inch it moved. With one hefty yank, she pulled it open and stared into a dark, gaping hole. She walked in and waved her hand in the air looking for the string. Where was that silly thing? She finally found it and the light bulb popped on, revealing many neatly stacked boxes on the floor and lining the shelves. Macey leaned against the doorframe and thought, *The first eighteen years of my life, boxed up and tucked away in the dark.*

Just the way she wanted it.

———◆———

An odd feeling of angst accompanied every movement to open each box. Then that feeling would attempt to mix with the warm memories evoked with the items she pulled from the boxes.

She found her old tap shoes from seventh grade when she thought her whole life revolved around dancing. And the mittens that her aunt Barb had knitted for her the winter of the Blizzard of '77. One box was filled with her old baby dolls, and as she sorted through them, she was surprised she remembered each of their names. The light-skinned, dirty-faced brunette with uneven bangs she had named Amber. When she'd tried to give the same treatment to her own bangs, her parents were forced to hide all the scissors in the house. Some of the dolls were clothed with outfits her mom had taken great care to sew, while others were half naked with missing limbs. Staring into their lifeless faces, their plastic eyes, their permanent smiles brought back the innocence of her childhood, a time when she understood so little and enjoyed so much.

Another box was filled with her old school papers. Poems about summer and dogs and watermelon, imagined stories of fairies and dragons, and even some particularly impressive crayon drawings.

Everything had been neatly stacked and sorted by age. It must've taken her mother weeks to do all this.

She studied her handwriting, block letters turning into bubbly cursive and then slanting and flowing, the curves less defined yet more elegant. From her first attempt at the alphabet to her last paper written on the rights of women in the workplace, each paper defined Macey in a way she hadn't acknowledged in years. She'd been a little girl with a love for life, an adolescent with an insatiable curiosity, and a young woman with a perspective on life that would eventually lead to her untimely exit from home.

A box high on the shelf tumbled into her hands when she grabbed for its bottom. She steadied it, lowering it carefully to the floor. Its weight had shifted unpredictably, and inside she found a disheveled group of framed pictures.

The top one had a gold frame, tarnished and muted with dust. She took the edge of her shirt and wiped at the glass, revealing a black-and-white photo underneath. There, in the tiny dimly lit closet, she stared back into the eyes of her father. The picture was taken less than a month before she had left.

She stood taller than her father, only because she was standing on a log, but the picture didn't reveal that. She had her arm around his shoulder, and their heads leaned in toward each other. It was clear from this picture whose smile she had.

Macey fought back tears and set the picture down. The next picture, just as dusty and missing the glass, was of the family on their one and only vacation. They had gone to the Ozarks. Each picture froze a tale in time; each told a story from her past.

The pictures were beautiful, depicting much happier times. Maybe these were more painful than the bad memories, because it was everything that she'd lost. The darkest moments of her life spanned only a week, while all the good times, all the love and laughter and joy, had occupied a large part of her life, only to be overshadowed by one mistake—one horrible mistake.

At the bottom of the box of pictures, Macey's hand touched something soft and leathery. A book. Her hand picked up a dark leather-bound Bible, of medium size and well worn. Macey laid it on the carpet in front of her and stared at it. It had been the Bible her father had given to her on her sweet sixteen, one of only two Bibles she'd ever owned. She carefully opened it to the first page. In black ink a handwritten message read, *To Macille, my dear daughter, may God bless your life and all that you do. With love, Daddy.* But she didn't need to read it. She already knew what it said.

She let go of the cover and it closed by itself. A few pages looked to be falling out, and she wanted to tuck them back in, but she didn't dare touch it again. It was as if it held a power over her. In one intense moment it seemed every Sunday school lesson, every sermon, every word ever spoken by God in the pages of the Book roared in her ear by way of the most deafening silence. Her hands covered her ears, and she squeezed her eyes shut. It silenced all the voices but one—her father's.

"Macey, I want you to listen to me. Are you listening to me, sweet angel?"

"Yes, Daddy."

"I bought this for you, just for today, your sixteenth birthday. This is a very special day for you."

"Yes, Daddy."

"I prayed today that God would always take care of you, and that you would always be in His hands. I also prayed that you would forever know right from wrong, and that you would always choose the right way, God's way. There will be nothing more important in your life, Macey. Follow God. Promise me you'll always follow God. And read this. So that you'll always hold His Word close to your heart."

"Yes, Daddy."

Macey's eyes flew open, and her chest heaved as she tried to catch her breath. She needed a drink of water but wasn't sure if she could stand.

"Get a hold of yourself," she said aloud, startling herself with her own voice. It was good to hear she still had it and that the other voices were gone now. She grabbed the edge of the doorframe and went to pull herself to her feet. After three tries she was standing, though her knees felt weak. She reached up for the string to switch off the light when she saw one final box, sitting back in the corner of the highest shelf. It looked like a shirt box, white and a little flimsy.

She paused, wondering what could be in it. She hesitated twice before finally reaching all the way back, gripping the box, and pulling it down. She took the box to her bed and set it on top of the comforter. It was extremely light, and for a moment she thought maybe there was nothing in it. But when she opened the box, she found a tiny piece of clothing—white, silky, and . . .

Macey dropped it, gasped, and stumbled backward. Her hand covered her mouth, and her eyes widened with each second she looked at it. She didn't know how long she stood there, several feet from her bed, staring at it, but finally she stepped forward and gently picked it up, as gently as she would a newborn baby.

Because lying in her hands, draped over her fingers, was a baby's baptismal gown. She held it out from her body, afraid of even holding it, and then carefully put it back into the box and closed the lid. A baby's baptism outfit? It wasn't hers. Her mother had made hers for her dedication, and it had burned in a fire a few years after she was born.

She rubbed her eyes, which burned from dust and exhaustion. Every time she blinked, they stayed closed a little longer. Overwhelming fatigue pulled her shoulders forward and hunched her back. Her feet felt like lead, and she wasn't sure if she could move.

She managed to lift her wrist close to her eyes and read the time. *Eleven-thirty!* How could it be eleven-thirty? She snapped out of the daze she was in and turned toward the door. Where was her mom? Was she still downstairs?

Macey rushed down the stairs, stopping at the bottom where she saw her mom still sitting at the table, asleep now. Evelyn sat straight up with her head tilted back, her mouth gaping open as she snored. Her hands rested on the computer's keyboard.

The night suffocated Macey. The ceiling fan whirred around as fast as it could, but she was still sweating, throwing her covers off, kicking at the end of the bed, tossing and turning, her mind screaming at all the voices screaming back at her.

Maybe she had stopped breathing. She awoke sitting up, breathless, panting and disoriented. It had been one nightmare after another, yet her exhausted body insisted on sleep. Her tortured soul, however, wanted anything but to be at the mercy of a mind that held so many dark secrets.

The T-shirt she wore was drenched, and her eyes were swollen slits. She swung her legs to the side of the bed. The air was hard to breathe. She rose and walked to the window. With weak arms she slid open the window and stuck her head outside. The night, though sticky with humidity, opened her lungs a little more. After catching her breath, she stood at the window and stared up at the stars. There wasn't a night sky like the one that could be seen from this Kansas farm.

She almost went to get her watch off the nightstand to see what time it was, but then decided it was useless. It didn't matter what time it was. The sky was still dark, the night still at hand. Whether it was two or three or five—it didn't matter. It was dark. And with darkness came the vulnerability, and with the vulnerability came the evil.

So, standing at the window, Macey tried counting the stars. If the house had been a mile and a half up the road, she could've counted Mr. Harmon's sheep. But on a night like this, there would be enough stars for her to count in a lifetime.

Her lifetime, however, wouldn't last long enough to rid her soul of all that darkened it.

Twenty

S he didn't remember going back to sleep, but summer's morning light was flooding the window when Macey was yanked out of bed by the shrill tone of her cell phone ringing. She fumbled around and finally found it sitting on the nightstand.

"Hello?"

"Macey, it's Beth."

Macey sat up in bed. Her eyes were so swollen, she could barely open them. "Bethie . . . hi. What time is it?"

"A little before seven. You're up, aren't you?"

"Yeah, yeah. What's going on?"

"I couldn't get you a flight out tonight, so it'll have to be Thursday morning, at 11:04, American Airlines. You'll make one stop in St. Louis, we'll pray you don't have a delay, and that gives you an hour to spare before your meeting."

"An hour?" The room blurred as Macey tried to pry open her eyes.

"Look, it's the best I could do. Everything else put you in New York two hours too late."

Macey sighed. "Fine. Thanks. How's Mitchell?"

"Hating Alexis more every day. I swear that woman doesn't have any business being in front of a camera other than her high cheekbones and perfectly white smile. I really should find out which dentist she uses."

"So he's cool with me?"

"I wouldn't say that," Beth confessed. *"He won't even speak your name. Maybe that's a good thing, I don't know."*

"Work on him, Bethie. Please. If I don't get the network, I'll need a job to come back to, know what I mean?"

"I'm working it, I'm working it. But he feels betrayed."

Macey fell back into her pillow and rubbed at her eyes. "How can he feel betrayed? He told me to take all the time I needed for family, and now that I am, he's freaking out."

"True, only you told him you'd be back, and I guess he took that to heart, especially when this story broke. He counts on you more than you know."

Macey was finally able to focus on an image in the room without it being blurry. "Okay. Just tell him I'm horrified, calling you all the time, crying . . . yeah, tell him I've been crying."

"Is that true—have you been crying?"

Macey paused. "Yes. And I'm completely stressed out."

"You must be. I've never seen you cry."

"Just send me the ticket info by e-mail, all right?"

"Gotcha. I'll talk to you soon."

Macey ended the call and lay in bed another ten minutes before heading for the shower. She let the hot water run out before finishing. She dried off, got dressed, and headed downstairs. Not surprisingly, her mother was already up and preparing breakfast.

"Good morning!" her mother exclaimed.

"Good morning," Macey replied, though making a poor attempt to sound as jovial. "What are you fixing?"

"Homemade waffles." Her mother grinned and then went back to mixing the batter. "How'd you sleep?"

Macey took a seat at the breakfast table. "Fine."

"Good, good. Well, my neck's a little stiff from falling asleep at the table. I reckon that shows my age, doesn't it?" She chuckled. "Thanks for waking me and getting me upstairs."

"You're welcome."

Evelyn poured the batter onto the waffle iron, then closed it and joined Macey at the table. "I have good news for you."

Though tired, Macey couldn't help but raise her eyebrows in anticipation. "No kidding?"

Evelyn moved around the table to the computer. She opened it, pressed the button to turn it on, and smiled over the screen at Macey.

Macey laughed a little. "You can turn the computer on by yourself?"

"Honey, you ain't seen nothin' yet."

Macey stood and walked around the table to stand behind her mom. She watched her open a document, type a few sentences, give the document a name and save it, and then hit the Print button.

A couple of seconds later the paper slid out of the printer, and Evelyn cried, "Ta-dah!"

Macey's face glowed with pride. She hugged her mom from behind. "Mother! I can't believe this! This is so amazing!" She read the paper. It was the first part of her mother's blackberry cobbler recipe.

Evelyn beamed. "I know. I can hardly believe it myself. The first time I did it, I thought I was seeing things. I got up early this morning to make sure I didn't forget how to do it."

Macey clapped and sat back down at the table. She was suddenly hungry and feasted on the fresh honeydew melon her mother had prepared. "We have a lot more to cover today. I hope you're up for it."

Evelyn nodded and grinned as she removed the waffle from the griddle. "I feel as if I could conquer the world."

Over warm waffles and savory maple and pecan syrup, Macey and Evelyn discussed other requirements of a corporate job. Macey explained the atmosphere in which Evelyn would be working, letting her know about corporate politics, backbiting, and the everyday pressure of making a huge corporation run smoothly.

Evelyn nodded and ate, nodded and ate, smiled and nodded, until Macey realized that although she was listening, she wasn't really hearing her.

After clearing the breakfast dishes, Macey promised to let her mom go out and gather eggs before they started more training. She followed Evelyn out to the chicken coop and stood by while she gathered eggs in a basket, but then felt herself drawn to the sound of the river. She walked over to the bank, several feet above the river. It was low but clear and moving steadily. The air felt cleaner, fresher down by the river. She stood amused by the way the light glinted off the surface and fascinated by the small patches of fog that rested just above the foam where logs and rocks diverted the current.

She soon found herself gazing in the direction of Noah's house. The wood was set aglow by the rising sun, and a long shadow spilled across the green grass west of his house. She had an urge to go see him, but she knew she had too much to do today. She walked back to the chicken coop.

"Mother? Are you about finished?"

Evelyn emerged with a basketful of eggs. "Gathered a dozen today. Enough for a quiche." She walked up next to Macey, and they headed to the back door of the house. "You're staying for dinner tonight, aren't you?"

"Of course," Macey said as she opened the back door for her.

———◆◆◆———

Evelyn was trying hard to concentrate, but her mind kept wandering. As her daughter worked on teaching her how to fax a document, Evelyn had other things on her mind. God had bought her more time, somehow, yet fear still suppressed her courage. Every time she tried to speak to her daughter about what had happened, something got in the way, and then Evelyn's boldness melted like butter on a hot crescent roll.

She mulled over all the consequences of talking with her daughter. She hoped, of course, that walls would come tumbling down and that healing would begin, for the both of them. But common sense told her that things wouldn't be so easy. Macey was rigid, that was apparent. She didn't seem to want to confront the past. She had more important things on her mind, like making her mother a working woman.

"Then you press this button. See, it says Send, and you'll hear a few beeps and then it'll go on through. Clear enough?"

Evelyn realized she'd only heard half of what Macey had said. All the buttons and flashing lights looked like a spaceship to her.

"Why don't you give it a try?" Evelyn slowly took the paper and couldn't decide which end of the machine to stick the paper in, so she simply guessed. She looked up at Macey, who was shaking her head. "No, Mother."

Evelyn pulled out the paper and stuck it in the other end.

"No, Mother." Macey sighed and took the paper from her mom. "You were right the first time. But remember, you have to pay attention to what side the text is on. I told you my fax takes text side down."

"Oh." Evelyn flipped the paper over, slid it in the correct slot, and stared at all the buttons. The green one looked inviting. Her finger started toward it.

"No, Mom. Remember, you have to dial the number first."

Evelyn swallowed. Dial the number? That must've been the part where her mind had wandered. She shrugged and walked over to her phone. Just as she was about to dial, Macey's voice pierced her ear. "What are you doing?"

Evelyn blinked and slowly put the phone down. Her daughter's face flushed with anger. "Um . . ."

"Why are you over at the phone dialing?" Macey's fists punched into the sides of her hips. "Do you have any clue as to what you're doing?"

"I'm dialing the—"

"At the phone? Didn't you watch me when I punched the number into this keypad? Weren't you paying attention at all?"

Evelyn hung up the phone and walked back to the table. "I'm sorry. My mind must've wandered."

Her daughter's eyes narrowed as she stared hard at Evelyn. "Your mind wandered? We've been at this for three hours, you've got an interview on Friday, and your mind's wandering? Do you know that I leave tomorrow morning, Mother? What are you going to do when I'm gone? How are you going to survive the interview, much less the job?"

Good question.

Macey blew air into her bangs and turned around, leaning against the table as if to catch her breath. Evelyn stepped forward and said in almost a whisper, "I'm sorry."

"No, Mom, I shouldn't have reacted like that. I know you're trying." She pulled out a chair and sat down. "I just feel like I'm trying to teach a foreign language to someone in two days. I mean, I'm attempting to show you the bare necessities. Mom, these are just the basics. I don't think you understand."

Evelyn sat down next to her and patted her on the knee. "You've been so kind to take the time to help me, dear. I'm sorry I'm not learning faster. Maybe we should just cancel that interview. God'll take care of me. You don't worry your pretty little head about that."

An angry glare swirled in Macey's eyes. "Mother, please stop being so naïve, okay? I have yet to see God drop a chunk of change down here for you to live off of. So until He does that, we're just going to have to make our own way."

Evelyn noticed her daughter's hands shaking.

Their eyes met and then Macey stood suddenly. "We obviously need a break, don't we? Why don't you make some coffee, and I'll . . . um, I need to go upstairs and splash some cold water on my face."

Evelyn watched Macey sprint up the stairs and close her bedroom door behind her. The heat of the afternoon was beginning to get the best of her, and she thought she could use a good nap. She yawned and started the coffee, hoping that would get her wound up again.

She'd bake a quiche later and then she would talk to her daughter. It would be her last chance. Then her daughter would be gone, for how long was anyone's guess.

As the coffee spilled into the pot and the aroma awakened her senses, Evelyn decided it was doing no one any good for her to just stand around and wait for it to finish. She walked over to the table and looked down at what once was a printer and now was a fax machine. She took the piece of paper off the table.

If it took all day, she was going to send this paper to Dallas.

———————◦◦◦———————

It had gnawed at her all morning and into the afternoon. Macey opened the door to her room, then shut it rather hard. She'd hidden the box at the back of the closet, not really knowing why. Maybe she was hiding it from herself. It hadn't mattered, she realized, if she had buried it out in a field. It seemed to call her name, and it was almost all she'd thought about in the last nine hours. Regrettably, it had caused her to be short-tempered with her mother.

She listened carefully for her mother's activities downstairs. She heard sufficient enough evidence to lay the box on the bed again and open it. Her hands clasped behind her back, and her posture straightened like a soldier's. She had something to prove to it, but she didn't know what. She didn't even know why it was there or what it meant.

A yellow tag barely sticking out from underneath the gown caught Macey's attention, and she carefully moved the material aside to read it. She hadn't noticed it before. In dark blue lettering across a yellow background, the word *Madeleine's* was written in overly fancy cursive. Could this be from. . . ?

She placed the lid back on the box and walked around the room in circles. Her heart thumped with every pace she took. If she didn't go, if she didn't attempt to find out, it would haunt her forever. She knew this for a fact, because she was so easily haunted.

Stepping lightly out the door of her bedroom, she stood at the top of the stairs, attempting to see what her mother was doing. She wasn't at the table. Maybe she was in the kitchen. Why wasn't she at the table? She was supposed to be practicing her faxing.

"Yes . . . yes, I'm practically a modern woman," she heard her mom say. She was on the phone. Perfect. She could run downstairs with the box, throw it in the car, and come back in with an excuse on why she had to quick run into town for something. She returned to her room and grabbed the box, tucking it under her arm. At the top of the stairs she could hear her mother's continuing conversation. "No, I actually did it myself. I never thought I'd ever touch a computer!"

She carefully placed each foot on the carpeted part of the stairs as she made her way down, hoping not to draw any attention to herself. At the bottom, she could see her mom's back and one shoulder, the cord of the phone swaying with her movements. She just had to make it to the front door.

Macey tiptoed across the entryway and to the door, turning the handle quietly. She glanced back to find her mother still had her back turned. But, at four o'clock in the afternoon, the humidity swelled everything from wood to fingers, and the door wouldn't budge. Macey tried both hands, and it moved half an inch but made a dreadful rubbing sound that caused Evelyn to turn around. Macey froze, but it was too late. Evelyn dropped the phone to her shoulder and said, "You have to bump it with your hip once or twice and then pull. Don't know why, but that's the only thing that'll do it."

Macey smiled and nodded. She knew this door usually required a hip check to open it but had hoped that just this one time she could open it the normal way.

"Are you going someplace?"

She held up her index finger, indicating she would explain in a moment. That seemed to satisfy Evelyn, who resumed her conversation on the phone. Had she seen the box under her arm? Had she even cared? Macey quickly turned to the door, bumped it twice with her hip, and pulled. The door opened as smoothly as if it had just been oiled, and Macey hurried outside. She threw the box into the trunk of her car and walked back in. What would she say if her mom asked? Did her mom even know what was in the box?

"Okay, yeah, call us later. We'll be here. . . . Quiche, I think. . . . Sure. . . . Okay, bye." Evelyn hung up the phone and turned to her daughter, smiling. "Patricia might join us for dinner tonight, if that's okay."

"Sure." Macey looked at the table. "How's the faxing going?"

Evelyn shook her head. "Beijing's the capital of China, isn't it?"

Macey frowned. "Uh, yeah."

"Well, that's all I know about China, and I know more about China than computers." Evelyn walked back to the fax machine. "I must be doing something wrong."

Macey felt her face tense up. "Why do you say that?"

"Because, every time I put the paper in, instead of going where it's supposed to go, it comes out the other end. I have yet to get anything to Dallas." Evelyn threw up her hands and shook her head.

Macey couldn't stop herself from chuckling. Did her mom actually think the little paper rolled itself up and shot through the phone lines to Dallas? If she only had an ounce of her mom's naïveté, maybe Macey's life would simplify to a tolerable level.

She smiled and said, "Mom, you're not going to believe this, but if the paper's going through the other side, that probably means you're doing it right." Macey walked over to the fax machine. "It takes a picture, sort of, of what you're sending, then transfers that into data it can send over the phone line. The paper doesn't actually go anywhere."

Evelyn's brows pinched together above the bridge of her nose. "Is that so?"

"Yep," Macey said. Pressing the black arrows, she retrieved the last few actions, revealing her mother had actually done it right. "Mom, I think you've got it."

Evelyn squealed and clapped her hands. "By golly, that's just a miracle." She looked at Macey. "What a feeling."

Macey patted her on the back. "Why don't you take a break from all this, maybe start working on dinner or something. I need to run into town for a bit."

"Oh, okay. Do you want me to go—"

"No, no. That's okay. It's just a quick errand, and you don't need to be out in the heat of the day anyway." Macey pressed her lips together and waited for her mother's response.

"Well, you're right about that. It feels like eighty degrees in here. Our air-conditioner never has worked all that well. I'll go fiddle with the thermostat."

"I'll be back shortly," said Macey. She walked to the door, bumped it twice with her hip, and as it opened she said, "And, Mom, I'm proud of you."

Evelyn grinned, her face as bright as Macey had seen it since returning. She quietly shut the door behind her. She hoped to find nothing significant about the little gown. But something told her not to hope too much.

Twenty-One

M acey turned onto Main Street and drove slowly, looking for the little store. If she remembered where it was, it should be only a block or two away. She approached each intersection with caution. She wasn't used to all the stoplights, and she'd almost floated through one. Back when she lived here, there were only two stoplights in the whole town.

Everyone seemed to be driving at her pace, so she wasn't too concerned with backing up traffic. After another block, she saw it. Madeleine's. Not far away was a parking space open on the side of the street. She wasn't terrific at parallel parking, but luckily the space looked quite large, and she cheated her way into it. The correct way to parallel park had never made much sense to her.

Adjusting the air vents so they all blew toward her, she waited until her nerves settled. What was she doing? Beckoning old ghosts? Was this an old ghost? She had no idea what this was, and perhaps that's why she had to find out.

She turned off the engine and fumbled in the ashtray for quarters. She didn't intend on staying long enough to get a parking ticket, but she wasn't about to risk having to stay in this town any longer than necessary. She paid the meter, opened the trunk to retrieve the box, and walked back to the store.

From the windows it looked almost exactly the same, except the clothes were more modern. In her day it had been a clothing boutique—a little expensive but the place to go when wanting the best. Macey doubted the woman who ran it, Madeleine

Chester, was still alive. She'd been in her sixties when Macey was in high school.

A little bell chimed when she opened the door, and Macey pushed hard against it, the air from the inside giving resistance. The smell of potpourri filled her nostrils, and as she stepped farther in, so did that of berry candles. In the back of the store she could see racks of clothing and shoes, while the front displayed picture frames, figurines, gift items, and a single stand of Hallmark cards.

A familiar classical melody was piped through the cheap sound system, something from *Swan Lake* she thought, the notes coming through flat and tinny. The floor tile was the same, kept presentable with a fresh layer of wax. The atmosphere struck Macey as serene, and she found herself strolling down each narrow aisle, her eyes inches from fragile crystal ballerinas and porcelain kitty cats.

She'd only been in the store a couple of times when younger, but she recognized that the layout was different. The checkout counter was closer to the door now, and on it sat a modern cash register. To her left, Macey looked at the dazzling watches and other jewelry inside a revolving showcase. She moved along the glass counter and then stopped at the wedding ring sets. *"Look but don't touch,"* her mother's kind voice rang in her ears. *Not to worry,* Macey thought. *All I've done my whole life is just look.* As the gold glimmered and the diamonds glinted in the fluorescent light, Macey sighed heavily, not wanting to accept the idea that marriage was never going to be for her.

"May I help you?"

Macey spun on one heel and found herself staring into the light hazel eyes of a very old woman, who leaned on a cane and looked up at her.

"Hello. Yes. I'm visiting my mother and I found this little . . . gown, and I wanted to know if you remember anything about it."

Macey held the box in front of her. "It has a tag from your store on it."

The petite woman smiled at Macey, and Macey immediately recognized her as Madeleine Chester. She was still alive. In her eighties now?

"Well, let's see what we have here." Mrs. Chester took the box and set it on the counter, her shaky hands fumbling with the box top. She finally loosened it and pulled it off, a joyful gasp following. "Oh! How precious! A baptism gown."

Macey stood back a few feet as the woman picked the gown up and held it in the light. She turned it over and examined every inch of it as if she'd sewn it herself. Macey held her breath.

"What do you want to know?" Mrs. Chester asked, studying Macey's face with curiosity. "Is there something wrong with it?"

"Not at all. I found it in my closet at home. I just wondered if—" Macey paused. This was where it was going to get tricky. How could she get the information she wanted without revealing who she was? She couldn't, she decided—"if you remember selling it to my mother or father." She spoke the words carefully. "Jess or Evelyn Steigel."

The woman's eyes enlarged as she peered up at Macey. "My goodness' sakes!" Her shaky finger pointed at Macey's face. "You're their daughter, aren't you? Dear, I can hardly remember my own name, I'm sorry. You're. . . ?"

"Macey."

"Yes, yes. Of course. How are your parents?"

"I'm afraid my dad died last week."

"Of course. I'd heard that. Oh, goodness me, I'm sorry. Your poor mother."

"She's doing fine. It was expected." Macey directed Mrs. Chester's attention back to the gown. "I was just wondering if you remember anything about this purchase. I know it was a long time ago. But I was wondering . . . if maybe my mother or father bought it."

Mrs. Chester laid the gown on the glass counter and removed the tissue from the box. "Ah, yes. Here it is. The receipt." She smiled at Macey. "I always tape it under the tissue so it isn't apparent that it is there, but handy if someone needs an exchange. I never minded exchanging things. I always wanted my customers to be happy."

"You've run this store a long time," Macey said. "Looks like you know how to keep your customers happy."

Mrs. Chester smiled again, her yellow crooked teeth showing only for a second before she self-consciously covered them with a bony hand. "How kind of you to say." She looked back at the receipt, and Macey realized how important this receipt would be.

"May I?" Macey said, reaching for it. Mrs. Chester gladly handed it over. Macey's eyes hung on six numbers at the top. She had to concentrate hard to keep her composure, and even that didn't much work. The numbers seemed to leap off the page and scream at her.

"Are you okay? Dear me, sit down over here," the old woman said as she guided Macey to a comfortable chair close by. "Sit, sit. Let me get you a glass of water."

Macey's body felt numb, the same way it felt when she'd heard her father died. The receipt trembled in her hand, and she found the courage to look at it one more time. There at the top, in faded handwriting, was the date, May 24, 1983.

Mrs. Chester's feet shuffled along the tile, the sound accompanied by the soft fall of her cane. She returned quickly with a paper cup in her hand.

Macey used both hands to steady it, looking up to see Mrs. Chester's warm eyes filled with concern. Macey tried to smile.

"It's the heat, I think. I must be dehydrated."

"You're pale as a ghost," Mrs. Chester said, then reached up to feel her forehead. "At least you're not burning up. Drink more of that water."

Macey obeyed. She closed her eyes, hopefully to regain control of her emotions. A thick lump rested in her throat. *May 24, 1983.*

Mrs. Chester took the cup from her. "My goodness, we haven't had this much excitement in this store in years. Can I get you more water?"

Macey waved her hand and answered, "No . . . thanks" with a strained voice. She took several deep breaths before asking, "So, um, do you remember anything about the purchase of that gown?"

Mrs. Chester returned to the counter, leaned on her cane, and looked at the gown again. "Why, yes."

Macey sat up in her chair. "You do? What do you remember?"

"Well, my mind's a little fuzzy these days, and maybe I'm just making this up, but as I recall it was your father who came in. I suppose it stands out in my mind because my store never saw a lot of male customers, as you can imagine. Occasionally we'd have a husband come in looking for a gift for his wife, and I remember your father, I think, because he just seemed so out of place."

"I can imagine."

"But he knew what he wanted and picked it out himself. Chose the most expensive one we had. See? It's trimmed in pure silk." Mrs. Chester felt the edge of the sleeve. "I also remember that he wasn't very personable." Mrs. Chester glanced at Macey. "I'd mentioned that this must be for a very special occasion, but he didn't seem too interested in carrying on a conversation. He wasn't rude, by any means. He just seemed a little tired. He paid for it and left."

Macey gripped the side of the chair and rose to her feet.

"Dear, you're still quite pale. Why don't you let me get you more water."

Macey shook her head. "I'm fine. Thank you. And thanks for your help."

Mrs. Chester placed the gown back in the box, but before putting the lid back on, she said, "Well, you have the receipt. It was quite a long time ago, but I'd be happy to exchange it for something else if you'd like."

"No. That won't be necessary."

Mrs. Chester smiled and handed her the box. "Of course not. What am I thinking? You'll want to keep this for your own child someday, won't you?"

A horrible burning sensation crawled up Macey's throat. She turned and walked briskly to the front of the store, pulling the door open. The bell rang again, only this time it sounded louder and more aggravating. Without looking back, she gave Mrs. Chester a little wave. In a near daze she returned to her car, tossed the box in the backseat, started the engine, and stared out the windshield, unaware a car had stopped and was waiting for her to move.

A short beep of the horn roused her, and she glared in her mirror at the old man waiting for her spot. She shoved the shifter into Drive, turned the wheels as hard as she could, and pulled out into the street, never looking for traffic.

At seventy miles an hour she headed back home.

⋆ ◆ ⋆

At five in the afternoon in Dallas, the traffic would be at a standstill. But the country roads here were clear, and her rental car sped along the pavement faster than the little compact was comfortable with. It shuddered a bit as it flew down the road. Or maybe she was doing the shuddering.

She'd avoided the topic of the past altogether during the week she'd been here, even though she sensed her mother had wanted to talk about it a few times. She hadn't come home to talk about it. She hadn't come home to rehash everything that had happened. She'd come to bury her father and help her mother, and that was all. Both of which she had done.

Her hands slammed against the steering wheel. Only hours left before she was going to leave! Why did this all have to come about now? She felt helpless, lifeless, her limbs moving only because some evil puppet master was pulling her strings.

No! She wasn't going to be yanked around by some heartless divine power. She controlled her destiny. She made her own way. She always had. Nothing was going to change that now.

Her fingers tightened around the steering wheel as her foot pressed on the accelerater. In her mind's eye, all she could see was that date. Yet, with all she knew, she still didn't know *why*. Or *what*. Or *how*. She just knew the significance of the date on the top of the receipt.

As she turned onto the gravel road toward the house, the wheels spun and she corrected the car as it slid. Sweat dripped from her brow. Her jaw muscles protruded in determination. She had to know. And she knew the one person who had the answers—her mother.

Slowing down the car, she turned into the driveway. All seemed normal and quiet. A light wind rustled the tops of the trees. How different from what was going on inside herself. Restless turmoil. Tortured memories. A dull ache, like the low, almost inaudible rumbling of distant thunder before a big storm.

Tears streamed down her face, and there was no stopping them. She didn't care. She wasn't going to hide the pain any longer. She would simply walk into the house, stick the gown in her mother's face, and demand the truth.

She turned off the car and swung the door open, reaching behind her on the backseat for the box. Her sweaty fingers slid off it several times, and she grunted with frustration. Twisting her body and grabbing it with both hands, she inadvertently smashed the edges of the box by holding it too tightly.

After slamming the car door shut, she marched up the sidewalk, climbed the porch steps, and kicked the front door until it popped open. *This is it. This is the moment of truth.*

Once in the entryway, she noticed the house was unusually quiet. When she rounded the corner and looked into the living room, she realized why. There was her mother—glasses sitting crookedly on her face, her feet propped up on a pillow—asleep on the couch.

Macey went outside and stood on the porch, sheltered a little from the heat by the shade of a nearby oak tree, its long shadow reaching all the way to the steps of the house. She held the box loosely in her hands. Only a few minutes before, every emotion had racked her body. Now there was nothing. No anger. No grief. No sadness. No pity. Nothing. And that was scarier. Her soul was like a black hole, where nothing could be retrieved.

Several long moments passed. Suddenly the air felt cooler. She glanced at the sky just as a low rumbling filled the air. Dark clouds had moved in from nowhere, and the smell of clean rain filled her nostrils.

Another clap of thunder, still in the distance. Looking out past the neighboring wheat field, she could see tall thunderheads towered on top of one another and stretched toward the heavens. She walked down the steps and saw lightning fall far away, made visible by the dark backdrop of rain.

The wind picked up then, and for the first time all day, she didn't feel hot. The sweat cooled her skin as the breeze kissed her face as gently as a butterfly's wings. More bolts of light streamed to and from the clouds. She stared at them, captivated by the beauty. It had been a long time since she'd seen a storm build up and approach like this.

Thicker clouds filled the sky now as large raindrops spattered the cement in front of her and hit her face and arms. She tilted her face upward and welcomed the wetness. The sun's fiery orange rays met with the black storm clouds, shooting purple streaks in all directions.

Then the rain came heavier and started pelting her, but she didn't care. Her clothes sagged as they soaked up the moisture. Instead of retreating indoors, she stepped out onto the grass. And then she took another step. And another. She tucked her tangled wet hair behind her ears and kept walking. Deeper, more ominous thunder rattled above, but again she didn't care. She kept walking.

Kicking off her sandals, she walked with her toes feeling every blade of grass. The noise of nature continued to roar above while the light of the sun became hidden, though glorious rays still shot heavenward behind the storm. She kept walking.

She reached up to wipe her face, and her fingers stained black with running mascara. Her feet quickly turned brown, with wet pieces of grass stuck all over them. Her clothes clung to her, heavy and cumbersome. She didn't look up and she never cringed. She just kept walking.

The wind picked up suddenly, swirling the tops of the trees and bending the smaller ones. Macey's hair flew into her face, and she combed it back with her fingers. The thunder continued to rumble, a low and steady groan, as if the earth were mourning. She steadied herself and strode into the wind, defiant, daring nature to touch her.

Before long, the rain stopped hitting her face, and the wind whistled by her in a harsh whisper. The sounds of the storm became slightly more distant. Macey realized she was standing on the sheltering porch of Noah's house, staring at his heavy oak door, drenched.

Before she could do anything else, the door opened and there stood Noah, silhouetted by the inside light.

Twenty-Two

His strong hand held her shoulder tight, and he guided her briskly, as if they were dance partners, over to the couch, where he helped her to sit. He squatted down in front of her, his eyes wide and serious. "Macey. What in the world are you doing out in the storm?"

Macey suddenly realized she was no longer carrying the box. Where could it be? Had she dropped it? Her breaths cut short. She started to stand, but Noah's hand kept her seated. She looked directly into his eyes. He waited patiently for an answer, but Macey had no answers. Her body hunched forward. "Where's the box?"

"What box?"

Macey's hands fell in her lap. Had she said that out loud? The windows rattled with more thunder, causing Macey to gasp. Holding her hair back from her face, she fastened her eyes on the carpet.

"Daddy! Daddy! It's a storm!"

Macey whipped around to find Savannah and Stephanie at the top of the stairs.

"Macey!" They both squealed and flew down the stairs. Macey tried to smile as they ran up to her, but the corners of her mouth trembled and tears welled up.

"Macey, you look sad," Savannah said.

Stephanie stared and nodded by her sister's side. Noah was no help, for there was no denying it. She was sad. There were no excuses left. She took Savannah's hand and said, "I am sad." Tears as big as the raindrops that had wet her skin fell from her eyes, and for the first time she felt a little relief from the agony that had plagued her. She had admitted she was sad. It had taken seventeen years, but she'd said it. "I'm sad," she whispered again to herself.

Savannah and Stephanie gazed at Macey, looking sad themselves now. Noah stood and took them both by the shoulders. "Girls, I want you to go upstairs and play for a while. I want to talk to Macey alone, okay?"

"Are you going to help her feel better?" Stephanie asked as the two headed for the stairs.

Macey didn't hear Noah's answer, but soon he was back by her side with a towel in his hand. "Here, you're soaking wet."

Instead of drying off, she used the towel to hide her face. "I must be ruining your furniture." It was the first rational thought she'd had for what seemed like a long time.

"Please. It survived the terrible twos and much more. It'll handle a little wetness." He left the room again, this time returning with a hot cup of coffee. "Here. I think this is how you like it."

After dropping the towel from her face, Macey gave him a weak smile, received the warm cup, and sipped from it. She wondered if her eyes were black with mascara but didn't have enough strength to care too much beyond that. Her back pressed into the couch, and she watched the rain falling in sheets through the nearest window.

"Mother must be worried," Macey sighed.

"I'll call her, let her know you're safe." He smiled as he stood. "I would always call your mother during storms just to make sure your father was there."

"Don't tell her I'm—"

Noah nodded, interpreting her thoughts. She could barely hear their conversation with all the racket outside, but he came back looking satisfied, so Macey didn't inquire any further. She continued to drink her coffee and listen to the rain. There was nothing she could say to release any of the humility she was feeling.

Noah joined her on the couch with his own cup of coffee, and the storm provided the only dialogue for a while. The lightning would call, the thunder answer, and every so often the wind and rain would shift directions and break up the monotony of it all.

"Macey . . ." Noah sounded hesitant, and Macey couldn't get herself to look at him. "Macey, what's going on?"

Macey shook her head. Any words would bring more tears. She didn't want to sob in front of the man who seemed to read her mind.

"You were standing out in the middle of a storm, soaking wet. Something's terribly wrong. I can see it in your eyes."

Macey looked the other direction, shivering, holding her coffee in one hand while gripping the towel with the other. She feebly wiped at her matted hair, which was tangled around her ears.

Noah leaned forward, his elbows propped on his knees. "It's difficult to talk about, I can see that. But you're obviously in a great deal of pain. If you ask me, you need to get some things off your chest."

"I didn't ask you."

"But you were on my doorstep. That means something, doesn't it?" His tone continued to be soft and sweet.

She swallowed down the last drop of coffee and tucked her dirty feet underneath her legs to keep them warm. She didn't know what it meant. She hardly remembered walking over the bridge and over to his house. Her head pounded as she thought of the box, somewhere outside. Where had it gone?

"You'll want to keep this for your own child someday, won't you?"

A deep groan emerged from Macey's throat. Why had she gone to the store? What could she have been thinking?

But just as thunder can roll across the skies and then disappear into silence, suddenly Macey's heart shifted in an unexplainable way. All those years she had kept a secret. All those years her heart pumped a sad rhythm. Could she even imagine any normalcy? Day to day, her life appeared good, almost enviable. A million people watched her smile and laugh and interact as if she had the best life a woman could have. Maybe she had tricked herself.

Yet she knew better. Her apartment was constantly filled with noise. She watched twenty-four hour news channels around the clock. CDs spun in the stereo, belting out music she didn't even care much about. She'd occasionally walk the malls, her ears tuned into the low murmur of indecipherable conversation. On the days when the ghosts of her past threatened to silence all the noise she created, she would find herself at the airport, standing near the large panes of glass, filling her ears with the tremendous noise of the jets and the busyness of passengers preparing for their destinations. She'd sit quietly, like a mouse, hoping not to be recognized, and listen to the robotic voices on the intercoms announce arrivals and departures. A strong urge always pressed her to board a plane and take off into the sky, but her sensibilities told her that at some point the plane would land, a destination would arrive, and she would be standing on earth again, trying to drown out voices from the past.

Noah rose and walked to the window. "What a storm," he said, his hands stuffed deep into the pockets of his well-worn khakis. "I love storms like this. When they first move in." He glanced back at Macey. "The sunlight still filters through the clouds, so it's raining and sunny all at once. Patches of sunlight almost seem to highlight individual blades of grass." He turned to Macey and leaned against the window frame. "If only I could capture something like that with my paints. But it's impossible. God's the ultimate artist. We can try, and maybe make some good attempts, but in the end He can't be matched. Nor can His creations."

Macey frowned. What was he trying to do, give her some subtle hint about God? Her hands curled into tight balls. She didn't need to be lectured about God. Her father had given her plenty to dwell on the last time they spoke.

Noah's next words came out carefully. "You know, ever since I met you, I felt like you had something to hide."

Macey glared up at him. Her chest tightened with anger. "We all have something to hide, don't we?"

"True," he said, walking a few paces toward her.

Macey stared down at the upholstery of the couch, clutching the towel in her lap. "I've never spoken about it since it happened." The words stuck in her throat. "Not one time."

"I'm listening."

Twenty-Three

There were rules. So many rules. They were good rules, and they kept me out of trouble, but I would've probably stayed out of trouble anyway. Or, I guess it could be argued, I would have gotten into trouble regardless. Either way, my father had a standard for righteousness that I could never obtain, even though I tried hard. I tried so hard that I lost friends, and by my senior year, I found myself isolated and lonely.

"I guess I still had a good perspective. I knew right from wrong. And I knew that the right choices made a positive difference in my life. I'd been a perfect little angel as a child, but innocence and purity went out of style the older I got. I still had a few friends, I suppose. I called those who waved at me in the hallways and talked to me at lunchtime my 'friends.' But somehow all those times I'd declined to go to parties and decided against certain movies left me searching for friendship in a way I never had to as a child.

"I remember the attic. My father spent a lot of time there studying the Bible and reading a lot of other books about the Bible. He'd built bookshelves up there to hold all the books he loved. The attic was unbearably hot in the summer and just the opposite in the winter, but he loved it all the same. It was his, and a place, according to my mother, where he would spend time praying for me.

"Even though I was kind of lonely, I still felt a lot of promise in my life. I knew my parents loved me and supported me. I made good grades and felt like I could get into a good college on a scholarship. My father thought I'd make a good nurse. It always hurt my feelings that he never mentioned I might be a good doctor. But I could see my father's idea of a woman's role in life through the eyes of my mother. She was a servant, a follower, and submitted completely to him. It made her happy, yet I wanted more out of life.

"A few weeks before graduation, I was more focused than ever. I was determined to ace my finals, and after that choose from several colleges that had offered me scholarships. I was looking forward to a fresh start in life, a new city, new friends, new opportunities. And that's when Harley Preston came into the picture. He was the school's quarterback and every girl's dream date. Except this one's. I hadn't even dared dream about Harley. He was so out of my reach that I was smart enough to know it would only hurt me. So I listened to other girls talk about him, passing him in the hall like a small insignificant shadow. I focused on my studies instead.

"One day, right after lunch—I'll never forget it—I was putting books in my locker when someone bumped into me from behind. I turned and found Harley Preston looking down at me with that goofy dimpled smile that always swooned all my friends. My heart skipped a beat, and I was sure it had been an accident, but then he said my name, and I almost dropped everything I was holding. He said he regretted not talking to me sooner, that he'd always been a little intimidated by me. I laughed out loud at that one, and I guess that made him even more insecure because he almost turned around and left. But when I asked him what he wanted, I was shocked to hear him actually ask me out on a date. He was fumbling his words, and his forehead was beading up with sweat. I probably looked confident because I was just so flabbergasted I couldn't move a muscle. Then, before I could think twice, I found myself saying yes.

"At home, Dad wasn't pleased and asked right away what church Harley went to. He questioned my logic about dating someone during April, with finals just over a month away, and then he scrutinized my intentions. It overwhelmed me. For the first time all year I was feeling accepted and liked, and my father was disapproving before I could explain anything to him. Yet, deep down inside, I knew there was nothing to explain. He wouldn't understand. His meaning, his purpose, his whole life's happiness was wrapped around his thick leather Bible. What did he know of life as an eighteen-year-old girl? He expected me to be naïve and innocent forever? I had to learn the ways of the world, and I knew my father would disapprove.

"I saw Harley in secret, and I knew after our first date I was getting in over my head. Harley had dated dozens of girls. He was the most sought-after guy at school. I, on the other hand, had shared an ice-cream sundae once with Peter Jameson, the head deacon's geeky son, at the annual church picnic. That was the extent of my knowledge of the opposite sex.

"So there I was—dating Harley Preston and wondering what in the world I was doing. I'd dismissed my studies and fallen hard for a guy I hardly knew. As the days passed and we spent more time together, I realized Harley's attraction to me was my innocence, and it frustrated me as much as it complimented me. I didn't want to be innocent and naïve. Yet I knew, even at eighteen, that my stability and maybe my nobility were what attracted him. He'd never had a girl with either before.

"I fell hard for Harley. And I knew I was in trouble, that I would do anything he asked. I couldn't find an ounce of strength to draw me back to the morals and standards that had been so much a part of my life. Each date we had, Harley began pressuring me to go further and further. I was so inexperienced in ordinary relationships that I had no idea how to steer myself in a complex one.

"But the significance I felt when I was with him, the way the other girls stared with envy when we were seen together in the halls, it was all I'd dreamed of and now it was here, within my reach. The quiet voice of my father's insistence of God's love and demand for obedience never compared to the louder and more exciting temptations that beckoned me every moment I was with Harley.

"I was able to keep my feet grounded the first few times we saw each other; I knew, after all, I was supposed to be Harley's stability. I was supposed to show him the way, the truth, and the life. But the way suddenly became broad and unpredictable. The truth was muddled. And the only life I cared about was the one I was living with Harley.

"On a dark, cool night, Harley and I found ourselves in the old rundown house across the river. Everyone was always warned to stay away from it. It wasn't safe. It was used to store hay occasionally, but that was it. Harley figured out a way to open the door and pry away enough of the boards hammered across the windows to let the moonlight stream in. What once was a dark and creepy old house now filtered light in a mystically beautiful way. We lay together in the hay and talked. I'd always assumed Harley was a shallow person, a meathead who worshiped sports. But he had depth, and as we grappled with our fears about the future, we connected in a way I'd never connected before with another human being. Maybe it was only for a moment. Maybe it wasn't even real. But I felt there was one person who understood me.

"Then I fell. The first temptation the devil had orchestrated for me knocked at my door, and I answered it. It came and went, and I felt shame like I'd never known. I could hardly think straight, and as much as I wanted to confess to someone, there was no one. I certainly couldn't tell my father. He'd had such high hopes for me, such grand expectations. I'd failed him. I'd failed God. I'd lost something I could never get back. The thought of that kept me in bed three days straight with unending nausea. And then I found out to my horror four weeks later that I was pregnant.

"I'd hardly spoken to Harley since that night in the old house. To him, it wasn't any big deal. It certainly wasn't his first time, nor would it be his last. But for me, it marked a downward spiral in my life and one that I wasn't able to stop. Now the unbelievable consequences of my actions could not be denied. The proof was in my womb. The evidence followed me to every toilet I hung over.

"It was a week before graduation, and I knew I had to tell my parents. I'd taken most of my finals and hadn't done well on them at all. Frankly, that was the least of my concerns. The dread that overcame me with each attempt to tell them was indescribable. I was in the greatest despair of my life, and I knew what I had to do.

"I spent an evening reading my Bible. I studied verses about forgiveness and God's unconditional love. I read about the woman who committed adultery and how Jesus forgave her. The more I read, the more comfort I found. I spent three hours reading those words until I found enough courage to confess what I had done. And I found comfort in knowing my father knew those words better than anyone. He'd been my picture of God my whole life, and now it was time to confess and be forgiven.

"I found my father in the attic. The sun hadn't quite set, but the attic was already dark except for the oil lantern my dad was using to read by. It wasn't often that I disturbed him in his attic, so he knew I had something significant to say. I sat in an old wooden chair near his reading chair. He closed his Bible and smiled at me. Before I could find the words to begin, he said, 'Macey, I'm so proud of you. You've been an excellent daughter, an excellent student, and you're simply priceless to me.' He rose, went to his desk, and pulled out a small box from one of the drawers. He said, 'I'm not sure what I'm going to do with myself when you're gone, but I know you want to go to college, and I can't stop you from doing that. You're much too smart to stay around here and help me on the farm.'

"I could hardly breathe. I didn't want him to say these things. I couldn't make my mouth move to try and stop him. He then said, 'I wanted to save this for after graduation day, but I might as well give it to you now. I've had it for months. I saw it in this little shop in Parsons and I couldn't help myself.' His hand opened, and he held the small box in front of me. 'Well, what are you waitin' for?' he said. 'Your dad's not getting any younger standing here waiting for you to open it.' He was smiling at me, and I could hardly keep myself from breaking down and crying. I took the box and stared at it. I had no idea what it could be. My stomach lurched and I thought I was going to throw up. He urged me again to open it and so I did.

"There, in the middle of a soft piece of cotton, was the most beautiful gold necklace I'd ever seen. Hanging on it was a small ornate cross. I gasped when I lifted it from the box. He said, 'Let me help you put it on. Do you like it?' I nodded as he helped me clasp it around my neck. My fingers felt the cross over and over, and for a small moment I drew strength from that. He was smiling at me and looking at the cross, so proud. 'I've never even gotten your mother a piece of jewelry like that. It was a little expensive, but you're worth it. I just can't tell you how proud I am of you. I probably don't tell you often enough, but I hope you know it. You're a fine young woman, and I'm lucky to be your dad.'

"Those words rang in my ears, and the tears came so suddenly I didn't even realize I was crying at first. My father said, 'Why are you crying? Don't you like your necklace?'

"I nodded and tried to smile. 'I love it,' I said, and then with all the strength and courage I could muster, I said, 'But that's not why I'm crying.'

"My father's kind and warm eyes dimmed with concern. He sat in his reading chair and looked at me. 'Well, what is it? What's wrong?'

"As fast as I could, I replayed all those words of Jesus. Staring at my father's Bible balancing on the arm of the chair, I said, 'I'm pregnant, Daddy.'

"He didn't say anything for a long time, so I finally looked into his eyes. I didn't recognize him. What earlier had been eyes full of kindness and love were now dark and mean. I started crying harder the more intensely he stared at me.

"He stood up and said, 'That Preston boy? Is that who did this?'

"I nodded, shaking so badly I thought I was going to pass out. 'I'm so sorry, Daddy. I messed up. I'm so sorry.'

"He turned his back toward me, and his head was lowered. I continued to cry, and that was the only sound in the attic for a long time. But then he faced me again. His face was red, and his eyes were wild with fury.

" 'Daddy!' I cried, but his lips were curled back, like a dog getting ready to bite.

" 'How could you do this?' he shouted. 'How could you go and do this? What have I spent all these years teaching you? I've worn holes in my pants praying for you!' He stepped toward me, and I clutched the side of the chair I was sitting in. 'What's everyone at church going to think? I'm the head deacon! I have to keep my family in order! How could you betray me like this? How could you betray *God* like this?'

"I shook my head. I had no words, no answers for his questions. All the shame that had been washed away by the words of Jesus now poured back over me like a flood. Because of the tears, I couldn't even see him anymore. He was just this dark blur towering over me.

" 'Was it worth it? Was it worth selling your soul to the devil?' He was almost screaming now, and I curled into the chair. I wiped my eyes to look up at him, just in time to see him start to say something. Our eyes met, and he stopped himself, but his lips were formed in a perfect circle to say what I knew he wanted to. *Whore.*

"He had stopped himself, thankfully. I might've died from a broken heart if I'd heard my father say that about me. And instantly, I knew he regretted even beginning to utter that word.

"But what he did next shattered me more than I can express. He grabbed the necklace around my neck and yanked it off of me. Then he left. I cried and cried, far into the night, and he never returned. My hand kept feeling for that precious necklace, but it wasn't there.

"By morning, I'd fallen asleep on the floor of the attic. It was early, and I doubted anyone was up yet. The sun was just starting to come up. Although they were early risers, my parents usually waited until the sun was over the horizon before getting up. I tiptoed downstairs wondering what I should do. As I stood at the kitchen window, though, I saw that my father's truck wasn't there in the driveway. He'd already gone.

"Mother was still upstairs. I went to the kitchen table, the same place it is today, and just sat there. I was numb, emotionally exhausted. My father's words haunted me until finally I knew I had to do something about it. My father had always been such a righteous man; he'd always worked so hard at pleasing God. And now I was going to humiliate him with my being an unwed mother. This was probably the most horrifying thing he could comprehend. I didn't want to lose my father's love. I couldn't. He meant the world to me.

"Two days went by and my father didn't speak to me. My mother was silent, too, but not out of anger. She just didn't know what to do. I didn't even know if she knew exactly what was going on.

"On the third day, I'd determined to make things right. My father didn't deserve the kind of humiliation that was going to come with this ordeal. In the middle of the night, I found the old milk jar he kept money in and counted out over two hundred dollars. I told my mom I needed to borrow the car to go do some things for graduation. Seniors didn't have to attend school the week before graduation, so she didn't stop me.

"I drove to Joplin, what I considered then to be a very big city, and found a clinic there. I'd heard one of my friends talking about her cousin getting an abortion at this same clinic. I looked it up in the phone book, found it, and made an appointment. Three hours later I was lying on a cold metal table and staring up at the ceiling. I didn't cry. All I could see were my father's cold harsh eyes. If this would bring him back to normal, then it was worth it.

"It took twenty minutes total. I drove home, hardly feeling any pain, and went to my room to take a nap. At around five I heard my father's truck pull up, and I watched him from my bedroom window. He came inside, and I heard him discussing the farm with my mother. Then Mom said she had to go over to somebody's house to deliver a casserole, and she left.

"I went downstairs and found my dad in the living room in his big chair, watching television. I remember being startled when he looked up at me. His look was different. It was softer. I didn't know why, but maybe he suspected what I'd done. Maybe he was relieved.

"He started to say something, but I interrupted him. I stood in the middle of the living room and said, 'You don't have to worry anymore, Daddy. It's taken care of.'

"He said, 'What do you mean by that?'

" 'I'm not pregnant anymore. Now you don't have to worry about what people will say at church. I used the money in the milk jar, Daddy, but I promise to pay it back.'

"At first I thought he was angry about the money. He literally pulled at his hair and glared at me in disbelief. I repeated that I would pay back the money, and then it dawned on me that it wasn't the money he was angry about. I took a step back as he got up from his chair.

" 'You killed that baby?' he yelled.

" 'No, Daddy. I didn't . . . didn't kill . . . I thought that's what you wanted. I thought—'

" 'You thought *murder* was the answer? You thought you could just go and murder this child and be rid of all your problems?'

" 'No, it wasn't like that. . . . ' My words betrayed me. I couldn't say what I meant. All the while I was trying to process what he meant. Was he calling me a murderer? Was that what I did? I was trying to make things right, to keep my father from being humiliated. But as his eyes burned into my soul, I knew I hadn't done that at all. In fact, I'd messed up so terribly I realized there was no correcting it. There was no turning back. I'd sent myself to hell, and there wasn't a single way to be redeemed.

"I ran upstairs to my bedroom. A few minutes later I heard my dad's truck roar to life. He sped away. Nighttime came slowly, and my father never returned. I packed a suitcase, trying to keep it light, only the bare essentials—jeans, a couple of shirts, extra pair of shoes, underwear. I also packed my little phone book. And my favorite nail polish, the one my father didn't let me wear very often.

"I was zipping my suitcase when the door opened. My mother stood there, her eyes wide and terrified and filled with tears. I turned and tried to hide the suitcase behind me, yet it was obvious what I was doing.

"She didn't speak a single word. Instead, she walked up to me, gave me a hug, and then opened my hand. She closed my fingers around something, hugged me again, and wiped away the tears that were streaming down my face.

"She closed the door behind her. When I opened my hand, there was five hundred dollars in cash. I sat on my bed and realized I was going to have to make a decision. I had to figure out where to go.

"It made the most sense to go to Texas. I'd likely received a full scholarship to Texas Tech, and that was my best bet for survival. I sat on my bed for five hours. It was the middle of the night. My father hadn't come back yet, and I knew now was the time to leave.

"I quietly walked downstairs with my suitcase and money, opened the front door, and left. I hitchhiked all the way to Texas. I never saw my father alive again."

Twenty-Four

I t was over in a matter of minutes. Macey blinked herself back to reality and was stunned at how quickly it had been retold. Could seventeen years of heartache, despair, and shame and grief and anger be summed up in several minutes? Impossible.

Her mind raced through everything she'd said. Had she left out any important details? Had she been explicit enough about how angry her father had been? She shook her head as more tears came. Only for a moment did sharing her story with Noah make her feel better. She'd imagined for years that when she finally said it out loud, some magical healing would take place and her heart would be mended. She'd been to therapy many times but never mentioned it. She'd always lied about why she had problems maintaining relationships. Each story was different, and she finally realized she was wasting her money by not being truthful. So she continued to wade through the pool of men the world offered her, trying to find someone worthy of understanding her fears and struggles. There had been no one.

Until now.

Macey looked at Noah. He sat comfortably on the couch, his face grim with concern, but his eyes still alive with some strange hope she wasn't familiar with. The story didn't seem to shock him, not nearly as much as it had shocked her in the retelling of it. And yet a perplexed look now crossed his face, something he wasn't understanding perhaps. He didn't say what it was.

Macey took a deep breath. For a moment she thought she was going to be okay. Tears flowed and her hands trembled, but she felt she was beginning to recover. That hope didn't last long, though.

Before she knew it, her body heaved as her heart cinched with anger and grief, as her mind replayed her father's horrible words to her, along with the condemning silence that had said even more.

If confessing everything wouldn't bring her peace, then what would?

Then Noah said, "I'll be right back. I need to get the girls ready for bed."

Macey nodded. She watched him walk upstairs and then laughed to herself. She'd confessed the darkest secret of her life, and *that* was what he had to say about it? Incredible. She leaned her head back against the top of the couch, stared at the ceiling, and waited.

Noah was upstairs for twenty minutes, tucking in the girls, reading them a story, reassuring them that the worst of the storm had passed and they were safe. The soothing patter of a gentle rain almost lulled her to sleep.

"I think I'll fix us some tomato soup," Noah said. His sudden presence and voice jolted Macey back to consciousness. He smiled at her before stepping into the kitchen. "It's a tomato soup kind of evening, wouldn't you say?"

Macey stretched her arms toward the ceiling and then stood and joined him. The air had turned cooler, so soup sounded perfect. The loud *whir* of the can opener awakened her even more. She checked her watch. It was after eight. Should she return home to her mother?

Noah seemed to read her mind. "You can stay until the rain lets up, can't you?"

Macey smiled warmly at him, then glanced down at herself. "I don't know. Just look at me. I look like a mud wrestler."

He laughed. "Yeah, I see what you mean." He handed her a fresh towel. "Maybe this will help."

"I doubt it, but thanks," Macey said as she scrubbed at her face with the towel. "Well, if you can stand looking at this dirty mug for a while longer, I'd love some hot soup."

He winked at her. "How fast can you eat?"

———◆———

Noah offered Macey the leather chair while he took the couch. They each had a soup cup filled with the steaming tomato variety. With each spoonful, a wave of warmth crossed her heart, though she wasn't totally sure it was all because of the soup. She and Noah traded smiles as they ate.

Finally Noah spoke up, saying, "That was pretty intense." Macey cocked an eyebrow. "I mean your story." He set his cup down. The spoon rattled inside of it, indicating it was empty. "That must've been a very hard thing for you to share." Macey's eyes darted in embarrassment, and her hand crawled up to her face and hid her eyes. "I'm proud of you," Noah continued, and Macey peeked at him through her fingers. "You're very brave."

A short tight laugh emitted from her mouth. "Brave? Hardly." She shook her head and all but lost her appetite for the soup. "It's just such a mess—that's what it is. A horrible, painful mess. And it always will be." Macey sunk into the leather chair.

"I'm sorry it happened," said Noah. "But it explains a lot." He shrugged. "Or at least a little."

"What do you mean?"

"There's always been a little bit of talk, you know," he said carefully. "Good-hearted small-town talk. Your father never spoke about it, but I knew him well enough to see the sadness in his eyes. The same sadness I saw in yours the first time I met you."

"Did he ever talk about me?"

"Not in so many words."

"Meaning?"

"Meaning, I know he always cared for you and thought of you often."

"You're just saying that to make me feel better," Macey said.

"I knew your father well," Noah insisted. "I had coffee with him twice a week. He and your mom have been like grandparents to my girls. He was a good friend. A kind man."

Macey tried not to glare at Noah. "Really? So it must be hard for you to imagine him doing those things, saying those things."

"A little. I know he was a very upright man. A very godly man. So it doesn't surprise me that he reacted to your news with . . . disappointment."

"*Disappointment?* You call that disappointment? It was rage in its purest form. He hated my guts, Noah. I'm sure the only reason pictures of me are still around in the house was so my mother wouldn't die of a broken heart. As far as I can tell, the day I left, he never spoke of me again. It was like I never existed. He shunned me and never looked back."

"Is that what you think? Your father hated you all these years? Really hated you?"

"What else should I think? That he was just a little too busy to come find me? That he was too embarrassed to apologize? I told him I was sorry. I asked for his forgiveness. He never gave it to me."

Macey noticed that Noah was looking down at the carpet, his eyes distant with a private thought. She wanted to go on, continue to vent her frustration over her father, but something quieted her. It was the look on Noah's face.

"It's sad," he stated, his voice struggling. "It's sad that you two had to end this way."

"It's not my fault," Macey said, her voice equally as strained. "I was young; I made a mistake. He wasn't willing to forgive me. What else could I do." It was a statement, not a question, and she eyed Noah, daring him to challenge her logic.

His lips pressed together, and again his eyes became distant. This time Macey's patience was growing thin. What was his hesitation? It wasn't as if he'd made it a habit of protecting her emotions.

"If you've got something to say . . ." Macey met his eyes.

Noah cleared his throat and nodded. The light in the room bounced off his eyes in a way it hadn't just moments ago, and Macey realized she was seeing tears. What could be upsetting him like this? She squeezed her hands together and tried to wait for his timing.

"I had always wondered," he began softly, "what your father was doing. I guess I never put it together, and he wasn't the type of man who invited personal questions. He liked to talk about the weather, agriculture, and the church. And occasionally his coffee." Noah smiled through his tears. "But every single Thanksgiving and Christmas, your father would—" Noah stopped and sighed heavily—"he would go to the bus station. And wait. For several days prior to and on the actual holiday, there he was at the bus station. People would see him, you know, just sitting there, that favorite old hat of his in his lap, just . . . waiting."

Macey's hands fell open, palms up, and her eyebrows rose. "Waiting for what?"

He looked directly into her eyes. "Waiting for you."

She heard the words yet didn't understand them. She stared hard at Noah, waiting for an explanation.

"I guess he never really expected you to step off that bus. I know he didn't." Noah paused. "Maybe it was some weird way of punishing himself. I don't know."

Chimes outside alerted her to the fact that the rain had stopped and a soft breeze had replaced it. She hadn't even known Noah had chimes, but they echoed a haunting melody as the last bit of daylight filtered through the windows. The storm had finally blown on through.

"The rain's let up," she said as she stood. She set her unfinished cup of soup next to her on the table. "Thanks for the soup."

She started toward the door, but Noah jumped up and took her arm. "This is a lot to process, I know. But don't let it go without taking it to heart. It means something."

Macey looked up at him. "Maybe it meant something once. It doesn't mean anything now. He's dead. And I never arrived home on that bus, did I?" Noah's eyes flashed disappointment, and he let go of her arm. She continued to the front door, where she turned and said, "Thanks again for the soup." She started to leave the house, but not before adding, "And for listening."

A small smile lingered on Noah's lips, and then Macey left, shutting the door behind her.

———— ◆ ————

Still barefoot, she walked slowly back over the bridge while enjoying the cooler temperatures the storm had ushered in rather dramatically. Grime and dirt plastered her body, but for some odd reason she felt clean. Clean and also confused. A little less tormented, though more aggravated now, more unfocused. Could it be that Noah had made up the bus-station story? That seemed more plausible than imagining her father sitting there every Christmas and Thanksgiving for seventeen years, no matter what his motivations were.

From where she stood on the bridge she could see that her mother was still awake, for the windows of the house glowed warmly in the impending darkness. This would be her last night here. She was thankful, but sad. So many questions left unanswered. Maybe it was better that way. The more she discovered, the crazier everything became. Wouldn't her life be better back in Dallas?

She watched as the water rushed under the bridge. The rain had swelled the river, increasing the current's power. Tomorrow's heat would lower it again. But for now, it was majestic and healthy. Then she saw it.

Down by the sharp and jagged rocks on the bank nearest her, a white muddied box, opened and wet, lay embedded in thick mud. From where she was standing, she could make out the gown's sleeve, almost looking as if it were reaching up toward her. She took several steps back and closed her eyes.

"You'll want to keep this for your own child someday, won't you?"

Macey turned and finished crossing the bridge, never looking back at the little box and gown.

Twenty-Five

At first she thought the wind was blowing the back screen—for four years Jess had promised to fix the latch yet never got around to it—but then she heard footsteps and knew Macey was finally back home. Evelyn greeted her.

"Oh, my!" she exclaimed, looking her daughter up and down. "What happened to you? Are you okay?" She reached out to touch Macey's face, but her daughter withdrew, though still offered a smile.

"I'm fine, Mom. Just got caught out in the rain."

Evelyn escorted her through the kitchen and into the living room, where Perry Como was singing "Rock of Ages" by way of a dusty old record she'd found earlier that evening. Her daughter glanced in the direction of the music.

"If you'll change out of those clothes, I'll put them in the wash. This mud out here can stain like the dickens."

"Okay," Macey said. She looked tired.

Macey climbed the stairs to go change, while Evelyn waited patiently downstairs, preparing a pot of bedtime tea. The water rumbled through the pipes, and Evelyn assumed she'd decided to take a shower.

On the dining room table Evelyn smoothed out the fabrics and tried to position herself in the light to get a good idea of the color. She'd never looked terrific in pink, but for summer she thought a nice pink floral pattern might do nicely anyway. Only fifteen minutes had passed when she saw Macey again, slowly descending the stairs, her hair wet and combed away from her face, a bunch of clothes under her left arm.

Evelyn met her at the landing. "Here, let me take those. I'll get 'em in the wash and have 'em dried by the time you leave." She looked at her daughter and tried to ask casually, "Tomorrow morning, right?" Macey nodded. "Don't you worry, these stains will come out. I have a few tricks up my sleeve." Her daughter nodded again but appeared as if she hadn't heard a word. Evelyn made her way out to the laundry room in the garage and started the wash. A side-by-side washer and dryer were two of her biggest luxuries. They'd purchased the set seven years ago, although she still preferred to dry her towels and sheets out on the line.

She found Macey in the kitchen, pouring tea. "Where's the honey?" she asked.

Evelyn went to the pantry and found the jar. "This is from Tex Bartlett. He's got a bee farm up the way, and you've never tasted honey like this. He sells it all over the country now. He's always given us enough at Christmas to last us the whole year round."

Macey added a little of Tex's honey in her tea, stirring and thinking some faraway thought as if she were the only one in the room. Evelyn stood nearby in silence, her own thoughts disengaging her for the moment. This was it. Her last night with Macey. She had to say something. She had to mention it. She owed at least that much to her daughter, didn't she?

Her daughter turned, and Evelyn lost her train of thought. "I have something to show you," she said, and her daughter followed her into the dining room. Evelyn swept her hand in the direction of the table. Macey walked over to it, her expression puzzled.

"Fabric?" Macey asked.

Evelyn smiled. "I'm sewing myself some business suits," she said, lifting the floral print for Macey to see better. "Just a couple. Enough to get me by until I can make more. It'll be tough, but I think I can do it by Friday. I once sewed a bridesmaid's dress in an afternoon when the bride's uncle dropped a cigarette on it and burned it to ashes. But that was in desperation, and I'm not sure I could do it again. I'm not the fastest draw on the sewing machine."

Macey walked around the table, looking at the different fabrics while sipping her tea. She looked so tired. Evelyn watched as she didn't even make it all the way around, but ended up collapsing into a chair and staring into space.

"Which ones do you like?" Evelyn asked.

"They're all nice. I like the floral, though." She said it while staring at another pattern, and Evelyn realized her daughter's mind was heavy with thought.

"I've been working hard on the computer, too," Evelyn said. "I'm faxing, I'm printing, I'm saving. I worked on it all evening. How's the tea?"

"Perfect." Macey looked into her cup. "Thanks for working so hard on all this, Mom. You've been a real trooper."

"I suppose I needed to learn all this a long time ago."

"No. No, you didn't. And I'm sorry that you had to now. All this . . . it changes a person." She glanced over to where the computer sat on the table. "It's a relief to know there are actually people alive still who live at a normal pace, whose lives aren't dictated by a machine." She sighed and sipped her tea. "Anyway, enough of that."

Evelyn pushed at her cuticles as she said, "What time do you leave tomorrow?"

"11:04."

"Well, I'll get up early and make you a nice breakfast."

Macey smiled. "I'd appreciate that."

Perry Como's soothing voice was now singing "Amazing Grace." It was the only sound filling the room, muffled only by the corner wall that stood between the dining area and the living room.

"How's Noah?"

"Fine."

"Good."

Evelyn stood and fussed over the fabric. "I don't know how good I'll look in a double-breasted blazer. I guess I'll find out. I'm going to lengthen the skirt to below my knees. That's only appropriate for a woman my age."

"You'll look terrific," Macey said absently.

"Had two chickens die today. The heat. Just keeled over."

"I'm sorry."

"No big thing. We usually lose four or five before the summer's over."

Macey nodded. Evelyn's heart fell to her stomach when Macey stretched her arms over her head and stood.

"I've got a long day tomorrow. I'm flying straight to New York. I better get to bed."

"Wait . . ."

Macey turned and looked at her. "What?"

Evelyn swallowed hard. She had to say *something*. "Macey," she began, her voice croaking in her throat. "I can't let you leave without . . . without . . ."

Macey leaned forward as if to help pull the words out of Evelyn's mouth. "Yes?"

". . . without, um . . ."

"Without what?"

Evelyn's chest cramped with fear. "Without giving you my blackberry cobbler recipe."

"Your blackberry cobbler recipe?"

Evelyn stared at the carpet. How could she be such a coward? She glanced up and their eyes met. Her heart pounded in her chest as she attempted it again. "No, not just that."

"Mom, I appreciate it, but I'm not much of a cook. I probably wouldn't use it."

"Wait," Evelyn said again. Macey had started toward the stairs. "There's something else."

Macey stood, one hand on the rail, waiting for Evelyn to speak.

"Honey, I just wanted to say I'm sorry. I should've called. I should've come to see you. I made a lot of mistakes." She couldn't help but hang her head as she spoke. It shamed her to think she'd let so many years pass with so little contact between them. Tears rolled down her face, and she tried wiping them away, but they were immediately replaced by more so she gave up and focused on what she wanted to say. There was so much to say. Her thoughts were jumbled. As she worked on sorting through each one, to say what needed to be said in a way that made sense, her daughter cleared her throat.

"You're not the one who made the mistakes, Mom," her daughter told her. "You have nothing to be sorry about." She then turned and hurried up the stairs, never looking back, quietly shutting the bedroom door behind her.

Evelyn was shaking so terribly she had to sit down. She lowered herself onto the bench near the entryway and stared at the empty staircase. The house was perfectly silent now, except for the hum of the refrigerator and the ticking of the old grandfather clock that sat in the corner of the entryway. The tears kept flowing, and with the silence came more.

Tomorrow would be the first day she would be completely alone. She hadn't said an ounce of what she'd wanted to say to her daughter, and now the opportunity was lost.

An hour went by as Evelyn sat on the bench. Complete darkness had set in, and as she listened more carefully, she could hear the familiar melody of the katydids outside the house.

She didn't have the strength to pray. What else could she say? There was no time left for miracles. If only her own time could run out as quickly. She glanced up at the grandfather clock, the numbers blurry without her glasses. She wondered how many times the hands would have to go around before time would stop for her.

Twenty-Six

"Now listen carefully, Mom," Macey said, talking between bites of eggs, toast, and cantaloupe. "You just be yourself. You're charming, nice, and personable, and that will go a long way in helping you to get this job."

Her mother sat across from her. She nodded and blinked through puffy eyes. Normally she was chipper in the morning, but this day there was a heaviness that Macey noticed.

After gulping down half a cup of coffee, Macey continued. Her eyes were puffy, too, although there was nothing new to her feeling exhausted. It was an everyday occurrence. "The woman there seemed very eager to help you out, and I hardly think there's a chance you can go wrong." That was practically a lie, but Macey knew if her mother didn't feel confident, she didn't have any chance at all. "I've written down all the information you'll need to know on that piece of paper. Make sure to arrive early, okay? I know you drive a little slow so leave in plenty of time. I've drawn you a map, but you know where it is, so I'm not worried about that. Downplay your weaknesses, okay? Don't tell them anything they don't ask. Emphasize all the things you do well, and make sure not to mention you just learned how to use a computer this week."

Her mother's expression turned worried. "What if they ask me?"

Macey paused midchew. There was no way her mother would lie, and she'd be wrong to ask her to. "Well," she said carefully, swallowing the eggs unchewed, "you can always just pick your words carefully."

Evelyn nodded.

"Mother, please, try not to worry. You'll do fine." She pointed to the piece of paper on the table. "I've written down my address, my phone numbers at work, at home, and my cell, and some other information for you." This brought a smile to her mother's solemn face. "We'll keep in touch, okay?"

"I'd like that, dear."

"Good." Macey wiped her mouth and finished off her coffee. She'd risen early, packed her bags, and spent as little time as possible reminiscing about her time here. It would only make leaving that much more difficult, and she couldn't afford to be distracted today. She had an interview with the network. She had to focus. She checked her watch; it was not quite eight o'clock. "Listen, Mom, I'm going to go over and say good-bye to Noah for a little bit." She met her mother's knowing smile with "He's a nice man. And I know he's been a good friend to you."

"Like a son."

Macey paused at that, then quickly let it go. There wasn't time for bitterness or regret. She hopped up from the table, offered to help clear the dishes, was waved on by her mother, and then rushed out the back door toward the Neosho.

She walked along its banks, listening to the river. Her shoes were picking up wet pieces of grass, but she didn't worry about it. A week ago she would've stressed about it, but now things were in a little better perspective, if that were possible.

As she stepped onto the bridge, her heart nearly stopped when she remembered the gown and that it might still be there in the mud. She glanced down and saw that the little box and gown hadn't moved, that it was still among the rocks, dirtier than before. She looked away as if she'd seen something obscene and continued walking over the bridge.

During the short walk from the bridge to Noah's house, Macey's mind, partially consumed with anxious thoughts about her mother's well-being, also entertained thoughts of her past. On the extreme outer edge of these thoughts was Noah's face, dimmed by everything else yet still visible.

She smiled as she dragged her feet through the grass, her hands resting in the pockets of her pants. He was kind, simple, and wise. She was drawn to more than his good looks and creative genius, to more than his ocean blue eyes and flirting grin. There was something else about him, a quality that spoke toward the good and the profound. As much as she tried to grasp what exactly it was, in the end she was unable to pinpoint it.

The morning sun had quickly made the air humid again, and Macey's skin perspired enough to cause wisps of her hair to cling to her forehead. Her silk summer blouse didn't welcome air to her skin like it had just minutes before. She waved her hand in front of her face to create a breeze while at the same time picking up her pace. She couldn't afford to look like she'd been wandering the Kansas prairies on a day like this. A small smile of satisfaction spread her lips as she thought of the network. *What a trip.*

At Noah's front door she listened for any sounds of movement, hoping everyone was up, before knocking lightly. No one answered, and Macey's hopes of saying good-bye to Noah dampened. She knocked again. Still no answer. She would've left a note had she thought to bring a pen and paper. Where could he be this early in the morning?

She rapped one more time on the door, then turned to leave. But before she could take a step away from the door, it opened and Noah greeted her with a smile. "Hi there."

Macey swallowed. His hair, normally tied back neatly in a ponytail, flowed over his shoulders. She'd never dated a guy with long hair. She'd once dated a man with an earring, which was a real stretch for her. There was a certain statement to his look; it was whimsical and free-spirited. As she stared, he took a band from his wrist and pulled his hair back with one motion.

"You arrived before I fixed my hair," he joked.

Macey hesitated. Should she go in? Or just say her good-byes here? What would she say? This was turning out to be harder than she expected. But then he opened the door wider and stepped aside. She took his cue and entered the house. "Where are the girls?"

"Oh, probably out in a field somewhere. Maybe in a tree. They like to play in the cooler part of the morning." She followed him to the kitchen. "Breakfast?"

"No, thanks. Mom just stuffed me with enough to get me through the week."

He smiled as two pieces of toast popped up from the toaster. He laid them on a plate and buttered them carefully on the island in the middle of the kitchen. On the other side, Macey watched for a moment, then remembered why she was here. "I was hoping to say good-bye to the girls . . . and you, of course."

Noah looked up from what he was doing. "You're leaving?"

"My plane leaves a little after eleven."

Noah set down his knife and leaned on the island. "No kidding."

Macey frowned. "You seem surprised. I wasn't going to stay here forever, you know."

Noah picked up his knife and continued his buttering. "Don't you have some unfinished business still?"

Macey didn't bother trying to keep her arms from folding in front of her chest in a typical defensive stance. "Unfinished business? I've spent the last two days training my mother on a computer. I've tried every conceivable way to secure her future. If she doesn't get this job, I don't know what I'm going to do."

"What job?"

"Mom's interviewing for a job tomorrow."

"Why?"

Macey felt irritation begin to simmer inside. She narrowed her eyes at him and tried to find his angle. What was he trying to do now? "It doesn't matter," she said. "What matters is that she gets it."

Noah took a bite of his toast and seemed to size Macey up. Macey stood tall and tried to look confident. She hated the way he always needed to know more, always seemed to read between the lines.

After a swig of juice he said, "That's not the unfinished business I was referring to."

"Oh?" Macey's voice jumped an octave unintentionally. "Then what unfinished business were you referring to?"

"You told me a lot last night, Macey. You really poured out your heart. I think you needed to. That was a lot to carry around for all those years." Noah paused, and Macey felt her face turn red. She didn't want to talk about this anymore. She wanted to say good-bye to him and ride all the way to New York wondering if there could've been something between them under different circumstances, in a different time and place. This was a safe place to stay—inside her head, wondering.

"Yes, but that's not why I'm here."

"You're here to say good-bye." He stood taller and put down his toast, brushing his hands together to rid them of crumbs. "But if you leave now, with things undone, what good will that do?"

Macey shook her head and stared down at the tile. What did he want from her? Why did he care so much what she took back with her? "I can't solve all my problems in a day," she insisted.

"No, but you can tie up some loose ends." He paused and then said, "If you don't intend on coming back."

She looked up at him. His eyes looked desperate. "I'm sure I'll return. Not next week, but I'll come back."

He blinked slowly as if searching for words, then said, "Macey, have you and your mother talked? Talked at all about what happened?"

"There's nothing to talk about." What a cliched answer, she thought. The truth was, there was too much to talk about.

Noah, of course, didn't buy the answer and cocked his head to the side, his eyebrows raised high on his forehead. "That's a lame answer."

"What did you expect? A tidy ending to my dramatic return home? Is that what you people think who sit in your little pews and pray and sing and listen to some man talk about how good you should be and how good God is, and how everything is just going to turn out so perfect in life?" Her voice trembled as it rose in pitch. "There *are* no easy answers, Noah. Of all people, you should know that. Were there any easy answers when your wife died and left you to raise two children?" Macey gasped and thought she might've crossed the line. She met Noah's eyes, and although they reflected a sadness at the mention of his wife, he didn't appear angry. "I'm sorry," she offered quietly, her eyes fixed on her shoes now.

"It's okay," said Noah. "And, no, there were no easy answers."

Macey glanced up at him. His expression was sincere. "I'm sorry I brought that up," Macey said again. "I'm being overly emotional, and that's when I say things I shouldn't."

"You're upset. It's okay."

Macey leaned on the wall behind her, her hands clasped against her lower back. "Noah, I know your intentions are good. A few days ago, I wasn't so sure. You always seemed to get under my skin. But I know you better now. I know you have my best interests at heart." She paused and looked into his eyes. "Please, don't press me on this. It was a big enough step to sit here and tell you my dark secret. Don't make me go to places I'm not ready to go yet."

Noah listened carefully and nodded, but something in his eyes told her that he still wasn't satisfied with her answer. "How does your mom feel about your leaving?"

Macey welcomed the sudden change in conversation. "I think she's going to be okay. I told her we'd stay in contact, and I intend to. I'm going to have to follow up on the job situation, anyway."

Noah started to say something but stopped. Instead, he drank the rest of his orange juice. Macey checked her watch.

"I better go. I've got a flight to New York to catch."

Noah set his glass down, wiped his mouth. "You're always checking your watch—do you know that?"

Macey eyed him. "Is that a sin?"

"Not a sin," he said with a half smile. "Just an indication."

"Of what?"

"Of a woman who's unable to stop, turn around, and swim against the world's current."

"How metaphorical," Macey quipped.

He shrugged. "Just an observation."

"You do an awful lot of observing of other people, don't you? When's the last time you looked at yourself? Seen any faults in that tall frame of a man recently?" She smiled, but it wasn't friendly. Did he think he had a right to size other people up without ever looking at his own problems?

"True. So what's wrong with me?"

Macey swallowed, not expecting this question. But, as long as he was asking, she decided to oblige him. "You're nosey, for one thing."

"Ah. Nosey like snooping around the outside of someone's house, uninvited?" He grinned at her.

"Very funny. You're also sarcastic."

"Well, I think it makes a great complement to your cynicism." Macey shook her head. "Anything else? You're on quite a roll here."

"No." She checked her watch again, then let her hand drop to her side as she rolled her eyes. "It's a habit," she told him.

He chuckled. "I understand."

"But I really have to go. I can't afford to miss this flight. I can't believe in a few hours I'm going to be interviewing for a network job." She turned to exit the kitchen and he followed her. At the front door she said, "Tell the girls bye for me."

"I will."

"And thanks again for listening. It was extraordinary that I spilled my guts like that."

"I know."

She scratched her forehead. "Well, next time I'm in town, I'll stop by."

"Please do."

"And if I get this job, and you come to New York, look me up."

"Sure."

Macey's heart tugged at her. She didn't want to leave. There was a certain peace Noah offered her. Shared with her. The idea of peace was a foreign concept to her, yet there was proof now that it existed, proof every time she looked into his eyes. "Take care," she said, smiling warmly while turning to step out the door. A hand rested on her shoulder then, and she turned back. Was he going to kiss her?

"Macey," he said, and he seemed to fight for his words.

"Yes?"

"You'll never find what you're looking for in New York." His eyes stared through hers, straight into her soul. "No amount of success will undo what has been done. Not what your father did. Not what you did." He paused and looked to be in pain. "You took an innocent life."

Tears stung Macey's eyes. She stood frozen in the doorway, horrified by Noah's words.

"No matter what you do, Macey, no matter where you go, who you meet, or how you get there, that will always haunt you." If his words didn't sound so sincere, Macey would've slapped him. But the shock of actually hearing them had made her numb. "I know you regret what you did. I know you understand that it was wrong. But don't you think that it's time for you to face it, time for you to tell the truth to the one other person it would matter to?"

Macey looked at him in disbelief. What was he talking about? What other person? She could barely choke out the words. "Is that supposed to help me, give me peace?" she asked angrily.

"I don't know, but it's a step in the right direction. The only one who can give you peace is God. He can forgive you so completely that what happened is wiped from the scope of eternity forever. But there's one other person who you need to ask forgiveness."

How could he stand there and condemn her like this? And who could she possibly need forgiveness from?

"I don't know him personally, but I know of him," Noah said, reaching out to her. She dodged his hand. "He works for his dad at the hardware store in town."

"What?" Was he talking about Harley Preston? He knew Harley? What did she need to ask forgiveness from him for? Just days after their big mistake, he'd hardly cared about her. And now? He didn't even recognize her in the restaurant. He would've probably paid for the abortion himself if she'd told him. "You're crazy!" Macey said through clenched teeth. "You're crazy if you think I'm going to go find Harley Preston and confess to him that I—" The words dropped back down her throat. Macey stared hard at Noah. "What good would that do? What possible good would that do for anyone involved?"

A small warm smile crossed his lips. "There are no easy answers to that."

"Aren't you just perfect at bringing everything full circle!" Macey snapped. "You've got a lot of guts telling me this. Saying these things. I sat here in your house and trusted you with my heart, told you my dark secrets, and now you're standing here condemning me for it. What a friend you are."

Noah's expression darkened. "I'm not condemning you, Macey. Not at all. We all have our dark secrets. We all have our mistakes we regret. But sitting in my house and telling me all those things isn't going to bring you any closer to freedom than you are now. I'm not the father of that baby. And I'm not God."

"Thank heavens for that." The rims of Macey's eyes, red and swollen, held pools of tears ready to chase the others. "So that's what *God* is telling me to do, huh? Go tell Harley Preston, a man who couldn't have cared less for me then and even less now, that I had . . . had . . ."

"Yes." Noah's own eyes glistened with tears. "Yes, Macey. As hard as that sounds, you need to ask for forgiveness. You need to tell Harley the truth."

"You know what I think? I think you're out of your mind. I think you people sit out here, surrounded by your prairies and your river, and you seclude yourselves from reality. You have cookie-cutter answers for everything. Pray about it. Do the right thing. Ask for forgiveness. Confess your sins. It's just a ridiculous formula made up by weak people to try and make sense out of things that will *never* make sense."

He reached for her again, but she turned and ran down the porch steps.

"I'm sorry I ever met you," she growled under her breath. She walked as fast as she could. She couldn't wait to be on a plane, up in the sky, as far away from this sick, twisted place as she could possibly get.

Twenty-Seven

They embraced this time like long-lost relatives instead of distant strangers. Evelyn hugged her tight and patted her on the back like she had when she was a baby. Her daughter didn't pull away, surprisingly, and it was a cherished moment.

As they stood on her front porch, Evelyn wiped the tears from her eyes as often as she wiped the sweat from her brow. Neither bothered her. She just wanted to hold on to her daughter, hug her longer, kiss her, tell her she loved her over and over. But there wasn't time for that she realized as Macey ended the hug and glanced at her watch.

"I'm cutting it a little close, but I don't anticipate a lot of traffic," Macey said. She smiled and patted Evelyn on the arm. "Are you going to be okay?"

"Oh, I'm strong as an ox," said Evelyn with a definitive nod of the head. "If the heat don't kill me, I'll be fine." She said this while tears trickled down her cheeks.

"Mom, I hate to see you so upset," her daughter said. "Please don't cry."

"Don't you worry about me. I'm just so glad to have seen you, to see that you're a fine young woman, strong and smart and successful. I couldn't wish anything more for my daughter."

Macey looked away as if embarrassed. "Mom, I'm not quite that great, but I guess mothers are allowed to see their children through rose-colored glasses."

Evelyn chuckled. "It's what we do best."

"Now, you've got all the information about tomorrow. And you've got my phone numbers so you can reach me anytime. As soon as I return from New York, I'll call to see how the interview went."

Evelyn smiled at her daughter. "We've both got important interviews, don't we?"

"We sure do," Macey said warmly. "You're going to do fine. They'd be nuts not to hire a terrific lady like you."

"Ditto."

Macey had already started her car to let it cool. Evelyn knew her time was short, and Macey was looking at her watch again. She had to say it. She had to tell her daughter, to explain and, if possible, make things somewhat right.

"Okay, I'll call you in a couple of days, at the most," Macey said, embracing her mother one last time. Evelyn melted in her arms and clung a little too tightly for a little too long. She didn't care. It might be the last warm body she would ever hold. "Okay, Mom, okay," Macey said, prying Evelyn off of her, chuckling a bit. "At least I know I'm loved."

"You are," Evelyn said, still unable to stop the tears. "So much."

"I know," Macey said sincerely. "And you are, too." Macey glanced at her car. "I better get going."

Evelyn nodded and watched as her daughter turned to walk down the steps. *Say something. Say something, you old chicken. Say something!*

"Macey?"

Now on the sidewalk, halfway to her car, Macey spun around and looked at her mother. "Yeah?"

Evelyn hesitated. The moment of truth. "Have a good trip."

Macey nodded, smiled, waved, and continued walking to her car. She slid in, and the car slowly made its way down the gravel driveway toward the road. Before pulling the car onto the road, Macey gave one last smile and wave. Evelyn waved back, but she couldn't smile. Her lips trembled, making way for gasping sobs. She pulled a handkerchief from her pocket and cried into the soft cotton. Soon all she saw was a cloud of dust sent up from the car's wheels on the gravel. Just like seventeen years ago, she hadn't said a word. Twice in her life now she'd let her daughter go without trying to make things right. Because of her being too afraid of angry words.

Too afraid of the awful truth.

Evelyn stumbled into the house, weary from the heat, weary from her grief. Her feet dragged along the wood floors. It hit her then that she had an entire day to fill up. What would she do for hour after hour? Upstairs she knew a half-sewn business suit lay draped across her sewing table. She'd have to finish that. She must call Patricia to have her hair done before the interview tomorrow. She'd need to feed the chickens.

A thought crossed her mind as she stepped into the kitchen. She would get a dog. Go rescue an old geezer like herself from the pound. She never much cared for cats. They were too sneaky, always seemed like they knew something more than they were letting on. But dogs were loyal, and it wouldn't hurt her none to have someone to help guard the house. Savannah and Stephanie would enjoy a dog, too, and could help take care of it. The idea of getting a dog brought some comfort to Evelyn, but not much. It passed as quickly as the cool of the morning.

In the kitchen she decided to make herself coffee. But then she saw she'd already made some earlier. There it sat in the pot. Yet it was old; she needed fresh coffee. She dumped out the old grounds, took out a new filter, and measured a new batch. That took less than five minutes, so Evelyn decided she would figure out what to make for dinner later.

She stared into her freezer and tried to think of what she could fix for one person. Nothing came to mind. Maybe she should start buying those frozen dinners Patricia was always raving about. She closed the freezer door and decided to tackle the problem later.

She called the church office to see if anyone had recently died or had a baby or needed any type of meal or dessert or beverage. Pastor Lyle said everyone was doing fine but thanked her for her concern.

She decided to feed the chickens, and that took about fifteen minutes. She watered the tomato plants, which took another five. Twenty minutes later the sun felt to be drawing closer to the earth, so Evelyn thought she'd better make her way back inside. The coffee was ready, and Evelyn poured herself a cup but left it sitting on the counter because suddenly it didn't sound good to her.

She went to the living room and straightened the pillows on the couch and then gathered some of the old magazines and threw them in the wastebasket, only to retrieve them after deciding to go through each one to make sure she'd read them all. She found two *National Geographics* she hadn't read yet. Taking the two magazines upstairs, she laid them on the nightstand in her bedroom.

It was 10:10 when she climbed the stairs. She made her bed, checked the hamper to see how much laundry was there. Three dresses and some underwear. Not enough for a load. She moved to the bathroom to put on a little lipstick just in case someone stopped by during the day. She rubbed in her wrinkle cream, too, just for something to do, and then lotioned up her hands.

At 10:17 she opened the drapes in her room, straightened a few items on the top of her dresser. By now she felt a little tired, so she decided to sit on her bed for a moment. A couple of minutes later she found herself staring at the small drawer of her nightstand. In the darkness of this drawer was the unsent letter. She pulled out the drawer, immediately revealing the stark white envelope with *Jess Steigel* neatly printed on the outside, along with their address. Macey's name was written at the top left-hand corner, along with the last known address Evelyn had for her. She thought about opening the letter and rereading it, but knew it would only make things worse.

Instead, she tossed the envelope into the small trash can by the side of the bed and stared at the clock on the nightstand. It was 10:21. She blinked away some stray tears, realizing she'd never been so aware of time in her whole life.

◆ ◆ ◆

Her bags hit a large man on his buttocks, and as she turned to apologize, the bag swung around and knocked a little boy in the head. Many in the crowd nearby scowled at her. She apologized as best she could while still on the move, racing toward her gate, weighed down by her briefcase and her suitcase, which she was hoping to get away with as a carry-on, thus making her venture through JFK much easier and quicker.

A tall, thin, overly made-up woman in navy blue confirmed her ticket and reservation, and finally Macey collapsed into a chair in the waiting area next to an elderly couple dressed in matching Hawaiian shirts. She found herself inadvertently glancing back to the metal detectors at the far end of the airport, hoping to see a handsome man with a dark ponytail, a foot taller than the crowd he was moving with, trying to get her attention. But no one of that description ever came, and soon the woman in navy was calling out row numbers to begin boarding the plane.

With their tickets in hand, the elderly couple stood and walked toward the woman standing at the gate's entrance. Apparently they were first-class travelers. Macey sighed. She'd been unable to fly first class until St. Louis, but she supposed she was lucky to get a flight out at all. She thought about calling Mitchell, but then quickly decided against it. Mitchell would be fine. He always was.

She slumped in her seat, clutching her bags, and thought of her mom. She'd left her to fend for herself, to make things happen, to survive. Macey had done that since high school. But did her mom have the same fight in her? Now that her husband had passed on, did her mom know enough about the world to live in it all on her own? Macey pushed the thoughts out of her mind, telling herself she would deal with this later, after she returned from New York.

Her thoughts drifted to the network and the exciting possibilities there, but these were soon replaced by one word—Harley. She'd stifled her emotions enough to think more clearly about Noah's suggestion. It still seemed absurd to her. Nonsense. A cleansing of the soul? It had been almost impossible to speak of the incident with a stranger. To imagine confessing her terrible deed to the man who caused it to happen in the first place? Harley would probably think she was insane for bringing it up. Anyway, he'd only recently been divorced from his wife. Did he really need *this* right now?

She doubted she could even get herself to go see him, let alone tell him everything and ask his forgiveness. She was strong, but she wasn't that strong. Noah's words echoed in her mind. Was it true she would never find peace? Had she hoped to? In one sense it seemed a very complicated step. In another, though, it struck her as straightforward and simple. What she had done *was* wrong, and she knew it. It had left her soul in shreds. Only in her thirties, she was already left feeling tattered and worn—tired, old, drained. Did she have all this to look forward to for forty, fifty, maybe sixty more years? If time healed all wounds, why then hadn't she gotten better? Why did the pain feel as sharp and real as it did seventeen years ago? Time had passed, and life had moved on. But something was missing. Even at her most irrational moment, she knew that for certain.

The woman called her group of rows, and Macey rose slowly, lifting her bags while trying to keep her ticket and driver's license available. She let a number of people go before her; she didn't know why. Usually she was plenty happy to maneuver her way to the front of any line.

The line moved quickly, and before Macey knew it the woman in navy, with maroon lipstick and sticky eyelashes, was holding her hand out and plastering a smile across her face. "Ma'am? I'll need your ticket."

Macey stared at the woman, her thoughts elsewhere. Again Noah's words rushed back to her mind, and suddenly she understood that what he'd said was the truth. She'd never once in her life asked a single person for forgiveness. She was too proud and too scared to leave herself in that vulnerable of a position. What if they said no and rejected her? What if they laughed at her? Yet what if this was her only way to peace?

"Ma'am?"

Macey looked up and felt the whole world staring at her. The woman in navy still held that same smile on her face, a smile that was definitely forced.

"I'm sorry," Macey mumbled.

"Your ticket," the woman repeated.

"Oh." Macey swallowed hard. She could still turn back. She knew if she left Kansas now, it would be a big mistake. She would never find the courage to come back and do what she needed to do. Noah's stinging words had to remain fresh in her mind or the dull drone of the world would become the norm again.

"Ma'am, please, your ticket," the woman said sternly.

Macey smiled as she apologized to the woman, explaining that she wouldn't be boarding the plane after all, then turned and tried to leave the gate.

She hadn't foreseen the chaos her change of plans would cause, and she was questioned for fifteen minutes as to why she refused to get on the plane. Luckily for Macey it was a female security officer doing the questioning, and although Macey couldn't begin to explain the entire story, at one point she simply said, "It's about a guy."

The red-haired woman shook her head. "Honey, it always is. Don't you go letting a man run your life, you hear?"

"I hear you," Macey said, and the officer let her go.

Before leaving the airport, Macey flipped open her cell phone to call Bethie. Someone was going to have to call Mr. Winslow in New York, and it wasn't going to be her. She punched in the shortcut to Beth's cell. It rang and rang and then her voicemail picked up. Macey ended the call there. Where was Beth? She always answered her phone. She'd told Macey she even slept with it next to her pillow.

Macey rubbed her forehead, wracking her brain, trying to come up with other options. As the seconds passed, her heart fluttered at the thought of what she was about to do. Was she really going to cancel an interview with the network? It was doubtful she'd get another chance. She was throwing her dream away to chase after inner peace. Only days ago she'd seen the job in New York as the means to finally achieve for herself a life of peace and happiness. So much had changed. Yet so little, too. She still didn't have answers to all the questions that had hounded her for years.

Outwardly the circumstances hadn't changed much. But inwardly things were different, and she knew it. Before coming home, canceling a chance to work with the network would've been the most irrational thing she could conceive of.

Now it seemed almost rational. Somehow it seemed right. And with no guarantee—no guarantee of answers or peace or happiness. She was taking a risk.

Macey activated her cell phone again and called the station. If Bethie wasn't answering her cell phone, she knew for certain where to find her. A few rings later the station operator answered.

"This is Macey Steigel. I'm calling for Beth Munson."

"*One moment, Ms. Steigel.*"

After a few measures of horrible elevator music, a woman said, "*Macey, hi!*" It was Starla Clover, one of the reporters. What was she doing answering Bethie's phone?

"Starla . . . hello. I'm sorry, they must've transferred me to the wrong phone. I'm calling for Beth."

"*I'm at her desk. I was looking for a pencil sharpener.*"

"Oh. Is she there?"

"*No.*"

"No? Where is she? It's like she's dropped off the face of the earth."

Starla chuckled. "*Not quite. She had an emergency appendectomy early this morning. Hold on.*"

There was indecipherable mumbling for a moment, and before Macey could identify the muffled male voice, Mitchell was on the phone. "*Well, well. Look who it is.*"

Macey's eyes rolled. "Mitchell."

"*Don't sound so glad to hear from me.*"

"Likewise," Macey said. "You were pretty coldhearted the last time we spoke."

The tension in Mitchell's voice eased up a bit. "*Yeah, well, I was mad. I'm slowly but surely getting over it.*"

"Good. Because it wasn't personal."

A pause was followed by, "*Are you in New York?*"

"Uh . . . no."

"*I'm assuming then you're on your way.*"

"No." The little word came easier than she thought it would.

"*No? Did your flight get delayed?*"

"I'm not going."

Mitchell laughed sardonically. "*You're not going?*"

"That's right. I'm not going," Macey repeated. "Some things have happened here. Things I don't expect you or anyone else to understand. But I'm canceling my interview."

She could hear Mitchell breathing heavily into the phone. *"Have you lost your mind?"*

"The jury's still out on that one," Macey said, only half jokingly.

Silence passed over the phone line for half a minute, and then Mitchell said, *"Am I to assume you won't be returning to Dallas, either?"*

"No, you're not to assume that, Mitchell." She shook her head and wished she could see Mitchell's expression, read his eyes. "I plan on returning home. I'm sorry this is hard for you to understand. But, as cliché as it may sound, it's something I've got to do."

The familiarly intense but friendly tone that Macey was so accustomed to from Mitchell returned. *"I don't understand it, but I guess that's not important."* His voice lowered to almost a whisper. *"I'm about to kill Alexis, so can you give me a time frame or anything? Will you be back next week?"*

Macey smiled. Mitchell was back to normal. "I will," she said. "I promise."

Her ear filled with Mitchell's heavy and relieved sigh. *"Fine. Then we'll just count on that."*

"Thanks."

"We'll see you soon."

"Okay. Bye. Oh, Mitchell, wait."

"Yes?"

"What hospital is Beth in?"

"Medical City."

"Thanks. Bye."

Macey quickly dialed information to get the number to the hospital, connected, and got the operator. *"Medical City Dallas Hospital."*

"Beth Munson's room, please."

"*Hold.*"

A few clicks pounded in Macey's ear like a jackhammer. So she had a little surgery. Surely she could still call New York for her. With all that was going on, she wasn't going to have to call New York herself, was she?

"*Hello?*" The voice sounded unfamiliar.

"Um . . . hi. I'm calling for Beth. Is she there?"

"*No. She's still unconscious. Who's this?*" The voice sounded slightly impatient.

"Macey Steigel. I work with Beth."

"*Oh. Well, she won't be at work today, I'm afraid.*" The voice was now irritated.

"Of course." Macey closed her eyes and managed to find her humanity. "How is she doing?"

The voice lightened up a little. "*They said the surgery went fine. She's in recovery right now.*"

"Are you a relative?"

"*Sister.*"

"Oh. Well, um . . ." Macey scratched her nose and realized her prayers would go unanswered here. "Tell her Macey called and I hope she's feeling better."

"*I will. And thanks for calling.*"

Macey pushed the button that ended the call, then groaned out loud, causing a couple of people passing by to turn and look. She would have to call New York herself. She found her phone directory in her briefcase, looked up the number, and slowly punched it in.

She never heard what the operator said, only that someone had answered.

"Uh, Mr. Winslow, please."

"*Hold, please.*"

The seconds ticked by and then, *"Mr. Winslow's office."*

"Is Mr. Winslow in?"

"He's with someone at the moment. With whom am I speaking?"

"This is Macey Steigel. I have an appointment with Mr. Winslow this afternoon."

"Yes, we're expecting you, Ms. Steigel." The woman hissed her *s*'s.

"I'm sorry . . . terribly sorry. I'm going to have to cancel."

Macey could tell by the short laugh on the other end that his secretary wasn't used to people canceling appointments with the great Thornton Winslow. *"Excuse me?"*

"Again, I'm terribly sorry. I'm just going to have to cancel."

"I see," the woman said demeaningly. *"Mr. Winslow will be disappointed to hear that."*

"I'm disappointed as well," Macey said. "If he wants to call, my cell phone number is—"

"We've got your numbers, Ms. Steigel. I'll give him your message."

The phone went dead, and Macey's eyes stung with the threat of tears. She stared at the ceiling and drew deep breaths in order to calm herself. She checked her watch. It was eleven-forty. She gathered her luggage and strolled through the airport, down the escalator, and to the rental car area. The same round-faced woman who had helped her only a couple of hours ago when she returned the car stood stoically behind her computer, waiting for the next customer. Several people were before Macey, so she waited her turn. When she finally stepped up, the woman peered at her over her glasses. "May I help you?"

"Need to rent a car," Macey said.

The woman's thin lips pressed together. "Didn't you just turn in a car earlier this morning?"

"That's me," Macey said whimsically.

The woman shrugged and began typing Macey's information into her computer. "And how long will you be staying this time?"

"Hard to say."

"And what type of car would you like to rent today?"

Macey smiled. "The smallest, cheapest thing you got."

The woman continued typing, and after a few minutes handed Macey her keys and confirmation papers. As she started to walk through the doors that led to the rental car parking lot, Macey stopped. With one swift motion, she pulled off her watch and tossed it into a nearby wastebasket.

Only time will tell, she thought, *if there is such a thing as peace like a river.*

Twenty-Eight

Evelyn walked slowly along the bank of the Neosho. She'd wanted to get out earlier and walk but had busied herself and lost track of the time, and now the sun was higher in the sky, the humidity thick. She took her time, though, and was careful to stay near the shade trees that, upstream from Stone Bridge, stretched forth their limbs over the riverbank. Still, the sweat rolled down her cheeks, and she decided it was time to head back to the house. She'd invited Patricia over for lunch and expected her to be arriving soon.

Before turning back toward home, she stood on the bank above the river, closed her eyes, and prayed. It wasn't a fancy prayer, and she certainly wasn't on her knees like her grandmother had taught her, but she figured the good Lord would hear it anyway. For a long time she listened to the burble and slosh of the river, which soothed her and reminded her of younger days when she and Jess would hold hands and walk here, with Macey trailing behind, skipping through the grass and searching for frogs.

Then there were the later years when they'd walk even slower and not as far, and although Evelyn never knew for sure, she guessed Macey was on Jess's mind as they walked.

A flock of crows flapped their wings, making their notorious racket, prompting Evelyn to open her eyes and stare down again at the water. She hadn't yet spoken a word to the Lord, though her heart prayed. Sometimes there weren't words to describe the feelings of the heart.

But finally she found two words that seemed to sum up all that burdened her. She uttered them aloud. "Help me."

It was all she prayed. Afterward, hoping she hadn't lingered too long, she turned and headed home. The sun easily burned her tender skin. She tried to pick up her pace, but this only left her gasping and out of breath.

She passed by Stone Bridge once again and smiled at the thought of how many times Stephanie and Savannah had run across it to visit her. She glanced over at Noah's house but didn't see anyone outside in the yard.

She stopped walking. Something caught her eye. It was a box, half opened, with something inside. Carefully stepping to the edge of the bank, she peered down and tried to steady herself. She had never been fond of heights.

"What in the world?" Evelyn said out loud and squinted her eyes to focus on the object better. It looked to be a small white clothing box. Whatever was inside the box also looked to be white, though very dirty. Had someone lost it?

Her feet inched closer to the bank's edge, and for a brief moment she thought about attempting to climb down and rescue it from the water and rocks below. But she dismissed the thought as quickly as it came. Nevertheless, something was drawing her to the little cardboard box.

"What are you doing?"

Evelyn whipped around, her foot breaking loose on the slippery riverbank. A strong hand caught her and pulled her to level ground. "Patricia!" Evelyn gasped.

"You looked as though you were gettin' ready to jump!" Patricia said, staring at her like she'd lost her mind.

Evelyn shook her head while trying to catch her breath.

"And what may I ask are you doing out in this heat?"

Patricia's eyes were wide with concern.

Evelyn's lungs finally caught up with her need for air. She pointed down to the river. "Look at that."

Patricia took a glimpse over the edge. "Looks like a box."

"There's something in it," Evelyn said.

"Ruined by now," said Patricia, taking Evelyn's arm and urging her back to the house. "It's all wet and covered with mud."

Evelyn stopped her. "Patricia, could you do me a favor and climb down there and get it?"

Patricia looked at her, a worried expression crossing her face. "Are you okay?"

"I'm fine," Evelyn insisted. "But there's something about that box." She glanced back down at it.

Patricia shook her head as she knelt down on the bank. "Pretty steep. But I've done worse." She turned around and lowered herself backward off the edge, sliding a couple of feet before finding her footing on some rocks. She jumped to a more stable area, hopped over a few more rocks, and then was down by the river and the box. Carefully balancing on the rocks sticking out of the river, she was finally close enough to reach for it. After two tries, she snagged it.

Climbing back up proved easier, even while holding the box out away from her body. Patricia was soon scrambling up over the edge and dusting herself off. She handed the box to Evelyn, then started scraping mud off the bottom of her shoes.

"What is it?" she asked, looking up at Evelyn. "Evelyn? What's wrong?"

Evelyn's whole body shook as she stared at the contents of the box. "Oh, dear Lord," she muttered.

Patricia looked into the box. "Looks like a baby gown."

Tears welled up in Evelyn's eyes. "It is."

It seemed to have become a routine these days: Patricia and Evelyn sitting together on Evelyn's couch, with Patricia patting Evelyn on the back while she sobbed into a tattered tissue. It was much the same grief she had felt the day she found out Jess had lung cancer and that there was nothing the doctors could do. It wasn't quite the end, but it sure had felt like it was.

Evelyn knew she'd see Macey again someday. The gentle kindness in her daughter's eyes told her so. But she didn't know when, or how, or even if it would be anytime soon. Her whole life had been filled with days marked by the predictable, routines she'd developed to perfection. She hadn't complained about it. In fact, there was a certain comfort in it. Now, the one time the Lord had asked her to be a little bold, to step out in faith and do the right thing, she failed miserably.

"There, there," Patricia said sympathetically. "It's not the end of the world. God's still God, and He's still in the miracle business. You know He works round the clock, seven twenty-four. He's not going to let you down now."

Evelyn nodded but still continued to sob. "But I failed Him. And I failed my daughter. I'm a coward, Patricia. A coward."

"Don't you say such things. It wasn't promising to be an easy thing, what you're needin' to do. God's the God of second chances, so we just need to be prayin' that everything comes around."

Evelyn shook her head. "He gave me a second and third and fourth chance already. I blew it every time. I'm a good-for-nothin' coward." She stared at her hands. "My poor daughter. Finding that little outfit. That's the only explanation for why it ended up in the river. What she must be thinking! Poor girl."

Patricia continued to rub circles on Evelyn's back, and Evelyn continued to weep. After a while, the grief faded into exhaustion and the tears dried up, making her eyes red and painful. The sobs had turned into slow and deep breaths, and she began to sense an inkling of hope. She didn't know from where it came, but for some reason her heart didn't hurt so much. She looked at Patricia, who smiled warmly at her.

"You okay, old gal?"

Evelyn nodded. "I'm sorry to put you out like this. I know you're busy helpin' folks much worse off than me."

"Nonsense. We're friends. Friends are there for each other. Besides, I was supposed to be out at Cal Courter's home, and he's so self-centered that it takes all my energy just to go visit him. Maybe me skippin' a day will make him appreciate me all the more."

Evelyn smiled. "Well, at least let me make you that lunch I promised you. I've got a whole fridge full of food and no one to eat it but me, and I certainly don't need it all."

"Sure thing," Patricia said. "You got any of Fred's roast beef?"

A relieved grin spread across Evelyn's face.

———◆———

Patricia and Evelyn sat at the kitchen table and ate lunch together, enjoying roast beef sandwiches, ice tea, and sweet pickles. Evelyn reminisced a little about Jess, the first time she was able to talk about their good memories without feeling complete heartache. Patricia admitted her fear of never getting married and how it was one of the more difficult trials the Lord had put her through.

As Evelyn listened, she quietly thanked God for this good friend. Even though a widow now, Evelyn wasn't totally alone. Patricia hadn't just been her husband's nurse; she was indeed a friend. She'd felt close to Patricia during the months Jess was sick but had feared their relationship would fade after Jess's death. Thankfully, that wasn't happening.

There were also Noah and the girls. She could see how much they missed Jess. He was always the one who would take them out on the tractor or let them feed the chickens. She so appreciated the way Noah took care of her in the way a son would. She'd always wished she had given birth to more children, but it never worked out that way. And apparently they hadn't done too well with the one God had given them.

As she ate, she kept thinking of the little baby's gown lying among the rocks down by the river. How had Macey found it? And when exactly? Evelyn closed her eyes and tried not to think about it.

"Let me help you with the dishes," Patricia offered as she finished off her sandwich.

"No need," said Evelyn. "It'll give me something to do for a while."

"You should go down to the community center in town, see what they have going."

Evelyn shrugged. "Maybe. I like this house. I never much left it when Jess was alive, but maybe things are going to have to change that way." She looked at Patricia. "I've got that big interview tomorrow at AST."

"That's right!" Patricia exclaimed. "Are you nervous?"

Evelyn shook her head. "No. I doubt I'll get it. Who would hire an old woman like me? But Macey wanted me to do it, so I will. If it doesn't work out, I'm not sure what I'll do next. I'll figure out something, I suppose."

"The Lord will help you." Patricia set her plate on the kitchen counter and swallowed the last of her ice tea. "What do you say we go into town for a little shopping?"

"Really?"

"I hear Sarah's Antiques just got a new shipment. June was braggin' about it at church Sunday."

Evelyn laughed. Maybe life would go on, after all. "I'll get my purse," she said.

Patricia nodded and headed outside. Evelyn was following her when the dirty, wet box and baby gown caught her attention again. It was sitting on some newspapers on the floor in the living room. She stared at it for a moment. She had lied only once to her husband in their forty-something years of marriage. She told him she'd thrown it away. But she hadn't. She'd hidden it in the back corner of a closet instead and hadn't seen it until today.

"Let's take your car," Patricia shouted from outside. "My old clunker doesn't have air-conditioning worth a hoot."

"Coming," Evelyn called. She thought about running the box and gown back upstairs to the closet, but then she decided against it. She'd had enough of hiding, enough of secrets, enough of dark corners in dark closets. She shuffled outside and shut the door behind her.

"Mother?"

Her words echoed off the silent walls. Macey figured she'd gone somewhere when she drove up to find Patricia's car there and her mother's car gone.

"Mother?" she called again. But there was no answer except for the old air-conditioner kicking on. She stood in the doorway, trying to decide what to do next. She could go in, relax on the couch awhile, wait for her mother to come home. She decided instead to walk over to Noah's, perhaps apologize for her behavior earlier and get some guidance on the next steps she should take.

As hot as it was, Macey felt energized and liberated. She rounded the corner of the house and headed for the river. The sun beat down on her skin, but she didn't care. Somehow it felt nice just to be out in the sun, breathing hot but fresh air, strolling through lush green grass beside a beautiful river.

She neared Stone Bridge and remembered the box and gown, hesitating for a moment. The tiny dress represented so much. Dare she retrieve it, hold it again? She smiled. Yes. If she could turn down New York, she could do anything. She walked to the edge of the bank and took in a sharp breath. The box was gone. She ran a ways downstream, searching for it. But there was nothing but rocks. Shading her eyes, she scanned the opposite bank. Again, all she saw was mud and rocks. A deep sense of loss swept over her. Just when she'd made peace with the thing, it was gone. She sank to the ground and braced herself with her hands behind her. It seemed her life had been one incident of bad timing after another. Though she'd been meticulous about time her whole life, somehow she knew that in returning, all would be different. She didn't know whose time frame she was on, but it wasn't hers. She blankly watched the river rush by, the grass tickling her hands and ankles.

"Looking for this?"

Macey whirled around and looked upward. She only heard a voice; the sun's bright rays blinded her so she could make out only a dark silhouette. She jumped to her feet and found herself staring into the eyes of her mother.

"Mom!"

Her mother looked down, and in her hands was the mud-stained box with the little gown inside. Macey's eyes widened, and her heart pounded inside her chest. Her mom had found the gown?

"Patricia retrieved it for me this morning," Evelyn said softly. "I saw it when I was takin' a walk. Figured you'd found it in the closet."

Macey took it from her and felt the gown's white fabric, still soft. She was speechless.

Evelyn patted her on the arm. "Well, I may be a little slow at times, and sometimes the Lord has to do a little yelling to get my attention, but the very fact that you're standing here tells me He's worked a good and true miracle, so this time I'm not going to chicken out."

Macey swallowed, unsure what her mother was talking about.

"Macey, dear, what do you say we go and have ourselves a little talk."

Macey sat in the lawn chair under the shade tree and waited for her mom to come back out of the house. They'd returned to the house in silence, both, she knew, deep in thought. The thermometer on the tree indicated ninety-five degrees, a much welcomed relief from the extreme heat they'd had only a couple of days ago. Thankfully there was a breeze, and Macey found herself quite comfortable, even with the baby's gown in her lap.

Evelyn approached her with a tray holding two glasses filled with ice and a large pitcher. "Raspberry tea," she said, setting the tray on the aluminum table between the two lawn chairs. She poured Macey's first, then hers, and finally settled into the empty chair.

"Perfect," Macey said, sipping it. "There's nothing better than ice tea on a day like this."

Evelyn agreed, and for a moment they both just sat and enjoyed the coolness of the drink. But soon the silence became dominating, and Macey heard her mom clear her throat. "Well, I put this off long enough," she said, "and it's just time for me to say it."

Macey felt her shoulders rise with tension. She tried to remain calm, telling herself she had to go with the flow, whatever was to happen. She hadn't returned only for the mild-mannered chitchat and good fried chicken.

"It's time you knew," her mother began, "and I'm going to tell you all that I know, and I hope that in some small way it will make

up for the terrible mess your father and I made of everything."
Macey shook her head and started to protest, but her mother held
up a firm hand. "I know you must think your father was a bad man,
and I'll admit right here and now that he made some pretty awful
mistakes. But he always loved you, Macey. And he always regretted
what he did to you."

Macey stared at her feet. If only she could believe it.

"You're probably wondering about that little baby gown,"
Evelyn said, pointing to it.

While stroking its sleeve, Macey said, "I went to Madeleine's,
found out Dad bought it there on the very same day I . . ." Macey
covered her mouth. To say it in front of her mother was an impossibility. "That same day. But I have no idea what it all means."

Her mother looked at the gown. "Your father felt so bad about
what he said to you when you first told him you were pregnant. He
had reacted out of anger, and as he prayed and thought about it, he
knew that God's forgiveness was abundant, just like He'd promised,
and that it would extend out to you no matter what. He told me
what had happened, and he decided he'd go and get a baby baptism outfit. He certainly wasn't in favor of any child being born out
of wedlock, but he believed a child raised with the principles of
the Lord, one raised in the church and with love, would be a child
blessed." Evelyn paused. "So he went out and got that outfit. Paid a
lot of money for it, too. It was . . . a gesture—" Macey glanced up at
her mom as she fought for words—"a gesture of love, a way for him
to ask for your forgiveness." Evelyn tried to smile away the tears.
"Your father was a proud man, as you know, and not one to admit
he was wrong very much. Most of the time he wasn't." She chuckled
softly. "So the baptism outfit was a way that he could tell you he was
sorry and that he had accepted the situation . . . that everything was
going to be okay."

Macey fought her own tears. "So he went out and bought this the same day I . . ."

Evelyn blinked at her. "Yes."

Macey stared at the gown. "I remember he was holding a box when I told him what I'd done. He was in the living room, in his chair. I didn't know then what was in the box, and then everything went so crazy after I told him."

"He did go crazy," Evelyn agreed. "I was upstairs in the bedroom and I heard everything. I was so scared, for the both of you."

A quietness settled as they both gathered their thoughts. Then Macey said, "He hated me so much that day, Mom. I was the apple of his eye one day, and the next the spawn of Satan."

"I know it seemed that way. You'd never seen your father's temper. Directed at you, anyhow. He said some horrible things, I know he did. But when it was all over and done with, when you'd left and the house was quiet, your father and me, we both knew that he was more angry with himself. He told me so," Evelyn said, glancing at Macey. "He told me it'd all been his fault. If he hadn't overreacted as he did, if he hadn't said those things, then you wouldn't have gone and done what you did. He was devastated, completely devastated."

Tears flowed down Macey's cheeks, and she doubled over with a heart-wrenching cry. Her mother's hand rubbed her back as Macey wept long and hard. After several moments she finally was able to stop sobbing long enough to sit up and look her mom in the eye.

"Noah told me that Dad used to sit at the bus station and wait every Christmas and Thanksgiving. Was he waiting for me?"

Evelyn nodded. "Every night he prayed you would come home. I don't suppose he ever really thought you'd get off a bus, but it was his way of expecting the Lord to do the impossible."

Macey shook her head and aggressively wiped away the tears. "I don't understand. If he was so sorry for everything, why didn't he come find me? Why were you the only one I ever got a card from?"

Evelyn held Macey's hand. "It's hard to explain. I think mostly he felt guilty, afraid that if he made that attempt, you would reject him. I'm not sure he could've gone on if that had happened. That's also why I didn't contact you as much as I should have. I sent a few cards, hoping you'd come home. And then when you moved, we didn't know where to find you. So we figured—" Evelyn sighed— "we figured you didn't want to be found."

Macey shrugged. "I guess I didn't. I was angry. Very angry."

"Understandably so. It just fell apart, and neither of us knew what to do. We're farm people. We go day by day and live a simple life. What happened was, well, it was complex and difficult, and I don't think your father and I knew what we were supposed to do. Especially your father. He felt he'd failed as a father in all respects. He felt he hadn't done a good enough job teaching you the Bible. Maybe he hadn't loved you enough, made you feel secure enough. What happened all those years ago he considered the biggest mistake and the biggest regret of his whole life."

Macey nodded, trying to take it all in. All these years it had been a mystery. And now she had the answers. The thought consumed her, and she found herself not knowing what to say.

"If there's anything for you to know, it's that your dad loved you—always."

Macey nodded, bowed her head, and began weeping again. The finality of her father's death left her heart aching. If only she'd come home. If only he'd found her. She covered her eyes with a trembling hand. If only God had answered his prayer.

Twenty-Nine

"I sure hope this thing thaws in time," Evelyn said. She dropped the roast to the counter and it landed with a thud. Macey couldn't help but smile. It delighted her mom to cook. And, she had to admit, she herself was beginning to enjoy the home cooking. "What time is it?"

Macey glanced down at her wrist and then laughed. "I have no idea."

Evelyn moved to the kitchen entryway and looked at a clock in the living room. "In this heat the thing's bound to not only thaw but cook itself! Boy, I love a good roast."

"Potatoes and carrots, too?" Macey asked.

"What's a roast without 'em?" Evelyn went to the pantry and started digging around.

Macey sat perfectly still, her eyes puffy. The coolness of the house let her breathe more slowly. For once in her life she wasn't on a schedule and she didn't care what happened next.

"Should we have Noah and the girls over for dinner?"

Macey hesitated in answering her mom. She had to think on it. When she left Noah earlier, she'd been angry. Though she doubted he was the type to hold a grudge, she didn't want there to be any awkwardness. "Let's keep it to just you and me tonight, Mom."

Evelyn turned and smiled warmly, nodding with satisfaction.

While thankful she'd learned the truth about her father and what had really taken place those terrible days so long ago, for Macey the knowledge was accompanied with a sadness, the kind that would stick with her, it seemed, for a very long time. It wasn't despair. Just sadness, plain and simple. Nothing could bring her father back, and nothing could make things right. She would just have to live with the consequences of what happened, which for her was hard even to think about.

"Oh, I'm such a klutz!" her mother cried, causing Macey to shake off her somber thoughts. Her mother bent over as if in pain.

"Mom, you okay?"

"Fine, fine," Evelyn grumbled. She stood with a pair of broken eyeglasses in her hand. "Knocked 'em off the counter, then stepped on them." Her mother tossed the glasses back on the counter. "Those were my good pair, too."

Macey rose to her feet. "Let's go into town and get you new ones."

Evelyn sighed. "Maybe another time. I've got another pair upstairs. They're not as fancy as these, but they'll do." She headed toward the stairs.

"Let me," Macey offered. "Where are they?"

"In the drawer of my nightstand. Should be right at the front."

"Be right back." Macey climbed the stairs and went toward her mother's bedroom, her feet scooting across the wood floor. Her body felt heavy with exhaustion, but her mind was clear, the exact opposite of her life before she came home. Before, she was physically fit, able to go around the clock, but beyond that, things were fuzzy. She never quite knew why.

And something else had entered her soul—a lack of rage. It felt strange. She'd been so temperamental and moody before, always on edge, never knowing when she was going to explode. The tension that so often rocked her world had mysteriously vanished. She smiled at the thought as she opened the door to her mother's room.

She sat on the edge of the bed and for a moment took in the room's atmosphere. She'd spent endless nights under the covers of this bed during storms. Her father had shown her their new puppy in this room. She oftentimes would take naps here, because it was cooler than her room. There was always the distinct smell of night cream and baby powder near the bathroom.

She remembered that her mother was waiting for the glasses, so she pulled open the little drawer of the nightstand and found them. Just for fun she tried them on, something she would've done as a little girl. To her surprise, everything was clearer, the edges and lines in the room having become more in focus. She chuckled. She'd have to look into getting glasses when she got back home.

She hopped off the bed when something caught her eye. If she hadn't had the glasses on, she might not have seen it. In the small trash can beside the nightstand was an envelope, addressed to her father. On the top left-hand corner of the envelope was written *Macey Steigel* with her former San Antonio address.

What is this? she wondered.

The flap of the envelope came unstuck easily, as if it might not have been completely sealed. She removed her mother's glasses, pulled out the letter, and began to read.

The *click click click* of the potato peeler was the only sound filling the kitchen. She'd probably peeled too many potatoes and carrots, but no matter. She planned on having a feast. She would bake fresh bread, put together a simple salad, and even make an apple cobbler if she had enough apples. She chopped the potato she'd just peeled and threw the pieces into a large pot. Behind her, she could hear the familiar thump of someone coming down the stairs. For years it had been Jess. He'd often skip the last step and hit the floor a little hard. With Macey, the thumping sounded lighter and quicker.

"Did you find the glasses?" Evelyn asked, picking up another potato, promising herself it would be the last. When no response came, she turned to find her daughter standing near the kitchen's entrance, her eyes upset and bloodshot. She held a white envelope in one hand, a piece of paper in the other. At first, she didn't put it together. But when she read the expression on her daughter's face more closely, she knew. The potato she was holding dropped to the kitchen floor and rolled several feet before coming to rest against the wall. Neither of them looked down. Macey's eyes stayed steady on Evelyn, and Evelyn reached out for a chair at the breakfast table and sat down.

"It was in the wastebasket in your bedroom," Macey said, not moving a muscle.

Evelyn's eyes lowered in shame. How could she have been so careless? Yet how could she have imagined her daughter would return home? She covered her mouth, unable to speak.

Macey finally walked over and sat at the table with her. "This looks like my handwriting."

Evelyn nodded but couldn't look her daughter in the eyes. "I used one of your old school papers from high school. I tried to copy it as exact as I could."

"The moth and the butterfly," her daughter breathed. A brief pause was followed by "You wrote an apology on my behalf? You tried to express to Dad how I might be feeling? What I was thinking? Why I had stayed away so long?"

Evelyn couldn't keep herself from trembling. Everything had been so good just minutes ago. And now this. "I . . . I thought, I just thought—" Evelyn stumbled over her words—"your father was dying, and I knew how much he grieved the fact that you two had never made amends. It saddened him more than I can tell you." Evelyn's voice shook with each word. "I couldn't bear to see him die with his heart so broken."

She finally glanced up at Macey, whose face appeared expressionless. Evelyn almost screamed as she waited with bated breath for some reaction from Macey. Then, to Evelyn's astonishment, a small but warm smile spread across her daughter's lips. Evelyn's eyes widened. What was she smiling about? Wasn't she angry?

Macey looked down at the letter, shaking her head and smiling even more. "I guess I should be mad, Mother. I mean, you lied. You deceived. But you did it with the best intentions. I can see that." She looked her mom in the eyes. "And for some reason, it brings me great peace to know that Dad knew how much I loved him, that maybe things were made a little more right between us before he died." Macey's face brightened. "Just to know that he didn't die wondering makes me feel happy." Evelyn shook her head and started to say something, but Macey continued, "Yeah, maybe it wasn't true at the time. When this was written, no, I didn't feel this way, but now I do. Now I know things I didn't know before. Everything's changed." Macey reached across the table and took Evelyn's hand. "Thank you, Mom. Thank you for doing this."

Evelyn pulled her hand away, rose slowly from her chair, and stood facing the counter and shaking uncontrollably. Now what? Should she tell her daughter the truth? Tell her that she hadn't sent the letter? She'd let her husband die believing Macey would never love him again. Could she let her daughter believe the same?

"Mother?" She could feel Macey behind her. "What's wrong? I said I'm not mad."

Evelyn shook her head and waved her daughter away. This was too much for an old woman to take. She scolded herself for ever writing the letter and then not being more careful in discarding it. She grabbed a potato and started peeling it. It was the only thing she could think to do. But two firm hands turned her around, and soon she was staring into the bewildered face of her daughter.

"What's the matter?" Macey demanded.

Evelyn pressed her lips together and resolved to tell Macey the whole truth. No matter how painful, she knew it was the right thing and that the future of their relationship depended on this moment. "Dear, your father never saw that letter." She said it more matter-of-factly than she intended to, but she was glad it had come out at all.

Macey stared at her as if trying to decide if she was telling the truth. "What are you talking about? I have it in my hands. It's addressed to Dad. It even has a stamp. . . ." Macey's voice trailed off as she looked again at the envelope. "There's no postmark."

Evelyn took a step back and set down the peeler. "I had intended to mail it. A couple of days before I thought your dad would pass on. I was even worried it might not make it here in time. But as I stood at the mail drop, I realized how deceptive it all was. I was trying to answer the prayer I had prayed. I was trying to play God. So I didn't send it. I wanted to so badly. I knew your father ached at the idea that you two would never see each other on this earth again. But I had to trust the Father more. It's hard when God says no to your prayers. I took comfort in knowing He had a reason."

Tears streamed down Macey's face now. She said through gritted teeth, "What possible reason could He have?"

"I don't know, dear. I wish I did."

Macey turned and buried her face in her hands. Evelyn let her cry. She didn't know what else to do and suspected Macey didn't need the comfort of two human hands right now. She needed something more divine than that.

Finally Macey turned back to Evelyn. "I thought this was my answer. I thought God had come through, that He'd somehow connected me and Dad across the divide and pulled us together again." Her daughter rolled her eyes toward the ceiling in an attempt to keep more tears from falling. "I don't understand this. I don't even know why I'm back here when I should be in New York getting the job of my dreams."

Evelyn bowed her head. She had no answer for that, either. She could only pray that her daughter's being here was part of God's plan.

"I'm going for a walk," Macey said, though she looked so tired Evelyn thought it would be better for her to lie down for a while.

Evelyn took a step toward her. "Are you sure? Where are you going?"

Macey opened the back door. "Somewhere where I think Dad might be."

———————◆———————

The walk wasn't quite a mile but it was uphill, and the heat made it feel more like three miles. She finally reached it, out of breath and sweating profusely, yet she was mindful of neither. She stood on the lawn and stared at the old chipped-up wood, the delicate stained glass, and the steeple that rose toward the heavens. When she had come here for church, she'd hardly noticed the structure. With all the people milling about, it had been insignificant. But now, with it empty, it truly seemed to be a house of God—reverent, noble, pure.

Macey walked up the narrow sidewalk, ascended the steps, and stared at the front door, a deep burgundy-colored heavy oak. In the center was fastened an ornately carved wood cross. Macey looked around. There wasn't another soul in sight. In the pasture across the way, a few cows grazed on scorched grass. The wind whistled by her, but that was it. She was totally alone.

It didn't surprise her that the front door was unlocked. No one here ever locked their doors and certainly not the church. It creaked as she pushed it open. She turned to shut it and found herself standing in the small darkened lobby. She moved into the sanctuary, which was ablaze with myriad colors from the sunlight filtering in through the twelve stained-glass windows, six on each side of the church. The dust in the air hovered in each beam of light, creating a hallowed scene close enough to reach out and touch. And she did, grasping nothing but air.

She walked forward, her body moving through the warm light with ease, her hands stuffed deep into the pockets of her pants. At the pulpit, a ghost of her father stood, and she distinctly remembered the time Pastor Lyle had been ill and her father had given the sermon. It was on unconditional love. She smiled at the memory. It had been one of the most exciting moments of her father's life. Macey recalled how proud she'd been of him and how perfectly natural he'd looked standing behind that pulpit, with his leather-bound Bible and his small reading glasses. He'd even bought a new suit for the occasion, and her mother had made herself a new dress. He'd started out with a joke, and everyone had laughed.

She stood at the altar, thinking about the peace she was feeling. All these years she'd never known peace like this. It had only been familiar to her as a child. She'd forgotten it long ago. But now the peace was back, and she basked in it. Nothing else seemed to matter.

The natural thing to do would be for her to kneel at the altar and pray, but instead she walked over to one of the stained-glass windows, closed her eyes, and absorbed the heavenly color and warmth that streamed through the glass.

She thought about the letter her mother wrote but never sent. In one sense, she wished it had been sent. But in another, something told her this wasn't the way it was supposed to work out. A surge of grief rose up in her as she thought of her father dying with such a burden. Guilt followed, and she wished she'd been level-minded enough to come home while he lived.

But nothing could be changed now. She blinked away the tears at the thought. Nothing could be changed.

Except one thing perhaps.

Macey swallowed hard, wiped her eyes, and laughed out loud at the absurdity of what she was about to do. Only hours ago it had seemed inconceivable. Now it hit her as something she needed to do. It wasn't something she wanted to do, for just thinking about it made her stomach churn. Nevertheless, it rang true in her heart, and she knew it might make at least one thing right in this otherwise very wrong situation.

As she stood facing the stained glass, she thought about praying. When she was a child, she had always found it easy to pray. The heart was pure, and God's love was abundant. Now, though, her life was a mangled mess, full of dark secrets and horrible deeds. Her heart had become like a twisted and knotted rope, fraying and barely connected to her soul.

So instead of praying she kept her hands in her pockets and walked out of the church. It was time to go see Harley Preston. Today would be the day of reckoning. And, she hoped, a day of restoration.

Then a chill of fear crept over her skin, and she decided to visit him tomorrow rather than today.

———————◦◆◦———————

"The roast beef is fabulous," her daughter said as they sat together for the evening meal.

"Oh, it practically cooks itself," Evelyn said. "I think the potatoes are overcooked, though."

"Taste fine to me." Macey smiled from across the table.

"Well, I guess a cook should take a compliment when she sees one," Evelyn replied, pointing to Macey's nearly empty plate. "I'm glad to see you have an appetite."

Macey nodded but avoided her mother's eyes.

"I suppose tomorrow's the big day," Evelyn said, and Macey's eyes shot upward, almost startled. Evelyn was confused at the reaction. Was the interview that big of a deal? "I tried on the suit last night. It's bunching at the shoulders, but other than that, it's a good fit."

Macey's posture relaxed. "Oh, the interview."

"What did you think I was talking about?"

Macey laughed. "Nothing. I'm just tired. Of course, tomorrow is your interview. Are you nervous?"

"A bit. I'm not sure I'll be a good fit over there. It's such a big place."

Macey asked for another helping of salad, then said, "You'll do fine."

As she handed the salad bowl across the table, Evelyn tried not to study her daughter too much. There was a change, that was for sure. Her eyes, once distant and cold, were now accepting and even the slightest bit joyful. Still, in the shadows of her face there was something troubling her. Was it the unsent letter? Or simply the overwhelming conclusion to seventeen years of mistakes, grief, and pain?

Evelyn set her fork down. "Dear, is something bothering you?" Macey looked up as if awakened from a light sleep. "You seem distant, and a little bothered."

She finished her bite. "No, Mom. I'm fine."

"Good, good," Evelyn said without being totally convinced. "Would you like more bread?"

Macey pushed her chair back from the table. "No thanks. I'm stuffed."

Evelyn finished the last bite on her plate, though her mother had always taught her that a lady should leave a little food on her plate, and stood to clear the dishes. "What'll you be doing tomorrow while I'm out at the interview? Maybe a little shopping?"

Evelyn had turned her back, but she could hear Macey helping clear the table. "I don't know." She set some dishes on the counter next to Evelyn. "Mom, eventually I'm going to have to go home. You know that, right?"

Evelyn nodded. She didn't want to believe it. God had returned Macey twice. Why couldn't He keep her here?

"I promised my boss in Dallas I'd return next week. But I want to see how your interview goes. Once we know that, we'll be able to plan a little better."

"You're still worried about this old lady?" said Evelyn, shaking her head. "I'm fine, dear. I'm in God's hands. What will happen will happen."

Macey's hands ran through her hair. "I know, Mom, I know. Just have a little faith, right?"

"It's simple."

"So they say," her daughter sighed, then continued to bring dishes to the kitchen counter. "You want this leftover roast wrapped up?"

"It'll make for a good lunch tomorrow."

Macey found some aluminum foil and began wrapping up the dish. "Tomorrow," she said, almost to herself. "A day never to forget."

"Come again?" Evelyn asked.

Macey looked at her. "Nothing, Mom." Her features clouded with that familiar resistance.

Thirty

"How do I look?"

Macey was sitting at the dining room table, engrossed in thoughts of seeing Harley Preston again. She looked up to the top of the stairs to find her mom in her new pink floral suit, adorned with pearls, her hair framed nicely around her face.

"Wow!" Macey stood. "You look like a regular office worker."

Evelyn shrugged and chuckled as she made her way down the stairs. "Well, I should've had Patricia come do my hair. I never can get it quite right. She has this way of ratting it."

"You look terrific," Macey reassured her, helping her conquer the last few steps. "And the makeup adds a nice touch."

"It's not overdone? I usually put on too much blush."

"It's perfect."

Her mother smiled and walked to the breakfast table, where she sat down to rest for a moment. "It's getting hot in here again. This heat's just getting unbearable."

Macey agreed. It wasn't yet noon and already the air-conditioner was having difficulty keeping the house comfortable. She sat with her mom, half listening to her mother's worries about the interview. Mostly she was wrestling with the idea of going to see Harley today. Was she crazy? What would possess her to do something like this? There had to be a reason why.

Maybe this was the last leg of the journey to healing. It sounded so formulated—too formulated. Twelve easy steps to forgetting your past and healing your pain.

As her mother was making another comment about her hair, Macey's mind wandered to that terrible day she'd gone to the clinic in Joplin. Although it would seem something so horrible would have plagued her every single day for years, it hadn't so much. It was almost as if it had waited dormant inside her soul, large but unnoticed, until one day it would explode.

Today, however, it would not only be in the forefront of her mind, it would be on her lips and tongue, and it would be spoken aloud, confessed, of all things. Confessed to the man who had the most at stake. Macey's mind played through all the possible reactions, and she couldn't begin to guess which one might come true. She could only hope that what she was doing would somehow bring closure to all the many chapters of despair that had unfolded throughout the years.

". . . but I figure she'll be able to see right through that."

Macey blinked. Her mother was leaning forward now and staring into her face. "I'm sorry, Mom. Did you say something?"

"You okay?"

"Yes. My mind just wandered a bit, that's all."

Her mother nodded and then waved her hand. "Well, I'm sort of a babbler, so it happens to me all the time. Anyway, I better shove off. It'll be quite a drive for me."

"You've got the map?"

"Yep."

"Yes."

"What?"

Macey smiled warmly. "Try to use *yes* instead of yep. It's a corporate thing."

"Oh. Gotcha."

Macey couldn't help but laugh as she helped her mother out the front door and to her car.

"Should I carry a briefcase or something?" her mother asked as Macey opened the car door for her.

"Not yet," she replied, steadying her mother into the seat. "Just relax. Be yourself. But don't downplay yourself like you're used to. No self-deprecating comments. Instead, emphasize your strong points."

Her mother looked worried. "My strong points are that I can iron a shirt wrinkleless and make the creamiest mashed potatoes this side of the Neosho."

Macey patted her on the shoulder. "Well, let's hope they hate dry cleaners and are hungry."

"You're going to be okay while I'm gone?"

Macey swallowed and smiled weakly. "I'll find something to do." She paused, then asked, "Mom, do we still have that property out on Farmer's Market Road?"

"Sure do. Haven't been out there in years, but we still have it. It's just sitting there, not doing too much except taking up space. Why?"

"Tell you later. You don't want to be late."

Evelyn nodded and pulled the door shut. Macey stepped back and watched her mother back out of the drive, two tires on the grass, and slowly make her way to the top of the hill and out of sight. This was it. It was out of her hands now. It was up to her mother or some higher power to make it work.

The middle of her back was damp with sweat, although she wasn't sure if this was because of the heat or the thought of her mother interviewing for a corporate job. That and what Macey was about to do next.

* * *

"I'm going to see Harley Preston," Macey announced after the front door to Noah's house swung open.

The tall man she'd grown to adore in a tumultuous kind of way smiled down at her and said, "I'm fine. How are you?"

Macey shook her head and stared down at her shoes. "I'm sorry. I'm just nervous." She glanced up at him. "After the way I left, I wasn't sure if you'd want to see me again."

"Hey, this is becoming a regular routine for us, and it always seems to work out fine in the end," he said, his customary grin taking away some of Macey's anxiety. "I am a little surprised to see you, though. I figured you'd be in New York by now." He opened the door wider, and Macey stepped in, following him into the kitchen. Stephanie and Savannah were seated on the couch, watching television.

"Macey!" they both cried, leaping up and running to her.

"Hi, girls," she said and embraced them both while looking up at Noah with a curious expression on her face.

"They love you. What can I say?" Noah responded with a shrug.

Savannah peered up at her. "You look happier today."

Macey smiled. "I feel happy." She winked at her. "My eyes, right?"

Savannah nodded. "Yep. You definitely look happier."

Stephanie turned toward the television. "C'mon. The commercial's over." They both ran back into the living room and threw themselves on the couch.

Noah walked to his studio, and Macey followed. He had been busy cleaning brushes when she knocked on the door.

"I didn't get on the plane," she said. "There were things I needed to wrap up here." His eyes understood every word she said.

"You threw away your dream job."

She nodded. "I guess so. Maybe it wasn't such a dream anyway. Maybe it was going to be more of a nightmare. I don't know. But I know I did the right thing by staying. Mom and I talked." She lowered her voice, but the girls were engaged in their cartoon. "I found out some things. I found out the truth."

Noah wiped his brushes carefully with a rag. "That's good. And you're okay with going to see Harley?"

"No, I'm not *okay* with it, really. But when I think about . . . confessing, I guess you could say there's this feeling that comes over me, a feeling of peace. It's like someone takes whatever has been resting on my shoulders all these years and lifts it away."

Noah's eyebrows creased in worry.

"What?" Macey asked. "Isn't this what you said I should do?" That familiar defensiveness began to creep in again.

Noah straightened his posture. "Macey, what do you expect to happen when you go see Harley?"

"I don't know. I'm trying not to think about it." She stared at one of Noah's unfinished paintings. "I guess I expect for things to be resolved. I mean, the past can't be changed. I know that. But with the truth comes resolution, right?"

"Sometimes," Noah said. He seemed to shake off his next thought and then smiled at her. "But whatever happens, you're doing the right thing."

Macey grinned with undue enthusiasm. "Hey, the truth shall set you free, right?"

Noah nodded, but there was something he wasn't saying. Macey let it go. She was resolved to visit Harley and tell him the truth, and Noah was the one who had advised her to. What else was there to say?

Macey released a tense sigh and said, "I envy you, Noah. I mean, I envy your life. Two beautiful daughters. A peaceful and simple life as a successful artist. Lots of friends. Sometimes it seems you don't have a problem in the world."

Noah laughed a little. "Oh, that's not true. I have you."

She smiled and handed him a brush he was about to reach for. "Thanks for the advice."

"You're welcome."

Macey waved good-bye to the girls on her way to the front door.

"Bye. Good luck," he said.

"Thanks. I'll need it." Macey strode down the small stone sidewalk. She didn't say good-bye. She knew she would see Noah again.

She could feel Noah's gaze still on her, but she didn't turn around. She sensed there was something else he'd wanted to say, only she didn't want to hear it. In her view, the man had a natural gift for complicating things. For once in her life she'd found the courage to do something bold, something good, and she planned on carrying through with it.

———◆◆◆———

Evelyn hardly needed a map to find the place. It loomed on the horizon like a daddy bull. Her old Pontiac lurched a little with each turn, temperamental as always in the July heat. The parking lot was packed with cars, but luckily she had her handicap sign to hang on her rearview mirror, the one Dr. Musser had given her ages ago when she'd had all those knee problems. She parked the car and dutifully hung her permit. She checked her watch. She was right on time.

Opening the car door let the heat rush in, though for once the heat wasn't the first thing on her mind. She stared up at the three tall buildings that seemed to pass by the clouds on their way to the heavens.

"My gracious me," Evelyn said aloud. Immediately she noticed all the people coming and going through the front doors of the main building. Most were young, strong-looking men and women, dressed in dark suits and expensive dresses. Evelyn looked down at her handmade creation. The powder pink print suddenly didn't seem like such a good idea. She tried to smooth out a wrinkle on her skirt, but it was pointless, so she grabbed her purse and shut the door.

The pace outside the building already flustered her. People brushed past her on the way to their cars, and Evelyn had to step aside several times for fear of being run over. It was as if they didn't even see her.

She finally reached the air-conditioned lobby. A large expensive-looking desk sat in front of a petite woman who didn't look to be very friendly. Evelyn shuddered when she realized the time. She swallowed, wished she'd brought some gum along with her, and then decided she probably looked pretty ridiculous just standing in the middle of the lobby. She approached the receptionist.

"May I help you?"

"I'm here to see Ms. Cunningham."

"Your name?"

"Evelyn. Evelyn Steigel."

The woman picked up the phone and dialed a number, all the while gawking at Evelyn's clothing. All Evelyn could do was stand there with her purse in front of herself and wait.

"Take the elevator to the fourth floor, make a left, and go to the second office on the right."

Evelyn's grip around her purse tightened. "The second floor, to the what?"

The woman's eyes blinked with slow irritation. "The *fourth* floor. One, two, three, four. Take a left. Then go two doors down and it's on your right. The sign says Human Resources." The woman looked at Evelyn suspiciously. "You *are* here for a job, aren't you?" Evelyn nodded and looked around for an elevator. Obviously agitated, the woman instructed, "The elevators are over there, ma'am."

Evelyn spied them across the lobby and began to walk in that direction.

"Wait," the receptionist said, handing her a piece of plastic with a thin leather strap through it. It read Visitor. "You put this around your neck."

Evelyn obeyed, then walked to the elevator, eyes wide with anticipation.

"Fourth floor," she mumbled to herself as she entered the exquisite elevator with a group of young people. The floor number had been punched before she got on, so she stood in the back, careful not to bump anyone, and waited for her turn to get off.

"Excuse me," she said, trying to make her way through a bunch of thin people who didn't seem willing to budge. Most were either reading newspapers or on their telephones.

The doors shut behind her, and Evelyn tried to remember whether she was supposed to go left or right. Ten or fifteen people rushed by her, none of whom looked friendly enough to ask for their help. She had just decided to go right when a tall attractive woman with glasses said, "Mrs. Steigel?"

"Yes?"

"Gosh, you probably don't remember me. Kimmy. Kimmy Trout. But it's Harrison now. I was a friend of Macey's in high school."

"Of course, Kimmy. Don't you look just positively stunning."

"You're looking pretty wonderful yourself, Mrs. Steigel. And you're right on time," Kimmy said, guiding her to the left. "Can I get you some coffee or anything?"

"Dearest me, no. I don't think I need anything to make me shake any more than I already am."

"Don't be nervous. Ms. Cunningham is a very nice person. She's my boss," Kimmy said with a wink.

Kimmy led her into a lavish office. She walked behind the desk and, without sitting down, picked up her phone and said, "Ms. Cunningham, Mrs. Steigel is here. Thank you." Kimmy looked up at Evelyn with a pleasant smile. "Go right on in," she said, pointing to the door behind her.

Evelyn looked at the door, took a few deep breaths, and thought for a moment she might start to cry. "Thank you, Kimmy," she replied and slowly opened the door.

From across the street Macey watched customers go in and out of the hardware store. They were mostly older men, and everyone seemed to know one another. She had hoped to catch a glimpse of Harley through the front window, but all she could see was a reflection of herself, standing like a frightened little girl, chewing at her fingernails.

She didn't know the exact time but figured it was somewhere between noon and one. The deli down the street had become busy. Harley was probably at lunch. Macey continued to work the pinky nail on her left hand until she tasted blood, then decided there was nothing left for her to do other than go in there and see if Harley was around. She hoped that Harley would be gone, at lunch somewhere, so she would have a legitimate excuse to turn around and leave.

She crossed the street, barely looking for traffic, and pulled open the front door to the hardware store. A plastic bass hanging on wood started singing "Stayin' Alive" while moving its head to the beat, but then thankfully the fish stopped as soon as Macey stepped out of the way of its motion detector. Her heart pounded in her chest with unbearable heaviness.

An elderly man with a gentle demeanor sat behind the register and smiled at Macey when she made eye contact. His name badge said BOB. "We got the thing rigged so it does that right when someone comes in. It used to sing the whole song through and that got pretty annoying. Now it just lets us know someone's here. We thought it was better than having the typical bell on the door. Everyone in town's got those bells." He leaned on the counter. "What can I do for the little lady?"

Macey tried her best to give a casual impression. "I'm looking for Harley. Harley Preston. Heard he worked here."

"He sure does."

"He's probably out to lunch, isn't he?"

"Not today. We got inventory coming up. It's always a busy time, when we all work a lot of hours. He's in the back."

"Oh, if he's busy, I can come—"

"Are you kiddin' me? Harley'd kill me if he knew I sent a pretty little thang like yourself back out into the heat. Go on back." The man pointed to a heavy-looking door down a dark hallway in the back of the store.

"Oh, okay."

Macey shuffled through the aisles, pretending to be interested in the assortment of screws, hammers, shovels, and other hardware items that lined the metal shelves on either side of her.

The door Bob was referring to hung on only one hinge, and Macey was afraid to touch it. A handwritten sign was taped to it: Employes Only. On any other day, the misspelled word would have made Macey cringe, but today she had much more important things to worry about.

She slowly swung the door open, and it hardly made a noise, seeming to hang in the air as she pushed on it. Somehow it didn't come crashing down, and Macey peeked around the corner. There was an office on the left and two on the right, all of them looking similarly cluttered. A strong smell of old coffee grounds clung to her as she moved forward. She stopped and listened and definitely heard papers being shuffled from the office on the left. Could she possibly do this?

She stepped forward, every inch as if she were trying to make her way through thick mud. Finally the office came into view and there sat Harley. He was hunched over his desk, staring at numerous pieces of paper with one hand on his forehead, supporting his head, the other clicking a pen furiously. Seeing him again, after so many years, about stopped Macey's heart.

"Um, Harley?"

Harley looked up, his eyes bloodshot with dark circles beneath them, far removed from the lean, muscular, smoothfaced boy she'd known back in high school. His hair was thin and wispy now, definitely balding, and he looked like he hadn't shaved in a week.

"Yeah?"

Macey stood in the doorway. "You probably don't remember me. It's Macey Steigel."

Harley frowned and stared at her curiously. "Macey Steigel." He smiled. "From high school, Macey Steigel?"

Macey managed to return the smile. "Yes."

Harley stood, dropping his pen to the desk. "I thought you looked familiar when I first looked up." He stepped around his desk. "You look fantastic."

Macey blushed while looking down at the gold shag carpet around her shoes. "Oh, uh, thanks."

"Here, here, sit," he said and pulled out a beat-up vinyl chair, one leg held together with duct tape. He repositioned his own chair from behind the desk and sat down next to her. "What are you doing here? Needing some hardware?"

Macey chuckled. "No. I wouldn't know what to do with a single thing out there."

He laughed and rubbed his eyes, as if he'd been staring at numbers for hours. "Where do you live now?"

"Dallas. I'm a news anchor."

"Really? Congratulations. I knew you'd end up doing something big." His eyebrows raised as he said, "And you're still Steigel . . . not married?"

"No. Still single. Heard you got married, though."

His head hung a little. "Yeah. To Ellie. But it didn't last . . . we're divorced now. Have some terrific kids."

"I'm sorry to hear that. About the divorce, I mean." He nodded, his eyes dimming with some painful memory. He then said, "Tell me, what brings you back to this small town?'

"Well, my father died."

"Oh, Macey. I'm sorry."

"Thank you."

An awkward silence compelled them both to glance around the room, looking at nothing in particular.

"So why have you come by to see me?" Harley asked.

The blood drained from Macey's face as she struggled to find a single word to begin.

Thirty-One

The petite woman known as Ms. Cunningham circled her desk and gestured toward an upholstered chair on the other side of her office. Exhausted, Evelyn sank into it.

The woman took a seat opposite Evelyn and removed her glasses before looking at her interviewee. "How are you, Mrs. Steigel?"

"Oh, me? Fine, just fine. A little hot."

"Did Kimberly offer you something to drink?"

"Yes. I'm fine. Just fine. A little hot. But fine." Evelyn closed her eyes, trying to remember if she was repeating herself. She tended to repeat things when she was nervous.

When she opened her eyes, Ms. Cunningham was smiling pleasantly at her. "I'm sure you're a little nervous. Your daughter tells me it's been a while since you last worked."

Evelyn nodded. *To say the least.* She remembered Macey's words about emphasizing her strong points. "A woman's work is never done, now is it?" She didn't know if that made sense, but she hoped it stressed how she'd been working her whole life, just not behind a desk.

Ms. Cunningham chuckled at Evelyn's comment before saying, "Well, you look lovely."

Evelyn straightened the jacket of her suit, aware that she was bunching between the shoulder blades. "Oh, thank you. I made this a few nights ago. I'm not sure I chose the best color."

"You remind me a lot of my mother," Ms. Cunningham said. "She passed away a few years ago. She was in a similar circumstance."

"Is that so?"

"I have a great deal of sympathy for women who've stayed home to raise their children and then must reenter the work force after several years. It's not easy, and it's certainly not fair."

Evelyn nodded. She didn't know what to say, so she just smiled and tried to stay comfortable in her chair.

"Your daughter says you have a few skills that might qualify you for a secretarial job."

"I certainly hope so."

Ms. Cunningham pulled out a file and opened it. "Before we go to the trouble of filling out an application, Mrs. Steigel, I'd like to ask you a few questions." Ms. Cunningham folded her hands together. "I don't want to mislead you. I can't hire someone who isn't qualified, no matter how sympathetic I am to his or her situation. I wouldn't be doing my job if I did."

"I understand," Evelyn said quietly.

"Good. Let's talk, then, about what you can do."

"Okay."

"What can you do?"

"Oh, um, well, I can type."

"Good. How many words a minute?"

How many words a minute? She had no idea. "Well, enough to keep me busy."

Ms. Cunningham's lips parted in a thin smile. "I see. Would you say seventy? Eighty?"

Evelyn paused. She didn't want to lie. But she didn't know what this meant. Was seventy good or bad? "Oh, I probably type as fast as anyone my age."

The woman's lips moved to say something that seemed painful. "So in the . . . uh, sixties?"

Evelyn smiled. "Yes, um, I am in my sixties."

The woman grinned as if relieved. "Okay. That's fine. Now, let's talk about what you can do on a computer."

Evelyn sat up straight. This was her moment to shine. "Yes, well, I can turn it on by myself, get into what they call that word processing program by clicking on the little picture. I can type a letter, hit that Print button using the little critter they call a mouse, print it out, and exit by clicking on the little X on the upper right-hand corner of that box. I can do that little shindig over and over again. If the paper jams, I'm able to take all the other paper out, remove the crinkled one, and then put it all back together again. When I'm writing a letter on the computer, I can backspace, correct a mistake, and keep typing. I can also use that tiny box that makes sure you haven't spelled nothin' wrong. I'd personally rather use a dictionary, but I suppose that's not as quick. I can also go to that place called Start and turn the computer off. Although, if you ask me, that's a silly place to turn off your computer, a place called Start, but of course nobody asked me, so I guess I should just keep my mouth shut." Evelyn suddenly realized she'd been talking for a long time, and as she looked at Ms. Cunningham, she also saw that whatever she'd said hadn't impressed the woman very much. In fact, Ms. Cunningham looked shocked. "I'm sorry, did I . . . um . . ."

Ms. Cunningham's jaw snapped shut, and she said, "Oh, no, I'm sorry. I . . ." Ms. Cunningham seemed at a loss for words, and Evelyn thought for a moment that maybe she had misread her, that indeed the woman was impressed. But then she said, "So, that's all?"

That's all? That was an awful lot, wasn't it? "Well, we haven't even covered that fax thing. I don't mean to brag, but I can fax a piece of paper as far away as Dallas."

Ms. Cunningham's eyebrows went up, though it seemed more out of amusement than anything else. The fact that Ms. Cunningham had stopped looking her in the eye and appeared more interested in the box of paper clips on her desk told Evelyn that maybe she wasn't doing quite as well as she thought.

Evelyn tried to sit up even straighter. "I'm very friendly and I can make a great pot of coffee, even in one of those automatic coffee makers. I'm a fast learner, too. I can sew a button on in fifteen seconds flat." Evelyn paused, remembering to keep focused on the skills an office job might require. "I can answer the phone. I'm great at talking on the phone. I do it all the time with my friends."

Ms. Cunningham was nodding, but she still wasn't maintaining eye contact with Evelyn. Finally Evelyn decided she'd said enough, so she sat back in her chair and waited for Ms. Cunningham to say something. After a few seconds of silence, the woman looked up as if only now realizing Evelyn had stopped talking. "I'm sorry. Were you finished?"

Evelyn nodded. She hadn't ever been in the work force, but she was smart enough to know disappointment when she saw it, and Ms. Cunningham, as nice and professional as she was, looked horribly disappointed, even with that pleasant smile on her face.

"Well now," Ms. Cunningham said, finally shoving the paper clips aside and looking at Evelyn, "you've got quite an array of skills, Evelyn."

Evelyn tried to smile. "Thank you."

"What about use of the Internet? The job I'm considering you for would require you to do some research on the Internet. Nothing complicated, just basic research."

"Are you talking about that e-mail thing? Because, yes, I can do that. I don't approve of it, though. People should be carrying on real conversations, not shooting words at each other like they're huntin' quail. 'Course nobody asked me." She stopped and looked at Ms. Cunningham. "I'd do it, however, if the job required me to. There are things that I won't do, like lie, cheat, and steal. But I'd e-mail if you needed me to."

Ms. Cunningham was licking her lips and then pressing them together, over and over again. "What about a CDRW. Are you capable of using one?"

Evelyn smiled broadly. "I appreciate you spelling it out for me; I can be hard of hearing at times. But I still didn't catch what you were trying to say. I think you left out a vowel."

Ms. Cunningham was now biting her bottom lip, and she started to say something a few times before stopping herself. Evelyn realized that whatever the woman wanted to say, it wasn't going to be easy.

She liked Ms. Cunningham. She seemed to be a nice and amiable woman. So Evelyn leaned forward as far as her tight-fitting jacket would allow and said, "Well, Ms. Cunningham, let's shoot straight here. Are you going to let me fill out that application or not?"

———◦◆◦———

"You look terrible. Do you need a drink or something?"

Macey nodded. She felt terrible. Light-headed. Sick to her stomach. Maybe she was dehydrated. She hadn't been drinking much water lately. Barely aware of Harley standing near her, she heard him going around to the other side of his desk, rummaging around, and returning to his chair.

She was staring at the floor when he said, "Here." She looked up to find Harley holding a large bottle of Crown Royal whiskey and a small cup. Macey's expression probably said more than any words she could've used, because Harley's face turned three shades of red and he quickly got back up. "I'm sorry. You meant water."

He left his office and soon came back with a paper cup filled with cold tap water and handed it to her.

"Thank you," Macey said, then sipped it slowly.

"You never were the type to do any sort of drinkin', were you?" Harley said, trying to sound lighthearted. Macey smiled, shaking her head. "I remember you came from a strict household. Your daddy had a lot of rules. I remember we had to sneak around those few times we went out."

Macey nodded and finished off the water.

"Do you need more water?"

"No. I'm fine now. Thanks."

He looked down at the whiskey bottle he was holding. "Well, let me put this away. I don't normally drink in the middle of the day. Things have been a little stressful around here, though, so I keep it around, just in case. But I'm not a drunk or anything."

"I understand," Macey offered, crushing the cup in her left hand. She watched him replace the whiskey in the top drawer of his desk and then return to join her.

"I sometimes wish my parents had been a little more strict. They didn't care much about how I lived my life, as long as I didn't interfere with theirs. My dad bought me my first beer when I was sixteen." He chuckled at the thought, but all Macey could think about was how lucky she felt that she hadn't married this guy. This would've been her life—married to a hardware salesman who drinks whiskey at lunchtime. That was her only comforting thought at the moment. "Anyway," he said, looking to want to change the subject, "I still don't know why you came to see me."

Macey nodded. It was now or never, and she'd come too far, gone through too much to turn back now. She hesitated, aware that Harley was staring at her with raw curiosity. She couldn't think of a stranger, more surreal moment in her whole life. She had a detached feeling, as if she were looking down, a bug on the wall, and seeing herself sitting in the old vinyl chair, spilling her guts to Harley Preston, once considered a high-school prince, now simply a down-and-out average guy working at his father's business, divorced and lonely.

Harley leaned forward in his chair. "It seems like this is something hard for you to say."

Macey finally looked him in the eyes. "It is," she admitted. "But I'm going to say it."

It took nearly fifteen minutes for Macey to tell him the whole story. She tried not to leave any details out, although she wasn't sure why. The details wouldn't matter to Harley. She stared at her knees while she told the story. She didn't want Harley's expression, or lack of one, to distract her. She thought even if he stood and stormed out, she would stay seated in that chair and tell the whole thing, from beginning to end, to nobody if she had to.

Once she got started, the words flowed easily from her mouth. She didn't ramble but felt as though she stuck to the point pretty well. From her view of her knees, she could only see Harley's shins and sneakers, neither of which moved an inch the entire time she talked. So she just kept talking until she'd finally said all she needed to say.

"So, here I am. To tell you this. To confess, I guess, and to tell you I'm sorry. If I could do it over again, I wouldn't have done it that way. But I can't, and I have to live with it forever. That's the tough part. But I want to ask for your forgiveness." Macey finally looked up at Harley, half expecting there to be tears of his own flowing down a face with a sorrowful expression.

Instead, his eyebrows were flat across his forehead. His mouth, in a straight line as well, quivered ever so slightly, and his eyes were narrowed, almost in disgust. Macey felt uncertain as to what she should do next. Say something? Let him process it? A sickening fear crept up her spine and raised the hairs on her neck.

Harley Preston finally rose, went to his desk, took out his whiskey and a paper cup, and poured.

The old man named Bob was suddenly standing in the door-way. "Hey," he said, "Brent Stile's on the phone for you. He wants to know about his order."

"Not now," Harley growled at him. Going by Bob's expression, Macey could tell he wasn't accustomed to being spoken to that way.

Bob glanced at Macey, then at the whiskey bottle in Harley's hand. "Little early for that, ain't it, Preston?"

Harley stared hard at Bob. "No. It's not."

Bob took one last look at Macey, as if wondering what on earth had just occurred to make Harley drink and snap all at once, and then left.

Macey stood and said, "Harley, I'm sorry. Maybe I shouldn't have come—"

"No, you shouldn't have," he said, his voice tight with anger. He guzzled the whiskey and poured another. "What kind of person would wait all this time and then come and tell someone all this?"

Macey shook her head, sort of wondering the same thing. "It wasn't something I'd planned. I came here for my father's funeral, and what happened was that—" She stopped herself, for Harley didn't seem to be listening to her anymore. His eyes had become distant and cloudy.

"What do you want me to say? What a hero you are for coming here and telling me this?" His face glowed with anger. "Here I am, minding my own business, trying to deal with my own troubles, and then you show up here out of the blue, telling me you got pregnant when we were teenagers, I'm the father, and that you had an abortion?" He slammed his cup on the desk, whiskey shooting up and splattering everywhere. "What do you want me to do about it? I ain't no priest! I can't forgive you!"

Tears began streaming down Macey's face. She stood quietly, hoping no one could hear Harley shouting at her.

"I think abortion's wrong! I always have. I think it's a sin." His eyes burned with rage. "I can't believe you'd go do something like that! You of all people, who came from that religious family."

Macey wiped her eyes. "I know it was wrong. Of course it was wrong."

Harley shook his head and fell into his desk chair, staring into space. His fingers tore through his hair. "What if I'd had a kid back then? I'd still be payin' child support, after all these years. Then I'd really be in debt, more than I am now." He looked up at her. "It was still wrong of you to do."

Macey felt her own anger returning. "You don't have to keep saying that. I know. That's why I'm here today."

"That's why you're here? *Why*, exactly, are you here? I don't understand. I haven't thought about you once in the last fifteen years. I didn't even recognize you when you came in. We went on three or four dates. I slept with you. So what? I slept with a lot of girls in high school. You were the one stupid enough not to be on some sort of birth control. I should've known you were too naïve for that."

Even just a few days ago, Macey would've lost her temper and hurled angry words at Harley. But now, though the words stung and the hurt deepened with every insult, Macey managed to stay silent, something she'd never been able to do before. She stood there and took it. And not because she was weak. It was because she was strong.

The air cleared a little as Harley stopped talking long enough to pour more whiskey. Macey cleared her throat and said, "I know this is going to sound crazy"—Harley shot her a look—"but I'm going to have a little service for the baby. I don't know why. It just seems right. I guess to acknowledge a life that could have been . . . that should have been. To say good-bye in some way. To close a chapter in my life . . . and in yours, too."

Harley laughed sharply. "How convenient. Have a little service. Say a few words. And it's over. It's like it never happened, right?"

"I know this is hard to deal with. I knew it would be."

"You should've kept your secrets to yourself. You should've just stayed away." He dropped the whiskey bottle back in the drawer. "I've got lunch in an hour and I've got a lot of work to do. So if you don't mind."

"Harley?" He looked up. "Please consider coming with me to bury our . . . I mean, to just . . ." The tears flowed once again. Macey took a minute to compose herself, then said, "My parents have some property, at the southeast corner of Farmer's Market Road and County Road 12. There's a big oak tree there on a hill, you can't miss it. I'll be there in an hour. Please . . . come."

Harley looked away. Macey turned to leave, and as she passed through the door, she heard Harley say, "Don't count on it."

Macey looked at him one more time, her eyes pleading with him to understand, to have compassion. They were met with a cold glare. "Please come," she repeated, which was all her strained voice would allow her to say. She walked past Bob in the hardware store, but luckily he was with a customer and didn't see her leave. The bass on the wall sang "Stayin' Alive" as she pushed the door open and escaped outside.

Thirty-Two

Macey stood at the large bay window that overlooked the river, her arms wrapped around herself as if she were cold. She wasn't cold. Just sad. Embarrassed. Confused. Yet, with all those emotions fighting for room inside an already crowded soul, Macey felt peace. As strange and unreasonable as that sounded, it was there.

The house was completely silent, which gave her some time to think. She pondered her life, from early childhood up to now. She let all the memories that wanted attention occupy her mind. Apart from one another, they were vivid and sensible. But when she tried to piece them together into something that made sense, the pictures became muddied and the feelings grew complicated. So she just let each one stand on its own, as long as it would stay in her mind, and as soon as it was finished, let another replace it. Some were good. Others bad. But each had its own place in her heart. As did the idea that there was someone else in charge, someone directing and orchestrating her life, putting pieces back together as she took them apart.

Macey turned to look at the clock on the wall. She had twenty-five minutes until the time she told Harley she would be out at the property. Hesitation sliced through her with every thought of what she'd planned to do, but she knew she had to do it. For her own sake, and also for the sake of the baby. Not for anyone else. Although if Harley did decide to show up, somehow the day would be more complete.

A loud bump was followed by the front door opening halfway, this followed by a second bump. "This door!" Macey heard her mother complain, and she rushed to her aid, helping her to swing it fully open. "It just sticks more and more. I'm going to have to get someone over here to fix that. By August I might have to come and go through a window."

Macey guided her mother inside and shut the door behind her. "You're back already?"

Her mother nodded without looking at her. She dropped her purse on the dining room table and headed into the kitchen to pour herself a glass of ice water. She took several swallows before finally turning to Macey. "It's so hot out there, I'm apt to wonder if the whole state of Kansas hasn't dropped to the pit of hell."

Macey smiled while trying to read her mom's face. She didn't want to sound overly anxious, yet she desperately wanted to know how the interview went. She let her mom finish her water before asking, "Well? How did it go?"

Evelyn sat at the breakfast table, wiping her forehead and brushing away the wisps of hair that stuck to her temples. "I'd have to say that apparently I'm not going to be a right fit out there." Her eyes met Macey's with painful apprehension. "I'm sorry, dear."

Macey tried to smile reassuringly but then asked, "How do you know? I mean, maybe you just *feel* that way. Maybe it went better than you think, but you were just too nervous to tell."

Her mother shrugged. "Well, I was nervous. But the lady, Ms. Cunningham, she was very nice."

"I liked her a lot. I thought you would, too."

"And she liked me a lot," said Evelyn. Macey sat down across from her mom, leaning forward eagerly. "She said I reminded her of her mother. I guess she passed away a few years back. We had a nice talk. I gave her my cobbler recipe."

"You gave her your cobbler recipe?"

"Yes. She said she liked cobbler, so I gave her mine. The easy version. Ms. Cunningham doesn't look like she cooks too much."

Macey let out a heavy sigh. "Mom, why do you think you won't be a good fit there? Did Ms. Cunningham tell you that? Did she say you didn't get the job?"

"Yes. She told me she couldn't hire me."

Macey's hands dropped to the table and she stared up at the ceiling, shaking her head. "Oh, no."

"I'm sorry, Macey," her mother said again, her voice shaky now. "I tried awfully hard. I bragged about myself more than I ever have in my life. I told her all that I could do, but she asked me a lot of questions, and some of them I couldn't answer. Sometimes I didn't even know what it was she was asking."

Macey reached across the table for her mom's hand. "Don't worry about it," she said, but her voice trembled a little, too. "I know you tried really hard. I'm proud of you."

Evelyn shook her head. "I tried hard, but it wasn't good enough." She looked her daughter in the eyes. "Now I'm in trouble, aren't I? I'm running out of money."

Macey didn't know what to tell her. Yes, her mother was in trouble. And she was no closer to an answer for this problem than she was to solving her own. Yet somehow, remarkably, the many years of shame and pain and regret were finally beginning to fade, not hurt so much. Something was changing in her life, and she knew she could take little credit for it.

"Mom, I guess we're going to have to rely on that faith you keep talking about. The good Lord." She smiled across the table at her mom.

Her mother's desperate eyes filled with light.

"I've got to go do something, okay?" Macey stood and her mom did, too. "I'll be back."

"Um, what do you want me to . . ." Evelyn tried to follow Macey to the door, but Macey was nearly outside already.

"Don't worry about me. I'll be fine. I won't be gone too long. Maybe you can think about what you're going to cook for dinner tonight, okay?" Macey gave her a quick smile and shut the door, pulling it hard to make sure it closed tightly.

———◆———

A richly green soybean field stretched for nearly half a mile to the east of her father's property. Macey parked the car on the dirt road in front of the old rickety fence that marked the property's boundaries. On the west side lay a wheat field, now freshly harvested and ready to be hayed.

Macey left the coolness of her car, armed with only a pen and pad of paper, and stood facing the small wooden gate, secured with wire that was twisted to a pole. She decided it would be easier to jump the thing rather than try to figure out how to get it open, so she climbed over the gate and landed on the other side with a short hop. She wiped her hands on the cutoffs she'd changed into after going to see Harley and headed the few hundred feet toward the giant oak that stood atop the only hill on the property.

Her sneakers cut through the dead grass as she pondered the land. At one time it might've been suitable as a pasture; now it was but dirt and dead grass. The towering tree in the middle was the only thing that set it apart and rendered the site interesting.

She reached the shade of the tree long before she reached the tree itself. Its limbs extended far beyond the trunk, heavy and strong, and were thick with leaves. Macey smiled as she looked up into the tree, recalling the three or four times she'd climbed it. It hadn't been easy. But with her father's help, she'd managed to get up in it, climbing twenty or twenty-five feet high until she was able to gaze across the land with ease.

Getting herself in the shade made a considerable difference to Macey's body temperature, and she found it easier to breathe. Tired and drained from the heat and emotion of the day, Macey leaned against the large trunk of the tree. After a while she sat on the ground, slumping against the tree and looking out at the beauty of the open landscape.

She hadn't prayed in seventeen years. Not once. Even at her father's church she hadn't been able to find the courage to offer up a prayer. But now, as things were coming to a close and as life seemed to be taking a clearer perspective, Macey Steigel had found peace. Somehow the pain she'd endured was dulled by the knowledge that God had been there all along and had finally brought her home. She closed her eyes and opened her heart up to the Lord, asking Him to search it. And she asked Him to stay.

After a long moment of silence, Macey remembered why she'd come to this place. Her lips trembled as she thought of the little baby whose life she'd ended.

She stood and found two sticks and then unstrung the shoelace from one of her sneakers. Then, waiting here on top of a hill in the quietness of the Kansas prairie, Macey prayed he would come. She prayed, once and for all, that this would bring some kind of closure.

Please, Harley, come.

———◆◆◆———

"Evelyn?"

Evelyn almost fell off the couch as she startled to consciousness, the magazine she'd been reading sliding off her lap and spilling to the floor. "What? Macey?"

"No, it's Noah."

Evelyn fumbled for her glasses, put them on and looked toward the front door. A looming shadow of a man stood holding the door partly open, backlit from the day's sun. "Noah? Come in, come in, dear."

Noah stepped into the living room as Evelyn adjusted her dress and steadied herself into a standing position. "I'm sorry. Did I wake you?" Noah helped her gain her balance.

Evelyn smiled and said, "I guess I dozed off. This heat always wears me out. Here, let me fix you some lemonade. Do you want something to eat?"

"That's okay," Noah said, following her into the kitchen. "I can't stay long." He looked more closely at her and said, "Is that makeup you're wearing?"

Evelyn turned away to find a glass for herself. "I probably look silly, don't I?"

"No. You look sophisticated."

Evelyn dropped ice cubes into the glass. "Sophisticated, huh? Well, you should've seen me in my business suit. I would've really impressed you."

"Oh, the interview."

Evelyn waved him off. "Don't want to talk about it. I didn't get the job." She opened the fridge to look for the pitcher.

Leaning on the kitchen counter as comfortably as if it were his own house, Noah said, "Evelyn, you look worried."

"Well, I guess that's because I don't have too much in the old bank account." She looked up at Noah just in time to see an amused and thoughtful expression cross his face. She was about to ask him what he was thinking when he spoke.

"Is, uh, Macey around?"

"No." The cubes rattled in the glass as she poured lemonade over them. "I think she was pretty upset about my not gettin' the job. She left; didn't really say where she was going. She's awfully worried about me."

Noah frowned. "She seemed upset?"

"Yeah. She tried putting on a front, but it was obvious there were things on her mind. A lot of things, I guess. This has been a trying week for her. I imagine she's not letting me in on everything, but that's okay. She's workin' through things, and I just gotta sit back and let the good Lord do His work."

Noah smiled but looked deep in thought. "Did she, uh, go anywhere today? To see anyone?"

"Don't know. I was at my interview, so she may have gone then. She did seem preoccupied, but I didn't make too much of it. Like I said, she's been havin' quite a week."

Noah stood tall, stuffing his hands in his pockets and staring down at the tile.

"Not you, too?"

Noah glanced up. "What?"

"You have that same look about you. That same look Macey had. Is something going on that I should know about?"

"Evelyn, do you have any idea where Macey might be?" He looked as though he wanted to say more but thought better of it. After a long pause, he added, "Maybe she needs some company right now."

Evelyn couldn't help but smile at Noah, and she allowed herself to imagine, just briefly, him and Macey together, married, with children. It was a nice thought, one that fit into a perfect world. Then again, this was no perfect world.

Evelyn thought more about Noah's question. "She said there was somethin' she had to do. Didn't mention what. It was like she didn't want to talk about it. So I don't know." Noah sighed lightly. "But she did ask about the land."

"The land?" said Noah. "You mean out on Farmer's Market?"

"You know about that?"

A wide jovial grin spread across Noah's face and he said, "I better go."

"Now?"

"I'll be back soon." He then hurried to the front door, hollered a quick good-bye, and left.

Evelyn moved to a window and watched him hop into his truck and back out of the driveway in a rush, leaving only a ball of dust in the air. She sighed and went back to the kitchen to fetch her glass of lemonade. She sat down, and the emptiness of the house became instantly apparent. She tried to imagine the good Lord at the table with her, drinking His own brew of lemonade. She smiled at the thought and turned the cubes over in her glass as she pondered the ways of the Lord. In her sixty-five years of life, she'd seen Him move in mysterious ways. She'd seen faithful men and women die of disease. But she'd also seen children healed on their deathbeds. She'd watched marriages crumble. But she'd also seen barren women give birth. It was the cycle of life, which frankly, never did make too much sense to Evelyn Steigel. She had the rest of her life to live out alone, at least in this house. That didn't make too much sense, either.

She took another drink of lemonade and pushed the glass away. It had a bit too much tartness to it this time, and she preferred her lemonade on the sweet side. Figuring it was best she didn't just sit at the table the whole rest of the afternoon, Evelyn decided to tidy up the place, starting with the living room. She stacked magazines, arranged coasters, and then picked up the heavy old quilt from off the back of the sofa. It probably needed a good shaking out.

Her life seemed to be like a good quilt, passed down from generation to generation, faded, worn, yet still unique and special. That was her journey. It had its purpose. It had its stages and uses. Like the quilt, it was made special with caring hands. Occasionally it had to be patched up and was known to spend a season or two in a dark closet.

But a good quilt can always be used for something. For the older it is
and the longer it's around, the greater its value, stains and all.

Evelyn laughed to herself, shaking her head at the thought of
herself as an old quilt. She folded it up, not bothering to match the
corners, and set it aside. She'd need something to do tomorrow.

She shuffled to the kitchen and stood by the sink, a spot where
she'd probably spent half her life. She tried not to think about where
the money was going to come from to keep things going. And she
tried not to think of what was going to happen with Macey. Her
daddy always told her that sometimes thinking too hard would just
get you into trouble.

Hanging in the kitchen window by a suction-cup hook was a
nice cross-stitch that Ruth Blair had made for her three Christmases
ago. It said, *Lord, grant me the serenity to accept the things I cannot
change, the courage to change the things I can, and the wisdom to know
the difference.* She'd always admired the beautiful handwork Ruth
had done, but it was the words that were impressed upon her now.
She made it her prayer, then went to the pantry for some sugar. She
added it to her glass of lemonade until it tasted just right.

Taking a seat at her kitchen table, Evelyn sipped her lemonade
and listened to the quietness of her very still house, wondering what
in the world she was going to fix for dinner.

Epilogue

Macey wasn't sure how long she'd been waiting on the hill. For a time she sat facing the road. But it was too disappointing watching car after car speed by without slowing. Her throat tightened with each one that passed, and each time she doubted even more that Harley was going to come.

It gave her time to think, though. With her back to the road, facing the western horizon, she had come to the conclusion that Harley's attendance at the little service wasn't going to bring closure.

She hadn't realized this immediately. It didn't dawn on her until after at least an hour of waiting, when she'd decided to go ahead without him. She began by tying the two sticks together with the shoelace, securing them tightly into the form of a cross. It was a little crooked, because the sticks weren't perfectly straight, but it was a cross nevertheless.

The ground was hard, void of moisture, and so she spent ten minutes chipping away at the dirt with another stick just so she could put the cross in the ground and make a small symbolic grave. By the time she had an adequately sized hole dug in which to anchor the cross, her hands, knees, and shirt were stained with dirt, mixed with the sweat that ran from her brow.

She tried to poke the stick-cross deep into the earth so it stayed upright, but it was useless. It kept falling to one side or the other. The ground was just too hard and she too weak to dig anymore. She sat on the ground breathing hard, angry at herself that she couldn't even get the grave right.

Holding the cross in her hand, she was about to fling it down the hill in frustration when a thought jolted her mind, one that surprised her in its depth. Her eyes widened as she stared at the jagged sticks, and she realized that this cross wasn't for the baby.

It was for her.

Her baby was gone, in heaven with God. But Macey Steigel was still here, still very much alive. And still very much in need of being saved from herself and who knew what else. She clutched the sticks in her hand, staring fiercely at them, determined to find out what all this meant for her life.

Suddenly, from behind her came a crunching noise, footsteps on dry brittle grass. Harley! She jumped to her feet and dusted herself off before turning around.

"Noah?" Her mouth hung half open.

"Hi there," Noah called as he walked up the hillside toward her.

Macey glanced around. "What are you doing here? How did you find me?" She looked down at herself and added, "I must look like—"

"A pig farm."

"Excuse me?"

He grinned. "That's why I'm here."

"To tell me I look like a pig farm?" Macey swiped the dirty sweat from her forehead.

Noah turned, gazing at the land. "Because of all this. Your father's land."

Macey shook her head. "I'm confused. What are you talking about?"

"Not long before your father died, a company approached him about buying this land for a pig farm. I handled a lot of your father's business after he became sick. But your father turned them down."

"Why? This land is good for nothing else. In fact, it's perfect for a pig farm. It's away from everything."

"True. Only that's not how your dad saw it. This land was your inheritance, and he wasn't going to give it to anyone but you."

Macey stared up at Noah. "Why? I hadn't seen or spoken to him in years. He didn't even know where to find me."

"I guess that tells you a lot, doesn't it?"

Macey surveyed the property. "But why are you here? Telling me this now? It's too late, isn't it?"

"I don't think so," Noah said. "They called me a couple of days ago, asking if the property was still available since your father had died. I told them I would get back to them. I didn't talk to you or your mother about it yet because I thought it would be better to wait until things settled down and life got back to normal. It didn't seem appropriate to bring it up in the midst of all the grieving." He looked at Macey. "I didn't know your mom was having financial problems. That's why you wanted her to go for that interview. It all makes sense now, but I didn't know then. I'm sorry. I would've said something sooner."

Tears of relief came to Macey's eyes, and she said with a smile, "No. I think your timing is perfect. How much do you think the land would go for?"

"I suppose around $150,000. It was appraised not too long ago."

Macey almost stumbled backward. "That much? I thought it was just a worthless patch of dead grass."

"Well, I guess it is if you're not a pig," he said with a grin.

"If I'd thought it was worth anything I would have looked into it instead of making Mom go through that interview. But . . . where's the deed? It wasn't in the lock box at home or at the bank."

"Your dad gave it to me along with a few other documents when he sensed he didn't have much time left."

Feeling overcome by the news, Macey lost her voice momentarily. They stood for a while, neither one saying anything. Macey looked out at the prairie surrounding her, letting it all sink in. Then she noticed Noah eyeing the cross of sticks in her hand.

"I saw Harley today," she said. "Told him everything."

"How'd it go?"

Macey shrugged. She didn't know how to answer that. It certainly hadn't ended up like any fairy tale, although she did feel as if she'd seen an end to a long nightmare. Maybe because she'd at last fessed up, faced her fears, and asked forgiveness, even if Harley chose not to grant it.

Noah was still staring at the cross.

"I made it. I was going to have a service, like a funeral or something, for my baby."

"Oh. Do you want to be alone?"

Macey shook her head. "No. I realized . . ." She tried to think of some way to put it, some way to describe what had happened in what seemed a blink of an eye yet had spanned more like an eternity. "Well, let's just say I ended up burying a lot more today than I thought I would." She smiled at him. "And to my surprise there was a resurrection or two, as well."

He nodded. "Boy. I never knew so much could happen on a little hill in the middle of Kansas." His hands found his pockets, and he rocked back and forth for a moment as if wanting to say more. Finally he looked at her, his eyes radiant. "Stay here."

Macey let out a nervous laugh. "What?"

"Stay here. In Kansas. Stay here . . . with me. Not since Emily passed away has a woman made me so much as glance in her direction. Not until you." He attempted a smile. "I want to take care of you. And God knows," he said with a laugh, "you need *someone* to do that."

She laughed, too, and wiped her own tears away. She'd never met anyone like Noah, and she knew without a doubt that she would most likely never meet anyone like him again. Still, there was something holding her back. Maybe it had to do with the epiphany she'd just experienced. Maybe, for once in her life, she felt strong enough to be alone. She couldn't say for certain. But she knew, at least for now, she would have to say good-bye to Noah.

"I need to go back to Dallas," she whispered, unable to meet his eyes with hers. Part of her hoped he hadn't heard it. "I have to process all this, to take the time to . . ." She finally looked at him and smiled. "It's not you. You're amazing. You're a pain in the behind, but you're amazing."

"Well, it's good to know we feel the same way about each other." He laughed and pulled her near, hugging her tightly. "I understand," he said, his lips close to her ear. "Just promise me you'll come visit your mom a lot."

"Not just my mom," she said, then took his hand and held it.

He took a few steps back and gave her a warm smile. "So what do you think the chances are that I can come over for a home-cooked meal tonight?"

Laughing, Macey answered, "I think the chances are, oh, around a hundred percent."

"Good." He started walking down the hill and then abruptly turned back to her. "You coming?"

"I'll be home in a little bit. I've got to do one more thing. Tell my mom I'm on my way."

Noah nodded and walked back down to where his truck was parked. Macey wanted to say thank-you to him, but the words stuck in her throat, and by the time she found her voice again he was too far away to hear. It was all right, though. She knew he understood.

She watched him drive away, waving once, hoping he would look back. When his truck was out of sight, she took out the pad of paper and pen she'd brought with her and turned to a clean page.

It was a medium-sized steno pad, the kind she'd used time and time again to jot down notes and quotes and facts all throughout her career. But this time she was going to use it for something different. It was time to write to her father.

Dear Dad . . . she began. The words flowed easily, and everything she had to say spilled onto the paper faster than she could write it. She allowed her pen access to every corridor of her heart and, without shame or regret, laid bare her soul. As each thought and idea formed on the page, Macey Steigel couldn't help but entertain a single overwhelming thought, one that kept her smiling and glancing skyward, sure at any moment she was going to see a hawk gallantly circling the clear expanse far above.

She was free.

Acknowledgments

I would like to express my sincerest thanks to:

My mom and dad, Susan N., Amy G., Cheri G., Sonja G., and Crystal D. for baby-sitting so I could have extra time to write. Amy, thanks as always, for a first read-through.

Laurie Ballweber and Heather Unruh for research help.

Fred and Carol Southern for a special gift that has made this whole process so much easier. *Thank you.*

Luke Hinrichs, my editor. Your talent on this project was astonishing. Thanks for pushing me and encouraging me all at once. And Dave Horton, an always knowledgeable, friendly, and available voice on the other end of the phone.

Janet Kobobel Grant—thanks for always believing, brainstorming, and just being you. I'm glad we're partners in this wonderful pursuit to write with passion and purpose. Randy I. and Susanna A., and the rest of the Mt. Hermon gang, for keeping me encouraged.

Sean—you keep me sane! Endless hours of baby-sitting, listening to me whine, and telling me I can do it. Thanks for helping me get this project completed through some difficult times. You're the absolute best ever. John Caleb—thanks for not having a clue as to what I do when I go and shut my door, turn on the computer, and tell you I'm working—and still loving me. To Cate for making 2002 a GREAT year!

And thank you, Lord, for all the reasons nobody else knows but you.